Worshipers

Hope of Freelandia

Kent Larson

Worshipers: Hope of Freelandia

Copyright 2013 by Kent Larson
Cover design by Michael Malone
Interior illustrations by Rebecca Ross

Library of Congress Control Number: 2013938257
ISBN Number: 978-1-939456-07-6

First Printing September 2013
Printed in the USA

Cover images purchased and used by permission of istockphoto.com and Malone Photography

Published by Search for the Truth Publications
3275 Monroe Rd.
Midland, MI 48642
www.searchforthetruth.net

The Freelandia Trilogy:
Book 1 - *Watchers: Guardians of Freelandia*
Book 2 - *Worshipers: Hope of Freelandia*
Book 3- *Warriors: Darkness over Freelandia*

A Note To Parents

This is the second installment of the Freelandia Trilogy. In Book one, we were introduced to Maria, a young blind orphan girl who has a supernatural singing ability. It is a gifting from God, a spiritual gifting the likes of which her world has not yet experienced. It touches not only people's ears, but down deep into their souls.

The first book takes place entirely within the highly secluded country of Freelandia, a land geographically isolated and blessed immensely with prosperity and peace for hundreds of years. Biblical New Testament spiritual gifts are widely exercised and even expected as being part of ordinary Christian life. In the first book, Maria's gift is discovered and she comes to live in the Keep, the capital of Freelandia. Her astounding gifting becomes widely known when she performs with a world renowned singer at a special concert. Within a short time Maria is befriended by quite a number of the most important people in the country. As she is taken in as a very special apprentice within the Academy of Music, life would seem rather idyllic …except for the ominous Dominion, a country bent on world conquest with Freelandia standing in its way.

We also met Ethan, the son of the Chancellor who also has a most unusual temporal supernatural ability, which is used to thwart an assassination attempt on his father.

Book One ends with Grand Master Gaeten, Ethan's exceptionally skilled mentor and one of Maria's benefactors, heading into Dominion territory to spy out their plans against Freelandia.

In Book Two we follow Gaeten as he uncovers information about the invasion the Dominion is planning. We are also introduced to the School of Engineers, where God's Spirit is actively at work with scientific creativity and inventiveness. Maria, meanwhile, finds that her gifting extends well beyond singing and impacts the entire Academy, and then the entire Keep, the country of Freelandia and even beyond. Ethan and the Freelandian navy are attacked by the Dominion, and God's people learn of a potent spiritual weapon to use against their true enemy.

You are invited to join the adventure. Please bring an open mind to the incredible awesomeness of our God. If you catch a spark of what living with the Holy Spirit's power might be like, if it makes you give glory to our wonderful loving God in any way, then all of the efforts to write it and get it into your hands were well worthwhile.

Kent Larson
Awestruck worshiper of the Most High God
2013

Acknowledgements

Writing a story that grows into a three volume trilogy is no small undertaking. I wish to thank my family for their patience both in releasing my time to write/edit and for their patience as I worked to create each subsequent installment … just think what reading this story would be like if you had to wait days for each new chapter! I also want to thank the fellowship group from my local church who weekly encouraged me to "keep going".

As the books took shape, one person in particular had the vision to see them published. A special thanks to Bruce Malone and *Search for the Truth Ministries*. Without a brother coming alongside to lead me through the publication process – I'm not sure these books would ever have become a reality. Thanks also to his wife Robin for the many encouraging words, the expert help of their daughter-in-law Beth for content editing and ideas for streamlining the storyline, and to Rebecca Ross for bringing the story alive with her beautifully detailed illustrations.

Finally, I would like to express thanks and appreciation for the encouragement of too many others to name – fellow believers who took the time to read and comment on the early versions of this story. May God reward your efforts as these books bless many lives.

Dedication

This book has been written to bring the glory of Jesus. To God be the glory for the things He has done! Praise to Emmanuel (the God-who-is-with-us), which can also be understood to mean "God-in-us". What a concept for every Christian, "God-in-me"!

About the Author

The author and his family: wife Sue, sons Ben and Matt,
daughters Sarah and Rachel (son Jonathan is not pictured)

Kent Larson's occupation may not be what you would expect for a writer of Christian fiction with a theme centered on the praise and worship of God. He is a material scientist at a leading chemical company. But he sees no conflict between these, as science proclaims the wonder of our Creator at every level for those who would simply acknowledge Him. The author and his family live in the middle of lower Michigan on nearly five acres - surrounded by a forest filled with animals - at the edge of where the Michigan population tapers off into a rural and rustic setting. On quiet evenings he and his family can step out onto their back porch, gaze at the starry host above, and feel even closer to the God who created it all.

Worshipers

Hope of Freelandia

Book 2 in the Freelandia Trilogy.

Chapter 1

Passengers to the Dominion

aeten carefully felt his way up the stairwell onto the moderately rolling deck of the Dominion merchant vessel that was taking him incognito away from his beloved Freelandia and into the heart of enemy controlled lands to learn about their plans for conquest. Gaeten had no way of knowing if the sailors were just as they seemed, but he assumed that at least some were disguised Dominion soldiers or spies. That did not particularly concern him. He certainly was a spy, and very much more than a simple soldier. And his disguise was nearly foolproof. After all, who would ever suspect an obviously blind, poor old man, one who had complained loudly to the captain the second day of the voyage that some scallywag had pilfered through his battered chest during the night and stolen the few coins he had saved up?

It only took a little exaggeration to stumble out onto the deck, his thin reed cane tapping along as he staggered his way to a side railing. Gaeten ignored the jeers and snickers the sailors made at his slow and awkward steps. Half-way toward his goal a mop handle was silently thrust just ahead of his feet. It was held by the sailor Gaeten had internally nicknamed Garlic Gone Bad, for he always reeked of days-old garlic. GGB, as the blind man thought of him, seemed to dog him around the ship, always trying to cause a trip or other accident. It was getting highly annoying. One of these days, Gaeten planned on showing the miscreant that it was exceptionally reckless to mess with a Grand Master of the elite Freelandian Watchers. Gaeten's lips curled into a dangerous smile. Maybe that time was now, at least in part.

Having sensed the movement, Gaeten had a clear picture in his mind of where the mop handle was. He pretended to stumble and it would have taken a highly acute observer to follow the exact movements of his feet as

he half-fell forward over the handle to regain his sure footing. While the offending sailor may not have exactly noticed the fancy footwork, he surely did notice the effect. Gaeten had landed one foot down on the end of the handle while the heel of his other foot had hooked backward to propel it sharply upward.

The blind spy was pleasingly rewarded with a loud "Oof" as the mop head caught the unwitting aggressor directly in the face and from the resulting guffaws of the other sailors laughing at the spectacle it caused.

Gaeten smiled more cheerfully and continued on as though nothing untoward had occurred, following his original path to a far more amiable encounter. "The sunshine is rather pleasant today, isn't it ma'am."

The middle-aged woman turned and smiled at the much older gentleman. Realizing he could not see it, she quickly responded back. "Yes, and the air is so very fresh out at sea. It surely beats staying down in that smelly hold. But tell me, isn't it somewhat dangerous out on the deck for … for someone like you?"

Gaeten smiled warmly. "Yes, but danger is my middle name!" He punctuated that exclamation with a deep feigned cough that would have done a professional actor proud.

"Oh … oh Mr. Gunter! My dolly Samantha wanted to come out to see the water and waves! Maybe she might even see a flying fish!" The owner of the high pitched sweet voice was the woman's little daughter, who had found a sure friend in the old blind man. A friend and an unknown protector. Several times during the night Gaeten had loudly snored and rolled about on his bed near these two females just as one of the sailors had been about to rummage through their belongings during the night.

"Well, be careful Samantha does not decide to go for a swim!" Gaeten was leaning on the railing now, filling his lungs with the fresh salty air.

"Oh, she would never do that! She always holds onto me really tight. Just you watch! She likes me to hold her way over the edge so she can pretend to fly in the air over the water. Why just yesterday she … AHHH!"

The deck pitched as it encountered a larger wave, shoving them all hard against the rail as that side of the ship leaned heavily down toward the water. The shock startled the little girl and she lost her grip on her precious possession.

Gaeten's response was pure reflexive action. His awareness of his surroundings was often considerably more advanced than a sighted person, and movement much too fast for anyone to clearly see his hand shoot out to catch the doll mere inches below where it had been dropped. It was not until he had handed it back to its rightful owner that he even considered how his action may have jeopardized his mission.

The little girl was half-sobbing and half overflowing with thanks to her doll's savior as her mother and Gaeten ushered her back below decks. Just before descending they passed the angry garlicky-smelling sailor nursing a bloody nose who watched them with eyes wide, wondering what he had really just witnessed. His fellow Dominion soldier-sailors ought to be rather interested that the old blind man was not quite the near-invalid he seemed to act like.

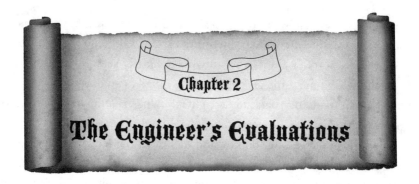

o, what brings you into my office at this hour?" Duncan had glanced up from the reports he was reading to see his wife Lydia come gliding in with her usual grace. It was a very welcome distraction.

Lydia smiled. "I just spent some time with Master Warden James. He is recuperating well enough from the wound he received from the Dominion assassin's arrow, though I think it will be a few weeks until he is ready to put in a full day's work. He asked me to stop by to help discern who should be delegated to lead several important projects that need immediate attention if we are to be even reasonably well prepared for a not-to-distant Dominion attack. I thought it was a great idea to not only ask for God's guidance, but then to faithfully utilize giftings He has already given to assist with the selections. There are other discerners he could have picked, but James said it would diminish decision dissention if the Chancellor's wife were actively involved in each case. God was quite clear on the choices too – the leadings were strong and clear on all of them … except one."

Duncan looked surprised. "Oh, what was that project about?"

"James wants someone to immediately begin assessing the projects and ideas of the engineers. It seems the Director of Engineering told him that there have been many new ideas, far too many to seriously work on, and so priority had been given to public sector works and none that might support our military defenses for quite a long time. James got the impression the Director might not be able to link the ideas to the needs of defending Freelandia. Furthermore, James felt that the formal procedure for project approvals was, well, overly institutionalized and lacked the speed and flexibility required when the Dominion threat seems so imminent. James had several of his senior Wardens and Watchers as candidates for doing the assessment, though he was not confident they could do it to the level required. We both agreed this could be extremely important and even critical to our defense. It did not seem to me that God was directing us toward any of those candidates, though the magnitude of the importance was surely impressed upon me.

So, my dear, I checked with your secretary and cleared out your afternoon schedule tomorrow. You and I will go meet with the senior Engineers to get an overview ourselves of some of their projects and ideas!"

Duncan's eyes had gone wide and he straightened his back. "Lydia! You can't just take over my schedule like that! I have meetings with the Council members who were giving rallies out in the district towns, and then I have several planning sessions! Really, this is not like you! Why do you think this meeting with the engineers is more important?

"Well ..." Lydia's eyes sparkled in merriment. "It was not my idea at all. As James and I were discussing what to do, I had a clear stirring in my spirit and I heard His voice say 'Go!' I saw a vision of us walking into the engineering headquarters. So, my dear, unless God tells you otherwise, I think we have a date!"

Duncan pushed back from his desk and smiled as the momentary tension melted away. "I will pray about it too, though I think it is pretty unlikely He would give me a countervailing direction! And you know, it might even be rather fun – certainly far different than our normal activities. Living with a discerner is never dull! Or perhaps more correctly, living by actively expecting and following the Spirit's daily and even hourly guidance is never dull! Is James sending one of his senior assistants too?"

"He wasn't sure. He said the problem was that few Watchers were really good strategists with imaginations – they tend to stick with tried-and-true methods that are often the best for standard warfare. However, James was thinking that the Dominion will NOT come with standard warfare techniques as the Watchers are typically taught. So he needs someone who is both highly practical and yet rather imaginative, who can assess how well a new technology might work even if it is developed for something non-military. They will also need to deal with the requirements for total reliability in situations where what can go wrong usually does. At least, that is how James said it. Oh, and he said he also needed someone who can work with 'thick-headed stubborn perfectionists who don't have the slightest idea of what is really important.' I think he was referring to the engineers, but then again Mesha had just walked into the room and I was not entirely sure if the reference was to the engineers or to a certain Master Healer who has been forcing rest on a very unwilling patient!"

Lydia grinned at the thought and then continued. "So I don't know if we will have accompaniment or not. Either way, I think you and I will be welcomed pretty well by the engineers – you have been quite supportive of their work and have funded many more projects than any of your predecessors."

"Yes, and we have all been the better for it. A few of those projects have tremendously improved crop yields, and their sanitation and water distribution systems have made the Keep the cleanest, most modern large city in the entire world. Some ideas have seemed truly inspired by God."

"Well, tomorrow perhaps we will see more of such inspiration."

"Tomorrow afternoon it is then."

"You have got to be the orneriest, most obstinate and obstructionist patient I have ever had the displeasure to argue with!" Mesha stood glowering at the seated James a moment longer and then continued. "You are in NO shape to go anywhere, not even for just a few hours! You will wear yourself completely out and then want to come crawling back here for our tender loving care and mercy. I tell you, if you walk or hobble out the front door I don't know if I will EVER let your stubborn hide grace the doors again!"

James glowered right back. "Is that a promise, your wind-bagginess? If I had known that I would have tried leaving already!"

"Master Warden, you surely try my patience!"

"Master Healer, you should try *being* your own patient! I can't let Chancellor Duncan and Lydia go off to the School of Engineering just by themselves, and I just can't find the right person to send in my place. This is a VITAL meeting; it could be one of the most important to the very future of Freelandia! If it kills me, then so be it – I won't live a second longer than God wants me to anyway. Now you can help me, or you can hinder me, but with you or in spite of you, I AM GOING!"

James looked on with fuming eyes and bunched muscles. It did not impress Mesha one bit, but it was obvious the Warden had totally made up his mind to go, and fighting it further was not going to accomplish anything useful.

"Alright Master Warden. You win." Mesha sighed resignedly. He still had one trump card to play, and he wanted the maximum effect. "I should have known better than to pick a fight with the head Watcher in Freelandia. I will help you in whatever way I can. But I will ask for two small favors. I realize you believe this to be an extremely important meeting, but if the strain sets you back very far you know you will have several more weeks here … under my care."

James looked smug at his victory, but that faded slightly into suspicion. "What favors?"

"Oh, nothing much, really. Just that I want you to promise to only stay as long as absolutely necessary – and please try to make it only a few hours – for the longer term sake of Freelandia? You really are needed back at your post in full health as soon as possible."

"Ooookayyy. You mentioned two?"

"Oh, well … I just think I should send one of my assistants along to help you out – you know, in case your leg starts acting up. You wouldn't want those engineers to see you fall over! And if you get over-tired you wouldn't want to fall asleep in front of them, now would you? That person would be your assistant for the meeting."

"Well … yes … I suppose so." James was somewhat suspicious – it seemed that Mesha was giving up much too easily.

"Ok then. Since you are graciously granting my two favors, I will fully support your *request* to go to the meeting. I will have your clothes sent immediately. I do want you to eat a good balanced lunch before you go, and I will instruct my nurse to be ready to give you some pain medication if your leg acts up – and maybe some stimulant if you get too drowsy. Remember, that poison is still not totally out of your system. You have been taking naps several times a day and your body needs that to heal properly!"

"I have taken RESTS, not 'naps!' And can I have some real food for lunch, not the leafy fruity rabbit food I have had to swallow down since being here?"

"My, you are testy. Give you an inch and you want a mile! I will see what we can cook up for you – maybe something spicier and with some greater substance?"

"Yes … YES! A slab of rare meat would be superb, but even some hot chili would taste powerfully good right now."

"Let me see. I will send an assistant with your clothes and see about your meal. I will stop by again before you leave." Mesha walked out with somewhat slumped shoulders, but as soon as he closed the door he straightened back up with a steely glint in his eyes. He sent an assistant to get the Warden's clothes and then another to get a carriage ready. Then he grinned, rubbing his hands together, and called for Head Nurse Abigail. The Master Warden had agreed to an assistant, but Mesha had the right to choose which one.

The School of Engineering was a beehive of activity. Each major project leader was scheduled to give a brief update, and for some reason the Master Warden had said he wanted to have a short show-and-tell of every idea that had been dreamed up and had at least a semi-workable model. That had resulted in a flurry of activity as dozens of apprentice engineers scrambled to build all sorts of contraptions and scale models. The Director of the Engineering School had cleared out their largest meeting room and set up tables and chairs in a "U" shape so that presenters could bring their inventions and ideas into the center where everyone could see and hear. The problem had been who to invite. Certainly every Master Level Engineer had to be present and maybe some of the retired Masters as well. The most senior apprentices should also be invited, and there were a few quite promising mid-level apprentices too. The problem was not in finding worthy attendees.

What was even a bigger problem was the other rule that the Warden had made, and it was still a source of frustration. He had explicitly wanted contrarian viewpoints – he wanted what he had called "healthy debate" and not just "status quo" brainstorming. Master Brentwood, the Director, liked to run a tidy ship, as he was fond of saying. He had in place a well organized methodology for evaluating projects that involved several lay-ers of formal project reviews so that what finally was funded was sure to deliver. The School had a success rate of over ninety percent on the couple of projects a year it delivered, and quite a few had proven to be highly beneficial to the welfare of Freelandia.

Of course, there were bound to be complainers – usually mid-level engineers who chafed at the slow progress of ideas and inventions that wound their way up through the formal channels. They eventually learned that you just couldn't work on everything, and low risk projects usually got the best funding. 'Slow and steady wins the race' was more than a motto – it was the guiding principle enforced on the School of Engineers from the top down. Therefore, to actually encourage opposing debate rather than the gentlemanly discussion he demanded was not to his liking at all. No sir, not one little bit.

So the Master Warden wanted a token contrarian present? Perhaps if he invited a rather outlandish eccentric the Warden would more easily see his mistake, and likely as not get fed up and dismiss the fellow within the first hour. And the Master Engineer knew just the person. He'd invite that young upstart Robert Macgregor! He was only tolerated at the School because, well, though he did not like to admit it, the man was a genius – but in a confoundingly eccentric way. He could fix nearly anything, often after just looking at it or hearing the details of a problem. He had often discovered flaws in designs that no one else saw or even believed were possible – until working models or even full scale units broke down and proved him correct. Yet he was nearly impossible to work with, and his thick accent supposedly from whatever country it was that he said he was born in did not help either. He seemed to flout the established norms and rules with abandon. He was wildly imaginative and was constantly babbling about some new idea or another – not that any ever made it through formal reviews … only rarely were any even submitted! And during the few reviews that he was reluctantly invited to, he was always interrupting with some crazy notions or suggestions. His critiques were useful, but few of the senior engineers whom the Director had personally groomed listened to him beyond those, and it was highly unlikely he would ever get past Apprentice Level Six – certainly not during Brentwood's tenure as Director of the Engineering School.

Yes, Macgregor was just the person to fulfill the Warden's ill-conceived request. Brentwood wondered how many minutes it would take before Macgregor would be kicked right out of the meeting! Perhaps that might finally make this odd-ball engineer come to his senses and conform!

Warden James was sputtering aplenty as he, Chancellor Duncan, Lydia and Head Nurse Abigail pulled up to the School of Engineering Headquarters building. He had to endure the indignity for a Watcher … for the Master Warden no less … to arrive in a *carriage*! He would have far preferred to ride a horse, or even to walk – but Mesha has been insistent, and admittedly this was indeed far easier on his leg. But it just was not a proper way for a Watcher to arrive at an important meeting. Harrumph!

The four of them entered the building – and James turned red when Abigail held the door open for him as he limped up – and were escorted to the meeting room. Master Brentwood ushered them to the front table with James and Duncan sitting in the center, flanked by Lydia and Abigail. Abigail made a fuss, and a young apprentice scrambled to find a short stool so James could keep his wounded leg somewhat elevated.

Most of the engineers were already in the room, with a few others wandering in to take their places. James noted that they were definitely dressed up compared to when he had visited before. He guessed that formal reviews required more formal attire. Precisely at the starting time for the meeting, Master Brentwood stood.

"Ahem! Please engineers, each of you take your seats promptly! This is not grade school! Several of you are tardy – that is NOT the way to start such an important meeting as this!" He glared sternly at the late comers. "Each Master Engineer will present on the projects they are in charge of, followed by the lesser ranks present in the room. The others will wait in the antechamber to this meeting room and will be called in one by one when it is their turn. Now, be assured, we have a tight schedule and so we will all be punctual to our allotted time – you all know how I feel about that and I will personally enforce the rule." Brentwood noticed that the furthest chair on the end was empty – the seat he had reserved for Mr. Macgregor.

"*Good,*" he thought, "*I did my part and the loud-mouth did not even show up! Perhaps this day will turn out better than expected!*"

James looked at Duncan and rolled his eyes. He had really wanted an open format brainstorming session with freely flowing ideas, but perhaps this method would work out ok, since they had quite a few projects and pre-project status ideas to review. Yet he knew that sometimes the best ideas were born of synergistic discussion built upon others. It seemed like Brentwood was rather rigid in how he ran meetings ... and by extension likely how he ran the entire School. James wondered just how beneficial this was going to be after all. At least it was better than being under Master Healer Mesha's baleful glare!

Brentwood frowned at those whispering in hushed voices before he spoke. "Engineers, we have the high honor of not only having the Master Warden here – and you must realize he is still recovering from the abhorrent poisoning at the hands of the Dominion – but we also have the very distinguished honor of having Chancellor Duncan and his gracious wife Lydia here as well. You should all be aware of the significant investment the Chancellor has made into our School over the last many years." Brentwood turned and belatedly looked over at Nurse Abigail, not sure who she was or why she was here.

Lydia stood and relieved his hesitation. "And this is Abigail, Head Nurse at the Ministry of Healing and personal assistant to Grand Master Mesha. She is here in an official capacity to care for the Master Warden."

James glared at Lydia with a stony frown. It was not like he wanted any attention to his medical condition!

Brentwood continued, "We want to give these good people a review of our work. I understand there may be considerably more funding available for projects that might assist in the defense of Freelandia. Now of course, that has not been much of a focus here for quite some time, and so the Master Warden wanted to take a fresh look at what we are doing to see if perhaps anything might have utility for that immediate purpose. I'm not so sure anything will strike his fancy, but we just may find that some of our projects can help the infrastructure, which can free up people for more specific defensive activities.

In any case, I think we can begin ... Master Hargrove, perhaps you can start?"

At that moment a commotion sounded in the next room, with shouting voices that spilled over into the meeting hall. The door between the rooms burst open and in walked a tall, lanky fellow with a thin reddish moustache and shortly trimmed beard. He was scowling and his head was turned to glare at someone in the other room. He was two steps into the meeting hall and was flinging the door shut with some force when he finally turned and noticed the room full of seated figures staring at him in shock – except for the stiffly standing Master Brentwood whose eyes were icy needles boring down toward the disruptive engineer.

The tardy engineer grinned sheepishly. "Ach … now I be surely sorry for me wee interruption gentlepeople. One or two of our apprentices needed a bit o' correction on their designs and didn't quite see me point, so I had to … persuade them more force-ably like!"

Master Brentwood was obviously not amused as his face turned a shade of angry red. "MR. MACGREGOR! You are unconscionably late! We have already started! You should have excused yourself and waited to enter at the scheduled break!"

"A thousand pardons I'm inclined to give ye. But it doesn't seem like ye be getting along too far in yer meeting yet. Least-wise it seems you be still do'in all the talkin'. But most importantly, sir, have the prayers been spoken yet? I sorely didn't want to miss bein' part of the blessing. Without God's blessing we're all just a wee bunch o' codgers dreaming up ideas in our own power. But now, under the power of the Most High and with our 'arts and minds stirred uppity-like by His Spirit, well sir, that be another story entirely!"

Master Brentwood sputtered. "I hardly think we need your preaching, Mr. Macgregor. Now please take your seat immediately so we can get on with the first project review!"

Duncan was grinning, already taking a liking to this late comer. "Ah, excuse me …"

Brentwood turned and assumed a more contrite attitude. "Yes, Chancellor?"

Duncan's grin turned serious. "I also think it is imperative we seek God's guidance on this meeting! The war that is coming is God's to win and ours to lose. I do not want to do anything on the basis of just my own power or judgment concerning the protection of Freelandia!"

Master Brentwood sputtered, "Oh … well, of course! I was just wanting to get the meeting started promptly … I know how important your time is!"

"Yes, I'm sure … though I did not see it listed on your quite detailed agenda. Regardless, do you mind if I pray for us first?" Duncan's question left little room for any other answer but one.

"Well of course not, Chancellor! Please … please invoke the blessing." Brentwood had taken on a placating tone but he was obviously uncomfortable, and not used to being overruled in his meetings.

Duncan arched one eyebrow. "I don't think I can "invoke" anything. I can, however, talk to our Creator." Duncan stood, eyeing the group. Several looked relieved, and Macgregor was beaming. Others were rolling their eyes and looked uncomfortable. Duncan noted those who seemed in agreement with seeking God's guidance. "Dear Father, thank You for Your inspiration. We seek Your guidance and wisdom today on how You might have us use the ideas You have already given, and ask for open minds to see anything new You may direct us toward. Please guide our thoughts and hearts to hear You, and let the words of our mouths and thoughts of our minds be quick to encourage and uplift our brethren, and to give You the glory and all the credit as the source of all knowledge. Amen."

"AMEN sir, and well said!" It seemed that Mr. Macgregor was rather … outspoken.

"Ah, yes. Thank you Chancellor for those … uh … stirring motivational words. Moving right along, Master Hargrove?"

James, listening to the exchange, felt his initial impression of Master Brentwood was perhaps overly considerate. He really did not seem to be the best choice to select and lead the efforts here to rapidly accelerate projects for the coming war effort.

Master Hargrove stood and beamed at the head table. He had a small-scale mock building with various tiny pipes attached. "The project I have been assigned to work on involves a rain water collection system for large buildings. One problem with tall buildings is providing water on the upper floors. My apprentices and I have designed a rooftop rain water collection system that can supply water to upper floors, or – and this is the true inspiration – it can be funneled and piped down to the ground floor and injected through small nozzles into the building's water supply. This can boost the pressure of that water thirty percent or more – to supply more water to the higher floor levels and provide higher water pressure for potential firefighting needs."

James tried hard not to roll his eyes or yawn. This project may be useful but did not appear to have much military potential.

Hargrove continued. "We have been working on this for over a year now, and are almost ready for a full scale trial on one of the newer tall buildings. Let me demonstrate on this model." He grinned even wider. "We spent several months perfecting this exact scale model. It will show the water pressure with and without the system in place by the water exiting a fountain that will fill the pond in the model. You can see the difference in pressure by the relative height the fountain water will reach."

Master Hargrove pulled out a narrow necked watering can and proceeded with the demonstration, filling his 15 minute slot with further details.

James groaned under his breath, just loud enough for those nearest him to hear. Nurse Abigail leaned forward with a worried look on her face, but the withering stare from James silenced her unspoken concern. Lydia suppressed a giggle with a hand over her mouth. Duncan, ever the diplomatic one, nodded appreciatively. "Thank you, Master Hargrove. Firefighting is indeed an especially important issue in a war situation, and the firefighters will likely need all the help they can get. What's next?"

Master Hargrove bowed low and busied himself with cleaning up – the fountain had over shot the miniature pond and made a puddle on the floor, but he had brought some towels along just for such a possibility.

The next several Masters described their projects, and while all had promise of improving the standards of living of Freelandian citizens, none showed particular benefit for the war efforts. The visitors were getting bored and James was now unsuccessful at stifling a large yawn. He wondered if this visit had been such a good idea after all.

Master Brentwood on the other hand was quite pleased. There had been no interruptions from Macgregor. "Next up is Master Oldive, who has a very clever use for one of our recently discovered new metal alloys of silarium." Master Brentwood sat down, look rather self-satisfied. So far each project review had gone without a hitch – the spilled water did not really count against that – and Chancellor Duncan in particular appeared rather impressed by each. He was sure the School of Engineering was going to show itself very worthy of greater funding and prestige.

Master Oldive was a pot-bellied shorter fellow with a balding head and a bright sparkle in his intelligent eyes. He had been one whose true piety Duncan had noticed. "Let me begin by saying that I have had the privilege to be assigned to one of the first projects incorporating the new metal alloy. As many of you have heard, silarium has many rather unique properties we are just beginning to explore – and as far as we know, Freelandia is the only current source for this metal. This first application is rather ordinary and simple, but the project was chartered to try out the new alloy in something plain and practical so we could get some history and familiarity working with it. So, while I really don't see a fit to the very urgent need of defending Freelandia, please bear with my simple demonstration."

He pulled out a small scale door on a frame and placed it on the table in front of him before continuing. "While others are exploring a variety of additional uses for silarium, we have focused on springs. You may or may not be familiar with these little metal spirals, but they can store up energy when compressed and then quickly release it. The approved project we have been working on is for automatic door closers." He pushed the small door open wide with minimal effort, and then let it go. The door promptly swung back to place, banging shut with some force on the frame in which it was suspended. "Of course, we would put some padding on the frame to keep it from banging like that, or let it swing clear in the other direction – the little springs here will dampen the oscillations nicely and the door will come to a stop in the shut position in just a moment."

"Thank you, Master Oldive. Do you have any suggestions for how this might work outside of, say, an office or shop?" Master Brentwood was obviously proud of this newest invention.

"Well, thank you for asking, Master Brentwood. I do believe it may be helpful on our ships for topside doors which would close immediately and automatically behind anyone exiting to the deck – it would minimize potential water entry, for instance."

"Splendid idea! I am sure Warden James will want to check up on that immediately! Now, next up is …"

"Wait up there a moment, if ye don't mind." Senior Apprentice Macgregor spoke up for the first time since being seated. "May I take a closer look at yer device there, Oldsy?" The last was said with a good natured chuckle and wink.

"Certainly Bobby, feel free to take it apart and tinker with it if you like. I don't think you've played with this one yet."

"GENTLEMEN, PLEASE!" Master Brentwood had jumped to his feet. "Please refrain from such casual bantering at this formal project review!"

Master Oldive had brought his door and frame over and placed it in front of Macgregor, then hastily retreated to his chair across the room. "Oh, I am sorry Master Brentwood! Please forgive me; I thought open discussion was to be fostered at this meeting." He nodded at the guests and took his seat.

James let out a barely disguised snort. So far nothing appeared to have any real utility. His leg was beginning to throb, despite what he had told Mesha – though he was not going to allow the oh-so-sticky-sweet Nurse Abigail to know about his discomfort. Who knows what that old battleaxe might try to foist upon him! Yet if something of interest did not turn up soon he may just as well leave – at least he had a good excuse he could use for needing to depart early!

The next Master stood and began to discuss his newest plowing invention which he intoned would reduce field work by at least fifteen percent.

Duncan's mind wandered and he was having a hard time concentrating on the speaker. His gaze shifted over to Apprentice Macgregor, who was totally ignoring the speaker and busily dismantling part of the door and spring contraption. He had some strange device in his hands that looked like a pair of pliers with a screw driver arm extending below it. Macgregor was pulling on the spring, turning it this way and that and testing its action. Then he paused a moment, obviously thinking. Something must have come to him, because he suddenly began to reassemble the parts, but not apparently in the same way it had been given to him. Macgregor then looked about surreptitiously and leaned backwards to grab some device sitting on the floor near him – likely a demonstration project of some other engineer nearby.

Duncan covered his mouth to hide a chuckle. Macgregor was removing a few parts of that other model while its owner, seated next to him, was intently listening to the next project review. The outspoken engineer was reassembling the parts on the rearranged spring contraption, presumably creating something entirely new. He made a few adjustments, and then pulled back on the smaller piece of wood now attached to the springs. He appeared satisfied with whatever he was doing on that part, and began carving out the end of the wood with what appeared to be a small blade he swiveled out from the other hollow handle of the pliers. Duncan wondered just what other tools might be equally well hidden in that most unusual pair of pliers.

A model of the new plow was being demonstrated in a pan of dirt, but it was not going exactly right as soil was being spun about and showering onto the nearest onlookers. The errant dirt was being brushed off with annoyance by the soiled audience while the speaker continued his monolog without even noticing.

After a small pile of shavings had been produced from his carving efforts, Macgregor looked about on the table this way and that. He reached over to grab a small plum from a plate of fruit which sat nearby. He pulled on the main plank attached to the springs, holding it back with some obvious effort, while his opposite elbow struggled to hold down the former door frame tightly to the table surface. With considerable dexterity he placed the plum in the now hollowed out area of the short plank.

Duncan was fascinated and he gently elbowed Lydia and directed her attention over to whatever it was Macgregor was doing, and then did the same to James on his other side. The plow presentation finally ended, and Master Brentwood thanked the speaker and then addressed the room. "Now, engineers and guests, perhaps we should take a short break to stretch our legs and take refreshments? Just for a few minutes though, we have many other equally interesting and important presenters to show us their work." Just as he finished, Macgregor let go of the end of the plank holding the captive plum.

The board slapped forward with considerable force, hurling the plum into the air. It sailed clear to the furthest corner of the room, where it smacked into the wall with great force, splattering the fruit in a large reddish purple spot on the white-washed walls.

There was dead silence in the room for several moments. Master Brentwood had first gone pale, and then his face rapidly reddened in anger as his eyes widened. He was winding up for a thorough and considerable rebuke when Macgregor spoke out first. "Did ye see that! Holy Father above!

Those springy-thingies have POWER! Think a wee bit what they might do in large size? Now I wonder 'bout that … what kind of range might a catapult have with a few o' these springy thingies super-sized? Hmmm – hey Oldsy, how big have ye made these springy thingies into?"

Master Brentwood's face was bright red and his eye bulged as his surging anger reached new heights and was now ready to explode in full gale-wind fury. "MACGREGOR! I – HAVE – HAD – ENOUGH – OF – YOUR – OUTBURSTS! You will take both yourself and that abominable contraption out of here this instant and …"

James was sitting up straight in his chair, staring alternatively at the plum-splattered wall behind him and back at the miniature device which had launched it. He very deliberately interrupted in a loud commanding voice: "And you will begin an immediate investigation into its possibilities as a long range catapult system! If I had not seen that with my own eyes I would have said you were crazy!" James laughed. "Maybe you are, but if so, it is a kind of crazy I like! You have my full support and as much funding as you need – make it happen, and fast!"

Brentwood's eyes were bulging out of his skull and he was no longer saying anything coherent, just sub-vocal sputterings.

Lydia reached over and touched the arms of Duncan and James, an intense look on her face as she spoke. "He is the one, James. Macgregor is the one who needs to lead the engineering war efforts. That is the direction I am getting."

James looked rather wryly over at Duncan. This was not going to go over all that well with the bureaucracy that Brentwood had clearly established in engineering stone. Well, it needed a shake-up, from what he could see. Duncan nodded in agreement with his wife. James could see that Master Brentwood was angry beyond words, his whole body trembling. Nurse Abigail hurried over to try to get him to sit, but even as she arrived Brentwood suddenly grabbed at his chest and collapsed to the floor.

Abigail was a head nurse and when she took charge she could put a senior Watcher to shame. She snapped out orders even as her nimble fingers untied Brentwood's tie and loosened his shirt. "You!" Her stare caught one of the nearby engineers in an icy grasp. "Get a blanket, now!" She turned to Lydia, who had rushed over. "He may be having a heart attack. We should move him to a bed or couch." Abigail caught another two engineers with her glare. "You two – is there a couch or bed nearby we can move Master Brentwood to?" As they fumbled out an affirmative answer she continued. "Then help carry him – gently – to it. And have someone else bring a glass of cool water."

The two engineers lifted the barely conscious Brentwood and carried him off with Nurse Abigail at his side, while another engineer trailed after them with a glass of water and the blanket the first man had just fetched.

James took control – he was particularly good at that in emergencies, and anyway, his nanny-nurse was now otherwise occupied and he intended to make the most of the opportunity. He stood to his feet and in a command voice ordered everyone else to be seated. James watched the procession leaving with the prone body of Brentwood, concern darkening his features. He cleared his throat noisily to get the attention of everyone remaining before he spoke. "Gentle people! Let us pray for Master Brentwood's healing and recovery." As James took a breath before continuing Engineer Macgregor leapt to his feet, a sorrowful look washing over his face.

"Beggin' yer pardon, Master Warden sir – as I am the likely trigger for poor old Brentwood's sudden affliction, might I be allowed to unite us in prayer on 'is behalf?"

James gave a critical look at the lanky young man, wondering just what kind of prayer this engineer might give for the man who appeared to be his nemesis, and how sincere it might really be. Perhaps this would be a quick check on the true mettle of this man. James looked Macgregor squarely in the eyes and nodded his head in acquiescence.

The engineer looked about the room slowly before he spoke. "Christian brothers and sisters, this is serious business. Let us come before our good Lord with united hearts and minds to intercede on behalf of our friend Master Brentwood." Robert closed his eyes and raised his arms and hands heavenward. "Dear Father above, we ask for your healing mercy to fall upon poor Master Brentwood. Please send Your Spirit to touch his body, to restore him back to full health. And even more, please open his mind and touch his soul to see his need for You. And help everyone here to know that this could be their last day here on earth and that some sitting here need to get right with You before it is too late." Macgregor sighed heavily and continued with obvious sincerity in his voice. "Thank You Father for hearing even me, forgive me for being such a thorn in Brentwood's side at times, and help me to learn to better support those whom you put over me. Amen."

A murmur of consensual 'amens" swept around the room. Robert remained standing with a concerned expression. "Friends, if anyone feels a need to be a'talking 'bout this later, please find me out. I'd be sure to stop whatever it was I might be do'in to talks with you. Please do take heed to what I said to our Good Father. There is no more important a thing you canna do but get right with God." He turned to look at James in the front of the room and nodded his head as he sat back down.

James nodded back. If he had been doubtful before, he was now sure this was indeed the right man. "Master and apprentice engineers, we do hope and pray that Master Brentwood will be healed. But we cannot wait. We need a Chief Engineer to lead a new Engineering Directorate for our war preparations. The person will report directly to me and make all decisions of funding and projects for the duration of the Dominion crisis. That person needs to be outside the normal chain of command, someone who can think and act very independently, and be able to make things happen quickly without regard to the established rules or bureaucracy. Both from what I have seen today and from what we have just discerned from God, that person is Mr. Macgregor!"

James did not wait for any response and now addressed the startled young engineer directly. "Will you accept that position, sir?"

Macgregor flinched, and then looked down. "I'm sure there be many more qualified engineers here, Master Warden. I am not even a Master yet! Surely there be others, like Oldsy there, who would make a better leader. I seem to be best at makin' our leaders here upsety-like."

Master Oldive stood. "No Bobby, I agree with the Master Warden that you are the one we need." He turned to Master James. "I think that is the right choice, Warden. Bobby is one of the most eccentric and opinionated people I have ever known, and he makes rather hasty decisions – but he is nearly always right! He is one of our smartest engineers with more raw talent than anyone I know, but he has been held back because of his 'unrestrained' and unconventional ways. He can and will make things happen like no one else in this room. And he has the respect – in his own quirky way – of everyone here and especially from the other apprentices. He is constantly helping them with their ideas and inventions, even when they have not had official recognition to continue the work. And most of all, he listens. Bobby listens both to his fellow engineers and especially to the ultimate Master Engineer, God."

Others around the table were nodding, mostly those Duncan had noted earlier just before prayer. He stood. "I agree, and believe God is leading us in this direction. Well, Apprentice Macgregor, will you help us?"

Robert gulped. This was certainly not expected! "I need to pray 'bout it first off – if it truly be what me God wants o' me, then woe is me if I be gettin' in His way! Can ye give me a wee bit of time, say by noon on the morrow?"

James smiled. "Certainly. Please come to my room at the Ministry of Healing and we will go out for lunch – my ... er ... Chancellor Duncan's treat! Meanwhile, I think we should cancel the rest of the meeting for today – with the change in leadership I believe we can let this go for another week – but we really, really are counting on you engineers to help us defeat the Dominion! And of course we all need to lift Master Brentwood up in our prayers. Thank you all."

The engineers filed out, with Master Oldive and Robert carrying the cata-contraption and deep in discussion. James had perked up and now was in a rather good mood. "Duncan, Lydia, let's head on back. I think we have done a good day's work here, and I expect tomorrow we will have a new Chief Engineer to shake this place up and report on what falls loose that we can use militarily. I think that calls for dinner out ... what do you say?"

Lydia grinned at James and said oh-so-innocently, "But James, I really don't think Head Nurse Abigail would approve! I am certain she has strict orders to escort you directly back to the Ministry of Healing and Mesha's care! You surely would not want to miss whatever thin soup or cream of mush they might be serving!"

"Oh, I don't know what her instructions might have been," James said rather magnanimously, "but anyway, she is going to be busy for awhile with poor old Brentwood – I am sure someone here can see that she has a nice carriage ride back when she is ready. Meanwhile, I don't think there is anything left for us to do here, so we might as well not just hang around – we should probably head on back. And if we just so happen to stop at a restaurant on the way … you know Duncan how you sometimes get hungry a might early some afternoons … then what could be possibly wrong than for three dear old friends to share a nice sit down meal together?"

Duncan laughed. "That's putting it on 'a wee bit' thick, my friend! I doubt you'd be missed for a few more hours … but if we are out too late Mesha will probably have the Keep Watchers scouring the whole city for you!"

James scowled, but it quickly changed to a grin. "I don't see any reason Mesha needs to hear about it. Our meeting ended early, Nurse Abigail is otherwise occupied, and our schedules are suddenly opened. Besides, I am powerfully hungry for some REAL food!"

Chapter 3

Bobby

Just before noon the next day James had a knock on the door to his office-room at the Ministry of Healing. He looked up to see Robert Macgregor standing there with a scowl on his face.

"I can't say I like visiting here – the place is chock full of sickly folks! Do ye think we could perhaps be gettin' ourselves off to somewheres else where we may be findin' some good eats? I tend to talk much better within' a filled up stomach. Otherwise it tends to talk back so much it seems to be carryin' on a conversation all of its own, if ye catches what I'm meaning now."

"Well, I think we could arrange that ..." James spoke up louder so the nurse out in the hallway could hear. "After all, you were promised a good lunch and we have some very important business to discuss. It just wouldn't do to try to have it here." He gave an exaggerated wink to the apprentice engineer.

"Ach, I do believe I can just feel those little sickly critters startin' to crawl up me legs – quick like, please Master Warden, can ye please be gettin' me out o' this establishment?"

"Oh yes, right away!" James stood and made a show of taking the cane that Mesha had told him to use. He made a pretense of walking with a rather heavy lean on it as the two men exited. Once they turned a corner James started to walk quite normally and carried the cane along. "It just seems to make the Master Healer less cantankerous if I pretend to need it now and then. I think that man is less and less happy the healthier his patients are – like he thinks he is going to lose business if we leave too early!"

"Ye surely have to be watching that kind with both good eyes in front, and with a spare pair behind yer head! I try to steer well clear of 'em – that and their nurses too! I'm not sure which is worser, the healers or the nurses! Not that some o' them are not unpleasant to rest your tired eyes on, now and again – but don't ye be turning your back on 'em or they're be likely to be poking or sticking you with something on the backside where no self-respecting ladyfolk should be caring fer!"

They both looked seriously at each other for a moment and then burst out laughing. James knew he had found a sure friend with a shared nemesis. They walked past several nicer restaurants, but Bobby – he had insisted that James call him that – said they seemed "a wee bit overly stuffy, where they probably served fancified itty bitty portions on huge plates with the latest sauces, where an honest man couldn't get his fill 'less he ordered up three or four platefuls." He did have a point, so James steered them toward a higher end tavern that he figured may be more to the engineer's liking.

They settled into a booth. "Aye, now this be more to me likin now! For sure the good Chancellor is pickin' up the tab? Good then, that is might decent of the man. He seems like a true God-fearin' man, the Chancellor, and his wife too. They seem to have a real love fer God and seriously rely on Him. How any intelligent people canna' see His handiwork all about them is beyond me."

"Yes, Duncan and Lydia are true followers of the Most High God. It seemed to us that quite a few of the engineers in the meeting room yesterday were somewhat put off when prayers were mentioned."

"Aye, that is a sorry tale to tell. It seems that Master Brentwood liked to keep everythin' in its own place, neat and tidy – including God. He just couldn't see that God is not so neat and tidy as he wanted. I fear that the good Master liked to keep God at a distance, serving Him more from the lips than from the heart and mind. 'Tis a sad thing for his heart to give way like that – I hear he is expected to be laid up with bed rest for several months and he may never recover enough to continue his duties at the School o' Engineering. We will surely be needin' a new head Master shortly, but those highest on Master Brentwood's list are cast in his same mold – if you follow me drift."

"I rather thought that, even from just the brief visit we had. It sounds like the place needs straightening out. Which brings us to our purpose for this lunch – what will you say to my offer?"

A waitress came by to take their orders, sparing Robert from having to answer just yet. After she left, he stroked his trim beard before answering.

"Well now, I prayed long 'n hard over that a goodly many hours last night and this mornin'. In general, I've no strong desire to be boss'in everyone around the place – I would much rather be doing engineering than boss'in. Yet as ye say, the School needs a stiff bit of redirectin', especially-like with the Dominion breathing fire down our necks. We have no time fer the normal slow inventin'. We have to make choices right quick, and push on the best idears like a bull wanting to git into the heifer's pasture. And the ideas have to work, work right, and work right away. I kin do that, Master Warden, I'm sure of it. What's more, I think it is what God is wantin' me to do too. As long as He is behind it, I'm your engineer."

"I am very pleased to hear that Macgregor … I mean Bobby. While under the War Preparations I officially have the authority to appoint you, perhaps it would be worthwhile if Chancellor Duncan made it very official – that might encourage any skeptics back at the School to take notice. As we said, we have no time to spare. As Chief Engineer for Freelandia, you have full authority over the entire School of Engineering and all Masters and Apprentices therein. You will also be on my Leaders' Council. You report to me directly, and I report to the Chancellor and the High Council.

You will need to support the defensive works around Freelandia, and that is going to require most of your manpower. The Dominion is very likely to come at us with a huge advantage in numbers of ships and fighting men. We really need you to help even things out, to give us "force multiplication" to whittle down their numbers.

I want you to talk with Minister Polonos to get a better idea of the enemy we face. Then touch base with the Master Shipbuilders and my Wardens in charge of the stationary defensive works at the Keep and our outer coastal shorelines. See what you can do to help them – and by all means evaluate every possible invention and idea that might fit with the needs. You have a nearly unlimited budget in this. Don't be wasteful of course, but spend what you think is wise. Speed is more important right now than expenses, and God has richly blessed us for many years – so our coffers are quite full.

I want a weekly update, but don't let that stop you from important work. If needed, send an apprentice with the update. If you run into roadblocks, work around them, break through them, or get me involved. Don't make enemies unless necessary, but don't let bureaucracy slow you down. And by all means seek God's guidance. Call on Lydia or anyone else gifted in discerning His will whenever you are unsure about a decision. This war is His, not ours. We mainly need to listen to His guidance and act upon what He shows.

Do you have any questions?"

Food was arriving, and Macgregor's eyes lit up as he drank in the savory smells. "Ach, it may be a wee bit difficult to think real straight-like with such distractions as this! I am sure to have a few questions along the way – probably startin' the minute I leave ye after eatin'! But as long as I know you will back me up and give me a decently free hand, I can git started immediately. Send someone along with whatever official-like pronouncement the good Chancellor cares to make, I'll nail that up on some wall somewhere for anyone who cares to see it. But now good Warden, I canna' speak and eat at the same time, and this lovely food is making me drool like a fox in a hen house. May ye speak a blessing over our meal and then dig in?"

Robert strode into the building he had left as a senior apprentice and was returning as Chief Engineer. Somehow things looked different. He no longer just worked here. Now this place was "his". Bobby laughed as he talked out loud to himself. "No siree, Bobby my boy. My heavenly Father owns this place. I am just a temporary caretaker, a steward He put in charge of the output of this 'vinyard' with high expectations. Time to git to work!"

He walked down the main hallway to a familiar office. "Hey Oldsy … guess what?"

"Hmmm – you look like your belly is full and you have a grin splitting across your face from ear to ear. I'd say we have us a fire-spitting new Chief Engineer!"

"And one who needs a senior advisor, mentor and friend! Oldsy, I want ye to be me Chief Lieutenant, my right hand second in command. I need ye – ye are one of the most organized engineers I know, and ye get along with everyone … ye can follow me around smoothing out the feathers I have ruffled and making sure the follow through happens. Ye know how I can flit about from one thing to another. What do ye say?"

Master Oldive was taken aback by the suddenness. "Well Bobby, I'm not so sure I can keep up with you, but I sure would like to try! You've got yourself a lieutenant!"

"Right proper of you, Oldsy! Now the first order o' business is setting up shop in new digs – we are going to need a lot o' room, and these old offices just are not going to do the job. What say you to us takin' over the front conference room – the one where Master Brentwood always had his final formal project reviews? I think in an hour we could convert that into a rather nice working area. I'ma thinkin' we will need to cosy up a bit, especially at first – we have a sore lot of things to accomplish in a wee time. Me marching orders from the Master Warden are clear … we gotta MOVE on things."

"That sounds like a plan. I think we should pull together a few like-minded engineers into that conference room right now and brainstorm ideas on how to get started, and then turn 'em loose to reorganize and shake up the whole school. We will rile some folks, but since yesterday they knew big change was coming – everyone expected you to take the Chief job, Bobby."

"Alright then, let's do 'er! And get the word out that I will come a visiting with each engineer, starting later today to hear their thoughts and project ideas. No formal presentations, I'm just a-wantin' them to shows me what they have. I wants to hear them all. We can go all night if we need to. Then I'll need a few good free-thinking engineers to hear about the Dominion, to check out the current defenses, and to bring that all back to the rest of us. We have a huge amount to do, Oldsy, and by God's grace we are going to move like the wind in a tempest to accomplish what we can!"

"Right-o Bobby." Oldive paused, then a sly smile broke across his face and his eyes narrowed with a glint. "I think we should first hear from Apprentice Arianna – she is the one who blew apart the barn a month back with that "bottled swamp gas" of hers. It seems to be one of the immediate things possibly more suited to the war effort …"

Robert stopped dead in his tracks and scowled. "Now just whoa there one minute! That engineer nearly killed two apprentices in that blast, as well as herself. Now I've done a wee few dangerous experiments meself, but I don't think I've endangered others doing them." Robby scratched his chin and thought a moment. "Well, maybe just once or twice, but the others were never in mortal danger, not really. But this apprentice Arianna, she seems to be a danger, a menace, undisciplined, contentious, a …"

"A woman?" Oldive interrupted with exaggerated innocence.

"Well … yes, that too! Engineering is most rightly done by menfolk! And besides which, she is just …"

Oldive interrupted again, this time much more forcefully "she is just too much like you? And she is just so pretty that you are terribly distracted around her so that you can't think straight?" Robert was sputtering and turning red. "Bobby, she is a bright engineer with more potential than a handful of most other apprentices combined. She can't help it if you go all gooey brained whenever you are in the same room with her. Now get past your prejudices, get control of yourself, and be sensible. We need to hear what she has been up to and assess if it can be harnessed for the defense of Freelandia."

Robert gained control with some difficulty. "Master Oldive, you surely have a way of baiting a body!" Robert swallowed hard. "But do you have to be always right? Arianna is indeed a clever one, and ye are right indeed, she has enough similar traits with me that I thinks I sometimes feel what Brentwood may have thought about me."

"Well, she has at least one mightily big difference over you. Huge, really."

"Now just what might you be think'n about, Oldsy?"

Oldive took a casual step closer to the door. "Well, she surely is a far mite easier on the eyes than you!" With that he leapt through the open door, a fraction of a second before a loose ruler went flying after him. Robert heard raucous laughter echoing down the hallway, followed by "I'll tell her the new Chief Engineer is anxiously wanting her presence in the formal conference room to thoroughly look her over … I mean her project!"

"O-l-d-s-y!"

Arianna hurried toward the conference room. She had been very late in the schedule for the presentation the previous day, and actually had given up on the idea that she would even give it. After all, Brentwood had put an immediate stop to the little project she had been working on and forbade her from ever working on it again. She was resigned to the likelihood of being assigned to some back woods farming community to improve their irrigation systems. Not that such work wasn't important, but it was so boring! She was fascinated with the concept of pressure in general, and the gaseous substance she had in large part discovered had such interesting properties.

She had been tinkering with another project, one which Brentwood had not heard of yet, involving boiling water inside a thick steel sealed pot with a valve she had invented when Master Oldive had run in, breathlessly saying that there was some new Chief Engineer – what kind of position was that anyway? – and he wanted to see her immediately in the conference room where Brentwood normally held his formal project reviews. Master Oldive had been rather … mysterious, not giving her any details other than to bring one of the pressure pot contraptions she had been working on.

Arianna had not anticipated this. Master Brentwood typically wanted engineers to be dressed up for formal reviews, and she had no time to change. As she hurried down the halls she tried to straighten and brush off her skirt and blouse and tried to do something with her long and often unruly auburn hair, or at least as best she could while lugging one of the heavy pressure pots she had made. The pot was still very hot, and so she had it wrapped in a thick towel. Even still, it was difficult to hold without getting burned. With her mind busily running through a rough outline she could use in a formal review, her coordination of juggling the weighty hot metal pot and still trying to brush off dust was just a bit more than she could manage. The open conference room door came up a tad faster than expected and her sudden change of speed undid the juggling act. Her grip on the towel and pot began to slip and she swung it higher in attempt to regain control. Arianna entered the doorway far faster than she had desired, and now the wrapped metal pot was dancing between her hands, not really in control of either one. Scrambling madly to get a firm hold on it, she stumbled and her last ditch attempt at control instead sent the pot sailing out of her reach.

Robert heard a commotion and looked up just in time to see a large dark spherical object wrapped in a towel sailing directly his way. He barely got his hands up in time to prevent it from careening into his face, and the weight and momentum of the heavy metal sent him arching backwards in the chair he had set up facing the doorway across the table. He somehow actually caught the pot and blanket, but its force rocked him powerfully backward. He looked up in astonishment at the frantic face of Engineer Apprentice Arianna as his chair leaned past the point of no return and tipped over backwards with him aboard.

Arianna looked aghast. "Oh no! Apprentice Macgregor – are you ok? Why are you here? I'm so glad you caught that. Where is the Chief Engineer that made me run down here in such a hurry – if I had to rush like that and he's not here – only you – I will be sorely vexed at whomever that person thinks he is …" When Arianna was nervous she could power-talk the equivalent of the contents of a thick book in minutes flat.

Robert moaned on the floor. The chair had splintered under him and he had cracked his head smartly on the hardwood floor. Somehow he had managed to hold on to the wrapped metal pot, which he now let slump to his side, though he thought it might have cracked a rib where it had slammed into his chest before he had stopped its forward movement. His vision was blurred and he began to blink to try to clear up the fog. Since that did not totally work, Robert shook his head to see if that might clear it further. That was a mistake as it seemed to jostle about the innards of his skull and he moaned again, louder.

He struggled to lift himself up on one elbow, though the effort was taxing. Then he felt gentle hands lifting and holding his head, which was next lowered onto something very soft and warm. His grogginess began to fade and his vision and hearing began to clear.

"Robert! … Robert? Can you hear me Robert? Don't you dare go and die on me, not before I've had a chance to tell you …"

Bobby's eyes finally began to focus and he was looking up into the deepest aqua blue eyes he had ever seen. The rest of Arianna's face came into clear view and Bobby realized he had never really studied her face before, certainly not from this angle or proximity. He knew she was a very skilled engineer, and he had noticed her praying before her lunch and regularly attending the nearby chapel services as he did himself. He figured that was what really attracted him to her; her sincere Christianity, her clever engineering and, he admitted to himself, she was as Oldsy said, quite pleasant on the eyes as well. Maybe he had indeed been too quick to pass harsh judgment. A moment later his brain registered her words, and he asked curiously "… tells me what lass?"

"Oh … you aren't dead! I'm so sorry Robert … are you all right?"

She was looking nearly straight down at him and somehow he believed he had never felt "righter."

"Aye lassie, I am either alive or else the nicest angel in all of God's heaven is carry'n me in that direction!"

"OH!" Arianna shifted and Robert realized that his head was nestled in the softness of her lap. His eyes shot open fully and he blushed in embarrassment. Arianna also suddenly blushed and moved to get up – which proved to be much too fast and Robby could not catch himself before her movement let his head drop back to the floor with a thud.

It hurt. A lot. Robby moaned again.

"Oh no, Robert! I am so sorry, let me help you!" She grabbed his arm and helped him get shakily to his feet. He lurched as he headed for a chair. He sat and gingerly felt the back of his head, wincing.

"Here, let me see." She brushed his hand away and began to gently probe his scalp. Her long hair tumbled over his face, and Robby sighed. For this he would willingly fall over more often! Then her fingers touched the bruised area and he winced. "I'm so sorry Robert! Master Oldive said someone he called 'the Chief Engineer' wanted to hear about my projects immediately – was waiting for me, and I was hurrying, and tripped up when I saw it was just you in the room."

Robert groaned again. "Oldsy said he was a'goin' to do that … I figured he was joking with me."

"So who is this Chief Engineer and why would he want to see me? You've got a goose egg forming up back here, but no blood. It is going to be a sore one for awhile."

Robby sighed. "Ah, well lassie, didn't ye hear of the decision from the Master Warden and Chancellor visit yesterday?"

Arianna took a step away and turned so she could look at him. "No Robert, I didn't hear any details. I was too busy working on the pressure pot you saved from crashing to the floor."

Robby reached up to touch his ribs where the pot had impacted and he winced at the bruises already forming there. "Aye, I saved it, but it was not so very kind to me. I think it may 'ave cracked a rib or two."

"Oh, did it hit you! Robert, I am so very sorry." Arianna looked into his face with such concern showing from her wide open eyes that his brain threatened to turn to mush. He stayed in control with some effort. How did she have such an effect on him? Robert was not sure, but for some reason he did tend to get somewhat fuddle-brained when he was near her.

But responsibilities called. "Well Apprentice Arianna, as much as I enjoyed your entrance, I think I had better get to business. I'd like to hear about your wee little invention thingy here, and your other rather ... exciting ... activities."

"Well, shouldn't I wait for the 'Chief Engineer' person? I mean, I'd be happy to talk to you about it – you are so very clever at figuring out ways around problems – but it does not make much sense to tell it twice. By the way, who is the 'Chief" person anyway?" Arianna moved to a chair and sat down after retrieving her metal device.

Robert sighed again. "Well, I've heard he's a rather plain-looking fellow, not really anything unusual about him, 'cept for a big ole goose egg bump on the backside of his head."

"Oh, do you know his name ... " Arianna's eyes went wide and she shot back in her chair. Robert rather enjoyed the scene.

"No ... you can't ... I mean, you aren't ... Robert Macgregor, you are NOT about to tell me that YOU are the Chief Engineer! Master Brentwood would never hear of it!"

Robert gingerly felt the back of his head and winced when his fingers made contact with the bruised area. "Aye, lassie ... Chancellor Duncan and the Master Warden themselves did it yesterday and today it is all official-like. You managed to nearly break the ribs and almost crack the skull of the new Chief Engineer of all Freelandia!"

"Oooohhhhh!" Arianna rolled her eyes in exasperation and then closed them and shook her head back and forth slowly. Her eyes snapped back open and narrowed. "Well if I had known that, I might have thrown my pressure pot even harder! You? Chief Engineer? Of all the engineers in the entire school, they had to pick you? Why didn't they choose some someone like Oldsy or another well respected Master Engineer? What are we going to work on now with you in charge?"

Arianna had begun to pace back and forth to work off some of her frustration. She stopped in front of Robert and took a deep calming breath, though she still had her hands defiantly on her hips and steel in her eyes. "Alright, Chief Engineer. And that had better truly be your new title mister. If this is some kind of sophomoric joke you are trying to pull you will be sorry. If the Chancellor and Master Warden have indeed put you in charge, then surely God is not surprised by it, even if I am. I've had to work twice as hard as most male engineers just to stay even with the likes of you, and with God's help I'll work even harder if I have to prove myself all over."

Robert's eyes had gone wide in shock at this outburst. "Now just hold on, lassie! Just a wee few minutes ago I was just agreeing with Oldsy that you were one of the cleverest and most promising apprentice engineers we have! And that is not a joke, nor is my new position. To tell ye the truth, I think I am just as surprised and mortified as ye at it all." Bobby slumped back in his seat and winced at the pain it caused in his bruised ribs. "I don't myself know just what to do. I did not ask for the job, but if God called me to do it, then do it I shall with His help! And both I and Freelandia are going to need the help of every engineer we have, most certainly including you. Will you help – even with the likes o' me steering the ship?"

Arianna studied him shrewdly, as if sizing him up for the task. Then a wry smile broke out as one eyebrow rose. "I will work as unto the Lord regardless of who is put in charge, as I always have. But I do have one condition for you."

"And just what might that be, lass?" Robby frowned.

"I want you to treat me just like all the other engineers. You are just like so many of the other engineers here. You look at me as woman first and as an engineer second. I want your respect as an engineer – as an equal to any other apprentices at my ranking for my ideas and skills. I don't want any favors nor obstacles."

Robert looked rueful. "Ouch! Guilty as charged, apprentice engineer." He sighed heavily. "I will try, Arianna. You are a sister in Christ, first and foremost. I will try to think of you second as a highly skilled engineer. I hope to think of you in the future as a friend as well. And finally as a lady. But I can't promise to treat you just like any other engineer. I was raised to give more honor to woman-folk, and I can't just change that ... nor do I think I really want to. But I promise you to try me best. But I warn you ahead o' time that I find ye quite pleasing to look at, and I may still get a wee bit distracted from time to time."

Arianna held her stance for a moment longer and then began to laugh. "Don't look so very dour, Chief Engineer! It can't be all *that* difficult, can it?" She batted her eyes coyly and Robert groaned while rolling his eyes heavenward. "And any lady likes to be treated as such by a gentleman. Thank you for your promise to try. That is all I could ask or expect, and I do really appreciate it." She smiled. "Quite pleasing, eh?" That was said with an arched eyebrow and a twinkle in her eyes.

Robert was entirely unsure what he was getting himself into. This engineer was complicated! He cleared his throat and shook his head. "Right then, apprentice engineer. I really do need to hear 'bout your work – Oldsy said it probably had the most potential of any new idea he has heard around here for quite awhile for the defense of Freelandia … or leastwise for demolishing unwanted old barns!"

"Ok Robert … Chief Engineer … now whatever am I supposed to say when I greet you?"

"Well, if it is anything like just now, I think 'DUCK!' would be pretty appropriate!"

"ROBERT! If you weren't the new Chief I would … I would throw something else at you!"

He laughed and Arianna could not help but began to chuckle too. "Well, that 'Chief Engineer' thingy is a wee bit over me' head. How about just plain ole 'Robert' – or better, me close friends call me 'Bobby'."

Arianna smiled. "I think I could get used to that … Bobby!"

"Right then, can ye show me proper what you launched at me?"

"Ok." Arianna's composure changed back to all business. "I've been working on two different ideas, though they very well may end up working together at some point. The first came to me while watching my mother canning vegetables. She has a big steel pot with a tightly fitting heavy lid. She gets the water boiling in the lidded pot, and when she lifts that lid she stands out as far as she can and picks it up the like it was a shield – which it actually becomes to block the steam coming off the hard boil. That lid is really thick and heavy, yet when the pot is really boiling hard it begins to rattle around as though it was thin sheet metal. I even put small rocks atop the lid, and in a few minutes the lid would still rattle and bump. I kept adding small stones until I had the top nearly covered, and it would still begin to rattle if the fire was really stoked up.

Then I made the mistake of brushing off most of the rocks all at once. Robert … I mean … Bobby … that lid shot right off the pot and nearly hit the roof. And there was so much steam it was like a fog in the room!

You see, the steam was somehow creating pressure inside the pot. I wanted a way to capture that pressure. So I designed a thick steel pot with a heavy lid that locks down, with a small vent hole on top. With a small amount of water in the pot and a hot fire, I get a blast of steam blowing out through that vent that shoots up several yards. You put your hand over it and can feel the velocity! Well, I figured I could make a locking lid with no vent hole, but the pressure inside would be all bottled up, with no way to use it – and if I was not careful the pressure might become too strong and blow the whole thing apart. I tried that on a really small scale version, leaving the room after stoking the fire. There was a mighty bang after a few minutes and I found metal pieces from the lid all over the workshop!

So I looked for a way to control the pressure, and yet be able to access it later when wanted. I looked at the valves Master Oldive had made last year for the water irrigation piping, and modified one to handle much higher pressure."

Arianna placed the pot on the table and carefully unwrapped it. "See the pointy valve on top? We are both glad that was not pointing at you when it hit!" Robert reached to turn the small handle, but Arianna pulled it away. "Not so fast there – it is still hot! I had a big pot somewhat like this in construction in which I had water boiling really hard an hour ago, and when the steam was shooting out I attached this. I let it go for 30 minutes, then closed the valve and removed it from the fire. I had to let everything cool down enough to be able to handle it, at least under these wraps. I have not tried it before, so be careful – I don't know how much pressure will still be inside!"

Robert stared at her. She was indeed a good engineer – curious, inventive and willing to try new ideas. Arianna pulled on a pair of leather gloves she had brought and slowly turned the handle of the valve. A high pitched whistle began to sound. Robert put his hand above the valve opening and felt the hot jet of air coming out at considerable velocity. "Very interesting – but how do ye think we can use this?"

"I have been thinking about that. My first thought was for irrigation – what if we bled some of this steam pressure into the water lines? It might impart greater velocity to the water, allowing it to be pumped further or sprayed farther. I also hooked this up to some of the gears used to give mechanical advantage for winches. I had to make the gears lighter, and with teeth that were much wider and larger – but the pressure would push the gears all by itself. If this were made in a much larger size, it could do a whole lot of work.

I was also thinking of gristmills – you know, where falling water pushes a big wheel that in turn is geared to large flat granite plates to grind wheat? Those can only be located where there is a decent vertical drop with plenty of water flow to turn the wheel. With enough steam pressure, I think such a mill could be set up just about anywhere you could make a fire. Think of that! Mills could be made anywhere, not just near waterfalls!"

"Hmm … that has real potential, Arianna! But I was thinking of another possible use." Robert found a small piece of wood and began whittling out a hollow spot that would fit tightly over the valve opening. He squirmed that down on the valve – it was indeed a tight fit. "Now hold onto the pot tightly, lass!" Then he opened the valve very rapidly all the way.

The small block of wood shot off the pot immediately, careening off the ceiling with considerable velocity, enough to shatter it into splinters which rained down throughout the room. Robert grimaced and pulled one out of his arm. Arianna just stared … "Well done, Bobby! I had not thought of that one!"

"You said you had a second idea?"

"Yes, more of an invention, or even a discovery. But it is going to take more explaining."

"Does it perchance pertain to your infamous barn destruction?"

Arianna smiled and her eyes twinkled. "You should have seen it Bobby! It was spectacular!"

Robert laughed at this description. Perhaps he had been wrong to prematurely judge this young engineer, especially without hearing her side of the story. "Well now Arianna, I could use a good tale that includes something exploding, told by a bright engineer – the only thing better would be having it over a decent meal. One o' the perks of bein' appointed Chief Engineer is a right decent pay. No more of the miserly apprentice wages the good Master Brentwood doled out. So I would be mighty pleased if I could interest ye in accompanying me to dinner tonight and laying out yer full story – what say ye to that Apprentice Engineer Arianna?"

Arianna was smiling but had a suspicious look in her eyes. "Chief Engineer, are you inviting me solely as an engineer?"

"Well … ah … *mostly* as just an engineer." Robby managed a weak smile in return.

Arianna rolled her eyes again and her hands went back to her hips. "Chief Engineer Bobby Macgregor, that is probably the best I can expect from you, at least for now. I think you have yourself a deal, but you had better be on your best behavior!"

Robert sighed heavily. "Well now, that be right kindly of ye, and I will try to be a proper gentleman, leastwise my own version! I am in a celebratin' mood, what with all my promotion and all. Hmm, now what sort of eatin' establishment ought we to grace with our presence? I was thinkin' perhaps someplace a wee bit special-like, not the run-of-the-mill taverns we lowly apprentice engineers usually frequent. Ah, a special occasion deserves a special location! How about we head down into the Keep proper? I've always wondered to meself how the Silver Chalice might be like …"

Arianna gasped. "Bobby, the Silver Chalice is one of the finest restaurants in Freelandia! We can't go there … it is much too expensive, and besides, I don't have anything to wear to such a formal place!"

"As fer the cost, I surely was planning on paying for us both, so that is not your concern. What do you need to wear? I was figuring on wearing me socks and shoes, and me shirt would most likely be tucked in, at least mostly."

"BOBBY! You most certainly cannot go in your everyday engineering clothes to such a fine place as the Silver Chalice! You would need formal attire, like the very best clothes Master Brentwood would wear."

"Well then, perhaps I be better off canceling me reservations. Maybe such a placey is too uppity for the likes of me – though it seems that with the proper getty-up you would likely fit right in with those high society types."

"Mr. Macgregor, was that a compliment or a criticism?"

Robert laughed. "Oh, a compliment for sure! Perhaps I should lower me sights a wee bit. We could always find a less formal place …"

Arianna was getting over her shock and now was reconsidering her opposition. "Now wait a minute there Chief Engineer … it seems to me you just invited me to a dinner at the Silver Chalice, and now you're trying to weasel out of it! If I can find a proper dress for the occasion, then you can find something nice too! You're not going to get out of this one so easily!"

"Now hold on ther, Arianna – I didn't figure on having to get all dressied uppy just to have a nice meal with an apprentice engineer. I don't have any formal clothing thingys! I canna wear what I don't have, now can I?"

Arianna's eyes twinkled and she smiled slyly. She cocked one eyebrow. "Well then, I guess we will just have to help the clothing-challenged Chief Engineer! Go find Master Oldive to help you out … I expect you can borrow something from one of the Master Engineers. What time to we need to leave by?"

"Well now, they seems to only serve their fancy victuals for late diners. I thinks we are supposed to arrive by half-past six."

"Then I want you to be here in the conference room no later than half-past five for me to check you over. And don't forget to order a carriage for us – it wouldn't do to be all dressed up and get dirty from walking all the way to the inner Keep."

Robert did not know how this had gotten so totally out of his control … wasn't he the one who had done the invitin'? And he did not want to seem too easy, not with the surprise he had planned. "But wait, Arianna … I mean, wouldn't we have a better time at someplace more of a compromise … where we did not have to be gettin' so formal-like?"

"Now Bobby, you are Freelandia's Chief Engineer! You will be expected to know how to dine out formally! And for sure you will need to have a wardrobe appropriate to you new rank. I suppose I will just have to help you with that too."

"But … but …"

Arianna again wondered how the person before her was ever chosen to be the head of the engineers. He was going to need a *lot* of help. "Bobby, you have a lot of responsibilities now. Part of that is to represent the School of Engineers everywhere you go in Freelandia. You will be speaking for the entire school. You will be our figurehead, like it or not, ready or not. And people who meet you will sometimes assess your abilities by how you look. It is not right, not logical and not even reasonable. But it will happen anyway. So you need to look and act the part.

You are not Master Brentwood, and please don't even try to be like him. But you cannot be the ultra-casual, even sloppy-looking old Robert Macgregor who tends to speak whatever is on his mind either." She shook her head, wondering about the magnitude of the job she had semi-volunteered for.

She saw the Robert stiffen in his seat and a look of defiant independence sweep over his face. "*Uh-oh*," she thought, "*maybe I went too far and too fast on that topic.*"

She reached over to touch Robert's arm. "I would be so very pleased to be taken out to such a place as the Silver Chalice. No one has ever invited me to such a nice place as that. And since you are the very newly appointed Chief Engineer, I expect people won't have too high of expectations of you yet. Still, appearances are important. And I certainly plan on wearing something formal to such a fine establishment – so you need to dress the part too."

Robert visibly swallowed down his righteous indignation. At least that was what he thought of it as. And he realized Arianna was right. Well, probably she was right. He would need to think about it more. He frowned in resignation. "Alright then, I guess I got meself into this here pickle. Least-wise I won't be in it alone. Perhaps I'll make a fool enough of meself so-as to get us both asked to leave early!"

"Oh no you will not, Mr. Macgregor! Least of all with me by your side steering you right!"

Robert looked up. He had already planned a further surprise for her – and now that she thought she had cornered him into an uncomfortable position, it would be even more of a surprise to spring on her. "Alright lassie, I give in. Besides, the reservation has already been made. Now before I go an' make a greater fool of meself, is there anything else I outta be knowin' about to go to such a fancy-lancy establishment? I think it will already be quite the picture now, a lanky engineer press fit into someone else's formal attire like a goat in a tuxedo, accompanied by the most fair young engineer in the country."

"I don't think it will be quite so bad as that, but I will reserve judgment until I see the best you can come up with to wear. But I do have one question." She was looking at him with her big round eyes and that twinkle that spoke of mischief.

"And what might that be lassie?"

"Do you really think I'm the fairest engineer in Freelandia?"

Chapter 4

Garlic Gone Bad

aeten found the ship travel quite tedious, and looked for ways to keep himself sharp while remaining the innocuous poor old traveler. One was invisibly sneaking up to the ship's deck at night. He stood near the prow in dark shadows, silently practicing some of his skills. He also found he could overhear conversations the sailors believed private.

❧

"I tell you, I saw that old codger move faster than anyone I ever seen! And you saw what he did to me with that mop handle!" The small garlic smell-laden sailor dramatically made the motions of a mop handle smacking him in the nose. "He ain't what he appears to be."

The audience of other sailors taking a short break at the stern of the ship in the dark shadows of late twilight had heard this now several times, with each rendition growing the old blind passenger's secret skills and exploits to greater heights. One of the other sailors spoke up with heavy sarcasm. "Next you will be telling us he snatches flying fish right out of the air or that he is a Freelandian spymaster! Dordo, I have had more than enough of your wild tales and excuses. He ain't nothing more than an old blind feller who was dirt poor when he came onto the ship and now is even poorer."

That brought a round of raucous chuckles from the other sailors, each of whom had visited the passenger hold to ransack whatever of value they could find. Several had rummaged through the old man's small chest and found the few small coins hidden among the clothes. Of the group, only Dordo had not managed to sneak in quietly enough not to disturb the other passengers to raid their possessions.

The other sailor spoke up again. "Now Dordo, if you try to make up any more excuses for your own clumsiness I swear I will cuff your ears right off your stinky little head!" With that the much larger sailor slapped out and connected with the hapless smaller sailor's head, effectively boxing the man's ear and sending him sprawling.

Dordo slowly regained his footing, toying with a knife handle at his belt. He thought better of even trying it and left the knife sheathed. "I'll show you. I'll show you all. I know what I seen," he muttered mostly under his breath as he began to slowly walk toward the front of the ship.

Gaeten grinned as he tossed the flying fish back toward the water. This development with the sailor Dordo – Gaeten still thought of him as Garlic-Gone Bad – could provide some interest. A plan started forming in his mind. Maybe tonight he should let the smelly sailor get a little luckier with treasure hunting ….

Gaeten stole silently away from the Captain's quarters. The door had opened quietly enough, and the darkness inside proved no hindrance to someone who could not normally see anyway. Now to get back to his bunk undetected.

Dordo waited until well past midnight before he began his burglary attempt. He made nearly no sound as he crept into the passenger berth section of the ship's hold, not even realizing his smell preceded his passage. Several passengers seemed restless in their sleep, turning and snoring before settling back into deeper slumber. With eyes now accustomed to the very faint light in the room, Dordo slithered forward. As he neared the bunk of the old man, Dordo froze in place. The blind passenger was tossing about in his bed, mumbling in his sleep and occasionally swinging his arms or kicking out with his feet as though he were trying to escape some dark monster in his mind.

Dordo nearly chuckled out loud, figuring it served the old man right to be haunted in his dreams if he indeed was not whom he seemed. With that thought the smile left the sailor's face and was replaced with a sneer. He'd show the others. He'd find some proof to show the old man was a spy, or at least up to some form of trickery.

The sailor reached the foot of the blind man's bunk and knelt to reach the small chest he knew the passenger kept there from what the other previous pilferers had told him. He was just beginning to pull it out when the geezer's dream must have turned more violent, for his legs began to thrash about more energetically, and one swung out to catch the sailor right across the forehead, sending him sprawling backwards to land with his head crashing into the floor boards.

Dordo shook his head to clear out the stars that seemed to be swirling in front of his eyes, expecting the noise of his fall to have alerted half the room. But no else seemed to be roused, and the old man seemed to have settled down. He more warily approached the bunk again, tentatively reaching out for the chest while keeping his eyes on the old man's legs. He carefully slid the small chest out from under the bed. Just as it cleared the old man again became agitated in his sleep.

"No .... NO! You can't take my last treasure! No!" Gaeten mumbled the words out while twisting this way and that on his bunk as though he was dreaming what was in actuality happening.

Dordo froze in shock, but then grinned evilly. "The old geezer is dreaming," he whispered to himself. "Well, this nightmare is gonna come all too true!" Dordo pulled the chest out the rest of the way and began to fuss with the latch.

The apparently dreaming old man swayed further, in the throes of what looked like an exceptionally vivid and gripping dream. Dordo looked up just as he finally worked the reluctant latch, sneering maliciously. His glance was just in time to see the blanket flying off the old man in a particularly violent roll. Then even the dim light in the hold went completely black as the heavy woolen blanket descended directly over his head.

Gaeten knew he was skirting credulousness. But he figured Garlic-Gone-Bad was not all that smart to start with. He made another sleep-sounding moan as he sat up to get within reach of the blanket shrouded sailor. "NO! You can't take that! It was my father's favorite! I … I must stop you!" Gaeten knew where the sailor was by his breathing, even under the wraps that the sailor was desperately trying to pull off. "Take that!"

Dordo was starting to panic. The heavy blanket effectively pinned him to the floor like a weighted net and now it sounded like the geezer was moving. The chest latch was undone, and Dordo hands scrabbled inside to find anything that might be of value. His questing hands found something hard down under the clothes and with a gleeful cry he worked to remove whatever treasure it might be.

Gaeten had to be quite careful now. It would be child's play – at least to him – to knock the sailor senseless. But that was not the plan, as much as he dearly wanted to do it. The blanket diffused the sounds of the sailor breathing and heart beats, so it was at least a slight challenge. Gaeten pondered just for a moment, then swiveled on the bed, swinging his feet out and wide, then bringing them down and together. Both heels precisely and instantaneously slammed together, sandwiching Dordo's head in a near-perfect ear box. At the stifled yelp of pain, Gaeten grinned. He could not recall ever having done just this exact maneuver ever before. He nodded to himself. Yep, he still had it all together.

Dordo had nearly screamed at the pain from his ears, and it was intense enough to make any wondering of how it had been accomplished evaporate completely away. He clutched the stolen object with one hand as the other tore off the shackling blanket. He did not even attempt to replace the chest but instead scurried away as fast as he could manage, with his head throbbing with a splitting headache. He surely hoped his prize was worth this much trouble.

Gaeten nearly laughed out-loud, consenting to hold his mirth until the sailor-come-incompetent thief had left the hold. He wondered how long it would take the Captain to discover his missing gold watch or find Dordo with it.

Chapter 5

The Silver Chalice

"Wow!" Arianna had just waltzed into the conference room-turned-office where Robert was being fussed on by Master Oldive. Robby stood open mouthed and wide eyed staring after his utterance while Oldive smiled warmly and at least maintained his composure and verbal capabilities. "Good afternoon, Apprentice Arianna! You look stunning!"

Robby himself felt that was a terribly gross understatement and he was instantly embarrassed by the dated, slightly drab and certainly out of style coat and trousers he had borrowed from one of the few Masters who was even close to his lanky size. As it was, the trouser legs were several inches too short, but Robert compensated for that with tall riding boots that while freshly polished still readily showed their age and utilitarian purpose. The pants were also too baggy, but a wide belt at least kept them from falling off.

Oldive continued, "I'm sorry Arianna – there is only so much I can do with this bean pole. Every stitch of clothing he had was grease or dirt stained – those that didn't also have holes. At least he is bathed and trimmed. It does look like my daughter's latest party dress fits you fairly well – that is her favorite ... and mine too."

Arianna smiled and gave a short curtsey toward Oldive. "And thanks again to your wife ... we had to make a few alterations to get it to fit right, but nothing that cannot be undone." She next gave Robby a critical look-over, while he continued gawking. "Master Oldive, you can only work with the clay the Master Potter gives you – and some are surely lumpier than others!" She looked up into Robby's face. "Bobby, you look ridiculous with your mouth hanging open like you were hoping to catch a few errant flies as an appetizer before dinner!" She said it with a mischievous grin and the infamous twinkle in her eyes.

Robby snapped his mouth shut and swallowed hard, but his eyes remained wide. "Arianna … ye … ye look … I mean … oh bother it all, why can't I get the words in me head out past me lips? How can I take ye out to a fancy eats with you lookin' like a royal queen or princess and me like your livery boy?" He was flabbergasted. There were only a few female engineers, and they were always dressed pretty much like everyone else – in dingy work aprons and greasy practical work clothes. Robby had never seen Arianna in a dress, much less a royal blue that made her eyes seem to downright glow … and her hair! It had been brushed out and partially held back with some sort of polished wood and bright metal clasp that he had never seen before. He was awestruck.

Arianna snickered. "Well, then, livery boy … did you remember to order a carriage?"

"I didn't forget … me Lady! And we had better be gettin' on now too, as we have a special stop to make before dinner." At least he had SOMETHING to keep up his sleeve and throw her a wee bit off balance.

Arianna's eyes narrowed. "And just where might that be, Chief Engineer? You did not tell me about that. What have you been up to?" She could just imagine him stopping off at some dusty hardware store or dragging her through a dockyard without the least thought of what it might do to their fancy clothes. And while this dinner was proposed as a work-related celebration, Arianna was slightly suspicious that it was also at least partly a date. Amongst the other engineers, Apprentice Macgregor had rarely shown much attention to her other than to offer suggestions now and again, though she had caught him staring her way several times, after which he had blushed profusely. That told her Robby had noticed more than just her engineering skill.

It was a balance that she struggled with herself at times. Arianna wanted to be known as a good engineer, but she did not mind being noticed as a woman as well. So she was flattered that Robby might think of this dinner as somewhat of a date, but at the same time she had very mixed feelings about him. She knew him to be eccentric but brilliant, and very obviously someone who loved God. That had caught her favorable attention, but he had such a way of getting under the leadership's skin, and his comments were often brusque and insensitive. He certainly needed social help. So what might this likable oaf have planned? She stared at Robby suspiciously.

Robby decided that looking deeply into her eyes was definitely hazardous to his holding back next to anything. She might be his sister in the Lord, but there was something decidedly beguiling about those two blue pools staring at him. Robby bit down on his tongue and then carefully answered. "Oh, that will be me bit 'o surprise for the night. Now if it 'pears I have passed your inspection, can we be getting along now?"

She gave him another hard look and fussed with his shirt collar. "I'm afraid he's as good as he will get, poor as it is", Olgive commented. Robby glared at him and then both men began laughing. "The Lady and the Livery Boy! Have fun you two. Bobby, enjoy yourself – you've earned it, and I expect you are about to become so busy you will likely not have another such opportunity for quite awhile."

"Thanks Oldsy – you are a true friend." He offered an arm to Arianna, who graciously accepted and they began to leave the room. "Oh, and Oldsy … pray for me tonight, will ya?"

The carriage ride was filled with small talk as they wound their way through the narrow streets of the Keep. As they neared the inner Keep's main commerce area the driver instead steered left, toward the business area. Arianna was too engrossed with the conversation to notice their whereabouts, so when the carriage stopped she had no idea where they were. Robby, seated across from her, exited and helped her down. "Bobby, where are we?"

"Ah, now that you'll just have to wait a wee bit to discover, me deary." They walked up to a large door set in the side of an impressively large townhouse in an obviously well-to-do section of the city and Robby knocked. The door immediately opened, with a large muscular man blocking the entrance. The Watcher looked them over – spending a considerable more time on Arianna, Robert noticed – and then let them in. As they walked through the entrance way, a melodious voice beckoned them to a sitting room.

"Hello Robert, how good it is to see you again! And you are even slightly early! But who is this lovely young lady with you?"

"Good afternoon … Chancel …er … Lydia – is that a proper way to greet you? I canna hardly say 'Chancellor Duncan's wife', now can I?'

Lydia chuckled. "I always prefer just 'Lydia'. Some will call me Mrs. Duncan, or I suppose even Chancelloress – but I have never liked that title much."

It was Arianna's turn to stand opened mouthed in shock. She turned with a helpless pleading look toward Robert just as Duncan entered the room.

"Oh, hi Robert – you are early, but that is fine." Chancellor Duncan strode up with practiced ease and shook Robert's hand warmly with a genuine smile. Then he turned toward Arianna. "Now who is your beautiful companion? You said you were bringing another engineer along, but I hardly expected such a lovely thing as this!"

Robby was grinning ear to ear, while Arianna seemed to be turning red and pale all at the same time. Even so, she was recovering rapidly. "Ah, sir Chancellor, this is Apprentice Engineer Arianna. Don't let 'er beauty fool you though, she's got quite a brain bundled behind those auburn locks, and she promised to tell us all about a quite interesting new project she was a' workin' on back before Master Brentwood put a stop to it."

Lydia stood and moved to Duncan's side as the Chancellor reached over to take a shakily offered hand of Arianna. At the last moment she regained enough composure to curtsy. Duncan smiled in a fatherly way. "I am very pleased to meet you, Apprentice Arianna. I would think you must be an exceptional engineer, to survive at all in a field dominated by menfolk."

"Well … yes sir, I guess so sir … I mean I work hard and God has given me some good ideas – and let me work with some really great other engineers."

"Well said, Arianna." Lydia chimed in. "And I just love your dress!" She reached to hold the younger woman's hand and steered her over to a richly upholstered sofa.

Duncan motioned for Robert to walk with him out of the room. When they had left, Duncan stopped and turned a critical eye on him. "Now I don't want to embarrass you, Chief Engineer, but you really do need at least one good set of more formal clothes to wear for such occasions as this. I presume these were borrowed from some other engineer … perhaps not quite your size and I expect quite a number of years older?" Robert nodded dourly. "Yes, I thought so. Well then, I am glad you did come early."

Duncan popped his head into the parlor. "Lydia dear, Arianna – would you mind terribly if Robert and I disappeared for an hour or so? I can send word to the Silver Chalice to hold our table longer … though I really doubt they will let it out on us!"

Lydia looked up from her conversation. "Well, certainly dear! I think a dark heather gray would make a fine choice." She smiled knowingly as though she were answering an already asked question. Arianna looked confused but Duncan smiled – his wife was particularly good at reading his mind.

"You sure you won't miss us?"

"Well of course we will miss you, but I suspect we have a lot of girl-talk to keep us busy!"

Duncan led a bewildered Robby out a side door of the house, picking up his usual compliment of security guards, and marched across the street to a high end tailor's establishment, at least from the understated but obviously highest quality items shown in a window display. "Well, hello Chancellor Duncan," said a short, thin and fastidious man with a cloth tape measure hung around his neck. "I did not hear that you were coming … did I somehow forget an appointment you had made?" The thin, short tailor peered up and down at Robert and sniffed disdainfully. "And you brought … a friend? Are you going to some comic costume party I had not heard of? Or did you truly unearth someone locked up in an old wine cellar with 40 year old clothes that fit exceptionally poorly? Tut tut." The tailor shook his head with strong disapproval.

As Robert began to draw in a breath to protest, Duncan began to laugh. "Yes … yes Master Alfredo – he may have been down there even 50 years by the looks of it! Now my good tailor, I have come specifically to you since I know you like a good challenge!"

At that, Master Tailor Alfredo grimaced. "I don't think I like the sounds of that, Chancellor. What do you need of my great talents …hmm?"

Duncan laughed again. "Well, this task may be too much for even you – and I know how busy you always are. I'm sure I can find another tailor who could whip up a passable suit of clothes for my friend here … the newly appointed Chief Engineer of Freelandia."

Alfredo looked hurt. "Chancellor Duncan! How could you say such a thing, after all I have done for you and your lovely wife! Another tailor indeed! I am THE master tailor of the Keep, I will have you know! Humph!" He began to size up Robert with his eyes, muttering numbers under his breath. "Now, what kind of suit is needed – what kind of occasion? And when can he come back for the second fitting?"

Duncan smiled. "Ah … well … we can probably come back a few more times for future needs, but for the immediate … we have a bit of a crisis, Master Alfredo, one that only someone of your consummate skills could possibly help."

The tailor lifted one eyebrow skeptically. "And what totally unreasonable, impossible, herculean task do you expect me to accomplish?"

"We have a dinner appointment at the Silver Chalice in less than an hour."

Alfredo staggered backwards and smacked one hand to his forehead. "You must be joking … tell me you are cruelly joking Chancellor Duncan! You nearly gave me a heart attack with that one …." He looked at the expression on the two men's faces and stopped. "I can work wonders, but you need to ask someone upstairs for true miracles. It is not possible to measure him, cut the cloth, make adjustments … I need many hours for such a task!"

Duncan looked serious. "Master Tailor, Lydia and I and a very beautiful young lady will accompany Chief Engineer Macgregor here to the Silver Chalice in an hour, with whatever clothes he has on at that time. What can you do for us?"

Alfredo was white faced with exasperation. "God Himself needed six days to create, not one hour! Oh, Chancellor … you … you seek to ruin my reputation … everyone who is anyone knows I am your personal tailor and if they see you dining with … with … with that …" He sputtered, then his eyes narrowed and his face took on a keen, determined look. "You ask the impossible! No tailor in all of Freelandia could do what you demand!

But ... but you will see what a true Grand Master Tailor can do! Step back and be amazed!"

With that pronouncement he snapped his fingers loudly and two apprentices scurried over. "Close the shop immediately – promise anything, but get all customers out. We have a Head-of-State emergency! Tell everyone to report to the fitting area pronto! Chief Engineer ... Macgregor was it? Please come with me." He eyed Robert professionally, noticing his apparent discomfort. "Have you ever even been to a tailor before?"

"Nay my good man, and I'm none too sure 'bout it now!"

Duncan stepped in to assist. "Robert, Master Alfredo is without doubt the best tailor in all of Freelandia." The tailor beamed. "It can take awhile getting used to what is coming, but trust them to do their job ... and put aside your manly modesty for an hour ... these are every bit as professional in what they are about to do as you are with your engineering."

Robert eyed Duncan worriedly. "What'dya mean, put aside me manly modesty? What are ye setting me up fer, Chancellor?"

Duncan just smiled thinly. "I will be waiting out here, looking over the newest fabrics. No need to have anyone tend to me, Master Alfredo."

"That is a good thing, Chancellor, since I will need every hand and finger I have in the entire shop! Now Mr. Macgregor, please come to the fitting area."

Duncan requested his ever-present senior Watcher to send word to the Silver Chalice that they would be later than expected and then stopped outside a curtained off area and began browsing. In just a moment he heard a loud exclamation from inside. "Now wait a bloomin' minute there Master Tailor! You want me to get all undressed in front of you! Tis not a proper thing for me to be a'doing sir!" There were murmured voices and then "Yes, Master Tailor, I know what the good Chancellor said to me, but does it really 'ave to be a'done in this here manner? .... Alright ... I guess. But this had not better be gettin' back to me apprentices at the School of Engineering none. I don't think a one of them would look me in the face without a'snickerin' in front of and behind me back!"

Apprentice tailors were scurrying in and out of the fitting room. In a few minutes Master Alfredo came back out. "Chancellor Duncan ... We will do the very best that God gives us the ability to do ...but next time, can you give us better warning? Now my guess is that your wife gave you some guidelines?"

"Master Alfredo!" Duncan feigned offense. "I am perfectly capable of choosing my own clothes and recommending something for my previously poor Chief Engineer."

"Yes sir, Chancellor, sir. Now what did she say?"

Duncan laughed good-naturedly. "She said a dark heather gray. What do you think for a shirt?"

"A fine eye for colors, your goodly wife has Chancellor. Let me take care of the rest. Now, a rather sensitive issue."

"Yes, Master Tailor, you can put the bill onto my tab. The Chief Engineer of Freelandia is going to need a wardrobe to match his rank, so keep his measurements. This one is on me, the rest I expect him to pay for."

"Very good, Chancellor. Now you mentioned he has a companion tonight … is the young lady in need of our services too?"

"It did not seem like it to me, Master Alfredo. She had a very nice blue dress that seemed to be very up-to-date, though perhaps not to your high standards."

The tailor sniffed. "I suppose we don't really have time anyway. A blue dress you say? Perhaps a white corsage with blue and gold accents … would that be appropriate?"

"I think the Chief Engineer would like very much to offer his companion something – and you will likely score two new loyal customers!"

Master Alfredo smiled. "Wonderful! I will get my wife working on it immediately."

Just short of an hour later Robert emerged from the fitting area. Duncan gave him a critical look over. "Master Alfredo, you have outdone yourself! I do not think any tailor in Freelandia could have done better!"

"Done better? Dear Chancellor, I do not think any other tailor could have even come close! With more time, we could have been perfect … but even so …"

"It is wonderful, Master Tailor. This is why I bring you all my business."

Robert was listening to the exchange with growing exasperation. "Do none of ye care 'bout me own opinion here? These fine clothes won't be walk'in themselves to dinner tonight now!"

Duncan laughed yet again. "Well Robert, what do you think?"

"It seems to me the neck is a wee bit too tight, and the trousers seem scratchy ... but it does indeed appear to be fittin' for a prince to wear rather than a lowly engineer."

"They fit perfectly! You are just not used to have such exquisitely tailored and customer fit clothing, Chief Engineer. A prince, eh? Well then, please present this to your princess!" Master Alfredo handed Robert a small box.

Robert opened it and pulled out a beautiful white flower surrounded with light blue ribbons and dark gold trimmed lace. "What be this delicate thingy? Ach, Master Tailor, you be the best! This makes up for yer asking me to disrobe and takin' all those measurements with me standing there in front of ye all in me under things. I'm sure'in to get on her good graces with a gift like this! Thank you sir tailor!"

The two men returned within a few minutes of their intended time. Duncan strode into the sitting room, where Lydia and Arianna were sitting next to each other on the couch, deep in conversation as though they were old friends who had not seen each other for years.

Lydia glanced up. "Hello Duncan dear ... I thought you were going to be gone for an hour – surely it has only been a few minutes?"

"No, my dear, it has been an hour as I requested. I trust you have kept yourselves busy?"

"Oh my yes! It has been positively delightful! Arianna, you simply must stop by to visit us again – and I mean that! Duncan, where is Robert? Did you lose him somewhere?"

"No, indeed I did not. I have the pleasure to present to you ... our new Chief Engineer!"

Robby stepped around the corner on cue. Lydia clapped delightedly and Arianna gasped. Robert stood in a dark heather gray suit coat and trousers that had hints of dark blue and burgundy interlaced within the woolen fabric and a white shirt with matching colored lines. Lydia stood and reached over to him. "Robert, you look so very handsome! Now you are more than fit for an evening out at the Silver Chalice!"

Arianna had also stood. "Robert ... Bobby ... you look so ... so ..." she curtseyed formally. "Chief Engineer of Freelandia, would you allow a lowly apprentice engineer such as I to accompany you tonight?" Her eyes shone, and Robert was more than a bit dazzled ... and extremely pleased.

He pulled his hand from behind his back and presented the small box to her. "Robert, what is this?" She opened the box and flashed a wide grin. "Oh, it is so beautiful!" She pulled out the flower and held it up to her dress. Lydia saw Robert's momentary panicked look and moved to help pin it on. She stepped back and appraised the effect. "Superb! You two will be the talk of the Keep's socialites – the unknown prince and princess!"

They all laughed and headed out to the waiting carriage.

The Silver Chalice was like an ornate ornament hung in the high income section of the Keep. Arianna had never been up close to the dark wood exterior so highly lacquered and polished that it seemed to reflect a thousand images of the oil lamps lighting up the streets. It exuded so much sophistication and culture that it had become somewhat of a legendary destination. An actual liveried servant opened the carriage door and escorted the two couples up the wide polished steps.

"Chancellor, Chancelloress ... welcome! We have not been blessed with your company in several weeks! We have your favorite table waiting. Ah, and who might your esteemed guests be tonight? Perhaps some dignitaries from abroad?" The owner was a very well dressed elderly man with a colorful vest of satin and a golden sash. He prided himself on knowing everyone who was 'anyone' in the Keep ... and here in front of him where two very well dressed unknowns dining with none other than the two highest ranked officials in all Freelandia. Who could they be?

Duncan toyed a moment with the idea of playing with the man. He was sorely tempted to introduce them as Roberto and Ariano of Engineeria, but instead just said "This is our new Chief Engineer Robert Macgregor and his guest, Engineer Arianna."

"Very good sir. Engineers you say? Both of them? I must say they are the best dressed engineers I have ever seen! Please, this way."

They were led to a private large table toward the rear, and their silent Watchers took up station unobtrusively nearby. They were seated and shortly a sumptuous meal of its signature roasted duck began to arrive in courses.

"Now Arianna, I've nearly forgotten the excuse I used to take ye out to dinner!" Robby said that with a wide smile and a wink. "You said you had a longer story to tell 'bout your other ... what did you call it, a 'discovery'? The one that leveled the old workshop barn?"

Lydia chuckled. "Surely you cannot be serious, Robert? It is hard to imagine Arianna here being involved with such a thing as that!"

Arianna grinned. "You should have seen it! Well, I have to back up the story. I was visiting with my cousins in the town of Omartis. There was some excitement while I was there – seems a few youngsters had to be treated for burns after giving a wild story of demon fire that attacked them the prior night. They claimed to have visited a local oddity, a muddy hot spring that bubbles and froths non-stop. They were out late – without their parents knowing it – and on a dare visited the boiling mud. Now the odd thing is, the soft mud there boils, but it is not particularly hot, and the smell is rather noxious. Everyone steers clear of the area, as any animal that falls into the mud within minutes dies, gasping as though it cannot breathe.

Anyway, the teens had brought a few torches with them – they knew enough not to want to accidently fall into the mud spring. It was getting rather late, and one wondered what the area looked like in the dark. He had the bright idea to toss his torch over the bubbling mud. Then something really strange happened. They all claimed that as soon as the burning torch reached a few yards above the mud, the very air itself burst into a huge fireball! It singed several of the youngsters who were closest to the spring – hence the so-called demon fire burns – and the whole town figured the place was possessed."

The others were in rapt attention. Arianna had a mischievous grin. "It sounded to me like something interesting! I went to the springs and watched the mud. It seemed to me that whatever it was that was bubbling out of that mud must have caused the explosion. It also seemed reasonable that it must be lighter than the air."

"Why is that?" Duncan was intrigued.

"Well sir, if it were heavier than the air I am not sure it would be boiling out of the mud, but even more so, if it were heavier than air it would have concentrated all in the hollow of the spring area and the explosion would have been much larger. When I examined the area, I found singe marks on trees, but only above the three foot mark – so it seemed to fit my theory. Now I was faced with a dilemma. I wanted to get a sample of whatever it is that was bubbling out."

"However did you accomplish that, Arianna?" Lydia leaned forward with interest.

"I had to think about that for awhile. I took a large glass jar and attached it upside down on a long stick which I then suspended low over the boiling mud. I left that jar for several hours, then pulled it back in and capped it while it was still upside down. I didn't know what was in the jar – it looked empty to me, but given the experience of the youngsters, I took careful precautions. The jar was brought to an empty field that was still wet with dew the next morning. Damp earth was packed around it and the lid was loosened but still held in place with a small rock holding it down. Next I attached a rag on a long pole, set it ablaze, and used it to push the cover off the jar."

Robert was looking at her critically. "I trust ye took a few bits o' precaution, knowing what happened to the others?"

"Yes Robby, of course … I may be dangerous, but I am not foolhardy!"

"Aye, anyone takin' one look at you tonight will for sure know ye are dangerous, woefully dangerous indeed!"

"ROBBY! Oh, you are impossible!" Her tone said he was in trouble, but her eyes told a different story. He chose to believe the latter.

"I was tucked in behind a rather large tree – and it was a goodly thing too. The explosion that occurred blew that jar apart, leaving quite a nice little crater behind, and creating a considerable fireball above! So I knew without a doubt that some kind of powerfully explosive gas was coming up through the mud out of the ground. But collecting it in jars was not going to be all that useful.

With some experimentation, I constructed a large covered wooden frame that could be pulled over the top of the mud spring, and sealed it all up with pitch – sort of like a tent to collect the gas. I didn't want the frame to sink into the mud, so I had to use as light of materials as possible. That took some trial and error, but eventually what worked the best were hollow bamboo poles. It took awhile to figure out the tent construction. Wood or metal were much too heavy, and even the thinnest canvas I could find still added too much weight. Cotton was light enough, but you can blow your breath right through it – it would never hold a lighter-than-air gas."

Arianna continued, "My mother had recently given me a silk scarf she bought from a merchant ship that was extremely light, yet very strong – it had a much tighter weave than I had seen before. The fabric was still easy to blow your breath through it, but the very thin cloth was still much stronger than anything else I had tried, and much lighter. I tried coating the fabric with various pitches, gums and waxes. I made sort of a pillow out of them, being careful to seal the seams well. I next captured some air in those, tied them shut and held them under water with a weight to see how long they would stay inflated. That was repeated with the best candidates over the mud springs, capturing that gas and then tying the bag shut and holding it under water with weights. I found several waxes that seemed particularly good at sealing the cloth, even though my clumsy attempts at capturing "mud gas" surely got a lot of air in too."

"Clumsy or not, ye were very methodical in yer approach, engineer Arianna. Very impressive! Did you find a different kind of wax worked best for this "mud gas" versus holdin' in regular air?" Robby was weighing out her tactics and could not find anything to improve upon.

"Yes – the mud gas must be different somehow than air … the wax that worked best for air worked ok for the gas, but another seemed to work even better."

"So lassie, what didya' do next?"

Arianna was in her element. "Next I obtained larger sheets of the silk and prepared a hot wax dipping for it, to apply as thin a layer as I could, just enough to contain the mystery gas. I stretched these onto my bamboo frame, sealed the seams, and then used ropes to pull the contraption over the top of the bubbling mud. That took a goodly part of a day, so I left the set up overnight. What a surprise was waiting for me the next morning!" She paused theatrically.

Lydia did not want to wait. "What happened Arianna?"

"I returned with a few young helpers but as we crested a small hill all the young men ran away, fearing the demons had returned."

"WHAT?" rang out three voices in chorus.

Arianna laughed and her eyes danced with merriment. "Maybe I shouldn't tell you – you will likely think I'm daft and not believe me!"

"Well now, me thinks we will have to judge yer 'daftiness' after ye speak out a wee bit more!"

"ROBBY! You are SO impossible! Well, as I was saying, as we came over the hill we saw an amazing sight. The bamboo tent was floating off the ground, a good 10 feet up in the air! I had not totally sealed one flap of fabric, and I think that is the only thing that was keeping the whole thing from sailing off into the sky! When I could rustle up the young lads, we went to lassoing the gas catcher with some ropes and pulled it down, securing it to trees and rocks. I had figured that the gas was lighter than air, but it appears it was a LOT lighter – enough to lift a few hundred pounds or more of my gas catcher right into the air! I'm not sure if that is useful or not … perhaps that is another project to consider!"

Arianna continued, "Anyway, then I had to work out my plan to bottle some of that gas into one of my pressure pots. I affixed a thin metal pipe to the only opening in the tent structure, and sealed the joint well. We added sections of the pipe onto that, moving perhaps 50 feet away from the mud spring. We attached a pressure pot with a valve on the end of the pipe and let it fill up for several hours. I filled up several pots that way to as high a pressure as it seemed they would take. When I cracked open the valve just a wee bit I could feel some pressure coming out, so I knew there was something inside besides just air. I doubt there was a lot of pressure, but I have ideas on how to improve on that."

Robby interjected. "I think I may be see'in where this be go'in next. You took one o' your little pots into barn to test out what that gas you had trapped might do?"

Arianna smiled brightly. "Just so, Chief Engineer. I knew it was very flammable, so I needed some ways to test it. I tried letting some of the gas escape into a jar to repeat my first experiment, but this time left the jar suspended upside-down on a wooden frame and brought a candle – on a long stick! – up to the opening. When the candle went into the jar itself, the flame immediately went out. If I brought it under the open jar at a small distance I got a nice contained explosion. So it seemed the gas needed to be mixed with some air to get any explosion or burning. I used many small jars to test that, and got a rough idea of what mixtures gave the best results.

Then I had another idea. I got a torch burning on a stand and aimed the pressure vessel at it and opened the valve. That nearly started the barn on fire – the torch burst into a fireball that was shooting out from the pressure pot, throwing a mighty flame over twenty feet through the air!"

"Oh my – that sounds dangerous!" Lydia looked apprehensive.

"Yes, but perhaps it could be a useful thing if you were up on a wall and a horde of Dominion fighters were swarming at you!" Robby was thinking hard about the possibilities. "But didn't the flame backtrack right up to the pot and make the whole thing go kablooey?"

Arianna smiled. "I was very worried about that myself! But the gas stream coming out had little air in it, I think, and needed some mixing with air before it would burn well – and that seemed to take a few feet of travel from the nozzle."

The first course of sweet breads arrived and they began to eat – with Arianna somehow continuing her story between bites.

"What I really wanted was a stump clearer – a way for farmers to clear tree stumps out of new fields. Now they have to team up horses and spend quite a time to get it done, and a really big stump requires a huge effort. I figured if there were some way to get the contents of the pressure pot to explode all at once in a confined area, it just might do the trick."

"So lass, you had to figure out a way to somehow mix in air with the gas to get a mixture that you could control and yet which would ignite all at once?"

Arianna stared at Robby for a moment. "Why, yes Robby … that is exactly what I figured needed to be done! And if it could be done in a confined vessel or area, the effect would be much stronger. That is what I was working on when we had the unexpected … incident. I am not entirely certain what went wrong. I had an empty container sitting out to mix in some of the gas and air. Without knowing it, another apprentice had been cleaning up the area where they had been filing and cutting some metal parts. I think some of the filings may have spilled into my container unnoticed. At least, that is what I think may have happened. I cleared everyone else out of the barn, and filled that container with a gas and air mixture. For some reason I just felt I should light it off from a further distance back than normal – that was obviously God's Spirit whispering to me. I hunkered down behind a heavy workbench and brought a flame close.

I had already made up some small mixtures and had what I thought was a pretty good idea of what to expect. But in hindsight I tend to think those metal shavings may have had some interaction with the gas, for I got much, much more than I had bargained on. When it went off, the explosion must have been hundreds of times larger than I anticipated. It blew the roof right off the barn and several side doors too. The solid heavy bench was pushed backwards – and me along with it, while a huge ball of flame passed over above me. It seemed like I could barely breathe, I was moving my lungs but it was like there was nothing going in! I was scared and prayed for deliverance. I felt a breeze rushing in from a back door that had been blown off its hinges just a few yards away and I got out as fast as I could. As I left I could see the rafters starting to burn along with anything else in the barn that was combustible. The barn was destroyed, but no one got hurt. Master Brentwood forbade me from working on the gas anymore and that has been the end of it."

Duncan spoke up. "Wow, what a story! It seems there may indeed be some possibilities with this gas material you discovered – though I am not sure how you will control it well enough. So I presume you will have to set up your gas collection and let it run awhile before you can really do much more testing? Won't that take quite some time?"

Robby grinned. "Now just wait-y a moment there, Chancellor! If this young lady is half the engineer I think she is, I have a sneaky suspicion there may be a wee bit of material held back in reserve … maybe a few o' those pressure vessels that had been filled and that may have been … misplaced?"

It was Arianna's turn to grin. "Why, Chief Engineer Macgregor … you just jogged my memory! It's coming back now … I think I may have a few such vessels stashed away!"

Robby turned serious. "This is going to need a very significant investment – think what such an explosive force might have against a rushing horde of enemy soldiers … or against a ship! Arianna, I need you to lead the effort, with a handful of senior apprentices, at least one Master Engineer, and a dozen or two of junior apprentices. This might just be the most important discovery and project useful to the defenses of Freelandia we have, easily as important as Oldsy's springy thingies. Are ye up to such as task, lassie?"

Arianna stared wide eyed. "But Robby, I am only a junior engineer myself! I can't be put in charge of more senior apprentices or a Master! A project with that many people and importance should be led by a senior Master Engineer!"

Robby smiled. "Arianna me dear, we have no time for such formalities that Brentwood imposed. We need the best people to lead the most promisin' projects, regardless of their … current … rank. If anyone has a problem with that, they canna speak directly with me! Besides, I think your project is going to be a needin' a might careful watching by a certain Chief Engineer." He reached over to take her hand across the table and looked deep into her attentive eyes. "And I be thinkin he just might be want'in to keep a closer eye on a certain project lead engineer too!"

Arianna blushed under the close attention and her eyes shone brightly, while inside her thoughts were in turmoil. Was Robby indicating he wanted to be more than just friends and fellow engineers? And if so, what did she – or should she – think about it? Lydia politely coughed – with a broad smirk on her face directed at her husband as she deciphered the play of emotions across the young girl's countenance.

"Ach, I be think'in I may have gotten a wee bit lost there for a moment!" Robby looked over at Lydia and Duncan and gave them a wink. "Not that I necessarily am wantin to be found right so quickly-like! But perhaps we have had enough engineerin' talk for tonight anyway. Let's enjoy this very fine meal … and the very fine company." He said that with a grin over at Arianna, who was still staring vacant eyed in his direction. Robert squeezed her hand gently and reached for his fork. He figured he was going to need to keep his strength up after tonight with plenty of new discovering and projects to be working on … and especially in regards to the one sitting across the table from him.

Chapter 6

Gaeten's Arrival

Gaeten shuffled off the gangplank, shoulders slumped heavily. He looked the perfect part of an old blind beggar who had just lost all his earthly belongings. He slowly tapped his way along with a long thin stick, to the jeers and coarse comments of many of the onlookers. The port was a rough one, and the dock area was especially so. Gaeten put on a nervous look and slowly made his way along, using his nose to steer himself toward nearby taverns. He rarely got a second look – it was obvious he had nothing worth taking, as easy as it apparently would have been to do so. Appearances, of course, are often very deceiving.

The Boar Head tavern was a greasy, dirty and very well patronized dock bar frequented by the rough mix of hardened sailors that plied the Dominion controlled city of Jazrek. Gaeten stumbled in the front door and was accosted by a gravelly voiced bouncer. "We don't allow beggars in here, old man." A large hand grabbed his shoulder and spun him around. It was a bit much to take for someone who had been cooped up on a small, smelly ship for over a week – yet it would not do to blow his cover by dislocating several joints of the first person he came into contact with the first few minutes in the new town. Gaeten allowed the hand to yank him backward, but somehow the stick he used to tap his way around turned with him even more rapidly and its blunted point stopped less than an inch in front of the man's eye.

"I was thinking I might buy a meal with the last few coins I have left … I presume my money is as good as anyone else's?" Gaeten held up a few coins with his free hand.

The bouncer blinked twice before his eyes uncrossed and moved from the end of the perfectly unwavering stick to the coins. Then he laughed coarsely and brushed the slight staff aside. "Sit where you like. But the next time you'd better use that stick without the warning … most folk around here are not as polite as I am and they might just call you on your nice little parlor trick." He laughed again and moved back into the shadows close to the door.

Gaeten sneered and edged into the tavern, shortly locating an empty seat at a low table. He expected his entrance had been noticed by a few of the other customers, but in a rough dockyard tavern many things are seen but few remembered. And besides, he did need a way to supplement his income, and perhaps gain some grudging respect that might loosen a few lips. That would come later, if it worked out the way he planned.

For now though, food was the next item to acquire. Gaeten waited a few minutes, and when no serving person wandered by he loudly slapped his walking stick down on the tabletop, nearly causing his nearest neighbor to spill his bowl of soup. "Hey old beggar! What do you mean by banging away like that! If you had made me spill I would have cut yer throat out for yer trouble!" The cruelty in the voice was likely real, which made the next part easier.

"And the next time if you don't move aside to give me more room I'll ram this stick down your own throat and then start whittling it to my liking. Food! Now!" The last was said with a loud yell and a dirty, smelly servant came scurrying over. Gaeten plunked down a few coins on the table, purposely allowing one to roll toward the churlish neighbor. "Give me mead and a bowl of whatever is in the pot on the left over there – the pot on the right smells like it has gone rancid."

The servant growled unintelligently and grabbed two of the three coins, leaving the one that had rolled furthest. The soup-eater noticed that immediately, and loudly banged down his own cup to cover the sudden darting of his right hand toward the coin.

Time for some fun, thought Gaeten. Faster than the man could see Gaeten whipped out a long, thin dagger, reached out and stabbed downward. The blade sank into the wooden plank of the table, actually grazing the coin just as the man's hand reached for it. His hand instead ran into the razor sharp blade, which drew a drop of blood before he could yank back his hand. "Why you dirty old beggar! That's the last time you will need a coin!" The man pulled back his hand and then pushed back his stool, reaching for a knife on his belt.

Gaeten had heard the bouncer coming up behind him and now he purposely turned away from the imminent attack and addressed the larger man. "What's the penalty in this tavern for stealing?"

The soup-eater had his own knife out now and was moving carefully toward Gaeten when the bouncer's presence suddenly filled the area and all movement stopped. While mainly focused on his intended prey, the knife wielder glanced up to see a short sword hovering at throat level, pointed at him. He gulped as he saw the size of the man holding it. "But Dawger, the old goat actually cut me ... look!" He held up his hand to show the few drops of blood. "No one gets away with that ... 'cept maybe you."

Dawger did not smile, nor did the sword waver. "Stealing and getting away with it is free. Stealing and getting caught usually is paid for with a finger."

"Dawger, you wouldn't ... you gonna side with this blind stranger over me?"

"You was caught, Greasy. You know our rules. As I recall, last year you even enforced this one when someone tried to lift your purse when you was drunk and they tripped as they backed away from ya."

"But Dawger, I didn't actually take the old man's coin ... I was ... I was just 'bout to pick it up and give it back to him!"

"Is that so, Greasy? Then why did you respond with your knife? What say you, blind man?"

"I'd say I was owed a greasy finger" Gaeten responded.

"NO!" Greasy screamed as two other patrons grabbed him from behind. Dawger sheathed his sword, clamped a big hand over Greasy's left arm, and forced the reluctant hand out flat on the table top in front of Gaeten. Gaeten held up his thin, long dagger. Greasy was blubbering in fear now. Gaeten reached over and traced the splayed out fingers in front of him first with a finger, and then with his knife. He next touched the large muscled hand and arm of Dawger.

"I have a wager for you, Dawger. I'll bet you that coin of mine that I can stab the table on either side of each of Greasy's fingers before you can count to three, without drawing blood from any of them – given that you hold him absolutely steady."

Dawger chuckled. "And if you miss?"

"Well then, you get my coin and I get the finger owed me."

Greasy was too frightened to do anything but stare wide eyed.

Dawger warily looked Gaeten over again. "For a blind man, you seem full of surprises. Let's make this even more interesting. "Hey, anyone else want in on the wagering? I get half of the take if the old man even nicks one of Greasy's fingers, and he gets half the take if he can do it … twice! Anyone in?"

There was a mad scramble as the patrons eagerly began jostling to make their wagers; the vast majority of course expecting Gaeten to lose. The tavern owner came out to act as the bookie, under the whole crowd's watchful stares.

Gaeten smiled. This was going well. He toyed with his knife, seeming to accidentally drop it and fumble a moment trying to find it. The theatrics brought on another round of bets against him.

"Ready?" Dawger sounded like he was enjoying this.

"Ready, I think." Gaeten changed his grip on the thin handled knife and tentatively brought its point down to the table top a few times to measure the distance. Then he moved closer to the whimpering Greasy. "Now I have what sounds like a goodly wager on this – so you had better not flinch, not move a muscle. Even a little itty bitty twitch might make me miss … and then I'd lose my bet and you would lose a finger … or maybe two if I get really distracted."

Several in the crowd laughed at Greasy's discomfort … it was obvious this crowd held few real friends. Gaeten lifted the knife. "Now don't you go cheating on the counting … GO!"

Dawger bellowed out "One … Two …"

Gaeten held back, but even so his hand was a blur of motion and the blade tip made a flurry of taps that were almost too fast to follow.

"Three."

Gaeten stopped, blade in midair. "I think that was two taps for each finger …" The crowd gasped and several stared down at Greasy's hand. Dawger lifted the hand high into the air, flipping it over a few times as Greasy winced. There were no blood spots. Two of the closer men stared down at the table and counted the knife imprints.

"He did it … the old blind feller did it!" one of them shouted in awe.

"Naw, he must'a just tapped the blade up and down, maybe he made those knife marks before we was watching", another man from the crowd protested.

Dawger remained silent for a minute as the crowd murmured, then he simply said. "You win".

"Hey wait a minute, I ain't so sure" protested one of the apparent losers.

Dawger looked surly. "I say he won. But ... could you do it again, just a bit slower so'es we can watch better?"

"Certainly. Hold him tight now."

Dawger slapped Greasy's hapless hand back down onto the table, and the crowd gathered around intently. Gaeten again traced out the fingers in front of him, and again checked the distance of his blade to the table top. Then he began to stab down between each of the splayed fingers. He started slowly, and then began to build up speed, though never reaching his full potential – some things were better left held in reserve. He suddenly stopped on a downward stab, leaving the knife embedded into the table top and sliding his hand down with the momentum of the stroke to land forcefully across two of Greasy's fingers. The sudden pressure and pain on his fingers was too much for the stressed-out Greasy – he fainted dead away and the crowd roared in approval.

Yes, it was a good start. And now the crowd should be much more open to talking to an old blind stranger.

The next day Gaeten was on a coach ride to the city of Kardern, three days to the southwest along the sea. He had been told there was a sizable dockyard there, with considerable warship building activity ... and a sizeable contingent of Dominion soldiers garrisoned. Several of the sailors at the Boar's Head tavern had been through that port, and none liked it very well – there were far too many soldiers around, even if they didn't enforce many regulations. And there were a few Dominion Dark Magicians too, whom everyone avoided ... and feared. They were known to make examples of people caught for minor offenses in ways that struck terror in all.

It had been a very profitable stop – both from the coins in his purse and from the information all seemed to readily share with a blind down-on-his-luck circus performer who could handle a knife better than any of them cared to acknowledge.

Perhaps he could learn something of military interest in Kardern.

Chapter 7

Music Academy

For Maria, the preceding week had seemed hectic. Suevey had helped move her into a dorm room at the Music Academy that Master Vitario had provided. It was one of the nicer rooms, and Maria was delighted that Kory was allowed to move in with her, and Kory herself was rather awestruck that they were allowed into an apartment right on the campus that was usually reserved for mid-level apprentices. It amazed them both that such a nice room was available just when they needed it.

Master Vitario had stopped by right after her very meager possessions had arrived and after Suevey had left. "Maria, you are now officially part of the Music Academy. We normally start people off as provisional apprentices, but given the talent you have already shown, I think we can dispense with the provisional part and start you off directly as an Apprentice Level One. Now, there are some difficulties in setting up a course of study for you. We normally start apprentices right away with learning to read musical score, but that of course will not work for you." He smiled at the thought and shook his head. "Instead, I have asked one of our teachers to work with you on a verbal memorization. The details are being worked out."

Vitario looked pensive for a moment as though he was considering an already made decision. "For now, you will join the other Level One apprentices, though they are part-way through their semester. I think you should also see Master Veniti right away – he is our most skilled vocal instructor, and he is particularly anxious to work with you after hearing your performance of Reginaldo's Masterpiece." At that remembrance Vitario smiled broadly and for a moment his eyes seemed to mist over. Then he sighed and turned to look at Kory.

"Kory, I am pleased you volunteered to be Maria's guide, with her in every class. I realize you have already been through these, but I need someone who can easily show Maria through the ropes, and I think this arrangement will cause the minimum changes for everyone."

"Oh thank you, Master Vitario! This is all so ... so wonderful!" Maria was genuinely amazed at all that was being done for her.

Vitario turned back toward Maria with a particularly pleased expression. "I am sure it will seem very different than where you were holed up in that utilitarian Watcher Academy! Tomorrow you will start your classes. We don't have any other blind apprentices, so it will take everyone some getting used to how to work with you. Please be patient! You will be starting with an introduction to musical instruments that all Level One apprentices take."

Vitario addressed Kory, "Kory, what have you covered so far?"

Kory was quite uncomfortable talking directly to the Grand Master, and her voice squeaked. "We ... we listened to several brass and wind instruments, and to some drums. We are just going to start with stringed instruments."

"Good. Maria, do you have any experience with playing musical instruments?"

Maria was in a quandary of how to answer that one. Before coming to the Keep she certainly did not have any experience at all. However, in her night visits she had stopped many times in rooms which had instruments left out. She had been in a terrible fright that she would be caught, and so it had taken awhile before her curiosity overcame her concerns. Maria had plucked, strummed, tapped and blown into nearly everything she had come across. Many were a mystery to her ... she just had not had enough time to figure them out. Others had made beautiful sounds, though Maria knew they must have much more potential when properly handled. There were a few stringed instruments she had worked on more diligently, enough to figure out where to place her hands to produce true notes. Some had what she learned was a bow that was used to glide across the strings. One she had found particularly captivating and so she had spent many hours with it.

So, how should she answer? Those night visits were done in secret, and Maria certainly did not want to get into any trouble ... "Well, Master Vitario, growing up as an orphan in a poor priest's parsonage did not exactly give me opportunities to play music!"

Vitario laughed. "No, I suppose not. Well then, tomorrow should be a very interesting experience for you. That class is in the morning, and then right after lunch I want Kory to take you to see Master Veniti. I may wander by a few times to check in on how you are doing your first day.

Now, to some other practical matters. While we don't have a formal dress code here, the state of most of your wardrobe is … how should I put it … let's say they appear very well used, past their prime, and Watcher workout clothes just won't do at all either."

Maria laughed. "Oh, I think that is putting it rather nicely, Master Vitario! Yet, they will work for me – after all, I can't see them anyway!"

"Er, yes, I suppose not. Anyway, there is no question that you cannot traipse around the Academy with the clothes you have."

"But sir … I don't have any way to pay for new clothes! Perhaps if you can find some odd jobs around here that I could do, then I could earn enough eventually to buy something … are you saying that if I don't have better clothes that I cannot … that I can't be here?" The last was said with a sniffle and Maria had tears forming in the corners of her eyes. To have come this far and now be faced with expulsion before she had even started! "Wait," she continued, "Sir Reginaldo gave me something … a tiara … perhaps I could sell that and …"

Vitario's eyes popped open and he took a step backwards in shock by this sudden turn in the conversation. "Maria! No! You belong here more than just about anyone I know. If it came to it I would pay for new clothes for you out of my own pocket! No, such a trivial thing will not stop me from finding out your true potential! As it is …" Vitario had been wondering how to tell her about the very large endowment that Sir Reginaldo had left for her, without letting on who it was from or how large it truly was. "… As it is, you have a benefactor who desires to remain secret. A certain sum of money has been placed into a bank account for you. I am the administrator of that account, and I was asked to make sure to cover all your needs. New clothes certainly fall within that directive.

Now I have taken the liberty of asking the head wardrobe director – you may recall she helped with procuring that lovely gown you wore at the concert? – to outfit a complete wardrobe for you suitable for your activities

here at the Music Academy. I might say, she was more than pleased to do so – though for some reason she said it was only under the stipulation that your rather intimidating Watcher friend not be present! She has made several formal dresses suitable for recitals and concerts, which undoubtedly you will participate in over time, and everyday clothes as well. I asked her to get started as soon as I learned who you were and your rather unusual circumstances. I think they may have already been delivered to your closet here in the apartment."

With that Vitario moved into the bedroom and opened wide a set of closet doors. Kory gasped. The closet was full of a variety of colorful dresses, skirts, blouses and other clothes, more than Kory had ever seen outside of a fancy store.

"What is it, Kory?" Maria stepped forward and first touched the closet doors, and then with that as a guide she swept her hand over the different fabrics hanging neatly in a row. She stopped in amazement. "But … but Master Vitario … these cannot all be for me? I've never owned more than one or two things since … since my father died. Surely all I really need is a simple shift dress or two." She thought a moment, and then stepped backwards. "The rest should go back, or be given out to others. This is much more than I need."

Vitario marveled – this was the first time he ever even heard of a female saying she had too many clothes and wanting them returned! "No, no Maria. These are for you. They were made to your measurements, and I am certain your benefactor would consider it very rude indeed for you not to accept his gift. And I might add, they are very pretty, and you will look marvelous in them. Now I won't hear another word of it. I think there are a few other items in the drawers over against the wall. Get some rest and be ready for your first class tomorrow morning." With that the Grand Master waltzed out, quite pleased with being able to offer such a rich gift to such a humble – and therefore eminently worthy – recipient.

Once he had left, Maria turned to Kory. "Kory … you and I are pretty nearly the same size, aren't we?"

Kory's eyes went wider still, if that were possible. "Maria … are you … are you suggesting …?"

"Suggesting nothing! If I have to wear all this finery, then no foolin' you are going to wear it with me! Now … let's try them on!"

Somehow both girls got a reasonable sleep and left for their first class the next morning with some time to spare. For Maria it was decidedly unnerving, being ushered through the busyness of the morning's crowd of apprentices and hearing the many whispered comments as they passed. It seemed like the whole campus was talking about "the singer from the concert", or more often just "the Singer". It appeared she had quite a reputation already. Several of the girls they passed also commented on their dresses – Maria had insisted that Kory select outfits for both of them – and those were a lot more comforting to hear, since the dresses must have been beautiful.

About half way across the Commons area toward their first class Kory abruptly stopped and Maria, not realizing the sudden halt, moved ahead one further step and collided with someone who was standing directly in front of her.

"Hey, watch where you are going, little blind girl!" The female voice was harsh and angry. "Who's your rich daddy? Such nice clothes for a poor blind orphan who thinks she can sing! I've heard about you. Who made you a princess to take over anyone's apartment you wanted?"

Maria took a sharp intake of startled breath. She instinctively took a step backward and even raised a hand to her chest, feeling the comforting cool metal of the whistle on its hidden string.

Kory bristled. "Back off, Vanessa! We had no part in choosing an apartment, and if you have any issues with that, take it up with Grand Master Vitario himself! Or ..." she looked a bit coyly at the older, larger girl ... "maybe we can ask him for you, since he told us he would stop by sometime today to see how Maria is doing!"

Vanessa's face went red and she lifted a clenched fist. "If I hear even a whisper that you try to get me into any trouble, I will pound you flat. So, the little singer is a favorite of the Grand Master himself, is she? We'll see how long that lasts! Nobody takes my apartment without paying for it dearly!"

She stomped off, and Maria could hear several other footsteps follow. "Kory, who was that?" Maria tried to keep her voice steady, but it quavered anyway, as she was indeed frightened.

"Nobody, that's who. It is just Vanessa. She is a Third Level Apprentice who has been passed over several times for Level Four. She and another girl used to stay in the apartment we are in – I heard that Grand Master Vitario had them moved out to the Level Two apprentice dorm, which is on the far side of the Commons."

"She sounds so angry and bitter. Do you think she will give us further trouble?"

"Naw, I doubt it. She will calm down in a couple of days and it will blow over." Kory's words said one thing, but her voice lacked conviction.

Senior apprentice Arial tapped a thin wooden baton onto the desk where she was sitting. "Apprentices, we have a new member joining us for lessons in Basic Instruments. This is Maria. And yes, she is "the Singer". From what Master Vitario has told me, she has little familiarity with musical instruments, so everyone please be patient and try to help out. As you can see, she is blind. I understand that Kory has been assigned to be her guide. Girls, please take the open seats in the back."

Kory led Maria to the back row, where the least skilled apprentices were normally seated. Kory grimaced – her normal seat was about a third way back from the front and she had been steadily moving forward. Maria, however, did not notice and was far too excited anyway – the instructor sounded just like the girl she had befriended out in the Commons area! Maria so dearly wanted to learn how to coax out some of the beauty she had heard come from the instruments in the Theater Hall. She sat up on the edge of her chair as Miss Ariel, an apprentice Level Six, began to tell the background of various stringed instruments and play a small piece on each.

After an hour or so, the class broke into groups and the instruments were passed around so each person could hold and experiment with playing. One was handed to Maria, and Kory laughed for a moment and helped

Maria hold it correctly. After strumming her fingers over the strings a few times Maria brightened up.

"Miss Ariel said this one was a mandolin … right?"

Kory smiled. "Yes, Maria – that's correct. You have good recall for what you've heard! Now if you shift your left hand along the neck and depress a string with one finger while you strum with your other hand and you can make different notes. Here, try pressing this string down here." She guided Maria's fingers and an awkward note sounded. Maria moved that finger up and down the neck, listening to the different notes. She shifted to another string and did the same thing. Kory looked at her inquisitively. Maria was moving her fingers rapidly over the strings, head bent over and intently listening to the sounds. Apprentices in other groups were randomly plucking and strumming and sawing, in general making an awful racket and laughing at the sounds. A few were awkwardly trying to make something akin to true notes, though few came very close.

Maria grimaced as a sour note sounded, and then immediately corrected it. Kory looked on in awed silence. Within five minutes Maria was sounding near perfect notes up and down the strings – it was like she had an intuitive knack for knowing how to play the instrument. Without prompting she tried holding a second finger on an alternate string, listening intently. After a few moments she had discovered simple chords and was rapidly moving through various combinations. The sounds from the other small groups died off, though Maria did not notice – she was much too absorbed in her discoveries. A part of her mind showed her sitting in a white-light area on a small stage with her special audience listening.

After a few minutes of further experimentation, Maria tried to play the simple piece their teacher had demonstrated. She made a few mistakes, but quickly corrected and shortly was playing it perfectly. She stopped for a moment, and then played it again, making a simple improvisation.

Apprentice Ariel slowly walked over, carrying a guitar that she had been demonstrating to another group. She looked oddly at Maria. "Maria, I knew you had some talent from when we met before, but I was led to believe you had never played any instruments! And here you are, practicing like a Third Level apprentice!"

Maria broke out of her intense focus. "Oh, sorry – I did not hear you for a moment. This is such a wonderful instrument! You called it a "mandolin," correct? I don't think I heard this one being played at the concert, though someone played something similar at the start – but the sound was not quite the same."

"Why, yes Maria. At the concert there was an opening piece played with two guitars. Later there was a quartet of cello, bass fiddle, viola and violin."

"Oh yes! The quartet was fabulous! I so enjoyed it ... can I learn to play those too?"

"Yes, Maria, I am sure you can ... but perhaps we should start a little simpler. Is this the first time you have played a mandolin? You must have spent considerable time and had lessons on some similar stringed instrument."

"I can't wait to try them! Yes, this is the first time I have played a mandolin. It seems pretty straightforward, though holding my fingers correctly took a few minutes to figure out. Can I try a guitar?"

"Sure. I have one here. Kory, can you take the mandolin?"

The guitar was handed to Maria, and she recognized it as one she had played before during her extracurricular visits of – was it only a week or two ago? To keep it a secret that she was already partly familiar with it, she asked to be shown proper holds and where her fingers should go. As she strummed the strings and picked out a few notes, though, she grimaced.

"What's the matter?" Kory asked.

Maria plucked one string again. "This one is not sounding quite right ... it is close, but off by a little bit."

The senior apprentice nodded. "Yes, I hear that too, but I did not correct it yet. Feel up at the end of the neck – do you feel those knobs sticking out? Those can tighten or loosen the strings. Trace the one that sounds off to its corresponding knob."

Maria did so and experimented with tightening and loosening the string to see what the resultant sound would be. She tightened it, listened, and then adjusted it a bit more. "There, now it is right." As she had been doing that Apprentice Ariel had found a metal triangle of the appropriate note and she struck it with a little metal bar. The note sounded out pure and loud, and Maria giggled delightedly. "Oh, that is beautiful! What a pure sound that makes! Please do it again!"

As Ariel struck the note again, Maria listened and plucked the same note on the guitar, matching it as exactly as a stringed instrument could. She had tuned it pitch perfect.

With the confidence that came from her achievements on the mandolin and her late night practices, Maria in minutes was strumming chords. She played the simple tunes she had heard Ariel demonstrate, and then paused a few moments. A determined look came over her features and she began experimenting with the strings again much more aggressively, beginning to produce much more complicated sounds that began to take shape into a melody.

Now everyone in the class was pressing around, all lessons forgotten. Maria was totally absorbed in whatever task it was she was trying to accomplish. Ariel picked up the mandolin from Kory and began to accompany Maria, or at least try to.

Maria did not know many tunes; in fact she only knew a few simple ballads and folk songs she had sung in Sam's bakery, and of course Sir Reginaldo's Masterpiece. She picked one of the simple folk songs and played it out by memory in the simple form in which she was used to singing it. Ariel recognized the tune and began to play a simple counter melody. Maria laughed out loud with glee and began altering the basic tune, working in more complexity … and playing faster. Several of the other first level apprentices began clapping at the nuanced version that was the common song they knew, and yet was being transformed into something far more interesting.

Faster and faster the two girls played, and where Ariel had been leading with improvisions, now Maria took over and the older girl began having trouble keeping up. Everyone was clapping and giggling as the girl's fingers flew across the strings, almost too fast to follow. Finally Maria strummed the ending and collapsed in laughter, waving and shaking her sore fingers in the air.

"Well done! Well done indeed!" Grand Master Vitario was standing just inside the door, along with several senior apprentices who had heard the music and had drifted in to listen and watch. All began enthusiastically clapping in appreciation, and the Grand Master joined in. Kory and Ariel hugged Maria and they all were laughing and clapping themselves.

When the commotion subsided, Master Vitario addressed the girls. "Either Maria has been fooling us all along about her supposed ignorance of musical instruments or Apprentice Ariel has a genius for teaching we had not fully discovered before … or is there some other explanation?"

Ariel, catching her breath, could hardly keep from tumbling her words. "Oh, Master Vitario! I had not heard you come in! Honestly, all I did was show her how to hold the guitar and tune it – she just picked it up and began plucking out notes, then chords, then she launched into a tune, and then …" the girl had to stop to breathe again … "then she started improvising along with me and we went faster and faster and faster …" She collapsed into giggles. "That was the most fun I have had in a long time!"

Vitario could not keep from chuckling. Ariel was a very talented musician, who had real potential to achieve Master status in the not-too-distant future. He cocked an eyebrow. "Maria … you just picked up the guitar and started playing?"

"Oh, no sir! I first learned how to play the mandolin!"

Kory interrupted. "That's right … she started experimenting with finger placement and got all intense looking, then within just a couple of minutes she was plucking out notes and then chords."

"Amazing! Maria, it appears you not only have a God given talent for singing, but for playing instruments as well. Tell me yourself what happened here this morning."

"Well … Apprentice Ariel played a delightful little piece on several different stringed instruments and then Kory and I were given the mandolin. I did not know how to hold it right, and Kory showed me how to work it. Then I … I …" she paused, thinking.

"I sort of listened to the instrument, to the sounds it made, and let my fingers match that to the music in my mind. Then the sounds kind of merged and grew and took on lives of their own … flowing along almost as fast as I could think …" She paused, searching for words. "Almost like a wind blowing and picking its way along a path, going in a certain direction toward a goal but having various routes it can take." Maria's face was screwed up into a concentrated look as she struggled to put words onto a process that was nearly indescribable. She was frowning with the effort, searching mentally for descriptors that just would not come. "Oh … ugh! It's like trying to describe how to talk, or lift your arm, or breathe! When

I am making music in my 'special place' everything just seems to flow, to almost be part of me, to be normal and natural."

"What do you mean by your 'special place'"?

Maria wondered how often she would need to explain it, but this time it was easier since she had found some words to use with Kory and Lydia. "It is a place – I think it's my soul – where I go to talk with God. When I sing or hum or make music, a part of me – a part of my mind I guess – goes there. I think God likes it when I play before Him."

Vitario's eyes were wide, but some of the other apprentices snickered derisively. He turned and silenced them with a stern look. "So just now, Maria, you were playing the guitar before God in your mind … um, your 'special place'"?

Maria squirmed awkwardly and a touch of embarrassment colored her cheeks. "Yes sir. Everything seems to flow better when I am there. And … and it always seems like God is pleased when I do it before Him and for Him. In that way my singing … anytime I am making music … really when I am doing just about anything … I can do it as a form of worship to and love for my Creator. Making music without doing it for God and His glory and honor is … is just forming sounds without purpose, just … just noise!"

The snickering turned into several guffaws and sneers, but Vitario's eye had misted and he stood in stunned silence. What this little blind girl had just said shook him to his core. Here he was, the leader of the Music Academy of Freelandia, one of the most skilled musicians in the country if not the world … and he had just been told he usually was only making noise. A part of him railed against the notion and his pride began to well up … but he recognized the feeling and promptly squashed it back down. This was … incredibly humbling, and required considerable more thought … and literal soul searching before God.

Vitario knelt down beside Maria and smiled broadly as he recognized a true God-given gift. He wondered just how much talent God had poured into this vessel, marveling at the gift he himself had been given to help shape and hone that ability – and to himself learn from. "Just where might this all lead to?" he mused silently. "Maria – it sounds like you may be a poet at heart too … and most truly gifted musicians are, as they struggle to use music as their repertoire of words." He reached over and took her diminutive hand in his. "Come, I think perhaps you may need a bit more 'challenge' than this class is designed for."

Maria let herself be gently pulled upright. She held out the guitar and Miss Ariel lifted it out of her hands. The other children cleared a pathway and Vitario led Maria toward the door. They had only gone about half-way when Maria suddenly stopped and turned back. Master Vitario did the same, looking back into the room. "Oh, yes of course! Kory – you come along too!"

As they walked down the hallway Vitario began to speak, half to the young girls and half to himself. "Ah, now what will I do with the problem of Maria? She is undoubtedly much too talented to stay in the beginner's classes, and yet still needs to learn much of the basics – though perhaps at a highly accelerated pace. Hmm. It seems to me she needs a more personalized training schedule, at least for right now. We normally don't do that, but we have made exceptions – for exceptional students." He slowed his pace and stopped, turning from his musings to look at Maria. The girls stopped walking too, uncomfortably wondering what they were supposed to do. To Maria, everything seemed to be happening so fast, and she was still flushed and tired from the guitar work-out. She was realizing God had given her some special gifting to sing, but it now appeared that singing was just one aspect of a greater talent. She had no idea what should or would come next.

"Maria, here is what I propose. Kory will introduce you to each of the beginner's classes – the instruments and other things that are covered. I expect that will take several weeks, and you still need to see Master Veniti for voice and singing lessons." He paused, wondering just how much Maria really needed lessons, and based on what she had just told him about her natural flow of musical talent, on how she would fare with the strictly methodical Veniti. "These introductory classes are really meant to give you an overview and familiarity with some of the major divisions of the Academy. Usually at the end of the first year of studies we have The Assessment." Kory inadvertently groaned. "Now Kory, it is not really that bad, is it?"

While a few weeks ago Kory would have never ever expected to even speak to a Grand Master, she was becoming more comfortable with it. "Yes it is! You have to learn all these new things, and then come before some senior apprentices and Masters and a vocational Discerner and they decide which division you must go to!"

Maria stiffened. A Discerner? She had heard about such people – who had a special gifting in knowing God's answer to some decisions. From what she could gather her new friend Lydia may have that spiritual gift. But a vocational Discerner? She gathered that was someone who matched people's talents and abilities to tasks and even careers. But … but what if you were skilled in something but did not particularly like it? Would you be forced to apprentice into a particular area even if you did not want that?

"Now Kory, that is only partially correct. We have several assessments of apprentices in the Academy. The first one is probably the most important. After you have been introduced to a wide variety of what we do here, and have been given an opportunity to try your hands – and voice – to them, we assess where your abilities and talents lie, and ask what you are interested in. Then each apprentice is directed toward the division best suited for them – at that time. We have apprentices who start in one division and stay there, others who rise to a certain level of skill and then decide to branch out to learn other skills. All divisions also cross-train people in several skills.

The Discerner tries to understand if God has a particular direction for a given apprentice for a given time. Sometimes there is, and sometimes there is not. Maria – you know Lydia – she is one of the more gifted Discerners in Freelandia. We have several people within the Academy who have a gift in this area. It is most helpful. However, we don't force people into any particular division or direction – they have to listen to what God is telling them too. If there is agreement, the apprentice is most often the happiest and content to go in that direction. But we do allow people a level of choice, and we especially support cross training. It is very common for someone to be particularly skilled on, say, one given instrument, but also be quite adept at other instruments in the same family, and maybe even in ones that are unrelated. We have many singers who also are quite good instrumentalists. However, we often find that people are drawn to one or two particular instruments in which they really excel. Most Master Musicians can play many instruments, but are only at a true Master level on one or two. Most singers have specialty types of music or styles in which they particularly excel. The sooner we can determine that specialty skill, the sooner we can concentrate on honing that to perfection ... and by perfection I mean to their peak ability. Everyone has a different set of giftings and abilities from God, and we want to bring people to as close to their full potential as possible."

Maria piped up. "So what does it take to become a Master Musician?"

"Well my dear, first it takes a great deal of effort! It also requires someone to have a considerable God-given talent in at least two areas, talent recognized by their peers and by a Discerner. It also requires that the person reaches close to their true potential in those talent areas – which is much harder to know. The more talented a person is, the more difficult it may be for them to attain Master level – they have to be very dedicated to attaining mastery of their talent. Of course, we hopefully never stop learning or growing, but we do not want to grant someone Master level when they are only half as good as they could be – even if they are more skilled than many of their peers. This also helps to encourage humility, especially among the most talented.

Pride is an insidious evil especially inflicting those whom God grants favor upon with particular talent. Pride is like an invasive vine that chokes out a young plant and stops it from ever reaching its full height and vigor. Many a young prodigy has fallen to its hold. They often do not last very long at the Academy. They are a flash-in-the-pan that creates a sensational promise, but then become 'too good' for us. They often are lured to the world of fortune and fame. They may become truly famous and rich, but they usually are sad too – knowing they could have developed even further. And some ..." Vitario paused now, and Kory noticed a small tear in the corner of one eye. "And some may realize their mistakes and humble themselves before God, and in time become far more than they ever expected."

Kory nodded thoughtfully but Maria tugged on Vitario's sleeve. "Will he come back, Master Vitario?"

"I think so, Maria ... I pray so. Now more than ever he has a reason to." Vitario gave Maria a long hug, and then they continued to walk down the hallway. Kory stood perplexed for a moment, wondering who they could possibly be talking about, then shrugged and hurried to catch up.

Chapter 8

Planning a Snatch

urdrock's ankle was only slowly healing from the fall he had taken during the assassination attempt of Chancellor Duncan. He rested in an abandoned lumberjack shack, cursing under his breath that despite the most potent healing spells and potions he had as his disposal, he still had to go easy on that leg. This assignment was turning out to be much more annoying than he had ever expected. Freelandia was weak – any fool could see that within the first few days of being here. The government seemed small and timid, allowing people to waste incredible time and efforts on whatever they seemed to want for themselves. They all lacked discipline. If he were in charge of one of their cities ... he chuckled sinisterly. Just think what he could accomplish – how wealthy he could become! *"All in good time, all in good time"*, he said to himself. With all the intelligence he was gathering, he undoubtedly would be in a superb position to be granted a governorship of some major city or region when Freelandia was 'integrated' into the Dominion. With a crack military police and spy network, he could transform these lazy people into a production machine to crank out whatever goods the central Dominion leaders commanded. With the abundant natural resources and a populace under his thumb ... yes, he could become a wealthy man, maybe even reach the upper ranks of leadership within the Dominion.

Yes, much was possible ... but first he had to deal with these dratted setbacks! The assassination attempt had failed most miserably. The hoped for civil uprising had also met with spectacular failure. Yes, there were a few more recruits for the new "Rat's Nest" gang now that he had replaced the weak Ramsey – and that new young leader Jarl had some real potential, though even he had failed to generate a single riot. It was bad luck, that was for sure. That and the spirits of this land must be stronger than expected. He would have to work even stronger dark magic next time.

And there would be a next time. Murdrock had sent a report back to his masters, whom he had earlier told of what a stunning victory they could expect. He needed to work on lowering their expectations, so that when he next succeeded it would look all the more glorious. It was a pity – a small pity – that he had to punish the archers. He knew they were totally dedicated and were unlikely to have missed on their own accord. Yet someone had to be at fault, and it surely was not going to look like it had been Murdrock! Regrettably he had punished them with the ultimate severity, but that really could not have been helped. Their tongues had to be silenced anyway lest they somehow castigate his own excellent leadership and planning. Besides, he could get more archers.

But even his skills would begin to be questioned by his masters if he did not plainly show success – and quickly. It also needed to be something big, something on a grand scale, something that would strike fear into the highest levels of Freelandia leadership. Something …. something …. something to do with that boy, that incredibly obnoxious young man who had somehow spoiled Murdrock's plans. And on top of that, he had just learned that this uppity boy was the son of that dratted Chancellor Duncan! That boy was becoming some kind of a hero in Freelandia, the tales of his exploits were becoming near-fables in the countryside, assigning supernatural abilities to the little mischief maker. He must have been just lucky or maybe some local god had helped – and the Freelandian leadership was manipulating the stories to be legendary to rally the commoners.

"A hero, huh? Son of the Chancellor, huh? A legend with supernatural powers, 'favored' by the gods of this country? We will see about that", Murdrock spoke softly to himself. *"I wonder what might happen if something … nasty … were to befall this Ethan fellow? What if he concocted some particularly nasty malady that ate away his flesh bit by bit? What if he was to become deranged and a lunatic?"* Murdrock knew of all sorts of poisons that could cause such mysterious happenings. Those could work, but then another thought came to him. What if this Ethan were to 'disappear'? It could not be permanently, or else the wretched priests here would make him into some kind of religious martyr and his legendary status could become even worse. No, he would have to re-appear again … somewhere.

And what if that 'somewhere' were deep within the Dominion? Murdock began a deep, evil chuckle. Oh, this could be truly grand!

What would the dear leader of Freelandia pay to get his beloved son back? Perhaps the sovereignty of Freelandia itself? Or what if this 'hero' showed up not only in the Dominion, but *joined* to it? Now THAT was rich! Murdrock also knew of several drugs that affected people's judgment, which could even put them into a mental stupor in which they would do whatever you told them to. What if the legendary Ethan showed up kneeling before the Dominion leadership, pledging loyalty to the Dominion, maybe even appearing at the forefront of the Dominion hordes as they went to battle against his very own Freelandia? *"And what would my masters do for me"*, Murdrock thought, *"if I were to deliver the little runt on a silver platter to them?"*

Murdrock had a new-found energy. He pulled out paper and ink and began writing a note to his superiors. He would keep many of the details to himself for now, but he knew he needed to show them a bold new plan immediately, to temper their anger over the failed assassination. And he would need them to begin other preparations: sneaking someone into Freelandia was rather easy, but snatching the son of Chancellor Duncan – and getting away with him without an all-out naval assault – was another matter entirely.

One thing for sure, though – he would need extremely good intel. He would have to get someone close to the boy, someone who would know his comings and goings, know his habits, and know his weaknesses.

Murdrock grinned with an evil thought. What surer way to befuddle and betray an adolescent boy than through the interests of an attentive woman … er … 'girl'? And especially one well funded by the Dominion itself! Of course, a few bewitching incantations and a potent love potion would help to seal the certainty. Murdrock could almost feel sorry for the boy … almost. He wouldn't stand a chance. Murdrock would personally make sure of it.

Chapter 9

Voice Lessons

ory led Maria to a different building, one that Maria had never explored. As they walked down a long hallway, they could hear many voices, but no one seemed to be singing songs – all they could hear was a variety of single notes and scales being sung over and over. Both girls grimaced. This did not sound like much fun.

Eventually they found their assigned room. As they entered, Master Veniti was precisely placing a piece of paper on a very neat stack. Kory could see his desk was nearly spotless with everything on it laid out in very orderly rows. She did not think that bode well either.

A deep and somehow fluid voice resonated in greeting. "Ah yes, we have 'The Singer' and her trusty guide! Please come in!"

The girls stepped into the office, but found there were no chairs to sit on. Master Veniti did not seem to notice. "Maria, I was at your performance of Sir Reginaldo's Masterpiece. Quite nice, quite nice indeed. Lots of raw, unrefined power and energy. Not perfect mind you, but for an untrained voice it was remarkably good." Maria smiled but was unsure how to take this … compliment?

The melodic voice continued. "Now I want you to know right from the start that I have had quite a few promising singers come through that door over the years, some whom I have been told have a "voice like an angel". Well, I cannot judge that, I personally have never heard an angel sing. But everyone I have met and worked with could be made better. Unfortunately, some of the most talented ones have the most difficulty – they seem to think they are some special case and are already near or at perfection."

Kory noticed the near scowl come over Master Veniti's countenance. Veniti drew in a larger breath that somehow made him look even taller and more imposing.

"Tut, tut! I am the judge of perfection, and that is my standard. I demand nothing less. I assure you, I can take what was passably good and raise it close to perfection. People come in here who think that they are highly talented just because they have years of experience singing at taverns! After I am done with them, they are fit to sing to Chancellors and kings!"

Maria felt her shoulders sag. She had been excited to come to learn more songs and maybe improve her singing ability, but now she was not so sure what this type of training was going to be all about.

Veniti continued. "Now let's take a little test to see what I have to work with, and how very basic I must start." He pulled out a triangle of bright metal hanging by a thread. "I am going to produce a perfect pitch tone. You try to imitate it as best you can." With that he took a small wooden mallet and rapped the metal sharply.

A pure tone sounded, and to Maria it was about as perfect of a note as she had ever heard. She cocked her head slightly so as to absorb as much of the sound out of the air as she could. She had such an intense look that Master Veniti allowed the note to slowly fade away without saying a word, just watching the girl's face. "*Interesting*", he thought.

Maria waited a moment after the note had completely faded before speaking. "Oh, that was wonderful! I have never heard such a sweet pure tone like that. That must be a very expensive bell, to peal so purely."

Veniti frowned for a moment, about to offer a rebuke of her ignorance, but paused. She was blind, after all, and supposedly had next to no exposure to real music. "Not a bell, Maria. Here, hold out your hands so you can feel it." She complied and felt the cold metal of the triangle and the warmer wooden mallet. "Now, this time I want to hear *you*. Try to repeat the same note, nice and loud please." He lifted the triangle and rapped it again with the mallet.

Maria smiled, lifted her chin and sang out an "ah" sound matching the note. "Good, that was quite good. Perhaps it needs more volume, and next time please hold it longer – as long as you can." Another triangle of a different size was lifted and struck. This time Maria tried to be louder and she held the note until her breath faltered away. Veniti frowned and shrugged. "Better. Let's test your range and see how low you can go."

A series of larger triangles came out, each of which sounded a very pure note at progressively lower octaves. After the third one Maria's voice choked up hoarsely as she tried to hold the note. "Ah, so there marks the boundary on the low end. With work, I think you might be able to master that one. Let's try on the upper scales."

Master Veniti pulled out a series of progressively smaller triangles and began to strike them in succession. As he hit the smallest, Maria's voice resonated with it pitch-perfect, and Veniti frowned. "That was very close, but I think I detected a slight warble at the end. He looked at her quizzically. "Do you think you can go higher?"

Maria frowned too. "My throat hurt on that last one, but I think in the Masterpiece I hit a note or two that were slightly higher."

"Yes, I thought so too, though I was not sure … I could not really hear it myself." He pulled out some straight and very narrow pipes that were hanging by threads in a wooden frame. "Our voices create vibrations, Maria. I have a series of tone pipes out on my desk now. When you sing the same note that these pipes produce when struck, they will slightly vibrate. I will touch them and know which ones you are singing, even if I cannot hear them myself."

Kory had been watching and listening the whole time, but now spoke up. "You mean there are sounds we can't even hear?"

"Certainly, but some animals and birds seem to be able to hear them just fine. Now Maria, start singing lower notes and work your way up as high as you can go."

Maria looked doubtful, but took several deep breaths and began a series of higher and higher pitched notes. Master Veniti began lightly touching the pipes as her voice went past what was audible to Kory, even though she was standing right next to Maria. He stopped about half way through the series of pipes.

"Hmm. Interesting. Very interesting. You have a considerable range, especially for someone as young and untrained as you are. No sense in trying to work on the high end, it is already well past where most people can hear. But you could certainly extend your low range." He moved the pipes back off his desk.

"Next I want you to take several deep breaths and then hold the note I sound as long as you possibly can."

Maria somewhat nervously took several deep breaths. Veniti watched with a frown and then struck one of the tones. Maria sounded out the note in a long drawn out clear voice, but in less than a minute she faltered and stopped.

"Tsk, tsk. That is not very good. You are breathing all wrong."

"What do you mean? I have been breathing like this all my life!"

"Yes, and if you want to just fill your lungs to breathe – fine. If you want to sing you will need to learn differently. Normally I would just show you … here, give me your hands."

Maria tentatively held out her hands while Master Veniti walked around his desk. "Kory, you watch too. You will need to watch Maria and make her do it correctly – and there is no harm in you learning also." He took Maria's hands and placed them on his stomach. "Now this is how you were breathing." He took several breaths, with his stomach extending out and then in. "You must learn to breathe with your whole body, like this." He took another several breaths, but this time his stomach did not move out. Instead his whole chest moved up and down.

"Oh, is that how I should breathe? Does it really make much difference?"

"No girl, I only do this for the fun of it! Of course it makes a difference! Feel." He took another tremendous breath and then sang out the same note Maria had done. Maria felt the muscles harden under her fingers and she smiled delightedly at the clear, strong and perfect note Master Veniti was sounding. It went on well past her effort … and on … and on.

The note was finally ended – and not with a gasp or a withering away, but with a finality that ended as perfectly as it has started. The sound had easily lasted three times longer than what Maria had obtained, and it had projected outward with significantly more volume and strength. She was rather astonished. "That was … beautiful! Can you teach me to do that?"

"That largely depends on you, young lady. It is hard work and hard practice. I have found few who have the patience and diligence to master it. And that is only one small part of becoming a 'voice master'. Will you be one of them? Hmm?"

Maria was thoughtful. "I honestly don't know. I have never tried these things. I have never really 'worked' on singing before – it has all just come to me from God. I do not know what I can accomplish."

Veniti grimaced. "Well, at least you recognize your complete ignorance. Most aspiring singers come in here and blithely commit with little clue as to the effort required ... or to their own impatience and limitations. At least you have that going for you. We will have to learn how really determined you are to achieve mastery in singing. And we certainly need to get some meat on those bones! Looking at you, I have a difficult time believing you had the stamina or projection to sing with Reginaldo."

The words stung, but Maria realized that they were true. Master Veniti appeared to be a very demanding and rather harsh instructor – well, maybe harsh was not totally correct, but he surely seemed to find fault quickly. "I ... I don't think I could have done it on my own strength either. The energy came from God."

"That would be about the only explanation that I indeed could believe. Now I want you to follow along with what I sing. Pay attention, I don't want to have to do this more than once." Veniti backed up a step from Maria and held a tone sounding like 'Ay'. It was rather low, and Maria diligently copied it, though it was near the very bottom of what she could reach. After a moment Veniti changed to a higher pitch sounding like "Ee". That was easier to copy. Next came an 'I' followed by 'O' and 'U'. These were each held for quite some time, nearly the extent of what Maria could do. Then he repeated through them, but much faster, going up and then down in the scale of tones.

"Reasonably well, for a beginner. You will need to practice those every day. Do it for ten or fifteen minutes at a time, spaced out by at least thirty minutes to let your voice rest. And certainly practice correct breathing – that is essential. If you cannot get that then you might as well quit any other voice lessons entirely. I want you to work with one of my junior apprentices to start with – I would put you into a class with all the other beginner students, but those classes have already started, and Grand Master Vitario requested that we treat you as a special case with more private lessons. I am not so sure about that ... but then again you somehow did sing the Masterpiece, and came up with an accompanying part. By the way, how did you do that?"

"Oh, sir, it was not me ... I heard Sir Reginaldo practicing and it ... it just came to me while I was softly singing it before God."

"Singing it before God? So you had a command performance before the Judgment Seat?"

Maria sighed. *"Here we go again"*, she thought. "Most of the time when I sing, in my mind – I think it is actually part of my soul – I see myself standing before God's presence. So I am not singing for myself or for others, I am singing for God … as part of worship I suppose. When I started humming along with Sir Reginaldo, I began to see the sounds of the Masterpiece. It is hard to explain, but after awhile I could begin to see a counter melody that wove around his notes. Without knowing it I must have begun to sing it … and he heard me."

Kory could see that Veniti looked doubtful, and he voiced his question. "So you snuck into the theater to hear him practice and just started singing whatever came into your mind … and that just happened to be the first successful duet part to the Masterpiece?"

"Well, I guess so – but it was God who must have showed it to me."

"Indeed. So when you sing, you say you picture yourself performing in front of God Almighty? That seems preposterous … and presumptuous."

Maria gulped. "Yes … yes sir. I … I want to sing to give Him glory … to please Him."

Veniti arched an eyebrow. "Well here, you will practice to please ME. If you want to sing to whomever you think is listening in your head, that is your business. You have potential, young lady … but so do many others. You are rough and unfinished … and we don't really know what you might become."

"Now tell me, what did Reginaldo do when he first heard you?"

Maria had slumped, and with a tired voice she answered. "He … he stopped singing and …"

"And what, child?"

"And he cried." Maria expected to hear a derisive laugh.

"Hmm." Kory could see Veniti looked pensive. "Perhaps there is more hope for him than I had expected or given him credit for over the years."

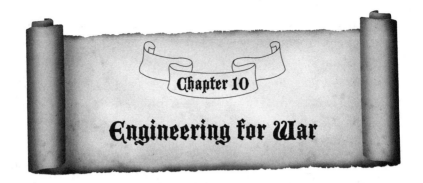

Chapter 10

Engineering for War

obby had more work to do than a single man had any right to. It was not that he didn't try to distribute much of it to others, but so very many of the top engineers had been brought up under Brentwood's heavy-handed directions that there just were too few willing to run with ideas on their own, to take risks. And, he did not have time to spare. Good engineering takes time to plan things out, to test, build prototypes, evaluate results and then repeat the process a few times until you got it right. The problem was there just wasn't time for all of that. The very existence of Freelandia was depending in part on what the Engineers could devise and implement – and he possibly only had a few months, almost certainly less than a year – to be ready.

First he had to reorganize the entire School of Engineers. Some non-war effort projects still needed to go on and be completed, but everything that could be put on hold was, in favor of evaluating ideas directly linked to the defense of Freelandia. Every engineer and apprentice was encouraged to find new ideas, and Robby had scheduled a weekly meeting where he, Arianna and select others would review them and vote on which to fund for further study. And already a few were looking very promising. Arianna's own swamp gas and pressure vessel research was moving along quite well, and was one of the top funded projects. It also happened to be the one he knew the most about, since he somehow found reasons to need updates on it every day from its highly attractive leader. But other projects needed attention too, even if their leaders were not nearly so pleasant to look upon!

Today he was meeting with Master Oldive at the Metallurgical Institute, a brick and mortar building with several large smokestacks that was built in the foothills of the nearby mountains, close to several mines. The chimneys belched out steam and smoke continuously as the engineers worked day and night on new metal alloys and on rapidly bringing the already planned production expansions online to make more steel, copper and other useful materials needed for building stronger and more modern defense works around Freelandia.

"Hey Oldsy! I forgot to bring me steak for lunch – it looks like you've got all de barbecues running full tilt!"

"Hi Bobby! Sometimes I think you could just slap down your steak on my desk over here and let it slow roast for a day! But come, I want to show you what we have been doing with that new silarium metal. It is a beast to purify and alloy, but when you get it right, you really have some interesting material to play with!"

Oldive led him into a shop workroom. Men were hammering away on various anvils, and small bellows were being pumped over stoves where red-hot liquid metals were being worked with. Over in a corner a small group of apprentices were tinkering around at a workbench on a variety of small items. As they neared, Robby could see bright pieces of what must be silarium – it tended to stand out from the other metals in no small part because it did not seem to rust or discolor over time like so many other metals did.

"Here, Bobby. Take a look at this." Master Oldive handed Robert a tube of the bright metal. It was surprisingly light, even taking account of it being hollow. Robby peered down the open end of the tube and saw a tightly coiled metal spring inside. "This is one of our early prototypes. Watch this." Oldive took a metal dart and dropped its end into the tube. It appeared to only have gone in a short ways. He lifted the tube and pushed the point of the dart into the wood of the workbench and began pushing. The dart's shank slowly disappeared into the tube. Master Oldive was straining to get the last lengths of the dart into the tube when Robby heard a "click" and Oldive stood up straight. He carefully handed the object to Robby, always keeping the dart pointed at a set of wooden planks about 30 feet away.

"Now you see this toggle on the side of the tube? That is the trigger. Hold the tube firmly now, and aim at the planks down range there."

Robby pointed the tube in the direction indicated and thumbed the small toggle. The dart launched out of the tube and Robby nearly dropped it from the suddenness and recoil. "Ye coulda warned me a wee bit more about that there recoil, Oldsy!" exclaimed Robby, looking over at his laughing friend.

"Oh, but I distinctly said to hold it firmly, Bobby! Now take a look at the results!" They walked over to the thick wooden planks and found the dart buried several inches into the hard wood. Robby cocked an eyebrow. "This is an early prototype? Oldsy, this surely would have gone right through an un-armored man!"

"Yes, Bobby, it already is a rather interesting weapon. It is too slow to re-load to get more than one shot off, but think if a solder had several of these at his belt – it surely would be deadly in close quarters and yet be nearly useless to the enemy if they captured it, at least until they could figure out how to fire and reload it. If every soldier used it at the first charge of an enemy, the initial wave would be decimated, without our soldiers needing to carry a bulky bow. Now, let's walk out this door and see the latest versions."

They exited a nearby door and Robby grinned. Before them stood a much larger tube mounted on a small turntable. "Now Oldsy, you did not just construct this contraption over the last day or two!"

"No, Bobby, this has been the project of a few of my junior engineers – we worked on it out-of-sight of Brentwood since I thought it had much more military potential than he would agree to."

"So I was not the first to think of using the springy thingies as launchers?

"No, sorry about that old chap! But their use in catapults was new ... we have been compressing the springs in these big tubes to launch larger and larger darts."

An apprentice was loading in a 6 foot arrow while another cranked on a wheel with handles mounted alongside the tube. Robby could hear a ratchet and gears at work inside the large tube, and he could see a small metal flag moving backward steadily as the wheel turned. Again, there was a loud click as the arrow reached its full depth. Looking down range, Robby could see stacked bales of straw perhaps 100 feet away.

"We just came up with several improvements on this basic idea yesterday." An apprentice brushed on a small amount of oil to the large head of the metal arrow. "We were penetrating at least one full bale before. Now watch this." With a nod, an apprentice sighted the tube at the straw target and pulled backward on a short chain. That obviously must have been the

trigger mechanism, for then the metal tipped arrow sped down range and there was a loud rasping metal clanging.

The group jogged to the target. Robby looked carefully. "Oldsy, did he miss entirely?" No sign of the arrow could be seen until they walked behind the bales. The head of the arrow had penetrated cleanly through four bales and the long shaft was now completely buried.

Oldive grinned. "We can punch through over a foot of hardwood, even at this distance. And we have not by any means optimized it yet, nor seen how big we can effectively make this thing. Think of what this might do if several were mounted on one of our ships?" Oldive was grinning ear to ear. "Now think if we made it hollow, or designed a break-off point just behind the head of the arrow – if it punched through a hull that would create a decent size leak! Or attach some lines with hooks to the end and shoot it through or over their rigging – it would tangle up the mast ropes – and now you have hooked quite a fish!"

"Oldsy – you are surely a genius! I am certainly glad you are on our side!"

"And that is not all, Master Engineer! We have another of these loaded up differently on the other side of this wall." Oldive led Robby to a solid wooden wall and a small door. He peeked in first to ensure the coast was clear, and they ambled over to another large mounted tube. An apprentice began to crank back the spring as they walked up. Two others were filling what looked like paper bags with small rocks. Three bags were placed inside a tall, narrow bucket that had a thin rope attached to its bottom. The rope was in a large coil with its end prominently tied to a large stake pounded into the ground.

"You don't have to use the rope, but we found we could control the spread of the projectiles however we wanted this way – to concentrate the payload with a longer rope or allow it to spread out in a much wider pattern with a shorter rope." Once loaded, an apprentice tilted the metal tube upward as though to lob its load a long distance down range. Robby peered in that direction. Dozens of small posts had been set up several hundred feet away, each with a man-sized piece of white cloth strung up onto them in a thin wire frame. In addition, several pumpkins had been rolled out among the posts, and there were also about a dozen thick wooden planks that stood facing their direction.

Robby looked quizzically at the intended target area. "Isn't that a might far distant away, even for this springy contraption?" Oldive just smiled and nodded at the apprentice, who took a final aim and triggered the launch. The now familiar rasping clang sounded which Robby understood to be the metal spring expanding and rubbing along the tube barrel. This time there was another whistling sound from the projectiles, and just a moment after launch the rope suddenly went taut and the pail was jerked to a stop in mid-air. A moment later Robby could hear a rapid staccato of impacts. He stared, first at Oldive, then at the spring tube, and finally down at the targets. "Oldsy … you didn't just do what I'm thinkin' ye just did … did ye?"

Master Oldive laughed heartily. "Let's see, shall we?" The apprentices had already jogged ahead and were excitedly mingling among the 'casualties'. Robby just stared. Only a few of the cloth combatants had survived unscathed. Most had at least one hole, and several were completely mangled into shreds. Robby walked around the targets. Many of the wooden planks had rocks buried deep into their surface, or holes corresponding to where rocks had punched cleanly through them, and two pumpkins had been hit squarely, with both entrance and exit holes indicating the force of the rock impact. Robby's eyes were wide. "Gracious God Almighty!" He said this in a soft whisper.

Master Oldive was quieted too. "Yes, Master Engineer. Think of a staggered row of these defending a pass. And we can reload pretty fast too. We have not determined effective range yet, and we expect even greater destruction with larger models and maybe with steel balls instead of stones. On a ship, think if we coated the rocks in pitch and maybe put a handful of live coals in the bucket first to ignite them during launch.

Of course these are not that much different than catapults, though they take up a lot less room, and so far we have not been able to quite match the range or power of our biggest 'cats … but these are much faster to reload and are easier to aim. We think we might get them down small enough that a two or three man team could carry them and within minutes could be ready to start launching a barrage of projectiles down range. The same tube that can send a big bucket full of rocks could also launch a bundle of burning arrows, or a larger single projectile. We have one team trying to up the payload while another is working on making versions smaller and lighter, and another experimenting with different payloads.

We had been doing all of this on the sly, with just a few apprentices sworn to secrecy, but frankly word was out among the younger apprentices and quite a few had voluntarily enlisted on my little 'black' project. So when we threw off the covers and said full speed ahead, why, there were already over a dozen trained workers and quite a few ideas that I had not even thought of that had been secretly put into practice. We are progressing much faster than I ever thought possible. The lads really have a will to work and it just seems like everything is going right."

"Lord Almighty, what are we inventing … how will it change our world?" Robby shook himself. "Master Oldive, I am doubling your funding. Your project is now second only to Arianna's – and if you continue to progress like this, you will take the lead. We need this technology moved as quickly as safely possible. I want you to be talking regularly with the Shipwrights, Coastal Defenders and with the Watchers setting up the Homeland Defense training. Also, do whatever it takes to increase silarium production – let me know what trade-offs are needed to make that happen. You also are going to need weapon production facilities beyond what this prototype lab can handle. Make me a list of what you need.

Oh – one other thing. Has the contingent of Watchers started to guard your work here? If not, get them going immediately – this is definitely a state secret we do NOT want the Dominion to know about if possible."

Robby got back to the School of Engineering in the late afternoon to a small mountain of paperwork. He did what he always did with that – he pushed it off to one side and would assign it to junior apprentices to go through and select only the most immediately important for his attention. Anyway, it was time to look at Arianna …er … Arianna's project.

Arianna looked up as Robby entered her pressurized container workshop. She beamed as always, that I-have-a-special-smile-just-for-you kind of grin, or so it seemed to Robby.

"Have ye seen any other might pretty engineers about, or are ye the only one today?"

"Bobby, will you ever be serious?" She scowled, or at least tried to. It was rather a difficult task while your eyes were twinkling.

"Ah, well, why should'st I start now? Ok, how's about one of the smartest engineers I know? So, been blowing anythin' up yet today?"

"Mr. Macgregor you are the most incorrigible lout of an engineer in Freelandia!"

"Guilty as charged, yer honor! I guess you will just have to lock me up and keep the key – I am as surely your prisoner as the tail on a hound dog." He put on a dour guilty looking face and held out his lanky arms toward her with wrists crossed in imitation of being bound.

"Oh … stop that Bobby!" Arianna's seriousness only lasted another moment and then she burst into giggles at the dejected expression Robby had assumed. He held it as long as he could, but her laughter was much too infectious and he had no real choice but to join in.

"Now Arianna, you really must be more serious about your so very important work!" Robby actually got that out without smirking.

"Oh you big oaf! You've made me entirely forget what I was about to do."

"Ach, I seem to have a way with beautiful women like that – the moment I come into a room they get all dizzy-headed and just fall all over me. It is such a difficulty. I guess the good God just puts such obstacles in path of engineers such as I to keep us surely humble."

Arianna's eyes flashed dangerously. "You … you …" she sputtered trying to find the right word and instead grabbed the nearest thing she could get her hands on, which happened to be a sizeable wrench. She swung the heavy wrench in a wide arc at Robby. He easily dodged aside and the weight swung through its arc, cleanly missing. Arianna obviously had misjudged the angular momentum and Robby quickly stepped forward as she spun awkwardly and began to lose her footing. He deftly caught her from behind in a tight hug as she whirled in place and stumbled, the wrench slipping out of control from her fingers and clanging loudly on the floor.

"Ah, there now lassie – you see exactly what I mean? I walk me-self into this here room, and the prettiest lady in all of Freelandia swoons right in front of me. And of course, being the kindly gentleman that I am, I step right up and catch her before she can as much as tousle that pretty head of hair!"

"BOBBY!" Arianna sputtered out and wrenched herself out of the too cozy embrace. "Sometimes you can be so very annoying that I wonder why I even think I might …" She caught her outburst before voicing the rest of her thought. Arianna took several deep breaths composing herself and letting her ire drain away. Then she leveled a steely glare at Robby. "The prettiest lady in all of Freelandia, huh? Well for that you just might be forgiven … just this once."

Robby rolled his eyes and groaned, figuring he had taken his joking too far that time. "I am oh so very grateful, that I am," he said with sincerity.

Arianna's expression softened but remained somewhat guarded. "Robby, can we just stick to engineering now?"

"I will surely try. But …"

Arianna raised a questioning eyebrow. "But what?"

Robby sighed and lifted his hands in resignation. "But I'm finding it more difficult to keep our arrangement … the one where I am 'sposed to only think of ye as me sister in the Lord."

"Yes, I've noticed!"

Robby laughed. "Ye mean I'm not too subtle? Me?"

Arianna laughed too, but then turned serious. "Robby, I've worked a long time to prove myself as a competent engineer. A competent *female* engineer that is dominated by menfolk. I want to get ahead by the merits of my ideas and skills. I don't want a relationship to jeopardize that."

Robby became serious too. "Arianna, you have already proven yourself. If I had even the wee smallest of doubts, your story at the Silver Chalice cleared them right out smartly. Your work here is incredibly important and valuable, and any fool can see that … even a big foolish lout like me! That is what … what attracts me so strongly to you. You are sharp as a tack, love the Lord our God, are pretty as God's own creation and … and you seem to even tolerate my wee attempts at humor."

"Wee indeed," Arianna agreed, but her eyes were caring and there was a tiny sprout of a smile working to show itself in the corners of her mouth.

Robby took that as an encouraging sign. "So, is there any hope for the likes 'o me?" His face took on an exaggerated forlorn expression as he looked longingly.

It was just too much. Arianna burst out laughing. "Now who is getting all dizzy-headed?"

"Guilty as charged, your most honoress! And what be your verdict?"

"You are rather direct, aren't you Chief Engineer?" Arianna still was not totally sure of her own feelings, but she was becoming rather fond of the lanky Robby. She smiled with a twinkle in her eyes. "I suppose there may be hope for even the likes of you. But I don't want any feelings you may have for me to interfere in the least with your responsibilities, nor with your judgment on the relative merits of my ideas. If the ideas or inventions of others appear more plausible to defend Freelandia, then you had better choose them over mine ... you get that mister?" Arianna brought steel back into her voice and punctuated her words with sharp finger points into Robby's chest.

"Ouch! I may be dense at times, but I get your points even without you having to pound them through me chest! It's a deal." Robby straightened up from the jabbing, threw back his shoulders and grinned. "Right'o then engineer, now, what have you been up to today?"

"Well, we have been working on a puzzlement actually. One of the apprentices is from the area where we collected the explosive gas. He mentioned what I thought sounded like a rather strange local custom. It seems the people who live nearby collect some of the clay around the pool. It is a grainy kind of clay that they press a kind of candle wick into and mold the stuff into shapes. Then they put these into small pots with a little water in the bottom and let the top part dry out for a few weeks. The water in the pot keeps them from totally drying out. Then they can light the wick and use the thing as a quite clean burning candle. I have one here."

She pulled over what looked like a small flower pot with a ball of gray putty sitting in half an inch of water with a short bit of waxy string jutting out on top. Arianna lit a thin reed at a candle and touched the flame to the wick. It lit up instantly and burned bright with not a hint of smoke. "Look at the fierceness of the burning – it seems to be combusting quite a lot hotter and faster than a normal candle, yet I am told this will stay lit for weeks.

Now even more interesting, I asked why they needed the water in the pot. I was told that if someone lets these things go dry the clay gets rather crumbly and powdery. If you bring a fire near it then ..." Arianna lit another reed taper, this one several feet long. She walked over to a small pile of light gray powder on a flat stone slab. When the flame neared it, the powder suddenly flashed and sparked into a small ball of intense fire.

"Great God Almighty!" Robby had taken a quick step backward from the ball of fire. "I expect they have had a few houses burn to smithereens when that there clay dries out!"

"Yes, I am told it claims a house or two every few years, sometimes with the occupants. It seems to burn very, very hot and very quickly."

"How long will the powdered clay stay like that?"

"I don't know – none of the local people let it go dry, and if they find any that has dried out they are mighty careful to remove it from any heat or fire source. They usually dump it into some water as fast as possible. Once it is damp it will still burn, but at a much slower and manageable rate."

"Arianna!" Robby turned and took her hands into his and looked very intently and seriously into her eyes. "You must promise me to be careful with this stuff! I don't want a single hair on your pretty head as much as singed."

"Why Bobby, you know I am a hands-on engineer! And anyway, how would you even know?"

Robby pulled her in close and made a show of sniffing her hair. "I guess I will just have to personally inspect this every day, just to make sure!"

Arianna demurely pulled away. "Is that a promise, Chief Engineer?"

Chapter 11

Workouts

Ethan walked over to one of the outdoor ranges within the Watcher Compound. His class schedule was rather chaotic compared to most apprentices, since his skills in most aspects of hand-to-hand combat were considerably above his peers. With that in mind, James and Gaeten had worked out a customized training plan, which relied rather heavily on Gaeten's personal instruction. In his absence, Ethan was trying to double up on some of his other practices while trying his hand out at new activities. He decided this week to focus on archery and hand thrown weapons.

A row of Level Five apprentices were at the archery range, with a steady stream of arrows flitting across a grassy field at targets about 100 feet away. A Master Archer was assessing everyone's style and making corrections. Ethan sidled up to an open slot at the end of the group. He fitted an arrow to the short bow. Even as he lifted it a blue line seemed to appear in the air. He moved the bow so that the blue line intersected the bulls-eye on his target. He just now had to concentrate to let go properly – even his superb guidance system could not correct for a flubbed release. The arrow flew true and buried itself into straw of the target in the center circle.

The instructor nodded, but then pulled out a long strip of cloth and proceeded to tie it around Ethan's head as a blindfold. "Try it again now, Ethan."

Smiling, Ethan felt for another arrow. He had done this routine a few times before. He lifted the bow and waited a moment for the blue line in his mind to settle down. He moved the arrow until in his mind he could see the line intersected with a pulsating blue dot downrange, and then he carefully released. Without even removing the blindfold he knew the shot was next to perfect. The instructor removed his blindfold anyway, and confirmed the shot. "Try again."

Ethan shrugged and picked up another arrow. He aimed, held a moment, and just before he let go the instructor suddenly waved a bright flag just within his periphery vision to his right. Ethan could not seem to help but look that direction, and the arrow missed the target completely.

"Ha! You may have great aiming skill, Ethan – but you have trouble concentrating when there are distractions!"

"That was not fair!"

"What – do you think the Dominion Bashers will come up to you in a nice orderly line? In a real battle there are multiple opponents and a great deal of chaos – but you must concentrate on your targets one by one, while still aware of all."

After a few more tries Ethan was able to continue to hit his target even with the visual distractions, but sometimes it was just barely. It was obvious he needed much more practice … not something Ethan was always patient for, as Gaeten had often reminded him. Resolved to improve – as much to show Gaeten when he returned as for any other reason, Ethan kept practicing. Sometimes, he thought, it might almost be easier being blind – his own eyes tended to be too easily distracted.

At lunchtime he collected a small serving from the cafeteria and climbed one of the higher tower lookouts within the Compound. He pulled out the small whistle Gaeten had given him and blew several long – though essentially silent to his ears – blasts. About five minutes later an eerie screech from a long, high distance answered and in a few minutes Sasha landed on an open terrace with a great flutter of wings and feathers. Ethan dumped out about half his meal onto the terrace, and Sasha hopped down to inspect it. It must have passed muster, for the gryph began to snatch pieces up with its beak and gobble them down.

Ethan was not sure how much the bird really needed his food as a supplement for what it caught out in the fields surrounding the Keep, and perhaps even out in the bay. Still, Gaeten has asked him to care for Sasha, and in all honesty he enjoyed watching the unfettered power and freedom of the great bird of prey. She had no responsibilities, no one to tell her what to do or having expectations of her. As Sasha left in a mighty leap to launch herself airborne, Ethan wondered what adventures Gaeten was getting into. He had all the fun … Ethan was just left here to continue on doing the same general training day after day. He was beginning to resent that. It was already getting boring without having Gaeten around. Ethan knew he could volunteer to help with other defense preparations, but he just did not particularly feel like it. He hoped something new and exciting would come along to catch his interest.

Over the next several days Maria was introduced to a variety of other stringed instruments. Some truly were brand new to her, others she had at least a most basic familiarity from her nighttime adventures. There were several she was more drawn toward, but realistically she loved them all. Her fingers were getting sore from all the plucking and strumming, but with each new instrument Maria became at least somewhat proficient within a few hours at most, and her mind cataloged the rich sounds each could make.

Voice lessons were another matter. They hurt. Maria's throat now hurt almost every day as her vocal chords were stretched on both the low and high side, but especially on the low notes. She had to practice her scales all the time. It definitely was not fun – one did not particularly sing through scales in one's special place before God. There was no aspect of worship or joy associated with this, just work. She felt drained and rather depressed over that instruction. So two days later when she heard that a group of junior apprentices was planning to put on a small vocal concert she was quite excited.

"Kory, where did the sign say the tryouts would be for the choral concert?"

"Maria, that is just about the fifth or sixth time you have asked! It is tonight, second floor vocal building room B. It says only Level Three and lower apprentices can try out … and I do not even know what level you really are!"

"Well then, I guess I can choose it for myself! I am still doing introductory level classes along with some more advanced ones, so I think I would still officially be somewhere around a Level One – what do you think?"

"I suppose that sounds right … and I don't think anyone will really argue with 'The Singer.' But they will not want you to show them up either – I mean, who would want to compete or even try to keep up with you?"

"Oh Kory, I would never do that … at least not on purpose! I am not asking or even trying for a lead singing role. I actually would prefer a back-up support role so I can learn more about singing in groups – I do not have experience with that. Well, really no experience at all outside of singing alongside Sir Reginaldo. And for the last week I have only been able to sing scales and hold a note. That is not real singing!"

"You're telling me … I have to listen to you!"

"Oh … I did not think of that … I'm sorry, Kory … has it been dreadful?"

"Well, I am sure it is better than if you were practicing trumpet scales! It is ok, but I am already tired of it. How long will you keep going with it? I can see why many apprentices do not stay but drop out."

"Well, I am sure going to try to keep going." Maria looked resolved, but she too found it tedious and frustrating and … hard.

"Make sure to remind me when we need to leave. Where do we need to go again?"

"M a r i a!"

Chapter 12

Kardern

It took Gaeten nearly a week to reach the river port town of Kardern, a bustling ship building city that was currently a bee-hive of activity. The coach ride had been uncomfortable, and three times Gaeten had to fend off thieves during the night, at least one of them had been one of the drivers, by the smell of him. Finally they arrived and everyone disembarked. The sounds and smells indicated they were near a food market, and when Gaeten had gathered up his few belongings, he cautiously made his way toward the shoppers. He meandered through the carts and stalls, clicked down his walking staff loudly and using it occasionally to probe his way ahead.

People reluctantly parted to let him through, but not without grumbling – and they did not think twice about bumping into him either. Within 50 yards he had been semi-professionally frisked several times by pickpocket thieves, who discovered nothing but found the prospects of a blind newcomer just too easy to pass by. Of course Gaeten could have apprehended or stopped them, but he was as much interested in gauging their skill as they were his pockets. One of them might do for his purposes, but he thought he might find a better candidate and he prayed for both opportunity and discernment. He did not have to wait very long. Gaeten heard a commotion of the sort he was particularly interested in. He gave a silent prayer that this indeed would lead to God's choice.

"Thief! Come back with that apple!" The man's voice was shrill and directed roughly in Gaeten's direction. A high pitched laugh sounded and Gaeten could hear the fast patter of light feet snaking rapidly through the crowd. He moved on an intercept course. Just as the footsteps scampered by, Gaeten's hand shot out and lifted the young vagabond completely off his feet and held him in the air.

"Hey, what'd ya think yer doing? Let me loose, quick!"

In a moment the shopkeeper caught up. "Thank you stranger, I'll give you a coin for your trouble. This will be the last time this thief ever uses that hand for mischief again!" The vendor reached for the boy menacingly.

"Wait a moment, good sir," Gaeten spoke slowly and, he thought, rather grandfatherly. "How much for the overripe bit of fruit this rascal snitched?"

The shopkeeper looked at the boy, then at Gaeten and a shrewd and even snide smile broke over his face. "That was a rare one indeed, a fine delicacy from the mountains of Kir far to the south. I was planning on delivering a basketful of those to the choicest restaurants in town – they are worth a very pretty penny indeed. Oh, I think such a fine specimen is easily worth …"

His sentence stopped short by the pressure of a staff against his wind-pipe. The staff abruptly was removed and laid lightly on the man's shoulder. "Now, good shopkeeper, I am sure you would not want to take an unfair advantage over a poor old blind man, now would you?"

The shopkeeper growled and his hand moved toward a knife in a sheath on his belt. In less than a blink of an eye the staff end was suddenly poking the man's arm just above the wrist, pushing it away from the knife handle. "Tsk, tsk. And here I thought you were an honest vendor! Perhaps this lad had good reason to appropriate your fruit? In any case, it smells like an apple a few days past its prime. I will give you a few coppers for it, probably still more than it is really worth."

Gaten, slowly put the boy down and whispered conspiratorially, "Stay put a moment, I'll make it worth your while". Then he fished out a few small coins from an inner pocket – one the thieves had missed earlier – and tossed them at the vendor while he returned his staff to his side.

The shopkeeper was not at all sure what had just happened, but he had a decent price and this old blind begger did not appear to be one he wanted to mess with, at least not now in the daylight, in front of a small crowd that was watching, and maybe not all by himself. "You steal from me almost as badly as that cur. I had better never see either of you again!" Cursing under his breath the man stormed off.

The skinny, curly-haired boy thief was munching away on the apple. "How many more did your friends just get while I kept the storekeeper's attention?" Gaeten asked with a chuckle.

"Oh, by the time he gets to his stall it would be better for us to be long gone. Say, you are pretty fast, especially for being ancient as dirt and as blind as a bat."

Gaeten laughed again. "You don't mince words do ya, boy? Quick, lead me to a safe spot where I can make you a proposition – and don't think you can walk me into a trap either ..." The walking staff appeared directly in front of the boys eyes such that he went cross-eyed looking at it ... "cause the first one to get killed will be you."

The boy gulped and then snickered. "Deal – for now. But it had better be something good you got for me. This way." He grabbed a sleeve of the older man and tugged him along down a side street. Gaeten was certain after a few minutes that the intention was to get him thoroughly confused and lost – which was nearly the case, especially in a strange new city. Eventually they slowed and Gaeten stopped.

"Whoa there lad, you're moving too fast for my poor old legs. And anyway, I smell a tavern across the way. Let's stop over there."

"Hey old man, I can't go in there! They'd box me ears if I took a step into a tavern. Don't you know nothing?"

"Not inside you lout, but it is a safe enough spot, just a few feet down from the door. We will look like an old beggar and his helper, and then I can make you my offer." Gaeten did not particularly want to let the boy take him into some back alley where he could be at a serious disadvantage in a planned ambush.

"Alright you old codger, but this better be good." They ambled over and sat down on the rough planks a few yards down from the tavern door. There would be enough noise coming from inside to cover their conversation, in case there were any prying ears about.

"Ah, there now. Time to conduct some business. First, what's your name, boy?"

"I'm called 'Nimblefoot', Nimby for short. What's it to you?"

"It makes it easier than just calling 'hey you' or 'boy'. I am looking for a quick-minded business partner who knows the city inside and out, and especially the ... shall we say ... seamier sections in particular. I want someone who knows the streets, and who knows ..." Gaeten lowered his voice to a deep whisper ... "how to run around under the noses of the Dominion without them so much as sneezing. Know anyone like that?"

Gaeten had made no movement to stop the boy from quietly and slowly drawing a knife from a leg sheath. The point now pressed lightly against Gaeten's tunic over his heart. "I don't know who or what you are, old man, but if you are trying to trick me into saying somethin' against the Dominion just so'es they can torture me like they did to poor old Scarl last month ... said he was to be 'a lesson' for us all to learn from ... then before you can blink those sightless eyes of yours I'm a going to skewer you through."

Gaeten chuckled lightly – any more and the blade tip would have punctured his skin. "So, a street rat with fangs, huh? Good, I like that. Means you might have the guts and skill to do what I will pay for."

The knife was not removed, but the pressure lessened slightly. "Just what kind of 'business' are you planning?"

"Let me tell you a little story. I used to have a decent job at a traveling circus, but ever since the Dominion came along people don't seem to have the time or money to come and get 'entertained'. We used to part fools from their money quite smartly, I tell you." Gaeten gave a rueful chuckle. We had a great thing going. We'd come into an area with such fanfare! People would come from miles and miles to see the wonderful, the exotic, the strange and unusual. And they would pay, boy would they pay! Then before they'd catch on to what was happening we would pull up our stakes and move a few days journey further along. But then came the Dominion soldiers. If they didn't like what you did, they'd just as soon stick you with a spear. They often wouldn't pay and anyone caught lifting a purse would be 'made into an example' – yes, I know all about that practice. Within months business was so low most of us had to be let go. So now I have to travel from tavern to tavern to earn a few coins to live on."

"Nice story. So what are you doing here, what do you want, and what is in it for me?" The blade had been pulled back now, but was still out and ready.

"I need someone who knows which taverns are safe for me to work in. I need to know when big ships arrive with new passengers. I need to know when soldiers are about to ship out and might be freer with their pay. I need to know when any larger groups will be leaving long enough ahead of time to work the people hard. I need to know when the Dominion is about to do a security sweep, and where to effectively hide."

"So ... the Dominion is looking for you?"

Gaeten could hear the wheels clicking … what would be worth more, turning in the old man or working with him for awhile … and then turning him in?

"Ha! I have kept a step ahead of them! But they do not generally look favorably upon people who empty the purses of their soldiers and workers at taverns! Let's say I sometimes earn a tidy sum, depending on how gullible the people are. And I am willing to share, say, ten percent of my take. Some nights that could net you a small purse of coins."

The knife came back up. "Ten percent old man? What do you take me for? Not a coin less than fifty percent. And I can find out anything in this town. I even got's some schooling too, before the orphanage got shut down.

Your arrival is pretty timely too … I happen to know the tavern where the main shipwrights work, and they've been talking about schedules to launch the Dreadnaughts."

"Dread-caughts? Sorry, I'm not much of sailor … can you figure out why?"

"Dreadnaughts, old man. Kardern is one of the largest shipbuilding ports in the Dominion, and they been building the biggest and baddest war ships anyone ever seen. Several were finished a few months back, and a couple more are nearly done to join them. New sailors have been swarming the dockyards. And worse, quite a few new soldiers been arriving and they be quartered near the river. Some of them are from the Deep South, or so I have heard. They have strange red eyes and smell funny. Now, how about it – fifty percent or you can take a blind stumble around this large town."

Gaeten gave a low laugh. "I sincerely doubt you are worth half of that."

The knife whipped back up and poked forward. In one fluid motion Gaeten's arm swept forward and snatched the knife right out of the boy's firm grip, swiveled it around and brought the point forward to prick Nimby's chin, drawing a single drop of blood. Had Gaeten been able to look, he would have seen the boy's eyes bulge nearly out of his head. As it was, he did hear the gulp and the quiver in Nimby's voice "Hold on, old man! Take it easy! I was just funning with you!"

"Ha! You would have just as quickly tried to find a way between my ribs with that blade if you thought you'd make better money or have better odds. Don't play innocent or dumb – I did not select someone for being an idiot." Gaeten pulled the knife back and reversed its direction, handing it back to the boy. Nimby snatched it back and paused, not really knowing if he should try to use the blade or sheath it. Caution got the better of him, and the knife was put away.

"I'll give you twenty percent, and if you prove particularly useful, I'll up it to thirty. If you are exceptional, you can come into the taverns with me – as a poor old blind man's guide – and get all the food and drink you can lift – and maybe a purse here and there too, if you are good enough not to get caught. But if you do get caught don't expect me to bail you out. You'll make more in a week than you probably do in a year, and you won't have angry shopkeepers chasing you around. Eventually one of those shopkeepers will catch you, and if you survive at all you'll be minus a hand or some fingers – and if that does not kill you your "friends" will likely finish the job since you will not be able to protect yourself very well anymore."

Nimby was quiet, pondering his options. "Ok, old man. I will see if it is worth it, but I'll cut out anytime I want to, leaving you high and dry."

"Good, Nimby. We can start tonight, and perhaps get enough income to rent a proper room somewhere. Now wipe the blood off your chin and give me a quick tour of the town."

Nimby dragged his hand over his face and saw the small blood smear with amazement. He stared at the blank eyes 'staring' across at him and wondered just how blind the old man really was.

Chapter 13

Choral Concert

The weather was sunny with a mild breeze, just about perfect for a concert in the outdoor amphitheater that opened outward toward the ocean bay a short distance away from the Music Academy. The 20 apprentices who made up the choir, mostly in their mid teenage years, were nervously standing on the stage as the last audience members filtered in and found seats. Performances were a rather common occurrence, but most were from older and higher level apprentices.

Maria stood in the second row, putting weight first on one foot and then on the other. She was not sure if it was better or worse to not be able to see the audience, though she could hear the muted conversations. She hoped she would remember the words and tunes, as most of the songs were new to her. She was glad she did not have a main part, so even if she did forget something her voice could hide among the other singers.

The try-outs had gone smoothly enough, once everyone got over the fact that 'The Singer' had shown up and that she did not have any desire for a lead role. Nearly everyone else trying out for spots was several years older than Maria, and all had aspirations for lead roles, where they thought they would be more noticed. Maria had insisted she was only trying out for a supporting position, and she was at a disadvantage right from the start since she did not know any of the chosen songs. She had to listen carefully to someone else sing it through, and then she sang it back with a simple harmony. When that did not seem to impress those in charge of the auditions she sang it again several times with progressively more complex harmonies that she could hear in her mind. That got her chosen quickly enough.

The group had practiced every evening, and all felt they were ready for a great performance. Maria shuffled again in her place waiting. The concert was just about to begin when she heard some commotion out in the audience off to one side. A loud group of female voices was slowly moving down the amphitheater steps toward the front. As they neared, Maria was certain she recognized one particularly loud voice – the bullying person that Kory had called Vanessa. The group sounded boisterous, but not in a happy sort of way – these voices sounded derisive and cutting. Maria could just make out a few sneering phrases that seemed to be deriding the upcoming concert. She was glad again that she was not standing out front.

Then Maria forgot all about nervousness and the loudly whispering girls in the front as the choir director stepped out and tapped on a small podium with a baton. The singers all stood up straighter while the lone accompaniment piano began the introduction to the first song. The audience hushed – well, Maria could still hear Vanessa – and then they began their first of a dozen scheduled songs.

The apprentices were good, though of course they were not Master level. For the first two stanzas Maria was too nervous to do more than sing the words rather mechanically, though still blending in perfectly. Then she settled herself and entered the special place in her mind where music transformed from simple auditory vibrations into colorful movement and sounds used to give glory and worship to her Creator.

Even in the interludes between songs, Maria kept herself in God's presence, silently continuing singing. All continued smoothly … until the eighth song, one of the most difficult for the lead apprentice girl during the practices. The girl valiantly started into her lead part, but immediately Maria noticed she was off slightly, not quite hitting the notes correctly. She had a loud voice that projected well, but now that was changing into a disadvantage. The rest of the singers were coming in after her start, and Maria could hear they were having trouble – the slightly off lead tones were pulling them off too. Some were on target, others were not, and a few were wavering. To a normal audience, this might not have been fully recognized, but at the Academy everyone heard the jarring slightly off notes.

Maria was frustrated. Her part did not come in for another minute or so, yet she could already hear murmuring in the audience, and in particular she could hear the voice of Vanessa and what must be the group of friends she had come in with starting to laugh and snicker. Even as the rest of the choir joined in, there was no clear lead – some were hitting their notes perfectly, while others were drifting off. Maria started, pitch perfect but to her very sensitive ears the sound of the group was ... terrible. In her mind, she could see the singers who were hitting the notes correctly as pure colors trying to weave together with others that were decidedly sickly colored and frayed.

Tears formed in the corners of her eyes. In her mind she tried to dance and worship, but it was very difficult to do with such glaring flaws. If only she could just reach out and fix the notes! Well, she could at least try to rally the healthy colors she saw weaving in the song.

All of this took at most a second, and then Maria took a deep breath – remembering to inflate her chest and not her stomach – and began to sing out more loudly, and, somehow, even more clearly. Those immediately around her were drawn in and no longer warbled around the correct notes. As they came fully into tune, the correct sounds became louder and more pronounced, which in turn drew still others to audibly link in. Maria's voice, though strong and clear, was still subservient to the lead singer. The groundswell of support singers made still further headway, yet the main lead female singer was still struggling. While now the other strands of colored sounds in her mind had become healthy and vibrant, hers still remained sickly and weak. Maria concentrated, willing the weaving sounds and colors to flow around and around that strand. Maria's own voice led the way, bolstering and uplifting that lead role to compensate for what was lacking. And finally, mid-way through the song, the resultant blend was nearly perfect. Maria smiled and danced for joy in her mind, all the while holding the complex weave of sound together without leaving her supporting hamony.

The song finally came to a close. Maria slumped at her spot – the effort had been quite tiring, but she was smiling – it had worked, at least to her ears.

Many in the crowd applauded, though Maria could again hear snickering from the front rows and a loud snort that must have come from Vanessa herself. The singers near her were whispering in excited though quiet tones, all wondering how they had managed to get through that song. They realized something had been wrong, and several even pinpointed the issue to having come from the lead singer, but none knew what had truly happened, or the source of the correction.

Maria was in half a mind to tell them, and was just about to put word to lip when she thought better of it. After all, she reasoned, she had just helped a little, and the main benefit was to bring greater praise to God, her true audience. She knew if she sought praise for her role, it would really be taking it away from God – and it certainly should ALL go to Him. So she remained silent, thanking God for the strength and ability to give Him glory, and even for the ability to sing at all.

The remaining four songs went on without a hitch, being led by others in the ensemble. When the concert finished she heartily congratulated those around her as the audience politely applauded. The choir began to disband, with several of those near Maria helping her down off the raised platform. Kory rushed up. "Maria – that was great! There seemed to be a bit of … of … well, of something happening on the eighth song, but I am not even really sure what it was … but then it cleared up and finished great. I could hear your voice too, though it was really difficult since it seemed to blend in so very well with everyone else's."

"Thanks Kory – that's the idea."

"So there's 'The Singer' herself! The concert would have been such a success too, if you had not been so off-key on the eighth song!" Vanessa's scorn was virtually dripping from every word.

Maria felt Kory move forward a step. "Vanessa, back off. Maria did just fine!"

"Oh she did, did she? And exactly how would a plebian novice like you even know? If you were a true musician you would know such things … if you could ever even reach such a lofty state."

"Vanessa, I would like to reach right over to …"

Maria grabbed Kory's arm and pulled her back. "It is not worth arguing about, Kory. Yes, we had some trouble there on the eighth song. Quite a few in the choir were slightly off for the start of the song, but about half way through we all came together and had a great finish."

Vanessa did not want to let it go quite so easily. "The song was a total wreck! You all are the laughing stock of the Academy! Just wait until to-morrow – it will be the talk of the whole campus. What goof-balls! Next time, leave concerts to the true professionals, like me. Just think … 'The Singer', part of such a fiasco! Your reputation is now quite tarnished, probably permanently. Heh, heh – maybe old Vitario will now think twice about having given you my apartment and send you two over to the beginner dormitory where you belong ... or even out of the whole Academy itself. Come on girls, let's go – let's leave these losers!"

Kory was bristling in anger but Maria held her arm tightly. "No Kory, let them go ... they are not worth the trouble. Besides, we did a lot better than she said."

"I'd certainly agree, young ladies. Far from perfect, but I'd say at least adequate for the skill and experience level of most of the singers."

Maria had been so caught up in the encounter with Vanessa that she had not heard anyone come up behind her. She turned with a surprise. "Master Veniti! I did not hear you! I take it you were in the audience?"

"Yes, Maria, I was sitting right behind those obnoxiously loud apprentices. Good thing for them they are not within the vocal division of the Academy, or I would see that they gave proper honor to performers. It is always far easier to be a critic than a performer ... or a problem fixer ... eh, Maria?"

Maria took on a guarded expression. "We did have a problem there on the eighth song, but I think by half way through we all came together."

"Yes ... yes everyone did come together, even Leslie, the lead singer, finally. She will be in my office tomorrow for a review. Making mistakes is normal – it is part of learning. But making them in front of an audience like this is unacceptable. If she did not have the song down solidly she should have recognized and admitted it, and let someone else lead. As it was, the song was being ruined terribly ... until a mysterious core group suddenly began singing pitch-perfect and the correction contagion spread to encompass the entire choir. I don't suppose you know what happened, Maria?"

Maria tried to choose her words carefully. "Well ... it seemed like some apprentices were struggling, while others were doing fine – but those who were off were unsettling the others and dragging people off-key. I guess a group of singers finally hit on the correct notes and that pulled everyone else back on target."

"A group? I distinctly heard one voice holding true, and then ... I cannot really explain it fully. It was almost like that voice reached out and uplifted the others, corralling them into the proper key and holding them to it. And yet, that voice stayed in the background ... it never became overbearing; it never dominated or moved outside of its proper place in the ensemble. It was … amazing, astounding … I have never witnessed anything like it ever before. I am still wondering what exactly happened, how it was done. Can you shed any light onto that, Maria? And might you know how one can do that? I mean, besides just singing the proper notes oneself, how does one seem to reach out and affect others around them, and even the whole choir itself … and all within moments?"

"Ah … well … I think it sounded to me like that voice … um … sort of weaved the other voices together into a coherent pattern that was back on track."

"And how might that be done, exactly?"

"Um … it might have something to do with a certain … 'special place' … and with the audience who is there."

"Is that so?" Veniti steepled his hands. "Interesting. Perhaps there may be more to that than I first acknowledged. Regardless of the source or how it was done though, the results were startling. I heard a couple of extra breaths needed beyond what should have been, but I could see you were at least trying to breathe correctly. All in all …" Master Veniti paused as though he was going to say something more, but then turned and began to walk away. He glanced back over his shoulders and coughed, acting as though it were only with great difficulty he could voice what came next. "Well done, Maria."

Ethan had gone to the concert too, and had expected to catch up with Maria afterwards. But he saw others talking with her and left, figuring she appeared to be doing just fine. *"There"*, he thought, *"my promise to Gaeten to keep an eye on Maria is covered, at least for now."* He wandered back toward the Watcher Compound that was becoming increasingly busy, but increasingly boring to him. Mainly because he was the Chancellor's son, Ethan had been asked to be on various inspection teams and everyone seemed to want to impress upon him how well everything was working, but how much even better it could be with additional funding. He was feeling rather useless – the teams really did not need him. They only seemed to want him for who his father was and not for his own skills. And now most of the Masters and senior apprentices were extremely busy with defense issues and had little time to spar with him.

Many were involved with setting up training for the stream of volunteers that were pouring into the Keep every day, responding to Duncan's call. At first they were coming in groups of tens and twenties, but now several thousand men were volunteering each week, requiring volunteer lodging and the creation of several barracks of tents. Most of those were temporarily being assigned to help build up the earthen ramparts around the Keep and other strategic areas, but as organization became stronger more were being assessed for other skills and sent to various Ministries to provide hand laborers. The Engineering school was getting most of the brightest and skilled tradesmen, but there was plenty of work for all.

All that is, except for Ethan … or so it seemed to him. He trudged back to his home in a grump. Even his parents were now preoccupied with so many activities that they hardly saw or had time for him. The whole country was gearing up for an historic fight. Yet to Ethan it seemed like nothing really exciting ever happened to him. He was starting to feel that he did not fit in, that it was not fair, and it certainly did not seem fun.

Chapter 14

Temptress Taleena

Taleena reminded herself to be glad to be alive as she finished packing the few belongings that she would not buy outright. Murdrock was not known for kindness or for looking over failure. He had told her in no uncertain terms that she had one last chance to redeem her life, and that she had better pray to her gods for favor and success – because if she failed a second time he would personally send her back to his Dominion masters so they could assist in drawing out every last detail of her memories of Freelandia in the nastiest manner they could dream up. She shuddered. At least he had not figured out who had put the soap on the stairs, which later caused Murdrock to fall and badly twist his ankle.

Her current mission, though, was an ocean away from the Dominion, and quite a difference from the kitchen scullery she had been assigned to before. This mission was much more suited to her and at least while it lasted it could be quite enjoyable. And the best part of it was, she had a considerably higher gold allowance – she had convincingly pleaded that she simply must look and act the part to even have a hope of success – which meant a new wardrobe of fine clothing, a small but somewhat elegant rented room – with a real bed! – carriage rides, fine dining and even modest jewelry and make-up. And, of course, several additional items for her potion bag more fitting to her new requirements. Those had been ordered through Murdrock and should arrive within a few weeks. Freelandia hosted a veritable flotilla of trading ships from nearly every port in the world – a number of which held Dominion spies and couriers.

It was almost too easy to get supplies. Ships were rarely stopped outright, and while the docks were well policed and cargo was checked, rarely was a ship really thoroughly inspected – and there were many places on a ship where things could be hidden. In addition, quite a few ships would dock to unload and then re-load cargo, and then put back out into the very large harbor to allow berths for new ships. While the cargo was more fully inspected and the ship itself was looked over, speed to open the berth again outweighed security concerns. The real interest appeared to be for commerce, and for the docked ships. Occasionally a ship at anchor in the harbor would be boarded for inspection, especially if it took several days of waiting before it could be berthed. Those ships would daily send skiffs back and forth to the docks for supplies and to give sailors shore leave. The docks therefore were an extremely busy, even chaotic place – ideal for spies and agents to slip through. And it seemed like Freelandia did not even care!

The threat of war would probably change that sooner or later, but until then it was to the Dominion's advantage that Freelandia was oh so trusting and believed itself to be oh so noble. The Dominion had no such pretenses. It ruled by fear, and enforced its whims with brutal and somewhat random violence.

Taleena tucked those thoughts away. She had first stopped at a smaller town outside of the capital and transformed herself from a scruffy kitchen maid into a young lady traveling in from a country estate. Upon arriving she had rented a nice apartment with the cover story that her parents had sent her for further education at the capital, and that she could pay for 6 month's rent up-front. Gold tended to shut questioning mouths when used properly. Then Taleena had an immensely pleasurable few days of buying furnishings and especially clothes and jewelry to support the image of a spoiled girl who looked considerably younger than her actual age.

Within a week she was gaily walking the streets of the Keep by day and integrating herself into the young people's nightlife. There was no lack of company – this was without doubt a rich city and even with the quite con-servative upbringing of most families there were considerable numbers of young men and women who seemed ready for rebellious evening activities at eateries that catered to their age group. It did not even take that much acting to fit right in.

It also did not take long to find out information about her target, Ethan. He was the focus of intense gossip amongst the girls, and of both admira-tion and jealousy among the boys. Taleena learned that he most certainly did not frequent the evening social scene in town, but was often either with his parents or at the Watchers Compound. She had no desire to get too close to either of those two places, though she thought she would prefer the Watchers over Ethan's see-right-through-you mother. So while there was a great deal of talk about him and his exploits (real or imagined), actual facts were rather scarce. One of the few things rather certain was that he stayed every night at his parent's house and supposedly started his intensely physical routine at the Watchers Compound quite early. Careful questioning pinpointed where the Chancellor's residence was located, and it took only casual examination to determine the most probable routes from there to the Watchers Compound.

Well, if Ethan would not likely come to where she was, she would just have to find a way to go to him – and attract his attention. Taleena smiled craftily. He was only a young teenage male – getting his attention should not be overly difficult, and she had a plan on how to keep it. She got busy with her preparations. Tomorrow was supposed to start with a light rain and that should work in perfectly with her plan. She also needed a quite early bedtime to ensure she was positioned at an early enough time and place for her planned rendezvous.

Ethan was not very busy but was getting very, very bored. Freelandia was preparing for war, and so Master Warden James had the Wardens and Watchers gearing up to meet the challenges of defensive preparations and training. Nearly everyone had additional responsibilities. Ethan had some also, but he was too young and inexperienced to be assigned to larger projects, yet too advanced to need to attend most of the new classes. And while his own skill level was considerable, he was not that good of a teacher – his gifting made it quite difficult for him to teach others anything but the most basic techniques and he just did not have the aptitude for that kind of slow pace. He supposed there were other useful jobs he could have sought out or even volunteered for, but frankly he did not really feel like it, at least not quite yet. Maybe later. Maybe when Gaeten eventually returned. Maybe.

His new-found near-hero status had also lost its luster and now was much more of an annoyance. People tended to gape at him and want to introduce themselves, and they again and again wanted him to tell of the adventure of saving his father's life. It was rather fun at first, but after a dozen times the retelling got old. With his best friend Gaeten out of the country, he just did not have the same enthusiasm and dedication to his activities. He had a work-out routine he continued to follow, though even that was slipping recently. He had extra time on his hands and everything seemed boring in his life now. It was getting to him. Nothing interesting was happening, at least not for him.

Ethan got up early the next morning hoping this blasé feeling would pass soon, that something exciting would occur that day. He supposed he could check in with the Engineers or shipyards that afternoon as something to do that at least was different. Maybe afterwards he could stand out on the docks and daydream about a big Dominion ship suddenly appearing, which he would single-handedly subdue and lead the captured sailors in a procession through the Keep. Ethan the Conqueror – he liked the sound of that.

His routine had him up earlier than anyone else in the home – aside from the assigned Watchers guarding the house that is, and he had his usual cold light breakfast and headed out toward the buildings that made up the Watcher Compound complex. It was toward the other end of town, nearly two miles away, but he never took a horse or carriage, preferring a light jog to warm him up for the more strenuous exercise planned.

It seemed like a typical morning, though it was overcast with a very light sprinkle of rain. Only a few people were up and about, mostly store-keepers busily preparing for another shopping day and bakers getting their kitchens started. Ethan was about half way to his destination when he came to one of the larger parks in the town. Some days he circled it a few times on his way, and he was planning to turn into the park pathways to do that when he noticed another jogger out in the faint light and mist directly ahead of him. That by itself was quite unusual – he had never encountered anyone else out for a run this early in the day, at least this distance from the Watcher Compound. The figure ahead turned into the park pathway. Intrigued, he picked up his pace and turned in as well … but as he neared the smaller figure a warning bell seemed to sound in his head and he saw in his mind a faint blue ribbon indicating a safe pathway that veered sharply away. He slowed his pace slightly, senses on high alert – but there was nothing out of ordinary that he could discern – no one else was out here, just the runner up ahead who now seemed shrouded in a red haze. Puzzled but not particularly concerned – after all, he figured he could get out of just about any dangerous situation that could present itself, and besides, there was no danger that he could see – he again sped up and soon was approaching the other runner.

Ethan could see the jogger was female – running made it rather obvious – but he did not recognize who it was. He admired the wavy black hair tied smartly back into a braid and particularly noticed the quite tightly fitting – and now sweat darkened – running outfit the young lady was wearing. All in all, it was starting to be a much more interesting day!

Just as Ethan drew alongside her, the girl glanced over, gave a slight shriek of surprise, and instantly sped away at much higher speed. Ethan grinned and loped forward, easily catching up with the bolting person. She seemed to put on a further burst of speed and Ethan laughed out loud, again easily pacing her. "Hey, it's ok – we don't have to race!" he panted out as he came alongside her.

"Oh, I thought you were chasing me or something! You startled me ..." the girl had turned her head to look at Ethan, and just as she was saying this her left foot seemed to catch on something and she stumbled badly, losing her balance and pitching forward toward the hard-packed earth trail.

Ethan instantly reached out to try to catch her but was only partially successful. She went down in an awkward roll and cried out in pain, coming to a stop clutching at her left ankle.

"Are you ok? What happened?" Eathan raced over to her side.

"It twisted as I stumbled. Why did you go and scare me like that, sneaking up behind me and then chasing me? Who are you, anyway?"

Ethan was taken aback. "But ... I did not sneak up on anybody! I run this path nearly every day about this time and have never seen you before!" His initial shock passed and, given the situation, he figured that being contrite might be the better pathway toward learning more about this rather attractive girl who seemed about his same age. "I'm sorry if I startled you. You run well – and you are pretty fast, at least when scared! Let me see that ankle, if I may?"

"Well ... ok. The girl winced as Ethan gently lifted her ankle and began to gingerly feel for any broken bones. "My name is Kaytrina, I'm new around here. What's your name?"

"Hello Kaytrina. I'm Ethan." Ethan watched her out of the corner of his eyes while looking busy with her ankle. Kaytrina had not given the slightest hint of recognition at his name. That was a relief. "Well, I don't feel anything broken. Can you put any weight on it?"

Kaytrina smiled sweetly. "That was very nice of you Ethan. Can you help me up?"

Ethan stood and offered her his hand. She gingerly pulled herself vertical but as she put weight on her left ankle she pitched forward and sideways … directly into Ethan's arms. He caught her awkwardly and she clung to him quite tightly. He found it rather nice, actually.

"Uh … I think I am going to need help, Ethan." Kaytrina had her face buried into Ethan's chest and as she straightened herself up it seemed she managed to brush most of her body over his. He blushed slightly at the unexpected and what seemed totally innocent yet intimate contact.

"Would you like me to take you to see a healer?"

"Oh no, I think it is just slightly sprained. If I can give it a few hours of rest I think I will be ok. Is there someplace close by where you could take me, and maybe keep me company while I can let it hopefully feel better?" Kaytrina said the last while looking deeply into his eyes, her face just a few inches from his, her eyes wide and pleading.

Ethan noticed a faint perfume – it was an unusual sweet odor that he could not place – and felt his face get warm in a blush. He normally did not spend much time with females, not having the patience for the frivolity and shallowness that most girls around his age demonstrated. Besides, most he knew seemed quite self-absorbed and more interested in being seen with the "legendary" hero than in really getting to know who he was. And here, out of the blue, a quite pretty young lady falls right into him – literally!

"I know of several small restaurants close to here. I'm not sure if any are open yet – but perhaps they might open early for us."

"Really? Do you really think they would let us in early? I have a hard time expecting that."

"Oh, I think they might." Ethan did not tell her that he doubted any shop in Freelandia would deny such a request from the Chancellor's son. "Do you think you can walk at all?"

"I … I can try." Kaytrina said that with a hint of pain in her voice. She clutched Ethan's arm tightly to her chest and tried to take a step.

Ethan's blush grew hotter at Kaytrina's seemingly innocent positioning of his arm. She leaned heavily on him and cried out as she stepped down onto her left foot. "I don't think … this is not going to work." She looked imploringly at him through thick black eyelashes and he again caught a heady aroma of her perfume. It was such an odd, but intriguingly pleasant odor, and he found himself leaning in closer, almost drawn in by the tendrils of smell.

Kaytrina – Taleena – saw the effects and leaned into Ethan even closer, pulling his arm yet closer to her as if to provide stability for her totally faked hurt ankle. Her voice lowered. "Do you think you could carry me – if it is not too far?" She wanted the close proximity so that the "perfume" had even more time to work to lower his defenses and bring him under her control. Between the potion she had made into a perfume, the incantations she had used and her own overtly feminine "charms", she doubted he had much of a chance to resist.

"Well, it isn't very far, and you aren't much more than an armful … but it would be easier to just get a carriage."

Somehow the top lacing of her tight running blouse had come undone. Kaytrina leaned over imploringly. "Pleeeasse Ethan … can it just be the two of us?"

His eyes strayed a moment, snapped away, then wandered back. "If you insist." Ethan was not overly broad shouldered, but his long training with Gaeten had kept him at peak physical condition and he easily scooped the young woman up, taking special care of her left ankle. Kaytrina snuggled into his grip, ensuring he had maximum contact and the best view. Then she leaned her head onto his shoulder, her perfumed hair inches from his nostrils. The walk was longer than expected, but Ethan never noticed.

Taleena smiled. This was going perfectly, even better than she had thought it would. A few hours at a café with small talk, and Ethan would find they had so very much in common, with just enough information left out to both make him more curious and protect the scaffold of lies. Then maybe her ankle would feel well enough for a walk, or a short ride, followed by lunch. Tomorrow, or maybe the next day she could likely work out a rough daily schedule she could feed to Murdrock. Within a week, two at the most, she figured she could deliver an infatuated Ethan to nearly anywhere in Freelandia Murdrock wanted as the abduction site. It would work in her favor to move things along quickly – she desperately had to avoid getting anywhere near that dratted Lydia, who surely would recognize her in an instant, even with the dyed hair and total change of costume.

She smiled sweetly up at her somewhat handsome "rescuer". He had actually blushed! She had not had a man blush around her for many years. It was rather cute, innocent and terribly ignorant. Her smile turned hard, just for an instant before she forced it back to sweet. He would never have the slightest clue a noose was tightening around his neck, and that he would even help her pull it tighter. Men, and especially young men, were so very easy to manipulate as long as you could keep them distracted. And there was no better way to distract them from thinking their actions through than with a little skin here, a quick smile and lowering of the eyes, a husky whisper, and maybe a pout if they did not go along with you quickly enough. Taleena smiled sweetly up at Ethan. In the skill of manipulating males, she was a Master with long practice.

Chapter 15

Countdown

Gaeten and Nimby walked slowly along the wharves, Gaeten affecting a shuffling step and hunched over stance. They frequently had to sidestep to get out of the way of people hustling along with handcarts or carrying large loads. Gaeten could feel the tenseness of the workers and passerby's.

"The docks are exceptionally busy today, grandfather". Nimby had suggested the ruse and most people did not give them a second glance.

"Hey there – old man and boy – what are you doing here?" The voice was gruff and Gaeten guessed it was from one of many guards and soldiers Nimby had mentioned seeing. There often were a handful of such along these docks where some of the naval vessels were located. They seemed to be the focus of much of the heightened attention.

"Oh, don't mind us ... we are just taking a walk along the docks." Gaeten put on a particularly old-sounding voice to accompany his affected slight limp and obvious sightlessness.

"Walk somewhere else! We are busy here, and you are in the way. Move along or I'll get you tossed into the dockyard prison ... or maybe just get you tossed into the river!"

The two edged closer to the soldier. "Why all the commotion, sir?" Nimby was turning out to be a fair actor, for which Gaeten was pleased.

"It's none of your business, street cur! Now move along!"

"Excuse me, young man." Gaeten tried to sound "grandfatherly". "Once upon a time ... before my accident ... I was on a frigate. I was right smart in those days! My eyes are long gone, but my hearing is still sharp and the smell of a voyage is in the salt air. Humor an old man who wishes he was still ship-shape. What is going on?"

The dock guard eyed the two up and down. He was about to shove them aside when a memory of his own grandfather came unbidden to his mind, who had also been a sailor. The guard's bluster subsided, and besides, the old man and young boy looked harmless enough. "Rumor has it much of the fleet docked here ships out tonight at high tide. Everyone is scurrying about with last minute supplies."

"The whole fleet you say? Good God – how many of our fine ships might that be nowadays?"

"I didn't say all fourteen ships were leaving, old man! But ten to twelve are likely heading out, based on what I can see of the supplies being loaded in. I hear that within a week most of the wharves will be filled up again with a slew of other ships coming from further south. I'm not sure I like that – means they will have a load of the Southerns, and I just get the willies around them. And if they are here, then for sure some of their Southern Dark Magicians will be coming too – and no one is safe around those crazies. You best make yourself scarce when they arrive. There is no telling what 'fun' they may want to have with an old blind man."

"Twelve ships heading out, you say? That is virtually a flotilla! Where would that many ships be heading? Out to quell some rebellious port or island I betcha. They won't know what hit 'em when our ships get there! Heh, heh!"

The guard quickly looked around to see if anyone might have heard. "Quiet down old man! No one is supposed to know where they are bound to. Anyone talking about it will lose their tongue quick-like."

"Oh … oh of course … secrecy's the word my boy. Sorry for asking. Besides, in my time the dock guards were never told nothin' anyway – they were the last ones to know what was really happening. I should'a known better."

The soldier bristled in indignation. "Maybe in your day, ancient one – but I happen to know that the fleet is sailing north … far north!"

Gaeten's hushed his voice to barely a whisper "Far north you say? But surely we are not ready yet for the invasion of those wretched Freelandians? Are we setting up a forward base somewhere closer? Or …?"

The soldier's eyes widened. "You had better keep your speculations to yourself, old man! I've seen men killed for such idle talk. Besides – those ships were not loaded with troops. I just know they are heading far north and I heard they were supposed to stay together – kinda in formation-like. That is going to be one fearsome fleet, especially if they git joined up with other fleets from some of the other ports."

"Is that supposed to happen?"

"Well, a friend of mine said he overheard one of the captains saying he did not want to ship out too early or they would just have to wait for 'the rest of them'. So I figure the final flotilla is going to be considerably bigger. That should scare them softy northerners right out of their wits – maybe even make them want to give it up to our inevitable victory."

"I doubt it would be that easy, young man – nothing ever is. And they wouldn't be bringing up all the Southerners here if they didn't expect an all-out war. Still … a one time epic defeat might indeed force some to re-consider their stance …" Gaeten's mind was whirling. He'd like to confirm some of this story, but he needed to get a message out immediately, and that was not going to be a simple task. How much time did he have? If this fleet was planning to meet up with other groups it conceivably could be several weeks or a month until they actually set sail toward Freelandia. If it were on the shorter side, he did not have much time to try to get word out. Even if there was no invasion, such a fleet could readily set up a strong blockade … and Freelandia was nearly inaccessible by land, so shipping was of paramount importance.

"Well, thank you sir for humoring an old sea-dog. Keep up the good work! Say, how long do you have to keep walking the wharves? When you come off duty perhaps I can buy you a drink somewhere."

"Maybe you can at that. I often stop at the Red Hog tavern after my twelve hour shift – about midnight. If I see you there I'll make you keep your word on that offer!"

"If not tonight, then another. You must get awfully tired – they make you work from noon to midnight every day?"

"Yep, that is the standard lot for wharf guards … twelve hours on duty, then twelve off. But it is still better than the merchant wharfs – those poor blokes work from mid-afternoon all the way till first bells at six in the morning. I had that job once … you can hardly keep your eyes open toward the end of the shift, but if they ever catch you sleeping, you'll be flogged or worse."

"But how can you stay awake all night like that?"

"Aw, most of 'em start walking around in the wee hours … course some just find a convenient hidey-hole where they are not likely to be found and catch a few winks when no-one's looking. Naturally, I never did such a thing!" The last was said with a conspiratorial wink and whisper.

"I'm sure such a knowledgeable and observant fellow like you would not … or at least would never let himself get caught!"

"Heh, heh – I never was caught, nope not a once! 'Course, what is going to happen down at the merchant shipyards anyway? The most that happens is when thieves try to lift some of the cargo, and that usually only happens when the captain does not pay enough for 'protection'. We was never paid enough anyway." The guard looked angry at that thought, then seemed to realize what he was just admitting.

"Now get along you two, and if I hear a single word of anything you never heard from me …"

Nimby spoke up for the first time. "What? Were you talking 'bout something? We never heard nothing, we'se just out for a simple walk, ain't we gramps?"

Gaeten assumed his dithering old man act. "What's that young'un? You know I can barely hear anymore. Who is this nice young man standing in our way – never heard him before in my life. 'Scuse me, sir … we are just passing through."

Nimby took the hint and Gaeten tottered off with him, leaving the guard snickering at their act. He watched the two disappear into the moving chaos of workers. A puzzled look came over him and he scratched his head, wondering why he had felt so at ease and talked so much. That wasn't like him. Must have been because the old man reminded him of his own grandfather. The guard's tension drained away as happy memories filled his mind. That is, until a laborer carrying a large box nearly collided with him. Then he snapped back to his old self, forgetting whatever it was that had been puzzling him.

Once they were well out of range Gaeten pulled Nimby in close. "Take me over to the merchant wharves next. I want to get a feel for that area and the sailors there too."

"You sure milked that guard good. Hope he doesn't remember us too long."

"No, I surely hope not either – and we will now have to avoid the Red Hog for at least a week or two. How much did he have in his coin pocket?"

Nimby stared at the blind old man. "How did you know I pilfered his pockets?"

"I could hear your fingers on his fabric and could tell you were moving about while we were talking." Gaeten suddenly grabbed Nimby with an arm across his chest, trapping the boy's arms at his side and squeezing him into Gaeten's larger frame. With his other hand Gaeten fished into one of Nimby's many pockets and extracted some coins.

"Hey old man, I snitched them fair and square – those are mine!"

"Ha – thought you could take a bigger slice of the profits, did you? If it was my pocket you were reaching into you would have several less fingers." Gaeten dropped several of the coins back into the boy's pocket but kept most of the larger ones. "Next time keep your snitching to the bars … you will get more money there than you have ever had. If that guard had caught you we would never had been able to move freely along those wharves again. Work with me and follow my rules … or I will find another boy to work for me. Understood?"

Nimby thought it over for a few moments. Then he nodded – and immediately realized Gaeten could not see it. So he began to shake his head "no" while saying "Sure gramps, whatever you say."

Gaeten was beginning to like this brazen young thief – he surely had spunk and his pick pocket skills were actually quite good from what he could discern. Still, he had to play his part correctly. He suddenly whipped Nimby around and dug one finger of each hand into either side of the boy's head, right back from his eyes.

Nimby's eyes went wide and he began to struggle to pull his head away – but it was firmly in a vice that seemed as strong as steel. He began to struggle even harder but then cried out in pain as Gaeten squeezed slightly inward and began to lift Nimby completely off the ground with just those two fingers. "You won't last long trying to fool me, boy. Learn that fast. Stay with me and get rich. Try to fool me and …" After a slightly increased pressure Gaeten pulled his hands away and Nimby dropped to the ground and curled into a ball, holding his aching skull between his hands. To his credit, he never cried out.

After a minute, he unfolded and got shakily to his feet. This old man was not one to mess with … but would the promised riches ever really come? He jingled the coins in his pocket – that was a good day's work already, even without the confiscated coins. And besides, he had hidden a gold coin in a secret pocket under his belt, and he bet that the old man did not know about that one, regardless of how amazing he seemed to be. He also doubted any of the rival gangs would bother him while he was with this strange old fellow. It seemed like a pretty good gig.

"All right, have it your way. But I keep anything I get when I am not with you – got that?"

"Fair enough. Now walk me over to the merchant wharves, and take me by some food stalls – no stealing, mind you, or I'll cuff you up good!" Gaeten laughed inwardly without the slightest trace showing. He wondered how valuable that other coin was.

After a thorough tour, Gaeten had Nimby lead him to an apartment in a low income but nicer area still fairly close to the docks. He paid a month's fee up-front for a small room on the second floor with a window – one high enough to discourage thieves yet low enough to provide an exit should the need arise. The door had a lock – of sorts – and Gaeten had felt scratches around it that were likely from amateur lock picks. No matter, he had little worth stealing, and he had his own ways of securing the door if needed. He offered Nimby the outer room to sleep in, and even purchased a thin bed roll for him.

That evening the two headed out for a tavern that would likely have a mix of both merchant and military customers, located roughly half way between both wharves. Gaeten had purchased a few clothes from a store catering to the dockyards, and he now blended in with the locals, as much as an old blind man with a walking stick and a rather young and scruffy companion could.

As they neared the tavern, Gaeten affected a slower shuffle and leaned heavily on his staff with drooping shoulders. His manners suddenly added an extra 20 years to his already ancient apparent age. Nimby chuckled under his breath as they shuffled up to the tavern entrance. Gaeten entered slowly, judging from the noises that the tavern was busy but not overly so. He did not particularly want his first night in town ending in a bar fight, and so had asked Nimby to select a location where it was not likely to get too rough – but this was still a sailor's tavern, so anything was possible.

The two entered and Nimby led them to an open spot near the end of a long table. They were eyed rather suspiciously by many, but then ignored – what harm could come from these two strangers? Gaeten ordered two small bowls of what passed for stew and paid with a few small coins.

"Now Nimby, give me a description of everyone here. Take your time. Tell me what they are wearing, how they look – skin and hair color, mannerisms, anything you notice. Don't look any of them in the eyes – that can come across to some as a challenge that you most certainly would lose. I need a feel for the crowd before I start. And when I do start, you watch your fingers – I don't want to have a one handed helper after my first night here. And above all, listen and observe. I will want you to tell me everything you have heard and seen. Remember, your percent of the cut is determined by how valuable you are to me."

Nimby nodded out of habit and then corrected himself. "Alright old man, but what if you need some help? Don't expect my knife to be always ready to cover your back."

Gaeten laughed. "Oh, I think I can take care of myself at least as well as you can. Now I can hear a small group over to my left that I expect are from Alexandria from their accent. Tell me what they look like."

Nimby began to describe the diverse crowd that represented dozens of countries. As he worked through the many tables Gaeten questioned him about several details and even pointed out a few things that Nimby had missed, based on his acute hearing and knowledge of the many customs and mannerisms. As Nimby described one particularly tall dark-skinned sailor Gaeten paused. "Tell me, does he have two rings on his left ear and three on his right? Is the back ring on the right smaller than the others? What color is it?"

Nimby looked strangely at Gaeten, and then surreptitiously at the tall man across the tavern. "Well, yes, he does have three on his right ear. So does his companion. The first man has I think a gold colored third ear ring and the other's is black. The one with the gold acts like he is the boss. Oh, and he noticed me looking, even though I was being really careful. He was acting like he was not noticing, but I swear he did."

Gaeten smiled. "Oh, I am sure both noticed. Those are Alterians, from an eastern country that has not yet been taken by the Dominion. They are some of the best sailors in the world, with smaller ships that can catch the faintest breezes. They love to travel for just the sake of seeing everything they can. Before the night is done they will stop over for a visit, just to satisfy their curiosity – they tend to be curious about everything. Here's a piece of advice – don't even try to lift anything from them. They will spot you sure enough … and they will be watching you work the crowd."

"Alterians, huh? I see them frequently at the docks, always two or three at a time, never more and never alone. There seems to always be a few of them around, though every day it is a different set. They stand out from most others, being a head taller than most everyone else and their skin is even darker than the Southerns. And they're always watching me, or so it seems. I guess they're watching everyone."

"Stay clear of them. Ok, now finish up with who is at our table. The gentleman three chairs down – he seems alone and has already had a few drinks, right? Describe him."

Nimby did, and asked "Is he your first mark?"

"Yes, I think he is a good candidate – or 'mark' as you described him. Now give me some room but don't wander too far yet. In a few minutes I will need you."

Gaeten quietly cleared a small area around himself and fished out a large copper coin from an inside pocket. He began to flip this into the air with one hand, adroitly catching it with the other. Higher and higher he flipped the coin, always catching it just before it hit the table. A few times he nearly fumbled the catch or the flip, but the coin never fell. The fellow down the table noticed and moved closer. Gaeten missed one catch, and the coin rolled toward the man. Gaeten scrambled to quickly retrieve it and began again to flip and catch.

The surly sailor stood and shuffled the few steps over to Gaeten – this floor was too flat and stable, not the pitching he was used to on a ship at sea. The man made to pass by and snatched the coin at the top of its arc in one smooth motion and kept moving as though nothing had happened.

Gaeten's walking staff seemed to miraculously appear in front of the man, blocking his path. "I think that is my coin, sir."

"What do you mean, old man? What coin?" The man sounded gruff, with a mix of surprise.

"The one you put into this pocket." The staff moved up to tap a small pocket. "Now if you want to keep that coin, you can win it – if you are quick enough."

"Win it? What kind of game are you playing, old man?"

"Oh, a simple game I use to pay for my grub. Nimby! Now where did that boy go? Come here and sit across from me a moment."

Nimby looked wary but sat.

"Now, that coin, my good man?" Gaeten held out an open hand.

The sailor grudgingly retrieved the coin and gave it back to the blind man. Gaeten put the coin on the table between him and Nimby. "Here's the game. At the count of three we both will try to grab that coin, and whoever gets it first keeps it. Simple. Watch, we will demonstrate." Gaeten placed both hands palms down on the table and Nimby copied the move. "When I say 'three' try to grab the coin."

"One … two … THREE!"

Nimby's hand shot out and slid the coin sideways just as Gaeten's hand came done where the coin had been. The boy gave a shout of glee and made to pocket the coin.

"Hold on there, boy. Best two out of three!" Nimby grudgingly put the coin back on the table, but slightly off-center and closer to himself. Gaeten reached out and felt for the coin. He frowned and moved the coin to a more central location. "Ready? Let's try that again. One … two THREE!" Gaeten said the last number must faster and shot his hand out, easily capturing the coin.

"Hey!" Nimby had been caught unexpectedly and was not too happy about it. Gaeten chuckled and put the coin back out.

"Old man, this time I count!" The sailor stood over them. "No tricks this time either!"

Gaeten scowled but put his hands out on the table. The sailor grinned unpleasantly. "One … Two … Three!" He said these evenly and two hands shot out toward the coin, passing over the spot nearly instantaneously.

Nimby was frowning as Gaeten slowly opened his palm, showing the copper coin.

"Ha – got it, you rascal! Now good sir, care to try your skill?"

Several others from the tavern had wandered over to watch. The sailor scowled but grabbed a chair and loudly sank into it. Gaeten carefully placed the coin. "Now to make this a true wager, you need to ante up – you put a comparable coin out too." The sailor frowned but fished out a copper coin of about the same size and placed it carefully on top of the other coin. Gaeten continued, "Now get ready and I will count".

"Hold on there old man – I saw what you did to the boy! We get someone else to count."

"Oh, ok. Nimby – can you do that for us?"

The sailor looked at the boy. "Nice and easy – no trickery or that will be the last time you use that tongue to count anything – understand?"

Nimby gulped. "One ….. Two …. THREE!" He had spaced the words out evenly and clearly. Both men shot their hands out and both reached the coin at about the same time. There proceeded a small scuffle but in a moment the sailor held both coins up high for the small crowd to see and Gaeten had a stormy countenance.

"That was my lunch for tomorrow! Let me try to win it back!"

"Ha, I won it fair and square old man! But if you insist, let's make it more interesting." He fished out a gold coin and smacked it down on the table. Gaeten gingerly felt the coin and gulped. "Come on old man, let's see what you have – or am I too rich for you?"

Gaeten clumsily fumbled in a pocket and withdrew another small gold coin. "Well, ok – but let's get someone else to count." He poked a finger out toward the crowd, moving it around until settling on one of the Alterians who had come over to observe. "You sir, will you count for us?"

A deep resonate bass voice answered. "This time, alright. Are you both ready?" Both men nodded, palms flat on the table. "One … Two … Three!" The voice had an even cadence that left no room for argument about fairness.

Even as the Alterian began to say 'three', Gaeten's left hand had risen slightly off the table without being noticed; everyone's attention was focused on the coins and the men's right hands. At the 'three' Gaeten slammed his left hand down very forcefully, causing the coins to bounce upwards just as his right hand swept through the air just above the table top, while the sailor's hand slapped down on the table just below.

Gaeten beamed as he held up the two gold coins for all to see.

The sailor glared in anger, his left hand reaching for his knife. The crowd burst into laughter, making the sailor even less amused. "Y o u cheated old man. Give me those two coins!"

"Ha, I won them and you lost! If you want them back, you will have to win them!"

The knife was out now, and Nimby's right hand was on his own, ready for fast action. "Old man, do that again and you will have one less hand. Put both coins down on the table. And since you think you are so smart …" the sailor frisked a few of his own pockets and pulled out a much larger gold coin, worth a week's wages. He plunked that down loudly on the table and glared at the old blind man sitting across from him.

Gaeten gingerly felt the coin and loudly gulped. "But I don't have that much!"

"Put out what you do have old man."

Gaeten made a show of emptying his pockets of coins, the total still coming to less than the single large gold coin.

"Close enough I guess – counting the gold coin you just stole from me."

Gaeten placed the two small coins in the middle of the table again and repositioned his hands.

"And this time, no table slapping." A sailor moved forward from behind Gaeten to place his burly and gnarled hand over Gaeten's. "My mates here will see to that."

Gaeten had heard another man move up behind him. He slumped visibly in this chair and took on a dejected look.

The Alterian frowned but asked if both men were ready. Gaeten shrugged yes but remained somewhat slouched. At 'three' he jacked his right knee up with tremendous force, bouncing the table considerably from underneath. He smiled slyly, showing the two coins he had snatched out of the air as he pushed back from the table.

The sailor across from him stood suddenly, his chair crashing backwards. "You cheating old fool! That will be the last time you take money from anyone!" His knife flashed out and he stepped closer. Nimby had his knife partially out but Gaeten just sat there, playing with the small gold coins in his hand. He cocked one finger over his upturned thumb and put the gold coin on it.

"So you want the coin back?" The sailor halted his forward movement slightly, looking at the calm but feeble-looking old blind man. He growled "I plan on taking more than that!" and lunged forward.

"Here you are, then." Gaeten's fingers snapped, sending the coin hurtling through the air and the attacker suddenly stopped just before reaching the sitting old man. The sailor's eyes bulged and his left hand clutched at his own throat. A thin rattling gasp escaped his lips as his face became beet red. The knife dropped to the table as his arm flailed in the air. The crowd backed away, giving the choking man room as he stumbled about in panic, his companions helpless and the crowd dumbfounded.

"Oh, now it seems you don't want it anymore is that right?" Gaeten had stood and moved close to the panicked sailor who was desperately trying to claw his throat and draw more than the tiniest of breaths. "You don't want it anymore, right?"

The sailor shook his head violently and began to stumble, arms flailing even more wildly. Gaeten grabbed his shoulder, straightened him up, and slammed his knee into the man's stomach in an upward arc. The sailor's breath explosively shot out, followed rapidly by the contents of his stomach. He convulsively gasped in life-giving air. Nimby gingerly collected the small gold coin from the floor – luckily it had landed well beyond the smelly mess that had followed.

One of the sailor's friends ran to his side to help, while the other began to turn on Gaeten, drawing his own knife. Before he could even unsheathe it Gaeten had retrieved the sailor's dropped weapon and its point was pressed to the man's chest.

"I think your friend needs some help getting back to his quarters – he will need a few hours before he is really up to doing much of anything. Perhaps you should help him, if you get my point." That last was said with a slight pressure to the knife.

The three quickly exited, with help from one of the bouncers. Gaeten followed his nose to the bar and offered the large copper coin to compensate for the mess on the floor, which the bartender gladly accepted as it was more than he typically paid one of the serving girls for a whole day's wage.

Gaeten took the offered beverage and asked Nimby to find him a different seat.

"How did you make out?" Gaeten said in a very low voice behind a hand that had reached up to scratch his nose. Nimby looked conspiratorial and whispered "There were several coins on the floor and a few extra left on some tables not being watched during your little game there, so not too badly – better than I typically made in a day."

"I told you. Oh, and of course I do want that gold coin back … now please." Nimby grudgingly deposited the coin into Gaeten's waiting hand. "Now we wait for information. I expect several sailors will wander over, if nothing else but to ask about the little game we just played. Who knows, I may even make more tonight! Now keep out of trouble and listen sharp. Buy yourself some food if you want."

Nimby wandered off. In a few minutes a man swaggered up – no question that it was a sailor by his awkward land-side stride. He plunked himself in a nearby chair. "Nice bit of work there with the coins – you sure had that barge worker taken for a ride. I have not laughed that hard in years. The look on his face was priceless – and even better once you popped that wee coin right down his throat. Where'd you learn to toss around coins like that anyway?"

"I was in a travelling circus for many years and picked up a few tricks. Wanna try it – no tricks, just see how fast you are?"

"Nah, I know I am not all that fast. So why did you leave?"

Gaeten lowered his voice. "Let's say that a certain new government did not exactly look favorably upon our type of entertainment. Now I have to freelance wherever I can pick up a few coins. It seemed to me a busy port like this may have decent pickings, especially from soldiers and sailors right after payday. Say, do you know which day of the week most of them get paid?"

"I git my pay on Mondays – the captain says that keeps most of the crew from disappearing over the weekend. Most of the soldier types get their pay on Saturday, from what I hear. I don't go near them any closer than I have too. There has been way too much talk of people being "pressed" into service – kidnapped and chained to a set of oars, never to be seen or heard of again. Slavery, that is what it is, pure and simple. But it may get better round here for awhile anyway."

"Oh, why is that?"

"Word has it that most of the warship fleet is packing up and slipping out shortly. They have been taking on plenty of supplies too, so business has been very good."

"Where might they be heading?"

"Well ..." the merchant sailor scratched his beard. "No one is saying for sure, but a friend of mine frequents one of the taverns over in that part of town ... he says one of the barmaids is rather keen toward him ... and she told him the talk around a few of those tables is that they are heading north ... far north."

"Freelandia?" Gaeten said that in a hushed whisper.

"Keep yer voice even lower - what do you want, for both of us to lose our heads? No one says that word in this town, not without placing great risk upon his life. But ... what else is far north? Just the same, don't be talking about it."

"Do you think this is the big one? The start of war or invasion?"

"Cripes old man, you really are new around here aren't you? No one knows such things 'cept the Overlords. All I knows is that the ships are gittin loaded up and are likely to set sail within a few days, a week at the outside. And there are more and more Dominion soldiers around than ever before. They are even loading up those two Dreadnaught giants. I surely would not want to come across either of those mountains of the sea coming at me! They say those ships have so much canvas that even a mere puff of wind will carry them miles. And the decks are loaded with catapults and all sorts of weaponry, the biggest and baddest the Dominion has. Poor Northerners, if those ships catch any of their navy on the open seas, they'll be fish food for sure. I don't know of any ship that could take those behemoths on – what could stop them? I doubt even a ram would have much effect, given the size of the timbers they used to build them, and did you know, they even have some metal sheeting over the hull that supposedly can stop just about anything you could shoot at it and keep the timbers intact from any other ship's ram. No siree ... I wouldn't want to be trying to oppose them at all."

Gaeten was lost in thought for a moment, then continued the conversation to glean as much as possible from this rather outspoken merchant sailor. After a few minutes he excused himself and spoke to the bartender.

"I need paper, ink and a brand new quill – can you get those for me?" He rolled out the smallest gold coin onto the counter.

"Yes sir! Right away sir!"

A few minutes later Gaeten was escorted to a more private booth and given the writing instruments. As awkward as it may have looked, Gaeten was well versed in the art of writing, keeping an image of it in his head as he put pen to paper. He had a thoughtful look on his face as he appeared to be doodling with the bare quill. Then after a few minutes he opened the ink, cut the quill, and began to write in earnest. After 20 minutes he carefully blew on the page to dry the ink, and when he was satisfied he placed a fresh sheet on top and underneath, and then rolled the three sheets into a tube. He dripped some wax from the candle at the table onto the exposed edge in three places, then pressed his thumb into each and made a few marks more with the pen. It would need more waterproof care, but he expected that to be taken care of by his chosen carrier.

Gaeten tucked the scroll into his clothing and sauntered back out to a more common table. A few other people stopped over, though none could be enticed to engage him in a game of coin. He picked up a few additional details that confirmed his fears – the Dominion was planning something big, something soon, and that something was against Freelandia. Gaeten figured it had to be the prelude to an invasion – the fighting ships would leave first, followed very shortly by the troop carriers. He had to get word out.

An hour or so later, while Gaeten was sitting alone nursing his drink he heard two sets of light footsteps approaching. One stopped in front of him, another just behind.

"Interesting show you put on." The voice sounded like it came from a long hollow log, deep and vibrant.

"Glad you liked it – it helps pay the bar tab."

"For one who has taken all evening to work on his first drink, it would seem the proceeds would last for quite some time for that purpose."

"Et illium est audia quoreum" Gaeten spoke the words clearly and slowly, though only loudly enough to be heard by the two gentlemen standing near him.

"Few in the Dominion know our ancient tongue, and fewer still have ever even heard of that particular dialect. May I see your hands?"

Gaeten held out his hands, which were taken in a large but gentle grip. "You once wore a ring. What color was it?"

"As black as the third ring on your right ear."

"We noticed your companion studying us. He has made quite a good take from the customers tonight, but has given our table wide berth. You gave wise instructions. How quickly do you want the scroll delivered?"

Gaeten smiled. Very little indeed missed the inquisitive eyes of Alterians. He was truly grateful they were on his side, though they might never publically admit it. He switched again to the nearly extinct tongue used for important business between Freelandia and Alteria. "It is of utmost urgency. I have specified a considerable reward for your efforts."

"Freelandians have always been quite generous – and loyal friends. We too prize loyalty, though it may be severely tested in days to come. Is there anything you need?"

"Not presently, but I have heard you keep a near constant presence here. I presume I may be able to use your services again if needed?"

"Our next courier ship will arrive in three days. We will leave at high tide, just before dawn. So far we have been given free passage, but that too may change. Our "neutrality" is still believed, but we cannot be seen taking a direct route north. It will take at least two weeks before your message can be delivered, more if the wind is against us."

"It will have to do. Go with God, my friends."

The Alterians left quietly. Gaeten was never sure with them just exactly how loyal they really were – which is why he had used three levels of security on the scroll. His thumbprint was known and expected, and he always did the imprint in the same manner. Second, the inked letter would seem rather simple – a letter to his Aunt Lydia that just described his recent travels in boring detail. Within that letter was a code that revealed a simple message. A more in-depth message was written in code without ink, just with the quill indentations on the back of the paper. That one was likely to not survive intact just from handling, but even portions would give greater details to his warning of an imminent naval assault.

Little did Gaeten realize that his message would actually aid the Dominion in one of its boldest endeavors.

Chapter 16

Kaytrina Begins

"But how will we stop the Dominion navy from just sailing right in and landing all their troops?" Ethan smiled. Kaytrina was so very unlike the fluff-headed youth he was more accustomed to dealing with at state dinners and formal events. She actually seemed to have a keen interest in things he was interested in – such as Freelandia's defenses and weaponry. While he was around her he seemed much more able to talk about what was on his mind – she truly wanted to listen to him, rather than steer the conversation around to talk about herself. That was rather novel. And without question she was pleasant to look at. Even her perfume was pleasant – it seemed to linger with him even after they parted.

What he did not understand, though, was that every time Kaytrina came near he would see a red haze around her and blue ribbons radiating away. Ethan could not understand; it was like his normally failsafe imaging in his mind was going haywire. He ignored it, and after awhile it did seem to subside.

Another thing that was odd was that Kaytrina was very firm about not wanting to come home with him for a meal or for any other reason. He at first did not see her point that his parents could be rather intimidating and nosey, but after a few days he caught on to what she kept on repeating – he could see how they could be demanding at times and always asking about what he was up to … what Kaytrina called prying into his own private affairs. He had not thought about it that way before, but her arguments seemed reasonable, and more so every day. Just last night his father kept asking who he was hanging out with each evening the last couple of days, even intimating that he wondered how that person was influencing him. When he had told Kaytrina that, she had acted aghast and personally affronted. It had taken Ethan hours to get her to speak more than monotone replies, though eventually she appeared to be mollified when Ethan also agreed that this had been a very unreasonable intrusion. And then his mother had nearly demanded that he bring whomever it was over so they could meet – more likely interrogate as Kaytrina put it – the person. Ethan had resented that. What business was it of his parents who his own friends were?

When he had mentioned that to Kaytrina, she had heartily agreed with him, wrapping her arms around him in a close hug. "After all, you are nearly an adult yourself, and you certainly have proven how important you are" she had said.

But now they were together again and he did not want to think about his parents or what they may or may not like.

Katrina noticed that Ethan's attention had wandered. She reached over, using a finger to pull his chin until he was looking directly at her. "I really like you, Ethan. In just two days you have become my best friend here in the capital. I hope I can be your best friend too." She had said that with such sincerity, while staring deeply into his eyes. How could he have said anything different? And besides, she was really cute!

"Well Kaytrina … did I even mention how pretty your name is?" She squeezed his hand that she was holding and snuggled in closer to him. "The Dominion ships may be bigger than ours, but our ships are much more agile and we have some really cool new weapons being outfitted onto them. And every ship has to come through the narrow mouth leading into this bay. We have multiple batteries of catapults up in the cliffs that can rain down destruction onto any ship trying to force its way in."

"New kinds of weapons for our ships? Oh Ethan, how do you know so very much? Can you tell me about them … or is that some sort of 'state secret' that only your parents are supposed to have the need to know about and would never tell you?"

"Oh, I know quite a lot about them. I go and visit the shipyards and engineer workshops occasionally to see what they are up to."

"But don't you have to ask your parents for permission? I'm sure there are things they don't let you know about."

"No, I don't have to ask their permission for everything I do! I have a pretty free run of the whole defensive works of Freelandia!"

"Wow – handsome and important! It's probably just as good though that you don't ask them – they probably would just say you did not have a need to know, and that you were too young to be trusted with such important information. Parents are like that, they seem to think we are just kids and not responsible."

He had to think about that, and it seemed that thinking was harder to do now. Were his parents holding information back from him? Did he really have access to everything? If he were to ask, would they truly give him permission … but did he even really have to ask for their permission? After all, he had saved his father's life and was rather advanced within the Watchers. Didn't he have the right to know?

"Handsome, eh?" Ethan smiled and puffed out his chest.

Kaytrina leaned in close and Ethan was very aware of her heady perfume and intriguingly curvy body. "Very handsome to me." Her lips brushed his cheek and he blushed. "So what about those new weapons?"

Ethan sighed contentedly. He had silenced those pesky red and blue images in his mind, shoving them mentally aside since they were obviously irrelevant. "Oh, they are rather awesome. I have only seen early prototypes, but from what I saw they could …."

Taleena smiled inwardly as Ethan divulged greater details. She was gathering quite an interesting dossier of Freelandian defense efforts. Each evening she carefully wrote down the details, then memorized them and destroyed the notes. In that way she left no incriminating evidence, and she could tell Murdrock that she had loads of information, but it was all in her head – that would make her much more valuable.

This Ethan was so very gullible. He was kinda cute and nice – not that this mattered in the least. He was like a ripe fruit in her hands, carefully manipulated to extract every last bit of juice out, squeezed dry, and later discarded. And it was rather fun to seduce him while staying totally in control.

She planned on pulling out as much information as possible in the three weeks Murdrock had given her, while spinning her web around Ethan. He already was responding to the potion she had made up into perfume – she could see redness developing in his eyes that was a sure indicator it was getting into his bloodstream. It was a good thing she had plenty of antidote to take herself. Every few days she was increasing the dosage, and soon she could begin slipping some into his food. That would prepare him for the massive dose she would use right at the end that would put him into an obedient stupor. Meanwhile, there was much she could learn as she expertly toyed with him.

She smiled sweetly – on the outside – and nestled her head onto his shoulder, pulling his arm around her. He resisted at first – she had to be careful not to go too fast, he still had some pesky morals and barriers she was working on undoing. But bit by bit she was dismantling his defenses and caution. And he was rather handsome, obviously quite muscular, and both famous and politically connected. Storekeepers fell over backwards when helping them. Hmm – maybe she could use that for added advantage. A woman could never have too many clothes or too much jewelry. Maybe she could insist that Murdrock pay for more, and then get Ethan or some merchant to give them to her. This was such an interesting assignment. Too bad it would end in three weeks.

Chapter 17
Instrumental Favorites

aria took a big breath and tried to pucker her lips further as she squeezed them over a mouthpiece. She pushed on two valves as she had been instructed and blew. The sound that came out of the large funnel end of the horn was anything but musical and before her breath gave way Maria burst out laughing at the sound. Kory was laughing too. "Ah, Maria? I'm not so sure this instrument is for you!"

"I think you are right, Kory! I just can't get my lips to pucker correctly. Let's try something else."

The instrument introduction classes at the Music Academy had many classrooms, most of which Maria had explored to some lesser or greater extent in her nighttime jaunts when she had first come into the capital. Kory led her through them at a record pace. She had plucked, strummed, struck and blew into what seemed like hundreds of instruments. Each was fascinating, especially when she had someone to show her how it should be held and used. Some were far easier to use than others, but all produced the most wonderful sounds. Maria felt she could have spent years just being introduced. She dearly hoped that someday there would be time for her to thoroughly learn each instrument – each made such interestingly unique sounds!

After trying her hand with several of the specialty instruments in one of the rooms she had never gotten to explore, Maria had laughed at the rattles, pops, squeaks and other unusual noises. "Kory, what could possibly be next?"

Kory was silent for a minute. "Kory, what is it?" Maria sounded a little worried at the extended silence.

"Well, there are three things left, and then we will have caught up with the other class of apprentices … and their assessment!"

"Oh, that cannot be too bad! And isn't it a relief for a Discerner to help you know what God may have planned for you?"

"Yes, I suppose." Kory did not sound too sure of that.

"What three things are left?"

"First, we get to go to a 'walk-about' concert this evening. Fourth and Fifth Level Apprentices are spread out all over the big stage at the concert hall and play several pieces in concert. The newbie's like us get to wander all over the stage listening wherever we want. Rumor has it that some of the Masters wander about too, both to give greater instruction to the players and to assess the new people. With you present, I expect quite a few Masters will be there."

"Oh Kory, that sounds like fun – not the Master's part … maybe it is good that I am blind – I won't even see them! But it will be great to stand right in the orchestra while they perform! What else?"

"Tomorrow we will get to tour the instrument museum. It is in a special room right off the stage at the great auditorium. That is where some of the most prized instruments are kept. There even are some that have been retired from use – they are considered far too valuable to even play anymore." Kory's voice had trailed off as she considered the collection in the museum. "Maria, they have instruments there from all over the world, the best of the best. Some are from master craftsmen from ages ago, which our best current craft masters still cannot perfectly duplicate. I have heard there are several pieces there that have not been played for over a century!"

Maria thought that was rather odd – instruments were designed to be played, not just looked at. "Then what?"

Kory gulped. "Then … then we have a recital. The new apprentices are put into quartets with Level Three and Four apprentices and we play several selections with higher-level apprentices and Masters in attendance. I have heard it is extremely embarrassing – I mean, most of the newbies barely know how to play anything. It is really part of the assessment. Everyone has to try their very best, but we are only starting apprentices. It is awful! I have heard of apprentices breaking from the stress – they have run out crying. Rumors say that some apprentices are washed out on the spot – that Masters tap them on the shoulder and they must immediately leave the Academy!"

Maria trembled. "That's … that's terrible Kory! To have come so far and then to be dismissed! Do the apprentices get to choose their instruments?"

"They are placed with higher level apprentices in quartets and have to use whatever the fourth instrument is. I have heard you do have some level of choice, but it is limited by what is needed to complete each group. Some of the new apprentices can do little more than try to pluck a string now and then or try to pipe in a note. I can just imagine how inadequate we must all feel! Ugh!"

The two girls exited into the late afternoon sun. It had been a long week and both were rather exhausted by the many classes. Kory led the way across the campus toward one of the small outdoor cafés. They had made it most of the way there when a voice steeped in sarcasm rang out.

"Why, if it isn't the star pupil gracing us with her very presence. Hey look, her feet actually do touch the ground as she walks!"

Kory's face went bright red. "It's Vanessa again!" she hissed through clenched teeth. "I wish she would just leave us alone!"

Maria heard heavy footsteps coming her way. "Vanessa, why don't you like me? I have never done anything to wrong you."

"What about stealing my room? Now I have to walk clear across the campus to my classes, all to make room for 'The Singer'! You think you are so special – getting my room, getting such fine new clothes, even having a baby-sitter to lead you around. And I hear you got special treatment and went through the intro classes in just one week – plain old 'normal' folks are forced through those dumb boring classes for close to six months and have to show we can play several instruments before we are allowed to pass. But no, not Miss Special. I think old Vitario must just have been feeling bad for all those others he made go through every stinking class, and so he is trying to make his conscience feel better by taking in a poor orphan and out of sympathy letting her get by easy.

Listen, missy – I have had to work hard for my place here. Some of us have to really work for a living. And we don't appreciate seeing someone get off so easy. No one showed any sympathy for me. I don't get any rich-girl presents. And I've got talent too, you know. Just because I can't sing that great doesn't mean I don't have talent. I should be a Fourth Level apprentice; I'm just as good as any of them! And you … you're just a pre-apprentice, not even officially a Level One yet! And anyway, you probably will wash out in the recital – where your precious Vitario cannot protect you like he is now. The recital is judged by the rest of the Masters, not Vitario. And I will be the first one laughing when they tap you out.

Oh, did you know that my friends and I are playing at the recital too – we will be in several of the quartets! Oh, I sooo hope you are put into MY group! Boy, will you ever be sorry!"

Kory was working up her nerve and now she forcefully stepped forward. "Vanessa, you are totally out of line! I don't care if you are a Level Three, if you don't stop I WILL talk to Grand Master Vitario, and boy will you be in trouble!"

"Oh, so the baby-sitter mouse has fangs, does she? The thing about mice – they get squashed if they get in the way!"

Maria heard movement and she backed up quickly. Then she heard a scuffle and someone crashed to the ground. Kory moaned at the impact from several feet away. Maria clutched at the small whistle hanging around her neck and almost brought it to her lips, but then thought better of it. She was not in real danger, and her feathered friend would not know enough to just scare the older girl away. She swallowed hard, but found strength knowing she had several friends in high places that could help. That gave her real confidence, and in a way, allowed her to respond with humility.

"Vanessa, I don't know why you seem so resentful toward me, but I hope you can let that go. Bitterness can drive a person to do things they shouldn't. I am sorry you were reassigned to a different room. I am sorry if there are things I do that seem to irritate you. I would rather be your friend. But if you have to take your anger out on someone ..." Trembling, she awkwardly stepped forward, toward the spot where Kory had been standing ... "then take it out on me, not on Kory. It should be easy enough; I cannot do much to protect myself from someone as big and strong as you, and I would not even see it if you swung at me."

Maria stopped, biting her lip so that she would not betray her fear and stood very still, waiting for the blow she very much expected.

Instead, she heard the older girl snort in derision. "Aren't you the brave one? No, punching you out or pushing you around would be much too easy. No, I have something else in mind for you, something much grander – and perhaps final!"

Maria held her breath, wondering what possible evil Vanessa was planning. But as she heard her stomp off, Maria slowly let out her breath and hurried over to where she had heard Kory fall. "Kory, what happened? Are you all right? Should I call for a healer?"

"No, Maria, I am ok, just had the wind knocked out of me when I fell. That Vanessa! This has to stop! I'm going straight to tell Grand Master Vitario right this instant, and I bet for sure she will be kicked right out of the Academy before morning! Oh, that will get her good!"

"No, Kory. That is not what God would want, I am sure. I think God would want us to try to love her, not want to get even. I am scared though of what she might be planning. We need to pray for protection and deliverance!"

Kory felt deflated – she had been working herself up to give a most thorough … and perhaps a wee bit exaggerated … tale of injustice she and Maria had already suffered from Vanessa. But Maria was right, as much as she did not want to admit it. They would have to keep a sharp eye out for the older girl from here on out … well, Kory would have to do that for both of them.

After dinner Kory helped Maria to get dressed for the walk-around recital. It took some time, going through the many splendid clothes at their disposal, and Maria again demanded that Kory choose something from the collection for herself to wear as well. Finally they were ready and the two girls made their way over to the Grand Theater Auditorium, which had the largest stage within the Academy. As they entered, Maria could hear various performers working on tuning and readying their instruments. She was rather excited – she had only heard a full orchestra once before, and she had been so nervous she had not been able to fully take it all in.

The two made their way up to the stage with the other early apprentices and Miss Ariel explained the evening's events.

"We have a full orchestra on stage, but they are spread out all over the area. That means the sound as a whole will not be as good as we normally would have, but you should be able to hear each set of instruments better this way. You are free to wander among the performers. You should try to visit each grouping, but don't hurry – you have several hours to experience the performance. The musicians have been encouraged to let you touch the instruments, but they are here to play – so don't pester them with too many questions! If you have many, I am here, and there are a few other more Senior Apprentices wandering about too – we will be happy to help. So now, enjoy!"

With that they were let loose on the orchestra. Kory saw that most of the apprentices veered off toward the stringed instruments and so she led Maria in the other direction, toward the percussion section. The conductor tapped for attention and then the musicians began a long and somewhat complicated arrangement that utilized most of the instruments on the stage. Maria gently placed her hand on one of the big kettle drums and nearly jumped out of her skin when it was pounded. She slowly glided from instrument to instrument, getting caught up in the sounds and the very vibrations pulsing through the air. It was marvelous!

Maria began to flit about the stage, no longer needing as much of Kory's help as her acute hearing placed each instrument and person. She moved about to hear first one sound, then another, then to various places to see how the sounds combined and swirled. She became rather lost to every-thing other than the music; in her mind the sounds and vibrations became colored ribbons that swirled in complex patterns and shapes. The vivid imagery became more and more real until it seemed as though she were stepping among the ribbons, feeling them brush past her. This was like her special place, even though she was not performing herself.

As the colorful patterns floated rapidly by she started to flow with them, feeling the sounds slip through her fingers and brush past her skin. As the ribbons scampered by she tried to catch a few to redirect their path, but they moved much too fast. She danced with the ribbons, flowing in and around her. As the musical piece reached its climax, she flung herself into the maelstrom of color and movement, becoming as much a part of it as the ribbons were themselves. The sounds died away gently as the piece ended and the color drained away to black and white in her mind as the ribbons fell to the floor, lifeless for now.

"Maria! Maria! Can you hear me? Are you ok?" Kory's voice sounded distant and frantic with concern. Slowly Maria began to notice hands holding her and she shook her head as though coming out of a stupor.

"Wh ...what happened? Where am I? What happened to the beautiful music?"

She heard Apprentice Ariel's voice and focused on that. "Maria, are you feeling well? You were … well, I guess it was dancing, twirling around – you looked more like an acrobat than a dancer, the way you were leaping and waving your hands about. We wondered if you were having some kind of fit."

"Oh, no … it was … it was the sounds! Did you feel them? Could you see them?"

Apprentice Ariel looked nervously up at Master Tolanard who had been conducting the orchestra. He frowned doubtfully down at the diminutive blind girl, and then he cocked his head to one side in thought. He knelt beside Maria and half-asked, half-commanded "Tell me, little one – what did you see and feel?"

Maria gulped. She did not know who this new voice was, and it sounded rather deep and dangerous all of a sudden. She shriveled up inside herself and with a cracking voice answered "I … it was the music, sir. I saw it." Maria's mouth suddenly became like a parched desert and a tear began to form in one eye. "I'm sorry if I caused any trouble. I really didn't mean to."

Apprentice Ariel was quick to catch on. "Maria, this is Master Tolanard. He was conducting while you were … were … experiencing the sounds." She sat down next to Maria and pulled her into a protective embrace. "It's ok, you're not in any trouble." Her voice was soothing and calm and Maria could not see the astonished stare being made at Master Tolanard.

He was slower to catch on, but then again this was a very different concept. "Maria, we just want to understand. Please tell us what you were doing. You said something about feeling and seeing the music? How can that be? You were not touching any of the instruments just now, and I don't mean to be rude, but it is obvious you cannot see. Tell us child, what was happening?"

Maria swallowed and knew she needed to explain it again. "Sometimes when I sing, it is as though the world around me fades away and I am in my 'special place' – a place all my own where the music and sounds seem to come alive. When I am there I can … maybe this sounds too silly, but there I can see. The sounds become colors and patterns, sometimes like a wind blowing this way and that, sometimes like a river gushing down its channel, sometimes … sometimes it is like I am on a calm still lake in the early morning, with the sun just starting to crest over the horizon. I don't really remember what that looks like, but I imagine it must be so very beautiful that you could not possibly tire of seeing it, that you would pay a king's fortune just to experience it." Maria was becoming caught up in her description, speaking with animation and energy.

"Just now it was different – but I have never been inside an orchestra before either." Someone nearby snickered at her description but she hardly noticed, too busy reliving what she had experienced. "I saw ... ribbons of color flowing through the air." This got a guffaw from a few people gathered around, but it was silenced by withering looks from both Master Tolanard and Apprentice Ariel.

Maria did not seem to notice. "It was as though I was in among the ribbons, seeing them all moving in patterns and even feeling them as they moved by me. I was somehow part of it all, and it was so wonderful! I tried to move some of the ribbons – really to redirect them, but they were moving too fast and I could not change them. Then the color started to drain away and the ribbons began to fall to the floor – I think the musical score was ending. And then I found myself here on the floor. That's all I know."

Master Tolanard looked very thoughtful. "Why did you want to change those few ribbons, Maria?"

She looked sheepish. "Well, I guess in part because I wondered if I even could ... but also I saw the pattern they were making, and I thought it would be even prettier if those ribbons were moved over to create a ... a ruffle, I guess, in the pattern."

"Hmm. Maria, I want you to listen for a few minutes. I want you to try to go back to your 'special place' if you can. Describe what you see for me."

Master Tolanard tapped his baton and motioned for the musicians to re-take their places. Then he pointed at one of the larger stringed instruments and a deep bass note sounded out, followed by an evenly paced string of consecutive notes.

Maria looked excited. "Yes – yes, I saw those! They were deep blue, such a wonderful shade and they felt like silk! Could you play a short melody?"

Master Tolanard nodded and directed the apprentice. The notes sounded out cleanly with a rich resonance. Maria smiled. "Yes, that's the one! It is so very beautiful, I think that one is my favorite."

Tolanard tapped again and another stringed instrument sounded, this one with a slightly lighter and higher tone. Maria clapped with joy and described what she had seen that correlated to the sounds. "Oh, that one is my favorite too!"

"Ok Maria, let's go through all of them, and then we can come back to focus on a few – and especially the ones you thought could be changed somewhat."

One by one, each instrument was played through a series of notes and chords. Maria was overjoyed, reveling in the unique sounds and beauty in a manner that perhaps only someone deprived of sight could fully experience. And it was just as good that she could not see the faces of the musicians, as some appeared rather annoyed at the process that seemed both incredulous and tedious.

"Well, that's all that we have out on the stage tonight. Now you have given us quite a description of each … I must say I have never heard or associated such things to these instruments before … but it is rather fascinating. Which ones did you try to change, and where in the work did you want to do that?"

Maria, her face flushed from excitement and wonder, slowly pivoted around. As each instrument was played she had placed its location firmly in her mind. She carefully walked through the people – she could hear the breathing of everyone in the room, but it was very complicated to place everyone unless they all stood still as they were now. She stood before an apprentice holding a small four stringed instrument with a bow. "This was one – it has such a beautiful golden silver blue color and the ribbon I saw from it was the most luxurious satin – surely this must be one of the most important instruments of all."

Master Tolanard smiled wryly. "Just so, Maria. The violin is indeed capable of incredibly beautiful music, and he who masters that instrument is often second only to the conductor. It can be a temperamental friend though – it can bring out your best or worst abilities with each move of the bow. Have you ever played one?"

Maria froze for a moment. She was pretty sure she had played one in her night visits, though she had not spent much time with it since she quickly learned she did not know how to properly hold or play it. "I don't think I have ever even held one properly."

"It is not generally shown much in the introductory classes – we usually prefer to start new apprentices with instruments that are simpler to work with. You said there were other instruments being played at the same time that you also wanted to 'manipulate'?"

"Yes sir, one in particular … it was a sorrowful sound, yet one that had hidden life just under the surface. Its ribbon was silver-gray that somehow had a rainbow sheen that sparkled just under the surface, as though it was waiting to come out." Maria walked over to another area on the stage, ignoring the snickering coming from a few of the older and new apprentices who were standing about and looking somewhat bored and annoyed by all the attention showed to just one novice apprentice.

Maria stopped in front of another musician. "This is the one. Its sound was simple, yet there seemed more to it – perhaps what was played was not where its true strength lies. I don't know … it is hard to describe."

"Maria, that is a flute, in particular a bass flute. It had a very small part in the orchestral piece we played tonight, but it has larger roles in other pieces and soloist parts as well. It is generally considered a somewhat simple instrument … but you seemed to see … or hear … more?"

Maria nodded. "It had a purity of beauty both similar but also unlike the others. It's hard to put words on it."

"Ok, maybe we can discuss this more later. There are only a couple of places where both the flute and violin sound together. Can you describe when you wanted to make the alteration?"

Maria pondered that a moment, and then began to point out other instruments whose ribbons had also been so vividly moving. She described which seemed to be louder or more vibrant, which were moving faster or slower, rising or falling, fluttering or flowing straight.

Master Tolanard looked over his sheet musical score, rapidly paging through it based on Maria's description until he came to a certain page. He ran this finger down the page and stopped, tapping gently on the paper. "Excellent description, Maria – though surely the most unusual one I have ever heard!" He looked up and sharply tapped his baton. "Orchestra! Turn to section 8, bar twenty-three; we will begin at the top of the page."

The musicians all sat up straight and began to play a short section. Maria listened most intently. She was not caught up into her 'special place', but she could still feel the music and recall what she had experienced. "Yes, that's the part. I tried to make the … flute … go to a higher counter note while the … violin" – Maria stammered and tried to find words. "Oh, I can't describe it right!" Her frustration was evident as she shook her head and wrung her hands.

Kory spoke up. "Maria, can you sing it?" That provoked considerable laughter and Kory's face flamed red while her countenance wilted.

Maria concentrated and then out came an aria whose sound was incredibly pure and perfect, even though she was just making simple vowel sounds. The musicians stopped, as did every conversation on the entire stage. Maria's voice seemed to do that – to catch and then demand your full attention. She lilted through the violin's part as played, and then began again but with the rendition she had visualized and felt during the first playing.

The violinist had not laughed. She nodded and played the piece as closely as she could to how Maria had sung it. "Yes! Yes! That is it perfectly!" Maria excitedly bobbed her head, and then she strode over to the flutist and sang out the part she envisioned.

The apprentice with the flute shrugged – he was not skilled enough to follow along by ear. Master Tolanard came over and held out his hand. The flute was given to him and in a moment rich sounds came out that matched Maria's notes. She nodded emphatically in appreciation. Master Tolanard nodded over to the violinist and together they played through the section with Maria's rendition.

"That's it! That's it!"

Tolanard smiled broadly and pulled out a pencil, scribbling notations down on the sheet music in front of the flutist. He handed the flute back to the boy. "Play this when we get here." The boy nodded and the Master regained his position as conductor.

"Everyone, we will take it up again at the start of section 3, but with the changes Maria suggested." He tapped his baton and they began.

Maria held Kory's hand. "Isn't it wonderful? The sounds come together with such majesty!" Kory squeezed her hand, though she did not entirely follow what had just been happening.

The orchestra played through and Maria clapped softly as her rendition sounded, adding a touch of flair to that particular spot that somehow both improved the whole and yet blended in so well it was at first difficult to exactly tell what was different.

When it ended, some people on the stage clapped and Master Tolanard came over and held Maria's hand. "That was beautiful, child. There have been several quite good alternate versions of this piece, but I don't recall ever hearing just what you suggested – and it indeed is an improvement. Never have we had a walk-through orchestra like tonight! I must ponder what you have said – and I surely will want to discuss some of it more with you later! This 'special place' you mentioned – it must be a very, very special place indeed. I only wish I could visit it with you sometime. But I suppose it is only for you, right?" He said the last with a heavy sigh.

"Oh no, Master Tolanard! It is not only for me – I don't see why everyone could not experience it. It is just … just a sort of a stage like this, I suppose. But I am never alone there."

"A stage you say? Then who is with you … who is in your audience?"

"Well … God of course! I am singing or dancing for Him! He is the true source for such beauty and wonder – after all, He created music and I think … I think He tuned us to experience its majesty, as though we could experience a small part of God Himself within the music." Maria suddenly became self-conscious. "I mean, that is what it seems like to me," she said in a small voice.

Master Tolanard had a tear that formed and ran down one cheek. He pulled Maria into a giant but gentle hug. "Maria," he whispered, "you have captured the very essence of music, and at such a young age! I think perhaps you can see better than most of us." He squeezed her one more time and then pulled back.

"Maria, I would like you to have a violin and a flute. I will talk to Vitario about it tomorrow. And lessons – he must schedule you for some lessons immediately."

He looked out over the stage. "I think that is all we will do tonight. More senior apprentices – I want you to consider what you have heard here tonight. It may sound strange and odd – but consider it. Sometimes we can learn a great deal when we look at commonplace things in very different ways. And an open mind is a key to greatness. Learning from something new and different is far better than laughing at it." He said the last very purposely toward the group where most of the snickering and derisive laughter had originated.

Vanessa, the ringleader, turned bright red and a dark frown came over her as she whispered under her breath, "Just you wait, you-who-thinks-she-is-so-special! I am going to fix you but good!"

The next day Kory was quite bouncy in anticipation of visiting the museum. It was only opened up to junior apprentices a few times a year.

"Maria, it is so special! You get to see all those historic and famous instruments. You can see ... OH! I'm sorry Maria, I forgot for a minute there that you couldn't see any of them. But ... but I bet they will let you touch a few of them – I don't think I have ever done that."

All the introductory apprentices were gathered near the theater stage where mid level apprentices would take them through the museum in small groups. The stage itself was being set up for the recitals, with small stools and instruments being placed into groups of four. As they neared the entrance to the museum room Kory suddenly groaned under her breath.

"What is it Kory?"

"Vanessa – she is one of the tour leaders! We need to watch out for her – it would just be like her to try to cause trouble for us."

Just then Vanessa looked over at them and smiled in what seemed to Kory a rather sinister way. Kory narrowed her eyes. "Oh, I just know she is planning something awful!"

"Kory, don't be so paranoid and afraid. Just watch – God will work out for good whatever evil may be planned for us!"

"If you say so, Maria. But just the same, I will keep watch out for her and her accomplices."

Master Tolanard was supervising the stage set up work and strode over to Maria and Kory.

"Maria, how good to see you again, and Kory – right? Yes. I picked a violin out for you for the recital – I realize you don't really know how to play it yet, but I would be honored to introduce you to it."

Maria gulped. A violin? She could not play that! She would sound terrible! "Ah ... thank you ... sir?"

The older man chuckled. "It really is not that bad. Come here, let me show you." He led them out of the line and over to the stage. Kory caught a glimpse of a terrible frown on Vanessa's face.

Master Tolanard led them to the closest grouping of chairs and picked up a violin. "This is the very one you heard last night, so you are already accustomed to the sounds it makes. Here, please sit on this stool." He guided her to the seat and placed her hands on the instrument. "Hold the body here at the neck and place the base under your chin. Then hold the bow in your other hand."

Maria held it awkwardly. She had plucked strings and even used a bow to saw a few times in her night time visits, but she had not known how to hold it properly. She laughed on the inside thinking back to how she had tried to play it like a guitar – she actually had had some success that way, enough to understand how to hold the strings to sound a few basic notes.

She slowly drew the bow across the strings. It sounded like a horrible racket and she heard a loud snicker behind her. Then she remembered how to hold the strings. The next draw produced palatable sounds, and with some rapid experimentation Maria produced some pretty good-sounding notes. She ran through the string holds trying this way and that to hear the various sounds.

Master Tolanard watched in appreciative awe, and then reached over. "Here Maria, let me a minute. You feel what my hands are doing." He hefted the violin and began a simple melody, drawing slowly back and forth. Maria felt his finger placement, gently following his movements. He went into a more complicated piece and she marveled at both the sound and how his fingers wavered to coax extra sound out of the simple strings.

After a few minutes he passed the violin back to her. Maria took it up and properly placed it under her chin. Then she began to copy his first simple melody, awkwardly but gaining confidence and skill as she went. She played it again, faster this time, and then again, trying out finger place-ment, movement and bow stroking. For such a small instrument it was very complex!

Master Tolanard looked thoughtful. Apprentice Ariel had told him about the guitar experience, and so he was somewhat ready for the very rapid familiarity Maria was showing with the violin. She made several mistakes, but rapidly corrected them and was intently listening and playing, learning as she went. She accomplished in 30 minutes what many apprentices took many months or even years to pick up.

"Alright Maria – you are already well past the skill level most of the other introductory apprentices are expected to show for the recital. If I let you practice too much more I think you will advance a level while sitting here! Please, take the museum tour and get ready – the recital is in just two hours." With that he gently removed the violin and bow from her hands and set them down on a chair next to her.

"Thank you Master Tolanard! At least now I won't sound totally ignorant of how to play such a fine instrument."

"That is quite alright Maria, the pleasure was mine. God has greatly gifted you. It will be most enjoyable to see how He guides you toward mastery of your skills."

Kory led Maria off the stage and over to the museum entrance.

"Well, if it isn't the child wonder. Maybe instead of people calling you 'The Singer' it should instead be 'The Plucker' … or maybe 'The Screecher'!"

"Vanessa, you leave us alone!" Kory was adamant but kept her distance this time.

"Oh, don't worry, I wouldn't dare do anything to you … right this moment. But I hope you are ready for tonight's recital. It should be *most* interesting."

As the girls joined the next tour group and began to walk away Vanessa continued, "By the way, you will have a very 'special place' tonight, special girl. You will be sitting in MY quartet. You will be playing with me, and if you screw up guess who will make sure everyone – and I mean everyone – knows about it? Heh, heh, heh."

Kory and Maria hunched their shoulders and hurried into the room, not seeing Vanessa move quietly off toward the stage.

The museum was really just a large room immediately to the side of the stage. As they entered through a wide door both girls wrinkled their noses at the musty odor. Directly inside they stopped with their guide and the other introductory apprentices. Their guide, a Level Three apprentice who introduced herself as Sabrina began what was obviously a "canned" talk.

"Directly in front of you is our first exhibit, and one of the most prized possessions of the museum. It is the famous Diamond Violin, the crowning work of the most celebrated instrument creators of all time, Luminarious III. This was the very last and best violin he ever crafted, using a type of wood and finish lost to our modern times. Only a few Luminarious violins are known to exist; nearly 300 years have passed since that legendary Grand Master walked the earth. It is only taken out and played at the most special occasions. The last time was 10 years ago when the King of Alteria, who is quite an accomplished musician, visited and was allowed to play it under strict supervision of Grand Master Vitario."

Maria pressed closer and began to reach her hand forward toward where she expected the instrument to be. She suddenly cried out as a small stick slapped across her outstretched fingers. "NO TOUCHING!" the guide harshly yelled out, followed somewhat under her breath by "and especially not for intro-babies, and certainly not for Miss Prissy here."

An older sounding man stepped forward rapidly. "Is anything wrong?"

"Oh, one of the newbies just tried to grab the Luminarious, that's all. It was her."

Kory gasped while Maria shrunk back quickly to the back of the group. The older man continued, "I'm SURE you all understand that this artifact is invaluable and meant to be preserved for future millennia! We certainly cannot have any of YOU actually touch it! Harrumph!"

Kory took up Maria's hand to inspect the red welt that was forming. In a quiet voice she whispered "I am so sorry Maria, I did not know what you were doing up there at first. Sabrina is in pretty tight with Vanessa. I think we had better stay toward the back to present less of a target."

Maria was crying softly, both from the sudden pain and from the accusation which stung even harder. As she sought control she asked "Tell me Kory, what does it look like?"

In a hushed voice Kory described "Well, first of all it has the classic dimensions of a regular violin, though it might be just slightly larger – its kinda hard for me to tell for sure. The wood is reddish but has other swirls of color too – I don't recognize ever seeing that kind of wood before. But the finish! It positively glows in the light with a soft hue. The finish must be very thin like usual, but it makes it look like it could be inches deep, like you are seeing much greater depth than it possibly could be. It must be the most beautiful violin – or other instrument – I have ever seen! It is in a polished rosewood case with glass doors. Oh, I wish you could see it!"

Maria had composed herself and her face took on a wistful expression. "I can now imagine it though – thanks Kory!"

The tour guide shuffled them off to the next display and continued a rather monotonous drone about the next item. With Kory's visual description Maria at least felt like she accomplished something, but in general the tour for her was rather useless since no one was allowed to touch anything. Her mind kept wandering back to the Luminarious Diamond Violin, wondering what glorious sounds it must make and what those would look like in her 'special place'.

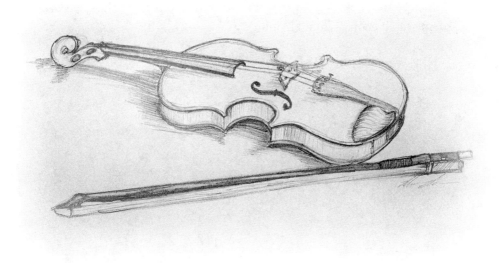

The tour ended and the apprentices were herded out. Maria could not hear the doors close, but she felt the air movement and assumed that is what caused it. As they moved off she could just hear the man's voice from the museum as he seemed to be speaking to someone softly but with some agitation. Something must have been decided as she heard what had to be his footsteps receding away at a quickened pace. Whomever he had been talking to must have either remained at the door or moved away silently.

"Kory, do we have enough time that I could practice again with the violin that Master Tolanard said I would be playing tonight?"

"I guess so, Maria – if they let us." She led Maria up onto the stage and looked around. Each set of stools were set up so that all of the apprentices could be on the stage at the same time in the prescribed sets of four. The closest group was where Master Tolanard said Maria would sit, and several other stringed instruments were placed on or near the stools all over the stage. Kory looked this way and that, and then did it again.

"Maria, I guess you can't – I don't see any violins out here, though I think most of the other instruments have already been placed about."

Maria shrugged. "Oh, that's ok. Maybe someone is waxing up the bow and getting it ready. Let's go get something to eat before the recital."

"Yeah, sure … ok." Kory gave one more look around, but the stage was absent of any people – and of violins.

Chapter 18

Recital Surprises

After a quick meal – both Kory and Maria were too nervous to really do much more than pick at their food – they just had time to stop at their apartment and change before walking back to the auditorium. With each step Maria became more nervous.

"Kory, what if … what if I go blank and can't even sound a single note! What if I don't know the piece we are to play at all – I certainly cannot read the sheet music! What if …"

"Maria, you're usually the one calming me down! I'm sure they will take your situation into consideration – remember, Grand Master Vitario is watching out for you! If you must worry, worry about me! I did not get to go through the whole introductory classes and I mainly listen to you blow everyone away!"

"Oh Kory, you do just fine – you know we work together! I think you are quite a bit further along that most of the other introductory apprentices as it is! God will help us, just you see!"

"Now that is more the Maria I know!"

They climbed the stairs and entered the hall. The echoes from their shoes clicking on the polished marble floors reminded them of the immensity of the hall, and of how small they were in comparison. They entered the main auditorium through a side door. Kory led the way to the stage. "Kory, tell me what everything looks like!"

"The stage is fairly well lit, but the windows are all draped over in the seating area, so it is pretty dark out there. The stage is lit only with candles placed mainly in the central area. It looks fairly bright and cheerful, but the outer edges of the stage and everywhere else are in shadows. I guess that is how it often is for recitals – but since there are only a dozen and a half groups they only needed to light up the main area. Most of the other apprentices are here, both our classmates and the Level Three's that will be doing most of the playing. I see Master Tolanard standing out in front of the musicians, and it looks like all the instruments are out too. I only see few people in the audience so far, but we were supposed to get here early."

As they climbed the short stairs to the stage Master Tolanard strode over. "Hello Kory and Maria, I am glad you're here. You both have time to check out the instruments chosen for you for a few minutes before we begin. Kory, you are in the third group to the right. Maria, I will escort you over to your seat."

Kory squeezed Maria's hand and scooted off. Maria felt a much larger hand enfold her own and give a gentle tug. "This way."

They had only gone a few feet when someone approached. "Master Tolanard, do you know where the bow wax is kept? I need more." He frowned. "There should be some behind the stage in the shelves where it is always kept – you should have taken care of that already."

A few steps later another voice piped up. "Master Tolanard, I cannot find Apprentice Frieda. She is supposed to be in my quartet and no one knows where she is … what will we do?"

Master Tolanard was getting irritated. "Why are you asking me, child? You know Apprentice Ariel is in charge of the assignments! Go find her and see who is scheduled as the first substitute – that person should be here also and ready to step in. Now go!"

They had not gone halfway toward their destination before another interruption came. "What now?" Master Tolanard asked between partially clenched teeth. By the time he indicated for Maria to sit down he was quite agitated with all the questions. "Sit here Maria. There is not much time to work with your violin anymore – sorry about that, there have been so many unusual interruptions. It is like everyone forgot what they are supposed to do!" He shook his head in exasperation.

As he left, Maria heard a low, evil snicker. "Seems like our conductor has become short-tempered, doesn't it? I sure hope no-one asks any more questions or that there are no more interruptions – he is likely to blow his top and ban that person from ever playing in the auditorium again! I hear he's done that before … anything else that goes wrong now will just set him right off."

Vanessa! Somehow it seemed like she must be behind the interruptions … but why? Maria did not even want to try to guess. She found the violin and bow. That brought peace to her and she hugged it close. It was alright now – she was seated, she had the violin, and even if Vanessa was sitting next to her, what really could she do now in front of Master Tolanard and the audience that Maria could hear filing into the auditorium?

"I'm sure everything will be just fine now." Maria fitted the violin to her chin and lifted the bow to get a few saws in while she still could.

"Oh, I sincerely doubt that, prissy."

Maria bristled at the comment and pulled the bow over one string. It was awful! She ran her fingers quickly over the end of the violin where the strings could be tightened. A horrified look flashed over her face – all four strings were limp; someone had completely loosened each. The instrument was completely out of tune and useless.

Maria felt hot tears begin to fall down her cheeks as she heard a muffled laugh from her side. Why did that girl hate her so? An enormous feeling of dread threatened to overwhelm her senses and instantly the familiar vision sprang up in her mind. Maria saw herself marching forward, unaware of the huge billowing cloud of evilness just ahead, seething in black fury, reaching out with tendril claws and with a gaping fanged mouth stretching forward to engulf and consume her. She should be turning and running in terror, doing anything and everything to escape the certain doom. Yet somehow Maria knew she had a duty to perform, a greater godly purpose that superseded her own welfare. And more, when she was doing God's work, she needed to relinquish her own safety, her own very life and simply follow His leading wholeheartedly and with abandon. And if that leading involved worshiping God, and even leading others to do so, as it seemed she was doing in the vision, then she should do it with all her might, with everything she had in her. She should … and she WOULD.

A fierce, grim smile came over Maria's face and the tears stopped. Without a word she quickly tightened each string, feeling the tension in each to get close to where she figured it needed to be. Then she began to quietly pluck each string, listening intently and finessing the screws. Vanessa suddenly began to saw on her large cello, trying to distract and drown out Maria's tuning. Maria just kept going – she had long ago learned how to tune out distracting noises – a must when hearing is your most valuable sensory input.

Master Tolanard had not noticed anything amiss yet, and he tapped for everyone's attention. He gave a brief introduction that Maria totally missed – she was still intently listening to each strum, feeling the sounds as much as hearing them to fine tune the strings. She had three done to the best she could get under the circumstances when she found she had to listen in on the final instructions.

"Ladies and gentlemen, we will now begin our Introductory Apprentice Recital. Each quartet will play through their prepared piece once without the new apprentice, and then a second time where the new apprentice will be expected to begin to play at least a little. They will then go through it once more and each apprentice is expected to give their best rendition. We will begin with the quartet to my left."

Maria sighed a quick thank you to God and kept at her rough tuning – the first quartet that was chosen was not hers, and now she might have time to get the last string at least close to being in tune – though without sawing she knew she would not be totally correct, and she had to do her work ever so quietly to not interfere with anyone else.

She barely heard the first group play as she concentrated. All four strings were roughly tuned, but there was just no way to do much more with them – she would have to make do and adjust her playing to try to compensate.

A second quartet was chosen and it was obvious that hers would be the third. This time Maria listened, and even through her nervousness she enjoyed the playing of the experienced apprentices and only winced once or twice to Kory's not-quite-close-enough notes as she played along. All in all though, Maria thought she had done pretty well.

All too soon that group ended. "Ladies and gentlemen, the next quartet includes someone you may recognize as 'The Singer', Maria. She has shown us already that she has much more talent than just a beautiful voice, and perhaps we will see some of it blossoming on the violin as well. Please be aware that Maria cannot see – she must play along solely by ear, on an instrument that she has had very little practice with. But that is one of the main points of the recital – to gauge raw talent that we hope to hone into real beauty here at the Academy."

Grand Master Vitario shifted in his seat. He had been watching Maria the whole time, and certainly had noticed something was wrong. He watched her feverishly tuning the violin she held. Why was that? All of the instruments were supposed to be ready for each new apprentice already!

The tapping sounded and the three apprentices next to Maria began to play. Maria recognized the orchestral piece as a simplified but equally long rendition of the same music played the night before, and she sighed in relief – at least she had a good idea of what to play even without seeing the music.

As the trio played, Maria lifted her violin and tried a few quiet notes on each string. She had no time for additional fine tuning, but her sensitive ear registered how each string sounded and she began a rapid mental calculation of where to hold and compress each string to compensate. She was NOT going to let Vanessa win! She prayed for mercy and grace to make it through.

The three other apprentices finished their first run through the musical score. Maria was determined to begin playing on the second pass.

They started again and Maria drew her bow across the strings with purpose, off-setting her fingering on the fly as she heard the tones and immediately adjusted to correct them. She smiled as the nearly pure notes sounded out. About a third of the way through she sawed with extra gusto where she knew it called for a strong sounding violin.

Disaster! Halfway through the saw one of the outer string snapped. Horrified yet again, she immediately compensated, shifting to the other three and finding the needed finger placement. No more than a minute later a second string first warbled off key and then snapped, and Maria could feel the bow strands shredding. As her hands flew over the remaining two strings she felt tiny serrations in several spots and came to the sickening realization that someone had carefully cut or filed the strings so that they could not hold up to the strain of use.

Without wanting to, tears began to form again and even before the last notes were finishing on the second run-through a third string broke with an audible twang rendering the violin useless.

Vanessa whispered "Now look what you've done – you have ruined the whole recital! Tolanard will surely dismiss you."

Maria hung her head. The fear of rejection hung over her like a heavy wet blanket.

Vanessa continued her low-voiced words. "I really did want to play this one more time though. Hey, I know where you can get another violin. I saw an extra one some apprentice had put just inside the extra stage room. It is right down the stairs to the right – the stairs are just behind us. I bet you could run down there and grab it and get back here in less than a minute – maybe you can save the day after all!"

Maria's mind was in a jumble, spinning this way and that, and she clung onto the words just spoken as if they were a lifeline thrown to a drowning person, not even really considering their source. She bolted up off her seat and felt the thin railing of the stairs, just where Vanessa had indicated it would be. She raced down and struck out blindly to the right, finding the wall and a doorknob. It turned and she raced in, feeling along the walls and floor of the musty smelling room.

Master Tolanard was more than a little upset. What was going on with Maria's violin … and now where was she going? The lighting was very poor off the stage and he could not see what had become of her. Was she running away because the violin strings had mysteriously snapped? But he could hardly imagine what he had seen and heard – Maria had played virtually without a hitch even as sting after string broke away and the bow disintegrated. If he had his eyes closed while she had been playing he was not sure he would have known anything was wrong. She had shifted – without hardly even knowing the instrument – to keep sounding her part quite faithfully.

Maria's hand brushed against something low along the inner wall and she clutched it. Its shape was that of a violin, and so she grabbed it and the bow that leaned on the wall next to it, whirled around and raced back toward the stage. The violin felt different than the other old and somewhat beaten up one she had been playing. This one was perfectly smooth with a hard surface and felt heavier than the other one. Maria noted that, but really did not pay much attention – she was highly focused on not ruining the recital. She charged out and up the stairs, retracing her steps back to her stool. "Thanks Vanessa!" she whispered. Maybe her nemesis had had a change of heart and now wanted to help.

"Oh, you are sooo very welcome," came a venomous reply.

Maria shrugged. Nice or not, she was ready to play the score again. She held the violin up and it cradled into her neck as though it were a perfect match. It certainly did feel different than the other one she had been playing, but Maria figured there may be various kinds of violins and each may feel different from one another. As she picked up the bow her mind cleared completely and she suddenly found herself in her 'special place', standing still and quiet. This took her by surprise, as normally this came on only when she was caught up into whatever she was singing or playing. In that place she felt peace and warmth and total acceptance.

Master Tolanard was rather taken aback at her sudden disappearance and reappearance, but seeing them ready he automatically tapped his baton to start up the third playing. The three older apprentices saw the instruction and launched into the quartet piece.

Maria sat perfectly still. In her mind she stood, feeling like the presence of God Himself was flooding into her awareness. He had always been there before too, but today it was with a swelling, rolling power that seemed to crackle with lightning. In a second that seemed like an eternity, God spoke: "Play for me, my Maria."

It was both a command and an invitation. Raw power surged around her. She raised the bow and joined in, remembering to revert to the normal finger positions of a perfectly tuned instrument.

The effect was electric. It was as though a power was welling up and spilling out of the diminutive form on the stool, at least for those aware enough to sense it. But both for those who did feel something and those that did not, all heard the sound.

Maria rejoiced in her mind. The purity of the sound coming from the violin was unlike anything she had ever heard. The ribbon of sound glowed brightly through prismatic color gyrations that danced across its surface as the ribbon flowed about in the space of her mind. It swirled

around, sweeping through the notes with exuberance and power, as though gleefully reveling in the presence of her most special audience.

To the other audience, it seemed as if the violin was somehow alive in Maria's hands. Her fingers flew over the notes faster and faster, and the tones produced became more and more vibrant and energetic. God's spiritual presence was enveloping Maria, who no longer was aware of any other reality than that which was more-real-than-life in her 'special place'. There, she was dancing and whirling within the colored ribbon of sounds, both producing the tones and somehow becoming an integral part of them as she manipulated the ribbon of her violin music as well as starting to do so with the three ribbons of her accompaniment.

Grand Master Vitario stopped dead in his tracks at the first note. It couldn't be! How? He took one more step toward the stage when God's presence swept over him. Movement was no longer an option as he stood enraptured with the rendition that was rapidly overshadowing every conversation and movement within the great hall. In a moment the only sound was coming from the quartet, the only movement the apprentices' hands sweeping over their instruments.

The spiritual energy and Maria's manipulations of the ribbons of sound were affecting her companion musicians. Their notes became better, blending in more cleanly and livlier than ever before. They were becoming lost within the music – all but Vanessa. She stubbornly refused and forcibly played her original part, while the others began to flow with the weaving improvisions Maria was literally fabricating. The energy washed around Vanessa, but did not force itself onto her, and her stony expression indicated a refusal to accept it.

On they played, through a second and then a third rendition, soon leaving Vanessa behind as their sounds cavorted through the score in merriment and wonder, underpinned by her stolid playing, which sounded more and more childish in comparison. Maria played with wild energetic abandon, caught up in her celestial performance before the King of Kings. And as it finally ended, wrapped up in a beauty as it had never been played before, Maria sensed one lingering impression … God smiling at her.

The silence that occurred after the last tones died away was almost palpable and thick. The spiritual energy slowly faded away, leaving a lingering sense of perfect contentment and an awe that everyone present had just witnessed, just been part of, something grander than anything they had ever experienced before. At first, no one moved in the still, peaceful silence. Grand Master Vitario was one of the earliest, and his total focus was on Maria. Even as he began to ascend the stairs Master Tolanard raced forward, red-faced.

Vanessa, the lone person in the room not awestruck, saw him coming. "Oh Maria, here comes your executioner now – and you should see how mad he looks! Oh, but you can't, can you?" Maria's head came up and she would have shriveled inward, but she was so full of lingering presence that she barely registered the words.

Master Tolanard reached them. His face was indeed red, as he wept unashamedly and knelt beside Maria. He could not even speak. He was so moved he just held onto her knees as tears streamed down his face.

Vitario reached them a few moments later. "I … I have never heard the Diamond Violin played so perfectly, with such power and grace!"

At that Maria did come back to earth, at least partially. What had he said? She nearly dropped the precious violin in a startled quake. Master Tolanard gently closed his hand around one of hers as Vitario picked the bow from her trembling other hand and spoke. "Sir Reginaldo donated this masterpiece to our museum many years ago, and I think we have done both him and it a disservice by leaving it locked up. Without a doubt, I am sure of what he would do with it right now." Grand Master Vitario used his other hand to gently lift Maria's chin. "Maria, it is with great honor that I humbly present to you a gift to be used again for its intended purpose – God's glory … the Luminarious Diamond Violin."

The audience – and that really included all of the apprentices as well – seemed to break out of their trance and began a thunderous applause. Everyone came rushing up, Kory making it to her friend's side first. "Maria … I could hardly tell that was you … it was so wonderful, so … she raised her hands up as words fled her.

Not everyone, though, was so happy. Vanessa stood just a few feet away, looking on in disgust and rising anger and hatred. Her anger boiled over and her face flushed with emotion. She stood, quaking with fury. She would take her vengeance out on that little girl right now! She grabbed the only thing at hand – the quite long and strong bow of her large cello. Grasping it two- handed she raised it above her head and strode forward, murderous intent in her eyes.

With all eyes on Maria no one saw Vanessa's rapid movement, and she was only a couple of steps away. The quite lethal weapon began its deadly swing downward with all the strength Vanessa's anger could supply.

Kory saw movement and glanced up. Without any conscious thought and with a speed that surprised even herself, she stepped forward and delivered a quite respectable uppercut punch right into the much larger girl's chin. Vanessa crumpled to the floor like a candle snuffed out between fingers, the large bow falling from nerveless fingers to the floor.

Vitario looked up with a dangerous frown. He motioned to two larger male apprentices and pointed to Vanessa. "See to it that one is delivered to the nearest Watcher immediately. Under my authority she is to be locked up – I will take care of the details later." He turned to Master Tolanard. "I think you had better also find out who her accomplices were – someone who had access to the key for the museum to start with. And I suspect someone tampered with the first violin Maria was playing. That should be checked out also."

Then the frown disappeared as he returned his gaze to Maria, who by this time was trembling rather severely from the combination of clashing events of the last several minutes and the confusion of sounds. Kory turned from the encounter of her fist with Vanessa's chin, shaking her slightly bloodied hand.

Vitario glanced over. "It seems like we chose not only a companion for you Maria, but a protector as well. Maybe she will show promise with more than one kind of bow!" Kory blushed and hid her hand behind her back. "No child, no demerit was meant – only praise. And I think I will stay out of the way of your right uppercut! Let me see that hand."

Kory held it out tentatively, and Grand Master Vitario pronounced it skinned, but otherwise intact. Maria had not even known what had happened. "Kory, what happened – how did you get hurt?"

"Later, child." Master Tolanard had finally found his composure, though he remained kneeling beside Maria. "Tell me, please, if you can, what happened?

Maria did her best to explain. When she got to the part where she began to play the Luminarious, Vitario interrupted.

"But when you got back to your seat and began to play a totally different look came over you. It was as though God was pouring out a measure of His Spirit directly onto and through you!"

Maria explained what she had experienced in her 'special place' and the two Masters looked at each other in awe. "Tolanard, did you hear the effect on the other two apprentices?"

"Yes Vitario, I did notice that. They began to play supremely well, at least two apprentice levels higher than before, maybe even three! All except that troublemaker Vanessa."

Vitario looked thoughtful for a moment. "Perhaps we owe her some gratitude. What she designed for evil God magnificently crafted into glory. We would have totally missed what we just experienced. I would not trade that for hardly anything! God sometimes works in mysterious ways, and He is certainly working strongly in Maria!"

"Maria – the violin is yours. I would suggest though that it is kept here, under a better security than it seems it had been in – it is an extremely valuable instrument. But you can play it every day if you wish. It has been kept hidden away far too long; it was made to be played and enjoyed and, I think, to help others experience more of God's glory and majesty. If you want something to play with at your apartment we will find you something else to work with – and not some knocked up practice violin like the first one. But nothing can quite reproduce what a Luminarious can achieve … unless, of course, God intervenes!"

Master Tolanard finally stood and dismissed the musicians and audience – it just was not possible to re-start the recital after what they had just been through. Maria handed the Diamond Violin over to Grand Master Vitario and Kory led her out of the building into the cool of the evening. The two Masters stood looking at each other for a few moments.

"Have we ever – in the history of Freelandia – ever had such a prodigy, such a gifting?" Tolanard asked quietly.

"Not to my knowledge. And she has only been here a few weeks! We still have no idea as to the extent of her talent and gift. At first I thought we had the world's greatest singer on our hands. Now ..." his voice trailed off. It picked up again a minute later. "What will God use that gifting for? His glory without doubt, but why now? Why when we are nearly at war with the Dominion, when no one has time for concerts and everyone is focused on defense preparations? How is He tying this in, and how should we get on board with His plan and design?"

Vitario was becoming even more excited. "Think Tolanard! What are our responsibilities? We have been given a not-so-in-the-rough diamond far more valuable than that violin. God has put us into positions to help shape and nurture – and protect – that 'mother-lode' gemstone! We have only seen a tiny portion of what potential may be inside that diminutive body that God has chosen to pour His grace into. Should we go slowly ... or push her to excel faster and faster?"

Master Tolanard spoke up. "I don't know if you will have much choice in that, my friend. Based on what has been happening – and what likely will be happening in the near future – I don't think the timing is in our hands at all."

Vitario nodded, but his mind was lost in deep thought. Again Maria had talked about her special place, where God's presence dwelt. She had said before she thought this was her soul, where part of God literally dwelled within her. Could such a place really exist? Could ... could it be within him? He had been playing music for many more years than he could remember, but only rarely had it ever seemed like he was truly playing for God. He knew he was a highly skilled musician ... but could there be more?

That night Vitario could not sleep. He could not get the thought of a 'special place' out of his head ... and so he tried to find it, to envision it. "Oh God," he whispered, "if what Maria said is true, if such a place really does exist in all of us ... please let me find it. I want my music to be for your glory, not mine. I want to play for you."

In his mind, a glimmer of a stage appeared. He felt a great peace fall upon him, along with a summons.

"Come, my son … I've been waiting for you."

Progressions

For the last several weeks Ethan's life had been a series of highs and lows. The time he spent every day with Kaytrina seemed so energetic and interesting. Progressively, however, his time at the Watchers Compound and at home was becoming almost unbearable. Everyone seemed to be on his case, prying into his life and complaining about everything he did. This morning his parents had actually nagged him that he was 'surly' and disrespectful. They just didn't really appreciate him, certainly not like Kaytrina did. He now tried to leave as early as possible and come back as late as he dared. He also had lost most interest in his workouts and in the measly unimportant assignments dumped on him by the Watchers – and so he began to skip them regularly. After all, they could get someone of lesser importance to do them. He had more important things to do. They were boring anyway, as was most of his life … except when he was with Kaytrina.

When he woke each morning he had been starting to notice an ache, almost a hunger to be with her. Maybe if Gaeten were here he would understand. But his best friend had left him alone, like he was not important enough to stay with Ethan. Hmph.

But not today. Today he was taking Kaytrina to see the coastal cliff defenses. She seemed quite interested in those and had been bugging him to see them. He was not particularly interested, but she could be quite persistent … and irresistible. Later in the week she said she wanted to see the mountain pass that was the only real land route into Freelandia. That would take a couple of day's travel. When he had brought it up with his parents they had at first been adamantly against it, when they learned he wanted it to just be him and Kaytrina. It was like they did not even trust him to be alone with her! How dare they!

Finally he had relented when he saw they were totally resolute and threatened to send a contingent of Watchers along with him. So he had seemed to acquiesce and said he would go alone. It was not really a lie – he would leave the house alone and no one in the city would see him with anyone else. Kaytrina had it all worked out. He would pack for a weeklong trip and head down to the docks. There were always ships heading off to the western ports of Freelandia, and he would arrange passage on one of them. But he wouldn't get on. He would meet Kaytrina in the bustling dock market at a pre-arranged spot and they would slip away. She said she would have horses ready for them, and they could even pick up food supplies they might want in the market. Kaytrina was so very smart like that. Not like the other girls he had met. They were all so … so … ordinary. When he was with Kaytrina he felt so … alive!

Ethan half-heartedly jogged around the park a few times in the very early morning light. He really was not running as well as he used to – for some odd reason he became out of breath and tired easier. Oh well, it was no big deal. And finally the pesky red lines in his mind were not so bothersome, he now tended to just see a reddish foggy blur most of the day and that was much easier to ignore. He had a hard time remembering why he had felt in the past that was so useful and important. Now it was just annoying.

As he ran down a park pathway he noticed an older gentleman sitting out in the early morning stillness. He was kneeling beside a rock bench in the area of the park set up as a small outdoor chapel. Ethan squinted. Wasn't that … the old missionary from the far southern Dominion? Ethan's route took him very near the old, sun withered gentleman. As he passed, the old man looked up quizzically with a puzzled look on his wrinkled brow. Ethan was relieved the old guy had not tried to stop him to talk – he really did not enjoy talking with others anymore … just with Kaytrina. But what had he been doing? A back part of Ethan's mind recognized the posture – the old man had been praying. That small part of his mind guiltily pointed out that Ethan had not been doing that now for several weeks. God seemed very far away and unimportant. Ethan's face screwed up. He did not want his own mind nagging him now like his mother and father. He purposely shut it off and continued on his slow jog.

After all, he would be meeting Kaytrina in half an hour and they could take the long horse ride to the coastal cliffs. There were some magnificent views along the cliff pathway, and from the highest spots you could view the vastness of the ocean and really get a feel for the protected bay. It would take all day, but the ride should be quite pretty ... and he would be sure to point out the very best spots for Kaytrina to view. She would like that. Oh, and of course some of the most important cliff defenses were along the way too.

Duncan and Lydia looked across the breakfast table at each other. Lydia started, "What do you think is happening with Ethan?"

"I am not sure. It is like he suddenly changed. Some young men go through such phases as they move through adolescence. Maybe it is just that. Yet it has been so sudden, so out-of-the-blue." Duncan shrugged.

"No, that is not it, or at least not all. I don't have a clear leading – but there is something else going on. I am sure of that. We need to do something, Duncan."

"Maybe you are right, dear. I could have Master Warden James speak to him, maybe have a younger Watcher keep a close eye on him for awhile – maybe Quentin. I think that lad worked with Gaeten quite a bit too."

"Maybe that would help. But there is something in the spiritual side too. Perhaps we could ask Chaplain Mikael to speak to him also?"

"Well, we invited the former Dominion missionary Polonos over for dinner Thursday. Perhaps there will be time for a discussion then. Ethan promised he would be here for that. I've missed having him here for most of the evening meals."

"That's it, then. We will have a good long talk after dinner. And Ethan leaves the next day for his review of the mountain pass. That will give him plenty of time to think – and to have some time away from that girl ... what was her name again? Kaytrina? Ethan will hardly talk at all about her. Yet I have had so many people mention that every time they see him he has this young woman hanging all over him."

"Yes, by the amount of time it appears they are spending together, it sounds like it might be getting serious between them. We will have to talk to Ethan about that too. Remember, he has had a very strong grounding in the Lord – he may be going through some rebellious phase, but he knows what is right. Give him time, he will come back."

"I guess." Lydia did not sound convinced. "I wish Ethan would bring her over so we could meet her. That is so unlike him. Yet every time I even start to bring it up he gets so angry and sullen. And have you seen how bloodshot red his eyes are becoming? It's like he isn't sleeping enough every night.

Let's see what happens Thursday night. Oh, and I think I will ask Ethan to clean up extra well before the dinner – lately he has had such an odd smell about him – maybe that also is part of the adolescent phase he is going through!"

Kory slowly strummed her small viola. She was rather attracted to its sound ever since she had to play it for the Apprentice Recital where Maria had played the Diamond Violin and had explained to Masters Vitario and Tolanard about how she seemed able to manipulate music in her 'special place'. Kory had heard the explanation of that place at least half a dozen times now. Yet she still did not really 'get' it. Her mind was usually a tumble of feelings and thoughts that flitted place to place in what some-times seemed like random pathways, and rarely could she seem to hold onto one thought for a very long time. Even when she prayed, it was more like shooting a prayer arrow or two upward before her mind would wander away again.

Yet for some reason, when she played the viola that Apprentice Ariel had lent to her, it seemed to calm her mind considerably. That was good, because she really wanted to just sit and think about what Maria had been saying. But the Music Academy was no real place to do it – there was much too much bustle and noise. In fact, no-where in the Keep seemed to fit … she wanted to get away to just be with God. Maria was busy at voice lessons, and Master Vitario had said he wanted to take her out for dinner afterwards, so Kory had the entire afternoon and early evening off. It was the time she had been looking for … now she just needed the right place.

As she sat in the Commons, a bird flew by quite close and landed to perch on the edge of the fountain in the center of the park. The splashing water reminded Kory of a pond with a small waterfall that was a little less than an hour's walk from the Academy, outside of the Keep in the nearby hills. It was a beautiful day. The pond would make the perfect backdrop for her ... for her ... well, what was it she really was expecting to do? Pray? That was certainly part of it, but not the kind of prayer flare she so often resorted to. Should she play her viola? That may help, but it was more of a tool. She pondered this further as she walked, the viola strung over her back with a soft sash belt to hold it in place.

What was it she wanted to accomplish? Well, she wanted to understand more about this 'special place' concept. It all seemed rather unreal – maybe fine for a special person like Maria or Lydia, but certainly not for such a plain person as Kory thought of herself. But she knew – or at least had been taught – that she had a soul. What was a soul anyway? She had never felt it within her. She had never really felt God within her either. She believed in God and prayed to Him – well, she sent up requests and concerns pretty regularly – but she had never really felt like she had a response, or at least not very directly. She did see God's hand on her life – just getting accepted at the Music Academy was proof enough to her of that. But she had never felt His presence like Maria described, never heard His voice, never really felt the kind of joyful exuberance that Maria described or the awe-filled reverence that Lydia had mentioned during their stay over. God was just ... out there somewhere, probably listening and maybe watching – but not like a person you could talk to, not a ... a... friend? Isn't that in part of how Maria described God? Maria had mentioned she regularly felt that God was pleased with her music, her singing, her dancing in her 'special place'. Kory wondered if she pleased God. How could you tell or know?

Without really noticing it, her musings had filled her time and she found herself at one end of the pond. At one end a rock outcropping made a natural place to sit where you could dangle your feet in water. Kory found a place that was fairly comfortable to sit and leaned the viola onto the ground beside her. After all, she was not trying to play in a concert – she only knew a few simple songs besides the practice chords she repeated daily.

As she gently splashed the water around with her feet, Kory picked her instrument back up and began to quietly strum. Her mind continued to try to unravel the tangle of thoughts, and she began to … not really pray she thought, more like just talk … to God. This was new for her … she could not remember ever sitting still (that was hard enough by itself) and just talking out loud to God.

"God … it's me, Kory. I am not very used to this … this just talking to you. But Maria and Lydia seem to do it, so I guess it must be ok with you … right?" There was no immediate answer, but Kory had not really expected one either. "So God, do I really have a soul? Is Maria right … is that where you stay when you are visiting … me? Is part of you somehow inside me now? I sure don't feel it." She splashed the water, noticing the many ripples that broke up and distorted the clear reflection of herself she had been peering at. The ripples bounced around and she could not make out anything on the wavy surface. But then as she ceased splashing the ripples slowly spread out and subsided, returning the mirror-smooth surface reflection. Now she could see herself clearly again.

That sunk in. Normally her mind seemed to flit from one thing to another. At times she could barely concentrate enough to do her lessons at the Academy. In truth, she knew it limited her training and advancement – she had a difficult time concentrating. When she was able to be still, she found she could play pretty well … she figured maybe some of Maria was rubbing off on her.

Was this … this busyness … also affecting her view of God and what He might be doing in her life?

Resolutely Kory tried to clear her mind of distractions and just concentrate on playing the simple tunes she knew, and to try to sense … God. One by one her errant thoughts were taken captive and she felt a greater peace than she could ever recall. Her fingers seemed to go on automatic as she felt the peaceful stillness in her mind and body – it was such a rarity that Kory could not recall ever feeling quite like that before. Into that quietness, it just did not seem right to ask anything of God – He was already giving her a special gift. Instead she wanted to thank Him. She had prayed with thankfulness before, but it was usually more of the over-the-shoulder 'thank-you' one would say as you sped off to your next activity. No, that would not do.

From far deeper within her, from what seemed like her very essence, Kory spoke to her Creator, though true words could not really convey her emotions or thoughts. "God ... I love you! Thank you so much for this peace – Your peace. You are so ... awesome!" Even those coherent words seemed weak compared to what she felt, and so wordlessly she just began to worship. A small part of her mind wondered if this was what Chaplain Mikael had once preached about when he said God wanted us to worship 'in spirit and in truth'.

Kory had no idea how long that went on ... she really did not care, she was somehow ... communing ... with her God. She had never done that before. And in the midst of her worship, she sensed His presence. There was no lightning or thunder, no earthquakes or explosions ... just a growing sense of awesome mightiness and power around her and ... in her. There, deep down inside, in her innermost being, she found His dwelling place. Kory laughed and cried with joy and wonderment. Without even knowing it, she began to sing along with her own accompaniment in a song she did not even know – but the words and expressions of worship came anyway, and she knew they were being supplied by God's Spirit. It was wondrous, beautiful and awesome.

So slow it was hard to even notice, the image in her mind faded and soon Kory found herself back at the pond, still right where she had been sitting on the rock – but she was a changed person. As her self-awareness came back, she noticed she was still playing the viola ... but now the sounds were far richer and smoother. Her fingers seemed to know right where to go and in her mind she could hear just what she should be playing, and her fingers somehow found the path to accomplish that.

Kory looked out over the pond, and it never seemed brighter or more colorful. She heard the slight breeze that had sprung up gently rustling the leaves in the nearby trees, and it sounded like a myriad of little hands clapping with joy to their Maker. There was a sense of vibrancy she had never noticed before. Without even trying, without the need to shoot up an arrow of prayer, Kory said a simple "thank you" inside, deep inside, to her audience of One.

Vitario found Maria singing voice scales with a senior apprentice. "Well Maria, how are the lessons going?" He took her by the hand and began to lead her out of the building.

Maria felt somewhat hoarse. She coughed. "Good ... I guess. This is hard work, and I feel like Master Veniti is never really pleased with what I am doing. It gets me frustrated and sometimes even depressed. Yet ... yet I think I can tell a difference. I can hold notes longer than I used to be able to, and I am hitting the lower notes far better than before. But my throat seems always sore and tired, and I never really get to ... well ... sing! The lessons may be making me a better vocalist, but they are a far cry from worship – I am used to singing in worship to God, essentially every time I would sing it was in my 'special place' before Him. But this ... stuff ... is not like that at all! For being 'The Singer', now I rarely really sing and instead mainly find His presence when I play the violin or flute."

They had passed outside now, and Vitario led Maria to a nearby café with outside seating. The warm breeze that had sprung up blew Maria's long hair and she shook it out with pleasure.

"Maria, about this 'special place' ..."

"Oh, do you want me to explain it again? I am not sure there is much more I can say about it. You do believe it exists though ... right?"

"Oh yes, Maria – I am certain of it being very, very real."

Maria cocked her head with a somewhat whimsical smile, which Vitario thought was particularly humorous when placed on a young blind girl. Inwardly she tried to slow her heart from prematurely rejoicing. "You have never mentioned that before."

"Yes, Maria. That is why I wanted to talk to you ... I am rather excited about it all myself. I think ... no, I KNOW that I too have found my own 'special place'! I feel like such a novice!" Vitario reached out and held one of her hands. "Thank you, Maria. God has used you to teach an old man something about music and worship he never really knew or experienced. I don't think I can ever sing or make music the same again!"

Maria laughed with joy. "It is all for Him, now – isn't it?"

Vitario began to half-laugh, half-cry. "Yes! Yes Maria! God created music – He had to, He created everything! He created the sounds, He created our ears to hear them and formed our minds to enjoy them. They are all His. Now when I play an instrument, I am finding it dull and boring – unless I am playing it for God. Then it becomes something wonderful and awesome, it is filled with a life and vibrancy I don't think I ever truly knew before. It is so enriching, so fulfilling, so … so much better than before. I cannot believe what I had been missing!"

"Oh Master Vitario – I am so very, very happy for you! It will never be the same now – it will be so very much better!"

"Yes, Maria … it already is. God is so good. I am so glad He brought you to us … brought you to me! And thank you, Maria – for being a willing vessel for Him to use. This revolutionizes my concept of the whole Academy. I have been leading it poorly. There is a whole other dimension that has been totally missing! I don't know, Maria … I don't know what to do next. Maybe I should resign …"

"Oh no, Master Vitario! God has put you in your position for such a time as this. God will lead you if you ask and listen!"

"I don't know, Maria. I just don't know how. But I do know I cannot do it alone. Will you … will you help me?"

Just then the breeze carried to them a beautiful melody someone was playing on a viola far away.

Chapter 20

Lofty Ideas

Duncan looked over the scale model of the Keep and surrounding area, and at a smaller scale version of the entire country of Freelandia. His Chief Civil Engineer was pointing out various local landmarks to ensure Duncan, Master Warden James, and the others in the large conference room could get their bearings before he continued. Chief Engineer Robert was already well versed on this map, though he did not know the entire content of the presentation forthcoming.

Duncan pointed to the main road from the dockyard that wound up through the warehouse district, across an open field and the ancient stone bridge that crossed Keep River, and finally into the city proper. "So this is the expected main entry route for Dominion forces?"

The engineer showing them the map spoke up. "Well, it may be one of them, but it is obvious – and it is not very likely the Dominion ships will expect to sidle up and dock at the shipyard! They surely realize we will have the docks sabotaged thoroughly. No, we expect that if any of their ships get past our navy and coastal defenses they will most likely land here, here and in these spots." The engineer tapped out locations with a long wooden rod. "The landing spot for the largest contingent of invaders is probably right here at the main beach to the west of the docks. It is the closest spot to the Keep, just a rather short run up the hills to reach us – or rather, it would have been just a short run. More on that later. If they arrive as expected during daylight, we think they will make bombarding passes, likely with the so-called 'hellfire' we have heard about. We believe that is a mixture of flammable pitches and tar, maybe mixed in with other ingredients that are even more difficult to quench. They would first target any coastal and shore defenses their catapults can reach, then they may try other targets, such as the docks and immediately surrounding areas. However, they may want to keep as many docks intact as possible for their own potential use.

Our shore 'cat's and the new spring launchers should be able to hold such bombardments away, but it is quite difficult to hit a fast moving ship, and impossible to keep up with a swarm of them. We have to assume they will overrun our distance weapons and actually land on the beaches. Obviously we hope to stop them before they reach our shores, but we are planning for the worst."

Duncan and the others nodded thoughtfully.

The engineer continued. "Now that is where some of the engineering projects that Master Brentwood had funded come into play. The rain water fire suppression system, for instance, may be particularly useful in buildings close to shore, and we have already begun installing slate tiles on roofs and outward-facing building walls. We expect that will help – and maybe quite a bit – but it will not protect everything and we need to expect heavy fire damage along the coast. Some of the new longer distance spring catapults are being installed on higher ground along the shore, and any ships coming very close will be running a gauntlet of suppression fire themselves. Our land based launchers will have significantly longer range than any ship mounted units – unless the Dominion tries to bring one of their Dreadnaught ships in through the sea channel at the coast. We doubt they will want to risk that … the channel is quite narrow. If they do, we will really have our hands full as they may have nearly the same range that we can deliver from shore from all but our largest cats and launchers."

The smiles obtained from the from the launcher and catapult discussion faded at the thought of Dominion Dreadnaughts maneuvering right off the docks of the Keep. Duncan looked more concerned now.

Seeing the concern, the engineer hurriedly continued. "We have some surprises planned for those beaches we think will look most appealing for off-loading Dominion troops. We are even making a few of them look more attractive than others by installing heavy stakes and floating logs chained in place as break waters. Several beach projects will look unfinished. At those beaches we are installing some other piping projects – we are putting reservoirs on high inland ground that will hold a large amount of wood alcohol and asphaltic liquids mixed with other ingredients. Opening up a few spigots near the shore will cause a flood of flammable liquid to pour out over the beaches, where we can easily ignite it to provide a very … warm … welcome.

The huge numbers of volunteer recruits have been of tremendous help. We are building high earthen berms at the various expected entry routes into the Keep and between the main beach and the nearest Keep gates. Many will have booby-traps that can be remotely triggered, and some of the most promising looking pathways will lead into high walled cul-de-sacs where our archers can wreak havoc upon them. Some of the local farmers have suggested other, shall I say, 'nasty' surprises for them also. The invaders that try to swarm inland, especially from the closest beach, will be in for quite a struggle. And if they turn toward the dockyard we have other plans being worked out to slow their progress."

He tapped the substantial outer wall of the Keep itself. "Teams are heavily reinforcing the outer and inner Keep walls, adding additional layered defenses. The goal all throughout here is to slow the enemy down and decimate their ranks with flexible defenses that we can continue to fall back from as the enemy advances. Here at the Keep itself the outer defenses are to start a 'harder' defense to stop them dead in their tracks … literally. And if they somehow break through, the inner Keep is being fortified to provide another bulwark to stop any that get by our outer walls. We are expanding the tunnels beneath the city to store large quantities of food, and our springs have plenty of fresh water. Still, we are not really well set up to defend against a long siege."

Duncan looked pleased. But then he frowned. "That looks pretty impressive for the Keep, but what about the rest of Freelandia and our other large cities?"

The two engineers looked at each other, and then to James. He took the lead. "We cannot possibly defend everywhere in strength. But we have begun to intensively train associate Watchers in every sizeable town and especially along the coastal areas. They could never stand up to repel invaders, and we have no intention of letting them get slaughtered trying. Instead, we are placing seasoned Watchers all over the coastal areas to organize guerilla units who can greatly harass an invading army, with caches of arms and food scattered all about. It is not likely invaders would settle into one location in the outer countryside, but instead they would more likely attempt a pincher movement toward the Keep. We have planned for that as well – but we believe the main attack will be an all out frontal assault on the Keep. The Dominion well knows that if they succeed here, the rest of the country will fall. As long as the Keep remains free, they will not have won. So we are predicting the huge majority of an invasion force will come straight at us here, expecting a fast, decisive victory. The Dominion has very rarely resorted to a long lasting siege."

"One more thing – what about the mountain passes?"

Robby fielded that question. "There are only a few, and it is highly unlikely anyone would attempt passage through the mountains in any sizeable force. Still, James insisted we be thorough. So at every pass we have built redundant landslides that can be triggered to totally block the passages."

Duncan smiled. "Well, it looks like you are well organized and that your work is progressing well. But how long will it take to really be ready? What if the Dominion came next week or next month?"

The Master Warden looked down, not meeting Duncan's eyes. "Honestly, if they came next week I doubt we could much more than send our fleet out and hope they could at least reduce the numbers coming ashore, and then fight hand-to-hand on the beaches and streets. I'd estimate than within two days the Dominion forces would completely overrun our defenses and take control of the entire Keep. Within two weeks of that they would totally control Freelandia."

That brought a hushed and morbid silence in the room. Duncan spoke in a muted monotone "And if we had a month?"

James looked up at that question. "Far better, though still not great. Work has been progressing faster and smoother than anyone had even wildly guessed. It appears God has given a tremendous will to work to the volunteers and professionals alike. Still, there is a great deal to do. A month from now we would be in better shape, but we still could not hold out – barring divine intervention of course. Three months from now? Then I would say our chances would be far better, maybe at least a thirty percent likelihood of actually successfully repelling the invaders."

Duncan still looked grave. "Only thirty percent chance, James?"

"Yes. Even if we had a year of full time preparations I don't think our chances would ever be greater than fifty-fifty. The Dominion navy outnumbers our own by at least a factor of four, and they are increasing the number of their fleet and the size of their vessels at a pace we cannot come close to matching. The longer they wait, the bigger that mismatch will be. The Dominion has a huge army, with most of them already trained and experienced in battle from their other conquests. We have the Watchers and Wardens, and tens of thousands of volunteers ... but at best we are at a twenty to one disadvantage in numbers, maybe even far worse. Defenders typically have perhaps a three or four to one advantage, but unless our engineers come up with spectacular inventions to even the odds, we will still be vastly outnumbered. By sheer volume of troops alone I must consider our chances of surviving to be ... well ..."

Robert was looking quizzically at the Master Warden. "So ye figure our chances be somewheres betwixt a doubtful maybe and non-existent?"

"I would not have said it quite like that, but essentially, yes."

"I must disagree with ye, mister Warden James. I must strongly be at odds with ye."

"Oh, and why is that, Chief Engineer?"

"I figure we have only two of what ye call them thar chances thingies. The chances are exactly zero or one hundred percent, depending on what God wills. Now I don't want to be in terror figuring on a sure defeat, and I wills meself to spend out me very last breath defending Freelandia – but I will depend wholeheartedly on God's coming to our rescue. I says we should expect to win one hundred percent, and work to our best ability toward that end ... never forgettin' that it is God who decides the outcome, not our best of preparations!"

'Well said, Robby." Duncan looked up, a glint now in his eyes. "We will prepare and we will fight with God's help and power. Any victory will be His, and any defeat will be accepted as part of His sovereign will, knowing His long-term plan is always best. If for some unknown reason God clearly indicates to us that we are to capitulate and surrender, then we will so do it with our heads held high. But unless we hear otherwise, we will fight with everything God gives us. So from here on out I do not want to hear of doom-and-gloom scenarios. God used Samson to defeat an army of Philistines. God used Gideon and a few hundred warriors to route an army numbered like the sands on the seashore. Our God is the God of unconquerable odds.

James, do you need anything more from my office?"

James spoke up. "Not presently. The main issue we are having is feeding and housing the volunteers – you know that they have been arriving at far faster rates and volumes than any of us anticipated. We have asked surrounding farmers to help with the feeding, and many have offered large portions of their crops free of charge. Still, the logistics are bogging us down."

"I will re-assign as many of our lower level managers as I can to support that effort. We should be able to convert several warehouses into dormitories pretty quickly. If there is nothing else, then I thank you all for the review. Freelandia's defense is in good hands."

Robby could not let that go by. "We are in the very best of hands – God's."

Lydia sipped her tea, seated at a small round table at a nearby café with Minister Polonos and Chaplain Mikael. Polonos spoke up first to her question. "So you say a young girl told you she sang and danced before God in her soul? That is … remarkable!"

Lydia smiled. "Yes, that is what she said. She spoke of a special place she would go to in her mind, where God resided. There she could talk to Him, worship Him, and listen to Him."

"Well, I don't know if that is my soul," Mikael said thoughtfully, "but when I want and need to listen to God I also go inward, deep inside of myself, and picture myself before an open door. God is inside. I must quiet myself before I enter, and then I go in and just sit in His presence. I ponder His majesty and attributes, and try to listen to what He wants me to hear. I guess I had never thought of it being my soul."

Polonos sat back in his chair. "I think she may be right. Regardless, I too quiet myself on the inside and put myself in His presence. I know he is always within me, always there, always present … but I still need to withdraw from the distractions around me, and especially from the distractions within me. I have not put words on it like this before, but 'special place' works well for me!"

Lydia nodded. "I too need to clear my mind to listen well to God. Sometimes He impresses something upon me even when I am in the midst of busyness, but usually I need to find quietness within myself to listen. I think Maria … at her tender young age … has discovered something it took me decades to learn. She is a singularly amazing young lady – and I believe God has great plans for using her … somehow … to help and protect Freelandia itself. How, I have no idea!"

"God does not look at the outside of a person, He looks at the heart. He looks at what someone could be, what He can make them into, if they will submit to His will. I agree though – to see God's hand strongly on someone so young is exciting. So very many young people are largely ignorant of God's word and work, and seem quite content with that state. So very few are really spiritually aware to see God's Spirit working in them … or for that matter the devil's." Polonos paused. "I just saw someone like that this morning. I got up very early and went to the central park to pray. A young man jogged by – I thought that rather odd, since it was quite early and I had not noticed anyone else out yet. My, what a spiritual darkness was upon him! It was like a thick cloud blanketing over his mind. I recall wondering if he even knew it – it just did not seem like he did."

Lydia's face had grown pale. "Someone who was jogging in the park early this morning?"

Arianna led Robby and the team of engineers he had assigned to her up to a tall hill that had a shear escarpment on one side. About 80 feet below were several wooden and canvas constructs in the shapes of a small ship, a hut, and even a comical facsimile of a pachyderm – those massive beasts from the deep southern areas of the Dominion which some Bashers rode into battle.

On top of the cliff was an indecipherable arrangement of materials. "This is a couple of iterations better than what I had first used with the swamp gas," Arianna explained. Spread out on the ground was a large silken sack of sorts, with thin ropes connecting it to some form of large pot.

"Girly, whatdaya have laid out fer us here?" Robby asked.

"Rather than explain it now, I think I will show it to you first." She nodded and an apprentice engineer pulled over a cart with a large metal cylinder. He connected a hose to it and fussed with the silken sack to find a small opening in the bottom. He then pulled a lever on the cylinder and all could hear a loud hissing. The silk began to ruffle inside and expand. In just a few minutes the silk was billowing out and upward until it had filled out into a large oval shape. As it more completely filled, it lifted off the ground and began to tug on the heavy looking metal pot to which it was attached. In another minute the pot began to rock back and forth a few times and then it too left the ground, rolling upside down. Soon only a thin rope was restraining the contraption as it strained to go higher. A light wind was pushing against it, and if not for the rope it would have sped upward and over the edge of the cliff.

Arianna walked over to a wheel where the rope appeared to terminate. She unlatched a small metal hook and began to turn the wheel, which in turn spooled out more rope and let the flying silken sack and pot drift out over the edge of the cliff. Robby looked closely and saw a thin black strand also playing out with the rope, but it connected down to the inverted pot.

When it appeared it was directly over the constructions on the ground below, Arianna halted and re-locked the wheel. "We played quite a lot with this. It is far from perfected, but we are making advancements on the design every day. We call the silken cloth a 'gas bubble', and the pot underneath is the 'payload'. This version is loaded with iron balls and the powdered swamp mud people have used for candle lighting. There is a small compacted ball of that mud mixed with sawdust in an upper compartment that is burning now like a small torch – it will stay lit for many hours, and I think we could even have it go for days if necessary. This little black string opens a tiny valve, which in turn releases a puff of the purified swamp gas over the burning mud. That will start things off. It was a lot of work to figure out how to get the construction design and timing right, but I think it is ready enough to show you."

"Just what are ye up to, lassie?"

Arianna smiled. "If everyone will please step up to this railing along the edge of the cliff?" The gas bubble was floating at about the same level as the people – just enough gas had been added to keep it barely buoyant – and the metal pot was now well below them. "May I direct your attention to the ground below?" When everyone was attentively looking down, she tugged on the black string.

For a brief moment nothing seemed to be happening. Robby was just beginning to turn and tease Arianna about this being a big ruse when a tremendous thunderclap made everyone jump and crouch to try to protect themselves. They stood back up sheepishly, saw no evidence of the gas bubble, and looked down.

The assembled constructions below were in shambles. "Great God Almighty!" Robby could hardly contain himself. "Did you just do what I think you just did?" He looked back down on what was left of the constructions below. They were largely smashed into pulp and splinters, and even from their height Robby could see what looked like hundreds of pock-marks in the ground below.

Arianna smiled. "There is randomness to the impact pattern, of course. We are working on that, and on scaling this up to a larger model. The Dominion's largest warships would hardly be stung by what you just saw, though anyone unfortunate enough to be on deck when one of these went off above them would be in a world of hurt. But on smaller targets, I think such a device as this could give our enemies quite a nasty surprise. And keep in mind this is just our latest prototype … our teams of engineers come up with multiple improvements daily, and we think we have just scratched the surface of the true potential of such devices."

"How many of these thingies do you think we can make?"

"I've got engineers collecting every whiff of that swamp gas, and we found we can gently heat the mud and extract more. Even better, we found a deep pond nearby where I found the gas that had strange bubbles coming up nearly constantly in one spot. We sank a pipe down into the bottom of that pond and are now getting quite a lot of pressurized swamp gas collected. I have also ordered as much silk as I could. How many we can make depends on how much time we have, how many people we can put on making them, and when we think we have a model good enough to stop tinkering on and move it over to production."

"So you think we could float some of these out over the bay? How far from land could we get?"

"I don't know yet, Chief Engineer. We have a lot to learn. I have a larger version to try that out in a few days along the coastal cliffs. I want to see if we can get out over the narrow strait that all ships must come through. Depending on the wind and weather, we should have your answer then.

We also have several ideas to increase the payload. For the next trial we will try to incorporate as many improvements as we can … we believe we can increase the damage you saw by at least ten fold, maybe even more. My lead apprentice has been tinkering with a much larger payload and even I have not seen all of his ideas. It is some pretty tricky engineering though …." her voice trailed off and then continued in a whisper mainly for Robby's ears "and we may need some additional, close assistance from the Chief Engineer."

Robby grinned ear to ear. "Closely working with my brightest apprentice is what Chief Engineers do best!"

Robby was incredibly busy, with status reports coming in almost hourly. It seemed like new ideas and advancements were coming out of the woodwork. Yet he knew there just was not time to seriously pursue most. He had several trusted staff engineers cull through them to find the most promising, and even still, he had few extra resources to assign to anything new.

But even with his workload, today there was a special event down at the dockyard. He had to convince Arianna to accompany him – he had told her he needed a decent secretary along to take notes, but barring that he would settle for her. At that remark he had nearly been clobbered, but then Arianna demanded he buy her an extra nice lunch for such a remark. At his acceptance of her terms, she had agreed.

Freelandia's Grand Master Shipwright was a short, swarthy man with rough skin and a raspy voice. He greeted the two engineers heartily and then got down to business. "We had already ramped up construction to make as many fighting ships as possible about six months ago, knowing it takes quite awhile to put seaworthy ships together. Thanks to the help of the engineers sent here over the last year, our ship building has been streamlined and we are now making ships faster than I ever thought possible!"

"Well, good sir, ship building is really partly engineering too – just of a specialized sort. Former Master Brentwood wanted to see if we could improve the shipping and fishery fleets, and I take it ye adopted the ideas toward defensive vessels as well?"

"Yes, and the latest batch of engineers you sent over have also been helpful. But can you tone them down from all their pestering suggestions? They want to tinker with everything they see! It is starting to drive some of my chiefs batty. Though, to be totally honest, several of their ideas have been pretty good. A fresh set of trained eyes can sometimes see past tradition."

"And sir, it takes a right open mind to accept new idears in suchy a traditional industry of fine craftsmanship – and especially from the likes of land-lubber geeky engineering types! I congratulate yer acceptance of new thingies, Master Shipwright! So how are you coming on the ideas to best those mountains-of-the-sea Dominion Dreadnaughts?"

"They are the challenge, aren't they now? We can't ram them. Maybe if a light ship were to run into one of those at full sail speed and hit it just right, maybe it could cause enough damage … but it would be a suicide mission since surely such an impact would destroy the smaller ship. The Dominion apparently is going after the ultimate in brute strength. We cannot out-brute the Dreadnaughts, but we surely can out-maneuver them – and make sure we stay out of their way. Our warships are the fastest and most agile on the sea, from what we know. But that does not matter a twit if you are just a mosquito bothering a pachyderm!"

The old one-time sailor smiled at his own wit, then turned serious again. "We could swoop in and attempt to board, but their crews would out number us twenty to one. We are also hearing reports that they are armoring their hulls with metal, and maybe other areas as well. That poses a mighty big challenge to breach their hulls with any conventional weapons we have. And the sheer size and especially height of those confounded ships makes traditional catapult attacks far less effective, and of far greater risk since those ships can carry such larger armaments with far greater range."

"One I am sure you have proposed solutions for?"

"Surely – or it would be time for you to get a new Grand Master Shipwright. Come on to the back workshops and I will show you what we have been installing on our ships."

The three walked from the front office area into a large warehouse building, filled with carpentry sounds. "We have taken some of the ideas from

Master Oldive and your companion there … seems to me, Chief Engineer, that she should be having the title 'Master' affixed to her name sometime soon, based on what she has been showing to us."

At that Arianna beamed, but Robby groaned. "Ach, ye dinna have to be saying such a thing in front of her, now did ye? It will all go a-swelling to her head, pretty as it is, and soon she'll get to a-lookin' like her gas bubbles! And anyway, she's been starting to assume the Master part toward me already!"

Arianna's smile turned into a growl and she swatted Robby hard across the back of his head. "Do ya see what I mean, man?"

"Oh … you can be the most obstinate, impossible …" Robby cut her off with a doleful look at the Master Shipwright. "Yes'im Master".

Arianna fumed and turned an ever darker shade of red while the shipwright roared, doubling over with laughter. "I'd heard you two were like mast and masthead, heading toward the same destination but not quite touching yet. But it looks and sounds to me like you are already married!"

Robby perked up with a big smile. "Not yet, me good man, but I am already practicin'."

"Robby, if you did not tend to make up so well I swear I would bean you every time you open your big mouth!"

"Right-o, and I surely get plenty of practice. Anyway, the Master Shipwright has better things to do than listen to a quarrel and make-up. Go on, sir ship builder."

Still smirking, the Master Shipwright continued. "We have been outfitting our ships with new catapults and with as many of Master Oldive's spring launchers as he can supply us. I think those latest launchers may be able to send a metal bolt through those big ship's hulls, metal plating and all if we can get in close enough.

We also have been trying some of Arianna's fire powder, mixing it with oil and tar – it creates a terribly hot fireball that just cannot be quenched, leastwise not with water. Even so, we need something better, something that gives us a standing chance against those sea mountains! One of our engineers is trying to pack some of that powder into kegs filled part way with stones that keeps it floating just at or below the waterline. If we can figure a way to get one of those to explode when it is up against a ship's hull, I think we could punch a big hole clean through any armor."

Robby looked at Arianna. "Would the trigger mechanism you were using on yer gas bubble thingy work?"

Arianna had a thoughtful stare and absently tapped one foot on the floor. "Maybe. But what if we put prongs all over the barrel that were connected to little levers that release some of the compressed swamp gas in an outer shell around the powder, which could then ignite from a pre-lit ember to set the whole thing off?"

Robby's face lit up. "That just might work. Could you send one of yer payload pot thingies here and show the good shipwright how it might work? Pack a barrel full o' that explosive mud and set it off against a Dominion Dreadnaught … I would surely love to see the result of that! Dominion sailors and soldiers, may I introduce you now to your Maker? What, you're a wee bit waterlogged, aren't you just?"

Chapter 21

Naval Maneuvers

The Alterian ship made very good time to Freelandia, even with the somewhat roundabout path it took to avoid Dominion suspicion. It sped through the narrow cleft in the cliffs from the open ocean and into the serene waters of the large bay. With full sails they made straight away for the docks, still several hours away. When no berths appeared open at the very busy wharf it pressed in close and lowered a small skiff, upon which two men embarked to tie off against a dock piling that had a ladder for access to the planks above. This was unusual enough to get the attention of the alert Watchers, and a small contingent met the skiff as it pulled into a narrow opening between two other ships.

"Ahoy, Alterians! What brings you with such haste?"

The Alterian sailor with two earrings glanced at the curious onlookers and made a quite inconspicuous gesture with his left hand while seeming to absently rub the side of his nose. The signal was noticed by the senior Watcher.

"This is highly irregular. I command you to come with us for questioning."

The two dark skinned men made a small show of resistance, enough to convince onlookers that some mischief had just likely been thwarted, and were shuffled off to the nearest Watcher station. Once inside the man with three earrings who was the Captain spoke up. "I have a message sent to Aunt Lydia from a certain old blind man I met in Kardern." He opened up a small tube and pulled out the scroll. The Watcher section leader jumped to his feet.

"I will personally see that it gets to the proper person immediately. Please, be our guests. I am quite certain the Master Warden will desire to speak with you." He ordered a carriage and assigned a senior apprentice to ensure the two men were brought to the Watcher Compound. Once the arrangements were complete, he hastily grabbed a horse and dashed off to the Capital building. Upon arrival he raced up the stairs and to the business office of the Master Warden.

Somewhat out of breath, he handed over the message tube with a short explanation and then retraced his passage back to the dockyard.

James looked up as his senior staff assistant unexpectedly hurried in. "A note sir, presumably from Grand Master Gaeten!"

James stopped everything else he was doing. "Let me see – have you opened it yet?"

"Yes sir, we first verified the thumb print – it was well preserved and matched our copy. We deciphered the code in the text, but before we do more we wanted to show it to you."

The Warden carefully unwound the scroll, noting the fine imprints on one side from a dry quill. He nodded at his assistant, who carefully dusted the surface with a special powder and then pressed a clean sheet of paper over the top. Next he rolled a heavy wooden dowel over the surface and then carefully peeled off the top sheet.

Careful not to disturb the now compacted powder, he flipped over the page and lightly sprayed a liquid onto the sheet. Text darkened immediately. The two men read rapidly. James spoke first. "Call an emergency meeting of the High Council – set it for two hours from now. Tell them we have a message from Gaeten of the highest importance that requires immediate action. Next, get the Master of the Navy, and of the Coastal Defense. I want them in my office within the hour. Put all Sea Defense Wardens on Alert Level Three. Send defense apprentices out to alert all coastal Wardens and especially the Cliff Watchers. Go!"

The man scurried off. James reached over to the wall behind him and gave three tugs to a rope, followed by three more. He then stood and strode out of his office with the scroll and sheet of text they had just read. He walked down a long hallway and stopped at one of the many open doors.

"Yes James?" In just the few moments since he had rung, Chancellor Duncan had cleared a space off on his desk.

"An urgent message from Gaeten."

The smile on Duncan's face froze for a moment, and then was replaced by a very serious look. James continued. "It is undoubtedly from him, but just the same I will question the Alterians who brought it. Gaeten said a large fleet of Dominion ships is gathering and there is a very high expectation that it is heading for Freelandia. Though Gaeten does not say for certain that this is the expected invasion force, I think we must consider that as a real possibility. I have called an emergency meeting of the High Council. I believe we should send out our fleet to meet them, per our phased defense plan. We are not ready, Duncan. We need more time!"

Duncan's face had gone pale, but he set his chin forward resolutely. "If it is war they want, we will surely bring it to them before they can bring it to our shores."

Master Warden James strode purposefully out of the Council chambers, his mandate fresh in his mind. He burst into the secondary meeting room he had set up, where not only the Navy Master was sitting, but also several of his most senior officers. They all stood as he entered.

"Send out the fleet. Find the enemy. If they approach within 100 miles of our shores, you have leave to defend Freelandia to the full extent of your abilities." The look on the Warden's face confirmed his words. All present nodded and hurried off. In their minds, the war had just begun.

Within two days nearly every warship in the Bay sailed out, outfitted as best they could be within that timeframe with the very latest engineering weaponry. Only a few ships were left within the Bay and the many that were still in various stages of construction.

Murdrock's plans were coming together rather nicely. The three Gallorian ships in the harbor had not attracted any undue attention – and why should they? The cargo of carpets and tapestries had been off-loaded and several had even sold at the dockyard market. The harbor master had already been told they were packing up whatever had not sold yet and would sail to other cities within the Freelandian Bay shortly. Everything appeared completely in order. No one had noticed a few extra deck hands, and the heavy carpets remaining on the ships had readily hidden a few decidedly non-merchant items stowed in the cargo holds. No one apparently was curious that two of the ships appeared to be the more common wide and heavily bottomed cargo ships, while the third was of a much lighter and faster design.

In just a few more days he would close the noose. Bold success always triumphed over past failures. His reputation would be salvaged and the Freelandian leadership would be thrown into turmoil. If the Dominion navy performed as planned, the path would be laid for Dominion dominance in the near future.

Within two days Gaeten knew his urgent warning had been premature, at least in part. It was very apparent that the Dominion soldiers planned to remain in Kardern – and therefore the ships that had set sail were not carrying an invasion force toward Freelandian shores. Whatever was planned, it was solely a naval exercise. Exasperated, he had no ready means to alter or update his previous message, as he and Nimby had not found any other Alterians near the dockyard.

Minister Polonos arrived at the Chancellor's house right on time. He was ushered into the sitting room where Duncan and Lydia were waiting for him. "Welcome, minister! We are so very glad you could dine with us tonight."

"Oh, it is surely my pleasure! I was afraid that with the sailing of the fleet you would be much too busy to see me."

"We wondered that at first too. But we have had other reports coming in that suggest the invasion is not imminent – but the war may begin nonetheless if our navies clash out at sea. There is also the possibility the Dominion is just testing us. We really do not know yet and God has not revealed the answer. So for now, we continue on as before, readying ourselves as best and fast as we can."

"Yes, and God will continue to bless you in your work and protect us, I firmly believe. But tell me, where is your son Ethan? I thought he would be with us tonight."

"He promised he would be here for dinner – but he did not say he would be with us any earlier. He has not really been himself lately. He seems so distant from us, even antagonistic. We had hopes that your presence here might be a good excuse to have an open conversation with him – he used to thoroughly enjoy long dialogs with our dinner guests, and particularly about things of God."

The conversation continued about Minister Polonos's fascinating work deep in the southern regions of the Dominion. In what seemed like almost no time a butler ushered them into the dining area to be seated. Lydia looked up with annoyance as Ethan suddenly slunk into the room and took his seat, with as little time to spare as possible. Even so, she put on a pleasant smile. "Ethan, we are glad you could join us. Minister Polonos has been regaling us with stories and information from his many years within the southern Dominion. It is truly amazing how God protected him again and again from the evil forces arrayed against God, and how he was able to escape from Dominion soldiers sent to capture him."

Ethan looked up with a dull surly expression below sunken bloodshot-red eyes. "Oh, I really doubt the people there are as evil as we have been led to believe".

Polonos had wrinkled his nose when Ethan had sulked in. "The people are certainly NOT evil, Ethan. But many of their actions are. While some have turned to the true God, most remain blinded by their superstitious fears and customs. And at least in the areas I ministered in, the witchdoctors kept the people supplied with a variety of 'medicines' needed to ward off evil spirits. The plant extracts they consumed kept most in a state of near constant stupor, where they were even more easily controlled."

"Really? I have heard other accounts lately." Ethan's scorn was evident in his voice. Duncan's hand slapped down on the table.

"Ethan, Minister Polonos is to be respected. He devoted his life to teaching others about God and brought light into a very dark area of the world. He is a genuine man of God, and we hold him in high honor in this household."

Ethan just slouched further in his chair, eyes on his plate. The food was served and an uncomfortable silence settled around the table.

Lydia tried again. "Ethan, can you tell Minister Polonos of your plans to leave tomorrow for a review of the northern passageway? It seems adventurous … a week alone, traveling up into the mountains!"

"It is MY trip, and I wish you'd just stay out of it! I can take care of it myself and I don't need your meddling about it!"

Duncan's eyes went wide while his wife's cheeks burned in embarrassment over the outburst in front of a guest. "Ethan, that was uncalled for. Apologize to your mother and our guest." Duncan's eyes flashed dangerously.

Ethan's chair slammed backwards as he suddenly stood. His face was screwed up in anger. "I'm not hungry anymore." With that he stormed out of the room.

"I am so sorry, Minister Polonos. It is as we were saying. Over just the last several weeks Ethan has turned from a sweet and kind hearted young man into a rude, sullen and angry person we hardly even recognize anymore. We are hoping it is just a phase he will pass through quickly."

Polonos looked thoughtful. "He is a very troubled young man. And he is indeed the one who I saw in the park a few days back. I can sense a great deal of spiritual oppression about him. Something is wrong, definitely wrong. We need to pray for him to see through the darkness that is clouded around him."

Some memory was nagging him, but just would not come into focus. Minister Polonos excused himself early after they had spent several hours in prayer together, and walked slowly back to his simple apartment, still trying to figure out what was puzzling him so.

Maria was overjoyed to have a violin all of her own that she could have in the apartment and could play nearly anytime she wanted. It was not the Diamond Violin for sure, but nonetheless it was a fine instrument. For the first few days she had happily contented herself on more thoroughly exploring the tonal capabilities of this marvelous instrument. Kory also had a small viola and was very rapidly advancing in her playing skill – Kory told everyone that perhaps some of Maria was rubbing off on her. Some of the most fun they had was playing together, and when they did that in the Commons during break they always had many other apprentices gathering around to listen and join in on the jam session. Often another apprentice would make an improvision or try out an original work, and Maria would excitedly pick that up and add embellishments until the work sounded like a professional piece written by a Master. And even a few of those started to visit the Commons during breaks too, and more than once a Master had brought an instrument and joined right in.

Life seemed so very, very good. But this morning Maria had woken up very early and troubled in spirit. Kory too seemed off, and they looked at each other helplessly. "What is it, Maria? I just feel this weight on my shoulders!"

"I don't know, Kory. I had a vivid dream, one that I have had before. I feel a burden too, down deep within me. It is almost a sense of foreboding … like something terrible is going to happen. Let's go over to the park near the Ministry of Healing – the fountain and smell of the roses there always seems to be so cheerful and peaceful!"

The two girls ambled slowly over to the park. While most of the people they met seemed to be going about their business as usual, some seemed to have a rather vacant, sad look, at least to Kory. They wandered into the park and as they rounded a bend in the trail they came upon two men who seemed to be in deep conversation. The sudden presence of the two girls appeared to have caused a disturbance to them, as their talk abruptly ceased and both looked up.

"Oh, sorry – we did not mean to interrupt." Kory quickly began to steer Maria around so they could leave.

"No, that is quite alright," Chaplain Mikael conceded.

Turlock looked at both of the girls quizzically, and then tilted his head in a short bow. "God bless you this fine morning, young ladies." As he straightened back up his eyebrows furrowed as he looked intensely at them. "Something is troubling both of you. And I do believe we have met once before; both of you were present with Lydia when my good friend Minister Polonos freed me of that … that demon."

Kory was at first taken aback by the foreign formality of the greeting, and then she took a half-step backwards, remembering that terrifying meeting and feeling uncomfortable under the scrutiny of this former Dominion magician. And the intensity of his piercing stare was rather unnerving to her.

Turlock eased his stare and smiled gently. "It is quite alright – I am a new person under God's control now. But I can sense something is troubling you. What could be so oppressive on your spirits?"

Maria turned toward the direction of that voice. "That is just it, sir. We don't really know. We both feel some form of heaviness or burden, but don't know why. It comes from down deep … like it is from my 'special place' where God dwells."

Mikael spoke up. "Ah, I thought it might be you, Maria. I don't think we have met. I am Chaplain Mikael. And your companion is …?"

"Um, I am Kory."

"Hello Kory. Mr. Turlock and I were just discussing that we too feel some kind of spiritual burden, like something may be happening in the spiritual realm that we should be aware of."

"Yes, that is it! But what should we do?"

Turlock's serious and intense look returned. "I believe it has something to do with the Dominion … I have a sensitivity to their actions and intents. I think we need to seek God's guidance … and protection."

Mikael agreed. "I suggest we all ask for God's wisdom and direction. Perhaps He will show us what we all need to do."

Kory piped up. "Can we do that now, here? I think whatever it is, it's very serious and important."

Captain Moorhead stared out into the thick fog with great uneasiness as his ship made slow progress tacking into a headwind as they sailed south. The Freelandian fleet had made excellent time over the last several days, and the light scout ships had darted outward to search for the expected Dominion vessels. But this morning a dense fog had rolled in on a contrary wind from the south that slowed their progress to almost a standstill. Their nautical charts, the very best from the Alterians, showed they were in open water. So there was no cause for concern about running aground, though even the Alterians might have missed something in the vast ocean. Fog was not common in these waters, but not unheard of and while unpleasant it should be just a minor inconvenience. But Moorhead felt there was something decidedly odd about this fog. His normal optimism felt dragged down and he had to actively fight against feelings of gloom and despair. It would be difficult to even know they were out on the ocean, if it were not for the sound their prow made through the still water and the gentle rolling of the deck. He idly wondered if others felt similarly, as he stared out into the dull grayness.

A few hundred yards away, the fleet's commander scowled. He too questioned if this were a natural fog – the time of the year was all wrong for it. He ordered hourly drills for the men as his flagship inched along in the lead of nearly 70 ships. The fog effectively neutralized one of the main advantages they had – no matter how fast or agile your ship was, in fog you risked colliding with other ships unless you moved very slowly and carefully. If they met the Dominion fleet under these conditions, the pitched battle with the much larger enemy ships could go very badly for the Freelandian navy.

They could not know that they were indeed heading directly into the jaws of the much larger Dominion fleet, with some of their largest and best armored frigates leading the way.

Ethan had already packed and woke from a fitful sleep very early. He stole quietly out the back exit of the house, barely acknowledging the alert Watcher stationed there. He hurriedly saddled a horse, loaded his bags and led the horse out as silently as possible. When he was a block away he mounted and headed off in a roughly northerly direction. He planned on going to the outskirts of the capital, where he would likely be noticed by other Watchers, and then sneak back in for his planned meeting at the dock market with Kaytrina. He decidedly did not feel very well, but this had become rather normal lately, and it went away within a few minutes of being with her. He wondered if that meant he was fully falling in love.

Murdrock opened his carpet stall in the market area near the Keep docks extra early, hanging out a sign that said that this was the last morning the merchandise would be on sale. He had a larger contingent of helpers present too, presumably to load the carpets back onto the waiting ship. The two other ships that had docked with it had already left their berths and were anchored further out into the Bay. Under the cover of darkness quite a lot of activity had been going on aboard those two ships. As the dawn lightened the sky extra carpets could be seen on the decks, draped over most of the railings. That made it nearly impossible to see any activity on the decks themselves.

All over Freelandia people awoke to the morning feeling a bit off. For some, the day just seemed dreary and they felt rather grumpy and down. Those more spiritually sensitive sensed that the oppressive gloom was unnatural and they began to pray, asking God for discernment and direction. Those that knew of their fleet's mission lifted hands southward as they prayed for protection. As the sky brightened, more and more felt an inward uneasiness and began to pray in earnest. Something seemed to be happening to the south, and many felt a sense of menacing evil welling up in that direction.

Maria and Kory hurried back to their apartment, still in the early twilight of the morning. They both felt that perhaps if they played their instruments it may make it easier to discern God's leading, as both noticed they felt closer to God when worshiping. But when they reached their apartment they both felt that was not the right place to be. After a few minutes of listlessly shuffling about their apartment, Kory spoke up.

"Maria, this just does not feel right. I'm having trouble focusing on my prayers and it just seems like we are supposed to go somewhere else."

"Yes, Kory. I feel that too, though I cannot really explain it. I want to be near the Bay, but also near the Music Academy. Let's wander over to the amphitheater. It opens out to the Bay so we can do both."

The girls made their way to the amphitheater with some sense of urgency, and Maria carefully felt her way down to the front bottom row and sat down, with Kory to her left. She turned her face southward as a strong and disquieting tug was coming from that direction. Her recurring dream was heavy on her mind, and she could almost see herself in front of a processional of musicians, with both they and she playing and singing out to God. And in front of them, directly ahead on the path they were taking, was the dank, dark, doom-filled black cloud that surely would engulf and utterly destroy them.

Maria began to play her violin. She really did not even play any songs or scores she knew, but just began playing simple tones to start with. Without even consciously realizing it, her mind slipped into its familiar special place. Today however, there was darkness to one side, with ominous red lightning flashes and pinpricks of white light floating nearer and nearer the darkness.

She saw the musical notes floating by in her mind, random slips of color without coherence. Then she felt a Summons – an undeniable pull of her attention to stand before the Almighty presence in her mind.

"Child, you must strive against the Dominion, for you are a chosen vessel for that purpose."

Maria stood in awe … God was speaking directly to her. While she had sung and danced in her special place many times, she could not recall ever hearing God speak. "But … but how?"

"Your singing and music are weapons of worship, and you were created to wield them as a mighty warrior."

"But … but how, Father? I am only a little blind girl!" Maria felt small and insignificant … and fear was welling up quickly. A mighty warrior? Huh?

"Out of weakness I am shown strong. The battle is not yours, but Mine, and I will choose to wage it as I see fit, for I know the past, present and future."

Maria shrank inward, frightened. "I … I don't know how … but I will try if you show me."

"That is my plan, child – I just desire a willing heart. I will give you strength, and more. Now follow my directions, for others are in great need."

Maria shuddered and shivered, but felt a strength rising from somewhere deep within her. She followed the direction she felt and began to play a hymn of worship in a strident, forceful manner, playing before her Creator. She did not know how this could be both worship and warfare, but she reasoned she did not really need to know. A burden had been laid upon her, along with a great urgency. She steeled herself. This was not the normal carefree, light-hearted musical jam session. This, somehow, was war.

Kory was somewhat absently moving her bow across the viola when she noticed Maria stiffen, cock her head to one side as if she were listening to something, and then begin to play with considerable determination. Kory did not know the song she heard being played, but as best she could she felt she should play along.

Ethan made his way to the market and nearly immediately saw Kaytrina waiting for him at the entrance. She looked fidgety, glancing furtively around as she pulled her cloak more tightly around her. Ethan figured she was nervous about their secretive travel plans. "Oh Ethan, I am so very glad you came, it means so very, very much to me." Unexpectedly she embraced him and kissed him forcefully on the lips. Her familiar perfume seemed especially strong today, and even her lips tasted of it. Ethan's stomach quieted almost immediately, and even the events of the last night's dinner faded to unimportance. The only important thing to him now was what was in his arms. He kissed her back, again being engulfed with her unusually strong sweet fragrance. She moved back after a moment and took his hand. "This way Ethan, I want to show you something."

Obediently he followed, oblivious to the red flashing in his mind and the dull headache that seemed to be coming on. That annoyed him – normally he somehow felt just so very much better once he got near Kaytrina. Not that it really mattered. With a somewhat idiotic smile plastered on his face, he let her lead him toward the farthest end of the market, closest to the docks.

Polonos woke with a start. The memory that had eluded him was clear and distinct in his mind. He bolted out of his bed and threw on whatever clothes were immediately at hand. Without a second thought he raced out of his apartment and began running. He needed to get to the Chancellor's house immediately!

Back out at sea, the fog bank was thickening noticeably. Every ship had flares lighted along the railings and ships tried to stay within murky sight of each other's warning lights. Captains all along the leading edge of the fleet were now running drills, even to the point of loading catapults and spring weapons. The fleet commander had the latest and largest of those newfangled weapons mounted in his bow, complete with immense metal-tipped arrows, tar-tipped fire arrow bundles, and even a couple of those strange engineer gas pots. He really did not trust them much though, and certainly did not understand them well. The engineers had said to light a wick and then launch it high above or even into the rigging of an enemy's ship, if possible. The captain was glad his Chief Gunny Mate had been trained with these new weapons … at least someone on board knew something about them.

He and others also had a complement of strange semi-floating barrels from the engineers that had what looked like overgrown porcupine quills sticking out all over. He was not totally sure what they even were, though his Gunny Mate had had a long talk with the engineers about them. Whatever. His boats were designed for a quick attack and quick flight, to dance around larger vessels inflicting damage from a distance. This blasted fog completely nullified any advantage he normally would have used.

A lookout in the rigging called for silence and all strained their ears for sounds different than the slight creaking of their own ship and water being sliced with their bow. Something … something out there was making a different set of noises, and it did not sound too far away. The captain ordered the bow lights to be extinguished and on a hunch loaded the engineering gas pot. Then they waited.

Maria played, though she knew only a few songs, and most of those somehow did not really seem fitting. Then she recalled some old hymns she had heard as a young girl. Some of those had a cadence of … of … marching? Somehow those seemed the most appropriate. She began to adapt a few of them from memory, adding more vibrant and strident notes, and then adding her voice with the words she could remember.

Kory recognized the basic tunes and began to play along more closely, complementing Maria's notes.

Even as she played, Maria kept pondering her conversation in her mind. Music as worship she understood – for her, all music was done in worship to her Creator. But as warfare? And against who or what? Somehow she knew it has something to do with those little sparkles of light and the dark and ominous cloud she could somehow see, and which reminded her strongly of what she dreaded in her dreams. As that thought grew stronger she began to change her focus. Normally in her 'special place' she danced and sang and played directly to the spiritual presence that seemed to always reside there within her. This time was different. In her mind she turned, and with that mighty Presence directly behind her, she began to direct her music toward the growing darkness that seemed about to engulf the points of light.

Even as she did this, Maria felt the infinite Presence behind her somehow grow even larger until it began to envelop where she stood. She nearly fainted away at the touch, but strength flowed into her. The ribbon of sound coming from the violin in her hand became super-charged, with sparks dancing along its surface and what seemed like fire glowing from within. The ribbon which normally danced and skipped around her began to change and now started extending toward the darkness, a tiny tendril of light and power flowing above the points of light and reaching toward the ominous shadowy cloud.

When the leading edge reached the darkness, small bolts of lightning seemed to start shooting from the musical ribbon, but the darkness seemed to overwhelm it. The sparks along the ribbon seemed to fade somewhat. It wasn't working. The darkness was winning.

Maria gritted her teeth and played with even greater stridency and began blending in the viola notes from Kory.

They had only been playing a few minutes more when she heard another instrument's notes begin to sound behind her, and then another. More joined in and soon there were a dozen playing and perhaps half a dozen voices added to hers – at some point she realized she had begun to somehow sing even while she continued to play. In her mind those other instruments and voices created additional ribbons of sound and energy that were at first incoherent but then began to join and mingle in with hers. As they did so they also brightened and sparkled with new-found power. Maria began to gather the ribbons of sound and shape them into a more coherent entity aimed toward the darkness. The small tendril of light became a thriving, pulsating, weaving vine whose end terminated in writhing ribbons of sound that danced through the air sending sparks in nearly all directions. Where her small ribbon had been ineffective at changing the darkness, the combined ribbons began to scatter the leading edge, seemingly vaporizing whatever darkness it met. Yet it was still a quite small scattering amidst the large dark cloud. But the darkness was at least no longer advancing.

Grand Master Vitario had been the third person to arrive, lugging his own viola, feeling a spiritual tugging like the rest of them. He could feel the music lifting, and like the others began to follow Maria's lead. Somehow he knew this was exactly what God wanted of them. As he began to play he could feel the power behind the notes, like nothing he had ever experienced before – which really was something, given the events of the past few weeks. He sat next to Maria and forcefully joined in, opening his mind and fingers to wherever God seemed to lead. He recognized the basic hymns Maria was playing, and began to add depth and richness to her notes, and after a minute he added his tenor voice to hers as well. She noticed and gladly accepted and incorporated the additions on the fly. Vitario's repertoire was immense, and he blended and added, sculpting the music to even greater levels. Even as he was doing this, he felt himself drawn to his own 'special place'. A part of him only wished someone were taking down the score – he did not think he could ever repeat what he was hearing.

More musicians joined in, each adding to the work. Most had no clear idea of what they were really doing, but all felt the call to come and to play and sing. The wondrous chorus soared out of the amphitheater, and even many of those who could not sense the call were soon attracted to the sounds and either joined their voices in or sat in silent appreciation.

Maria felt a growing urgency and the ribbons in her hands were now like a mighty cable of living strands. As she immersed herself in the effort, she noticed little whiffs and puffs of bright light rising in her mind from all around that were drawn into the cable of ribbons and seemed to add additional energy. She had not recognized what they were before, but now somehow she knew what they were … prayers. God was calling His people to intervene … but in what? And why had He chosen her to be both a conductor and Watcher, locked into combat?

Polonos was rather fast for a man of his age. He reached the Chancellor's residence out of breath but with fire in his eyes. At his insistence a Watcher woke Duncan and Lydia, who had slept in after a long evening of discussion and prayer. As they dressed they both felt an oppressive weight, and worriedly looked at each other. They hurried downstairs and into the parlor where Polonos was agitatedly pacing. Duncan spoke first. "Minister Polonos, what is the matter?"

"I could not put my finger on something last night. Did either of you notice the odd smell when your son entered the room?"

"Well, yes – he told us it is the odor of his girlfriend's perfume."

"WHAT? What would your son's girlfriend be doing with a Dominion love potion?"

The fleet commander noticed the change first. A slight wind was starting to be felt from the north and the fog began to lighten slightly. A rolling puff of fog blew away from them for a moment, and with great concerned surprise the commander saw the outline of a much larger ship close before them with the unmistakable demon-monster figurehead favored by many Dominion ships. Without hesitating he gave out hushed instructions for immediate action to his crew. Then another bank of fog rolled over them, obliterating the view. The commander was skeptical of new-fangled technology, but the fog did not allow many options. All over the Freelandia fleet, every captain was coming to the same conclusion.

The Dominion commander was not particularly concerned. He did not expect to come across any Freelandian ships for another few days, though he cockily felt ready to take on their entire fleet at the drop of a hat. He had wanted to have one of the massive Dreadnaughts for his command ship, but his superiors had wanted to save the few they had of those for the invasion fleet.

Oh well, it did not really matter – those were overkill anyway. His frigates were still considerably larger than anything his spies told him the Freelandian navy could float. Besides, his attack fleet outnumbered the entire Freelandian navy, though he anticipated only encountering scattered groups of patrol ships. He could only wish to meet up with what he considered a more worthy adversary for his attack armada. Regardless, he thought, within a few days he should thoroughly crush the Dominion's latest enemy and they would rule the seas.

His magicians had assured him a heavy fog would accompany his fleet, with a steady wind from the south. Yet all of a sudden the wind had just turned contrary and was now coming from the north. At this circumstance the fog would likely lift. That was not according to plan. He had been assured of wind and fog that should bring them right to the coast of Freelandia. Of course, it was not like this was the first time the magicians had failed to fully deliver.

"*Magicians,*" he thought, "*you could never really depend on them.*" Nearly half their promises never materialized, though they always had oh-so-real excuses. He would just as soon pitch the lot overboard. Yet they did have some strange power … you could sometimes feel it when you were near them, a cold darkness that would raise goose bumps on your skin and make the hairs on the back of your neck prickle whenever they were close. He did not really fear them like the common sailors did, but nonetheless he gave them wide berth.

So, the fog was lifting prematurely. It really did not matter much – and perhaps he could use this as leverage against the lead Dark Magician on board. Regardless, he had at least another day or more of travel before coming anywhere near the Freelandian coast, where he would set up a blockade. If all went according to plan, a large portion of the Freelandian fleet would be trapped in their own bay. If they attempted to exit, his much larger fleet would pick them off one by one. And he dearly hoped whatever vessels were already out at sea would try to break through the blockade … he was itching for real battle action. Nothing got you promoted to admiral faster than battle victories.

They would starve out the secluded and isolated Freelandia in preparation for their invasion. No one would get through … except for a few ships of their own for which he had been given very specific instructions to allow immediate passage. He did not know what that was all about, nor did it matter. A noose was to be tightened around Freelandia, and he had the privilege to be the one holding the rope.

Taleena impatiently steered Ethan toward a large carpet stall and nodded at several of the men standing nearby. Murdrock took a quick survey of the area and motioned for two sets of men to lift carpets which were laid across tables. As Taleena led a dull looking young man forward to the stall, one set of men unfurled a large carpet and began to walk out into the market. They turned, effectively blocking the carpet stall from the sight of everyone else. The other two men had followed, but turned around sooner, holding their carpet more like a net. Taleena squeezed Ethan's hand and lifted up a handkerchief that Murdrock had handed to her. Ethan had even watched the transfer, but in his drugged stupor he had no idea what it was, nor did he care.

Taleena rapidly brought it up to cover Ethan's nose and mouth and held it there against his weak struggling. He never even felt the heavy folds of a thick carpet suddenly roll over him. The men wrapped him up like a sandwich and then lifted their burden to their shoulders. A third man joined them to assist, lifting in the middle. The three made their way the short distance to the gangplank of their ship, and brought their burden below decks. To anyone watching, they were just loading another large carpet back onto the merchant vessel, the third of the morning. It did not raise any suspicions; the carpet seller had mentioned he was closing up shop early this morning. Rapidly, others followed until all the carpets were loaded. Murdrock and Taleena were the last on board, and they too immediately went below. Hastily, the ship was loosed and sail was raised. The sleek ship moved out from its berth, heading toward its two companions. Not a single shout was heard. So far the snatch was a complete success.

Chapter 22

Victories and Losses

Arianna felt the spiritual oppression too, but she had to put it aside after a quick prayer. She and Robby were partway up on the cliffs, at a spot where the rock wall plunged into the sea on the relatively calm inland bay. She was making last minute adjustments to the immense gas sack on the ground before them. Unlike others, this one was secured with ropes to a large basket.

"So lassie, just what is this contraption tied to your silken sack?"

"Robby, if we want to use these to be launch points for anti-ship bombardment, there is just no way someone from shore could accurately trigger the payload. Someone must be with it to guide its position and to know when and if to fire the pot. We have figured a way to get some level of steering on the gas bubble, but again, it really cannot be done from shore. The bubble here is large enough so that when it is full it can lift both the gas bomb and a person. Both can float out over the Bay, tethered to shore by a stout line."

"Ok lass, I see yer point. But there is simply no way I am gonna allow that person to be you. Uh-uh – no way, no how. You can bat them pretty eyes of yers all day long and I won't change me mind. You are much too valuable an engineer to risk it. I donna care if you've been up in this contraption a few times already like you told me. I just will not stand for it."

Arianna's eyes flashed. "Robby, I think your judgment is clouded by your feelings for me."

"Guilty as charged, but it doesn't change a thing – you are not goin up in that thingy with a bomb hanging below ye that you actually plan on detonating!"

"Robby – if it was your invention you would do it." Arianna's steely voice drove the sharp words in deep.

Ouch. Robby knew that to be totally true. He would never have let anyone else attempt it. But this was different! This was …this was the woman he cared about, who, he admitted to himself, he was starting to love. But did he care about Arianna enough to let her be the engineer she was? The war continued to rage in his mind, but he already could see the outcome.

Robby sighed heavily. "You win." He took her hand. "But promise me, no heroics! I … I just couldn't bear the thought of losing you."

"Why Robby, you really do have a great big soft heart in there! Don't worry. We have tried this a dozen times now – albeit in shorter test runs over land and small lakes. The gas bubble will hold me up, no problem. And the basket floats like a raft, and I can swim like a fish. The Navy also has one of its ships out as a spotter for us – it was in the dockyards to fix a leak, but the captain said it should be fine in the harbor – it just isn't fully seaworthy for the open ocean."

"Still lassie, floating out over a few hundred foot cliff does not seem the wisest thing to do – it's not like God gave you wings!" He cocked his head and grinned. "Though I'ma supposing they might just look exceedingly good on you, angel that you are!"

Arianne rolled her eyes. "Can you at least help me climb into this basket?"

Freelandia's fleet commander was impatient. A few minutes ago he had caught a glimpse of the enemy, still in Freelandian territorial waters, and they were close. Yet this strange oppressive fog interfered. Then, like the morning sun fading away the darkness, the fog around his ship dissipated. Behind him from the north the sun was shining brightly and a breeze was picking up. Directly ahead of him, right in front of his ship, the thick fog bank lingered, but its upper edges were fraying into thin wisps as he watched. The commander was standing near the bow, right next to the spring gun. "Steady now … the second we see a mast, let this thing loose on them."

He cocked his head to one side … the breeze seemed to be carrying a very faint almost musical sound, but he could not quite make out what it was.

All over Freelandia people were stopping and dropping to their knees, lifting hands, hearts and prayers heavenward and southward. Duncan and Lydia and Polonos felt it too. As the other two dropped into prayer, Duncan raced to the outer room where his senior Watcher guard was stationed. With one look the Watcher came instantly on full alert. Duncan shouted "FIND ETHAN!"

Maria felt an added surge of power and the ribbons shot out sparkles of fire into the oppressive darkness. The heavy feelings of doom and terror were fading away. The evil that seemed overwhelming could not stand against such an onslaught and began to retreat back upon itself. Maria could see and feel that they were winning. With buoyed spirit she played on, continuing to draw the music into a coherent weapon launched against the dark evil.

On every Freelandian ship, all eyes were straining forward into the thick fog. The fog was thinning more rapidly now, dissipating from the top down as the sun burned it off and the favorable wind scattered it. A dark pole suddenly appeared to the forward port side of the Freelandian flagship. It was moving northward and was well within range, though the rest of the ship was still shrouded in fog. It could not be anything else but a Dominion naval ship based on what could be seen. The commander clapped the chief gunner on the shoulder, but he was already swiveling the spring tube and adjusting the elevation. With a nod a mate lit the fuse of the payload pot and the gunner pulled the release latch.

Murdrock smiled as he stood on the deck of his ship. They were nearing their companion vessels, which were already raising sail and turning out into the Bay. With the southerly breeze picking up they should be at the mouth of the entrance into – and out of – Freelandia in a few hours. Still no alert had been sounded, and even if it had been, there should only be a few patrol ships left in the entire harbor – the naval fleet was otherwise occupied … and hopefully being decimated even as a very special cargo was being whisked away right under the noses of the entire capital. This was certainly going to be a momentous day for the Dominion!

The clang of the spring launcher was not terribly noisy, but in the dead stillness of the lifting fog it sounded like the crack of thunder. Lookouts on several Dominion ships instantly reported it to their respective captains. On the ship nearest the sound, the captain ordered all hands on deck to man battle stations, just in case. Everyone rushed to the deck anyway to peer into the foggy air. Probably just a whale breaching and over-active imaginations of our lookouts, the captain thought. Nevertheless, he also took up his station on the upper deck near the large steering wheel. The lookout atop one of the masts reported that the fog was dissipating way up there, but so far he had not reported observing anything of interest.

The projectile arced high into the sky. The chief gunner had only shot a few prototypes before, and so was far from an expert with this strange weapon. He had not known for sure how high to aim, or what the exact burn time of the fuse would be. He knew he did not want to just fire it into their sails … the metal pot itself would not make much of a hole, and in this fog he really could not target the mast itself very well. So, he had aimed in a high arc to try to get the pot to come crashing down onto the main deck. The fuse however was shorter than he had expected. The small fins on the projectile helped to orient it downward, and a few seconds into its trajectory, near the top of its apex, a spring in the back popped to release a small cloth attached with strings to the tail. The cloth instantly caught air and billowed out, slowing the movement and orienting the payload so that its tip was now pointing directly down.

The burning fuse was timed with the spring, and moments later the leading sparks reached the first chamber where the gas was located, instantly igniting it. With a massive thunderous BANG the projectile split apart in prearranged sections. Inside the main cavity had been packed hundreds of small metal balls, coated in tar and packaged in slightly damp powdered swamp mud. The ignition of the gas instantly dried the powder and propelled the metal balls into a high velocity hail, hurtling directly down at the unsuspecting Dominion frigate, the flagship of their fleet.

The Freelandian captain did not wait to see what effect his first shot might have. While that tube was being reloaded he ordered his two smaller catapults to fire. They were loaded with more common payloads, bundles of arrows whose heads were wrapped with highly combustible tar soaked hemp. These were ignited just before launch. The sharp twang of both catapults sounded and the force of motion turned the ship slightly.

The commander also ordered those strange barrels to be jettisoned after their fuses were lit – he really did not want them around when the fighting started anyway. The four were strung together along a rope and a sailor in the stern shoved the first one over the side, careful not to push against any of the strange spines poking out. After the first one hit the water the rope attached to it played out, and in a few moments the drag from the first barrel pulled the others off in order.

As the pressure pot bomb went off and its payload of metal balls was just beginning to break apart, a secondary fuse burned clear of its protective wrapper. Extra mud powder had been used to fill in between the balls, and that formed a white cloud that was rapidly spreading out behind the tar coated balls. In a split second that powder ignited in an immense fiery flash high above the Dominion ship. The additional energy wave added even more velocity to the metal hail streaking down, and ignited the powder and tar coating them.

To the crew of the doomed Dominion ship, it was as though some angry demon above had just unleashed a thunderclap of fire and brimstone down upon them. The noise of the explosions drowned out the shrieking and cursing of sailors as well as the splintering of wooden decks. Those not killed or badly wounded outright valiantly tried to suppress fires started all over the ship, though downed rigging and torn decking made movement very difficult.

The other Freelandian ships nearby heard the launch, even though they could not yet see the enemy. Then they heard the catapults just as the sky directly to the south lit up with a tremendous flash followed by what sounded like a huge and terrifyingly close thunder clap. The flash acted like a giant light, illuminating a half dozen other Dominion ships still having their decks shrouded in the fog that now hovered only a few dozen feet up from the water. With such nicely highlighted targets, nearly a dozen Freelandian ships fired their own weapons nearly instantaneously.

The crew of the Dominion flagship had little warning and no chance of escape. Burning metal cascaded downward over the middle and rear of the ship's deck, tearing sails and rigging and splintering wooden spars as it showered down. Several sails caught fire and only a small handful of sailors on the deck survived that initial assault. Fires started all over the affected area both on the top deck and even below where burning shrapnel had penetrated through. A moment later, burning arrows came shooting downward in the front and middle sections of the ship. Of the original complement of the mighty flagship, the pride of the Dominion fleet, less than ten percent survived this very first contact.

The steersman somehow remained standing, though one side of his body was riddled with wooden splinters that had showered outward as metal balls had plowed right through the deck around him. While the ship still had some forward momentum, he turned the rudder hard about toward the slowly moving small Freelandian ship nearest them. Even with torn and burning sails, he still had greater forward speed from the wind that had been blowing in their favor for the last several days. The narrow gap between the ships rapidly closed. The steersman smiled through his pain. With their mass and metal shod hull, even with their ram raised high, they would plow right through the small ship like a hot knife through butter. Then maybe they might even make him a captain!

The Freelandian commander was turning his ship to engage other enemies when he saw the large Dominion ship, fires raging all over its deck, turn sharply and bear down on them. Even with the breeze from the north picking up minute by minute, he knew he had no time to escape. "Prepare to be rammed!" he shouted out to his crew.

Multiple other flashes and bangs were sounding in the retreating fog bank, and catapult twangs were coming from further east and west. It sounded like a large portion of the Freelandian navy was engaging an enemy of unknown strength.

The Dominion flagship had closed two thirds of the distance when it struck the first barrel directly on the prow, where the metal sheeting was thickest. A loud retort sounded and a geyser of water shot upward. The big ship shuddered, but continued on. The explosion was insufficient to punch through the hull plating. The plating only covered the very front section of the bow, however. The wooden beams further down along the sides had no such outer protection when the second and third barrels hit, having been swung around by their tethering rope connecting them all together.

The second barrel did nothing – its primers had gotten wet from a flawed seal … it was a dud. Number three, however, worked properly and as its spines connected with the hull the barrel exploded. Partially cracked by the blast from the first barrel, the structural integrity of the hull beams and ribs could only take so much. A section of hull nearly 10 feet long at and below the waterline was blown completely out of the side. The huge flagship immediately listed heavily to its starboard as water gushed through the gaping hole, effectively stopping its forward momentum. Fifty feet from its intended target it listed over on its side and in just a few seconds it sank with no survivors.

At that range, everyone on board the Freelandian ship had a nearly perfect view of the carnage on its deck as it vanished from view below the waves. A few noticed the fourth barrel, whose tether rope had been shorn free from the blast, floating off into the fog where other Dominion ships without doubt were coming.

The Freelandian commander turned from the sight. One ship was down, but only God and the enemy knew how many others remained. At least the wind was picking up. Now he could maneuver his fast ship. He ordered a course change toward the next nearest large Dominion frigate, just coming out of the low-lying fog and engaging with two other Freelandian ships. He had one more firepot projectile for the big spring gun, but he chose to keep that in reserve for the moment and instead had loaded a very large metal tipped arrow. The gunner aimed low, targeting just at the water line amidships. The sailors on the Dominion ship were scurrying about putting out fires, though several were still burning merrily away. All enemy eyes were on the first two Freelandian ships, which were rapidly cutting through the water to the port side. They did not see the lethal danger from the starboard.

Maria was tiring, but kept playing as the darkness in her mind retreated and shrunk. A few musicians had dropped out, but she and others pressed on. Even as it now appeared the darkness was being defeated, Maria still felt something was not totally right, though she had no clue as to what it might be. She was also becoming acutely aware of her own lack of repertoire. The music was doing its purpose, but more out of brute power than out of finesse. Not that what she was playing was at all bad, it was just not really suited for the purpose at hand. Maria gritted her teeth. That would have to change, and she felt a heavy burden falling onto her diminutive shoulders.

"We located Ethan's horse, but it was down at the dockyard market, not towards the outskirts of the capital," explained Master Warden James to Duncan and Lydia. "We are questioning everyone there. I expect another update shortly."

Lydia turned toward her husband in near panic. "What would his horse be doing there? Where could he be?"

Duncan took her hands into his own and held them tightly. "I don't know, dear. But Ethan has always been in God's hands. Whatever is happening is not surprising God. We can trust Him in the scary times as well as the calm. God loves Ethan even more than we do. And James is doing everything within his power to find and bring Ethan back to us safely. All we can do now is wait ... and pray."

Arianna felt like a bird in flight – well, almost anyway. The basket she was riding in had lifted off the ground easily by the gas captured in the silken sack above and the breeze was gently pushing her out over the Bay, now several hundred feet up into the air. It was absolutely exhilarating. She saw the old scow that was to be her target, being towed by one of the inner bay patrol ships. So far everything was working out perfectly. Even the light breeze from the north aided her in drifting out over the Bay. It was just about time for her to begin to lower the pot and payload that were secured directly under the basket.

This was a much larger version of what had been installed on some of the naval ships. It had several major advancements based on ideas, workshop tests and a few small-scale test firings they had made. This was to be the first time all of the ideas and components were being brought together into one weapon. If it worked like expected, the results should be spectacular, easily a hundred times more powerful than anything they had tried yet. But to really test out the true potential of this first prototype the delivery had to be made from higher above the target than current spring guns or catapults could readily accomplish, and the much larger payload made it impractical to try launching from simply larger versions of those land- or sea-based systems. It should be quite a spectacle if it worked right.

Arianna hoped she would be high enough … the engineering team she led could only make a rough guess of what to expect, and she had lowered their initial estimate as being much too optimistic.

Duncan dismounted his horse near the wharf marketplace. A knot of people were talking excitedly to some of the Watchers there. The most senior noticed Duncan and ran over. "Sir, several of the market sellers report seeing a young man accompanied by an attractive young woman here early this morning. They recall seeing them inspect a carpet seller's stand, but that is the last place they remember seeing him."

Duncan looked around. "What carpet stand?"

"That's just it, sir – the merchants said that seller had planned on leaving today, but before hardly anyone began walking around the marketplace they very suddenly and quickly packed everything up and hauled it all off to their ship."

"And the ship?"

"It lifted anchor immediately."

Duncan ran to his horse and galloped off to the Watcher tower on a nearby hill, which maintained a record of all ships coming and going. His Watcher retinue barely had time to catch up when he was met by another Watcher coming out of the tower.

"Oh, Chancellor Duncan – I was just going to come find you. We were investigating a ship that left the docks earlier than expected this morning. It seems it sailed directly out to meet with two others. We were told its itinerary was to go along the Bay to stop at several other cities. However, strangely enough, it turned south, out into the Bay toward the cliffs. One of the spotters here trained his telescope on the ships, and he said he saw considerable commotion on the decks. Before they were out of sight he thought they looked to be constructing or mounting something on the stern deck."

"A weapon?"

"He was not sure sir, but that was his best guess."

Duncan's face went ashen as he contemplated the possibility that Ethan had been abducted aboard the ship. He ran the few steps over to the signal launcher that had just been installed, replacing the arrow launcher that had been kept there. The coast of Freelandia had many of these, each located within a prescribed distance of each other. While crude, they could shoot arrows several hundred feet into the air, each with a thick tar that could be coated over their fabric- wrapped tips that would burn with one of four colors easily distinguishable to sharp eyes. An array of such launchers was at each station, giving the capability of sending up a variety of color coded alerts. In the bright daytime the burning arrows were more difficult to observe, requiring successive launch sites to relay the message toward the coastal cliffs. At night it was much more effective and faster since considerably further out stations could easily detect and decipher the burning arrow code.

Duncan did not hesitate. "Escaping ships – they must be stopped but NOT sunk." The attendant swallowed hard but immediately dipped four large arrow heads into the appropriate colored tars and loaded them into the launchers in a specific sequence. He sure hoped they worked. When they had been first installed there were several misfires during practice sessions – the launchers were still very new and all of the bugs had apparently not been worked out of them. He lit each arrow head and bright red, yellow and blue flames shot up. Next he stepped away from the tubes and collected the firing ropes, which all came together in a large metal ring. He glanced at Duncan, who nodded. He yanked the ropes.

Two red and one yellow burning arrows shot skyward. The fourth remained stubbornly in its holder. The attendant ran up and began fidgeting with the spring release mechanism, which had jammed. He bent his back, tugging on the release lever. With a mighty yank it released, but his forceful action had bent the tube holder and the flaming blue arrow shot harmlessly – and invisibly to the other stations – out into the water in front of them. He looked up helplessly at Duncan, who eyes had gone quite wide.

"What … what message was sent?"

The attendant spoke in low tones. "Stop escaping ships – by any means!" They both looked at the hopelessly bent launch tube. No second corrected message could be sent.

Both men looked southward along the coast of the Bay. Already they could see a second set of signal flares launching into the sky. The message was being sent out quickly, but it was the wrong – or at least incomplete – message.

Murdrock was happy, as happy as he had ever been in this enemy territory. Everything seemed to be going so well! Their convoy of three ships sped toward the narrow channel leading out to the open sea. In a short time they would pass through, and then there was nothing between them and Dominion territory except a week or so of ocean … that and the most powerful naval fleet the world had probably ever seen that should even now be mopping up the smaller Freelandian navy.

The sea battle was not over, but by now the outcome was all but secure. Dozens of Dominion ships were too badly damaged to continue fighting and had turned tail and were limping southward, including the remaining two of their largest frigates. Thirty other enemy ships with lesser damage had taken up protective positions around them, and another few dozen ships still in fighting condition were engaged in a pitched battle to give the others more time to escape. All told, the Dominion had lost at least forty vessels, several of which had been boarded and were now slowly sailing toward Freelandian ports where they could be studied in greater detail, if they could be kept afloat that long. The Freelandian fleet commander was quite pleased, though his own navy was not without their own losses. The Dominion had only sunk ten of his ships, though many more were damaged. A contingent was still fighting minor skirmishes, but it was clear the Dominion fleet commander had decided to withdraw and had turned back … this time. While the majority of the Freelandian ships would now begin more serious patrol duties, the damaged ships could themselves limp home for repair, though it would take several days to reach Freelandian docks against the headwind.

The commander looked southward. Had the Dominion pressed on without regards to their casualties, their superior numbers could likely have still prevailed, especially with the new explosive munitions from the engineers having been totally depleted within the first half hour of the fighting. He had been doubtful of them at first, but a substantial majority of the defeated Dominion ships suffered considerable damage from the new inventions. The Commander knew many more would be needed. *"At least our first battle was decisively won"*, he thought. Then he reminded himself: one battle does not a victory make.

Maria slumped, her numb and raw fingers lifelessly holding the violin. She was utterly, terribly exhausted after non-stop intense playing for nearly four hours. Kory was softly crying nearby, holding her raw and even bleeding fingers in front of her. Master Vitario was likewise feeling wrung out, but tears were streaming down his cheeks as well. He had never, ever, remembered playing so … so powerfully and so well before, and never so totally enthralled before his God. It was remarkable and awesome. Somehow it seemed that when he joined in with Maria, his own remarkable musical talent had been amplified. He turned with a compliment on his lips, and watched as Maria's numbed fingers dropped her violin and as her thin, frail body collapsed to the ground.

The signal actually circled the Bay quite rapidly, as it was designed to, until it reached the cliffs overlooking the entrance and exit to the sea. Lookouts spotted three ship masts just visible on the northern horizon coming their way. Orders were shouted out and all available catapults were loaded. The senior shore Watchman only wished he had some of those longer range newfangled spring shooters at his disposal, but none had been lugged up to the cliffs yet. Still, he could just about reach out to the center of the channel with the catapults he had, and those on the opposite cliffs were being made ready as well, having also seen the signal arrows. Why was he always the last to get anything new?

Then he had a thought. Wasn't the Chief Engineer just down the cliff a short distance, testing out some new weapon? Maybe, just maybe ...

He raced down the pathway, catching his breath only when he reached the overlook area where Robby stood. Too late, he thought. Arianna must have been close to a thousand feet away now, well over the channel. The old target scow was anchored nearly under her, but the older patrol ship had noticed the signal flares and had taken up station further toward the other side of the main shipping lane. The captain likely figured any fleeing ships would see the old scow and be unsure of what it really was, and so might veer his way.

"Chief Engineer!" the older gentleman gasped for breath from his run. Robby looked at him quizzically.

"What on God's green earth are you all a'runnin round fer? And what might be those pretty colored arrows shootin all up and down the coast ... is there some kind of parade happening?"

"It's our coastal signal flares. They are reporting that we must try to stop – at all costs – vessels fleeing from inside the harbor. Look! You can just spot them now, off to the north! They will be here within thirty minutes for sure."

Robby squinted and peered in the direction indicated, while his mind was whirling over what could be done about this new development. "Well man, what will you do to stop them?"

"Our catapults are armed and ready, though it is not an easy thing at all to hit a fast moving ship in the center of the channel. With our navy out to sea that old patrol ship is the only real fighting vessel we have at ready. Now if any come in closer, then you might see some mighty fine shooting! My men are some of the best shots in all of Freelandia!"

"So man, are you saying we just have to sit up here and watch those three ships gang up on our wee little patroly boat out there while the most we can do from here is throw pebbles and hope they may bean someone?"

The cliff Watchman's eyes widened with indignation. "Chief Engineer – if you got us some better weaponry we might stand a chance of doing more! I have not seen you out here before asking what we need or how you can help! We are doing the best we can with what we have."

"Ok, sir, ok! No offense meant at all, I'm not blaming you, I'm just frustrated we canna do more. I had not realized our limitations out here. Be sure that will be remedied! But is there nothing else we can do now?"

"Well, Chief Engineer, I was hoping to catch yonder engineer before she up and took wing. I was wondering if there was any possibility of her trying out that strange new weapon on something bigger than that old scow?"

Robby scowled and began to pace. He was already concerned with having Arianna so far over the water and it horrified him to have Arianna doing any real shooting out there – what if something went wrong? At the same time, he knew if he were in her place, he would jump at the opportunity, and especially with the otherwise limited options presently available. But that was him, not her. He could consider putting himself in danger, but it was another matter entirely with Arianna. Robby paused in his pacing, coming to a full realization that he really did … love her. He could not condone putting her into danger. Yet he knew she would not have a second thought but to help in whatever way possible, danger or not. The resolute denial showing on his face melted away. He knew Arianna's safety was not in his hands, it was in God's. He sighed heavily and looked back over at the Watchman.

The older gentleman had paused, but now continued. "But I see I got here too late. She is already up there and with the wind I am sure we are well out of yelling distance to let her know what we want. I guess we will just have to make do."

"Now holdy on there, good sir. We canna yell up to her, but we might just let her read our thoughts."

"What in the world are you talking about?"

"Quick man, find me a hollow reed that would fit over your thumb. I don't suppose you have any paper and a pencil or quill and ink about you?"

"No … I don't. What for?"

"Don't worry about that now. You find me that hollow reed, just a short piece an inch or two long, as light as possible. I think one of these large leaf fronds might work for paper, if they are tough enough. Keep an eye out for a bird feather. There sure are enough birds up here on the cliffs."

The Watchman hurried off and began hacking away at some dry reeds. In a minute he had a piece close to what the Chief Engineer seemed to be wanting. He strode back to find Robby, who had a semi-dried out stiff leaf.

He was bending it this way and that, and seemed satisfied with its strength and flexibility. He also had a white feather from one of the millions of seagulls that frequented the cliffs.

"Chief Engineer, here is your reed."

Robby stood it on a rock. The reed was rather strong and he had to use a stone as a hammer to get his knife to produce a narrow cut lengthwise. He took it over to the rope tethering Arianna's contraption to the ground and with some work slipped it on. It moved freely along the rope without falling off. "Ach, now I need ink ... or something else to write with." He looked about and scowled. Then he took his knife and reversed its direction and pricked one of his fingers. Bright blood welled up and after cutting the end of the quill he dipped it in and began to scribble quick words on the leaf. He had to repeat his pricking a few times until he was satisfied with his work. Then he blew on the frond to dry it.

The Watchman looked on quizzically, thinking perhaps the engineer had gone daft. He watched Robby cut a small circle out of middle of the leaf and a thin slice so that he could fit it over the smooth piece of reed that was on the rope. He next wrapped some twine strands in front and behind the leaf, securing it rather well to the reed.

"Engineer, I have seen many things in my life, but I am stumped as to what you expect to do with that. Do you think you somehow can push that reed and leaf all the way out to your friend out over the channel?"

"I won't need to push it at all, my good fellow. The wind will do that for me rather well. Watch." With that he pushed the reed up the rope, using a long stick to get it high enough so that the leaf frond could catch the breeze. It did, and the large leaf acted like a sail, sending both it and the reed shooting upward along the rope.

The Watchman looked on in amazement as the little message steadily climbed. Robby whistled loudly and Arianna looked their way and waved. Robby waved back and then pointed to the rope and its elevating message. They could not see her expression, but shortly they saw her lean out to snag the rising reed. The message had been delivered.

Both men looked out at the rapidly approaching ships. Robby began to play out more of the tethering rope so that Arianna would move yet further toward the middle of the channel. She was rather high, but he knew she could easily adjust that herself by letting out some of the gas trapped in the silk sack by means of a little string attached to a small flap near the top. Now all they could do was wait and watch. The senior Watchman left to attend personally to his armament, leaving Robby alone to wonder if they were really doing the right thing. He felt so helpless now – but there was one very important thing he still could do. He knelt and began to pray.

Arianna had noticed the flares, but like Robby she had no clue as to their purpose. His note had cleared that up. She could readily see the three ships approaching. She only had one payload, and she readied it as best she could. Trying to sink an old anchored scow was one thing – a fast moving ship was quite another. Not to mention that this ship may also be trying to shoot her down at the same time. She was not overly concerned about that, though. She planned on staying well above any vertical range they might have. If the weapon worked as planned, she had no need to be very low, and it would likely work best and be safer if she remained at some higher elevation. Arianna lit the fuse, knowing it would burn safely for hours. The trigger was activated by a small strong string attached to a tiny lever on the large metal pot. The pot itself was much too heavy for her to manipulate. Instead, it was held tightly against an opening in the basket floor and could be lowered with several pulleys and ropes.

Once the pot was hanging thirty feel below she began to adjust her height. She had no real control over any other direction of movement. The channel narrowed to only a hundred feet in width, surrounded by jagged spires of rock which jutted out of the water at odd angles before the cliff faces loomed upward. That left only about fifty feet of navigable room for vessels to move through. Ships would line up from quite a ways out to shoot through the cleft. Robby had given her enough rope to be close to the center line, though she was still a ways from the actual cliff channel – it would not help matters if she struck a high pinnacle of rock in her fragile carriage. The patrol ship was to the east and the scow to the west. Now she could only wait – though at the speed the ships were approaching, that would not have to be very long.

Murdrock and his companions had no idea what that thing was up in the air. "Bad magic" was what the crew was muttering, and he was tempted to believe it. Was this some new sorcery the Freelandians had concocted? Was it supposed to scare them? Hah! Regardless of what it might be, they were going to get through that channel. One of the larger companion ships positioned itself to intercept the small patrol boat. It had several large catapults on its decks now, with experienced crews manning them. They all knew enough not to go near the cliffs and so be within range of the mounted shore catapults. The other Dominion ship headed off to the other side ahead of Murdrock, to engage with what looked like a derelict scow – but they were not going to take any chances. That left his own ship – with its precious cargo – heading directly in the middle, directly under that … that … whatever-it-is.

Vitario lifted the limp Maria in his arms, cradling her form as he carried her back to her apartment even as Apprentice Ariel, who herself was exhausted from playing along with them, had led a wobbly Kory off to the Healers. Maria feebly smiled up at him. "Did you feel it, Grand Master Vitario? Did you feel HIM?"

"Yes Maria, I surely did. God was moving mightily in our music this morning. And He was mightily using you as well."

"But …but it could have been better, sir. The music … it was ok, but not really suited best for that task. Can you teach me better music for this? I need to be ready for the next time."

"The next time, Maria?"

"Yes." Even in her exhausted state she stirred and struggled in his arms with energy. "We must be better prepared. We must be ready. I need you to help me, Grand Master Vitario." The last was said with considerable determination and seriousness.

Vitario gazed down at the little girl in surprise. Maria had said this with deep conviction, and even maybe with a touch of authority. He was rather taken aback. What change had just taken place in the naïve and innocent child who just yesterday was lost in delight learning to play the violin? And what had God shown to her that was coming?

The two larger Dominion ships surged ahead to engage possible enemy targets. The Freelandian patrol ship darted in, per their usual tactics. But the leak in the hull had allowed considerable water in, and the ship was not nearly as agile and fast as normal. Against a wide-bodied merchant ship this should not have been too great a hindrance, but this merchant ship had sharp teeth. As they neared each other, catapults on both ships sent deadly arrows arcing toward one another. The Freelandian captain had expected as much, and the instant his ship fired he turned sharply away, so that the rain of burning Dominion arrows fell just off his starboard side. He turned inward again to get another shot, noticing his first volley had hit, but done very minimal damage. He stared at the other ship … what were those things hanging from the railings and across the decking? It looked like carpets!

The Dominion captain had fired too soon, but at least the burning arrows from the Freelandian ship had been easily absorbed by the thick carpets doused thoroughly with water that he had spread out all over the ship. That smaller patrol ship was turning in again, likely thinking to slip astern and try to come up on them from an unprotected flank. He chuckled. A normal merchant ship might only have a single small defensive catapult, but his was no ordinary ship. As the Freelandian ship came closer astern he waited, drawing them in. Then both the stern and amidships 'Cats' fired again, this time with far better results.

Meanwhile the other larger Dominion merchant ship neared the scow and confirmed it posed no threat – indeed, it had no crew at all. Satisfied, the captain ordered an abrupt course change back toward the central channel.

Arianna readied her firing line. She was quite nervous and excited all at once. She looked through the hole in the center of the basket floor where the metal pot had been fixed and saw the smallest of the three ships coming up directly beneath her. A large man limped on her deck, pointing and gesturing up at her. Maybe more sailors would populate the deck – all the better, for what she had in mind.

The Freelandian captain knew he was in serious trouble. The last two volleys from the Dominion ship had killed several deck hands and shredded his sails and mangled some of the rigging. He had just lost his main advantage of speed and maneuverability. He veered his vessel away and fired a half-hearted volley at the larger ship which was bearing down on him. They altered course to port and only a few of the chains and small metal balls they had just launched landed in the enemy's sails. Then the big ship turned on an intercept course toward the fleeing smaller vessel. The Freelandian captain had only one real hope, and he prayed – very literally – that it would work.

Arianna took one last look at the ship that was rapidly approaching on a course that would take it directly below her. She had to time this right. The new weapon below her was different than others, and had a greater lag time. Arianna counted to three and then pulled the trigger line.

Murdrock looked up again. He did NOT like coming anywhere near that … that … whatever it was. Extra sails had been unfurled and his ship sprang forward with added speed even as the larger merchant vessel veered into a nearly parallel vector.

The firing line activated a small lever on the pot, which allowed a burning fuse to ignite an inner layer of swamp gas, much like the other versions. This exploded with a large bang and flash of light, but at first it did not appear anything else had happened. A very thick white puff of finely powdered mud formed into a quite sizeable cloud above and just in front of the fleeing ship, perhaps a hundred feet or so above its masts.

Secondary fuses burned through their wrappings. A certain amount of the swamp gas had evaporated out of the finely misted powder, and the burning wicks immediately ignited that, which in turn ignited the powder. The entire payload of powder had formed a cloud multiple times larger than the ship below, and it erupted instantly in one tremendous, gigantic, never-before-witnessed flash. A wave of superheated air blasted outward and especially downward with stupendous speed and energy.

Arianna watched in amazement, even though the brightness hurt her eyes. Everything on the deck of the ship – and most of the deck itself – was incinerated to char and ash by that flash. Then the pressure wave hit. The large ship was flattened as though a giant hand had slapped down onto the water where it had stood. Every remaining beam splintered into thousands of fragments and even the water itself was violently shoved aside by the force. Arianna was actually looking down into a deep depression on the surface of the water covered with the scattered fragments of what had once been a ship. She thought she even saw flashes of the rocky bottom of the floor of the Bay itself.

Then the air and water came rushing inward to fill the vacuum and void. Water churned forcefully, obliterating all sight of where the ship had once been. Arianna gasped at the destruction. That was the last thing she remembered as the reverse percussive wave of air slammed upward into the basket she was riding in.

The captain of the Dominion merchant ship and all his deck hands turned at the humongous thunderclap of sound, and they stood transfixed in disbelief at what they saw – it was as if some sky demon had breathed fire down even as a water monster had opened it huge gaping maw and swallowed their entire companion ship. Thus preoccupied, none saw the sharp spires of rock just below the surface of the water directly ahead of them, which the Freelandian captain had just avoided with a last-minute course adjustment. With a horrible sound of splintering wood the Dominion ship impaled itself on the hidden reef. The first rock pinnacle rising from the depths tore a long gaping hole through the ship's hull, and the ship struck a second spire squarely and stuck fast upon it. A few sailors were thrown clear off the deck. Those less fortunate had no time to escape as the ship broke apart nearly in two and immediately sank.

The Freelandian captain turned his ship about to collect survivors. He had heard the thunder behind him, but had not witnessed the destruction of the other Dominion ship. He disappointedly watched the third ship pass through the cliff channel and out into the open sea. Then he scanned the sky above. Where was that floating silk bubble?

The coastal catapult crews watched in mute awe at the destruction out in the channel area before them. The crew chief was slow to come back to his duties. "Quick men! Aim at that last ship … FIRE! The big 'Cat' jumped and its payload of smooth stones sailed out in a long, high arc, falling to pelt the water fifty yards behind the fleeing Dominion ship. They only had time for that one shot before their quarry shot through the cleft.

Robby had at first thought the new payload was a dud, as after the first minor explosion all he could see was a cloud of white forming underneath it. His jaw dropped open in utter amazement when that cloud became a giant flare in the sky directly above a vessel. From his distance he could not totally see all of what was happening, but what he could see was a massive fireball pound down to the water's surface, obscuring his view of the second of the two ships that were in the vicinity. When the flash faded, there was no second ship to be seen. As the loud thunderclap reached him, he looked up and in horror saw the basket tumble through the sky in great swinging arcs, still tethered to the silk bubble. Then the rope beside him went limp as the gas bubble tore apart in several places. The wildly gyrating basket and the deflating sack began to rapidly drop. With a gut-wrenching feeling in his stomach he saw both strike the water far, far from the nearest shore.

Chapter 23

Lessons Learned and Yet to Come

than stirred into semi-wakefulness. He wondered where he was, though in a moment he knew it was on a ship at sea based on the rolling motion. The last thing he remembered was looking at carpets with Kaytrina. Oh – they must have boarded one of the ships at the harbor and were headed northward on their journey to inspect the only land route into Freelandia. He smiled. She was such an interesting girl! With that thought he sat up, or tried to. Something was restraining him, holding him tight. In his drug-dazed state he did not understand.

It was semi-dark where he was, and after awhile he could make out a few items in the hold of the ship. He could just turn his head enough to see strong cords binding his wrists to a wooden frame, and from the feel he expected some similar arrangement held his ankles. What was this all about? Was Kaytrina playing some kind of joke on him? Whatever it was, it was not funny.

The hold was stuffy and dank and smelled strongly of ... carpet? With that question on his mind he heard footsteps and a door opened somewhere out of view, flooding the area with light. Two people walked in.

"Oh, I see he is finally awake." The voice was deep and harsh, and with a few more steps its owner came into view. The large man had a limp and a dark complexion. His accent was not Freelandian, and he did not seem like a particularly nice fellow. "What is that stench about him – it makes the whole area reek!"

Another voice sounded, and it made Ethan immensely more at ease. "It is a potion I made for him, making him as meek as a kitten and very easy to manipulate. It may be wise to let it stay – it will keep him much more compliant. And maybe ..." Taleena rested her hand on Murdrock's thick arm "… even you might grow to like it." She moved in closer to him, making sure her thick and scented hair brushed against his face.

Ethan frowned at the apparent show of affection to someone else, but had no further time to think about it.

Murdrock growled, "Ha! If you think your potion will work against me, think again!" Murdrock roughly shoved the small woman aside and she stumbled to the floor. Ethan strained mightily against his bonds, infuriated at the rough treatment of Kaytrina. How dare this oaf push her around? "Look, your boyfriend wants to protect you … how utterly quaint."

Taleena slowly stood, shaking with rage.

"Don't get any mischievous thoughts, either," Murdrock continued. "Remember who is in charge – and who will be giving a report to our Overlords. Oh, and don't think that just because you did not write down all you discovered about their defenses that such a ruse will protect you. The Overlords could suck it out of your little skull, leaving little else behind. And of course, we have the original source here now too, don't we? Watch your step, or I may decide you are more of a nuisance than a help and toss you overboard. Or maybe the Overlords will find a use for you – or maybe not. Oh – and I found your pitiful attempt to hide the jewelry you purchased out of MY money. Did you think that was yours to keep? Ha! Now go and write up your report for the Overlords … or maybe there are some scullery duties in the galley – as I recall, you have plenty of experience and are ideally suited for such jobs … surely the captain of this ship would be highly interested to know we have such a valuable passenger!" Murdrock roared at that thought, with half a mind to carry through with his threat. It would sure put a stop to the haughtiness Taleena was showing, as though she had done some especially difficult assignment in assisting in capturing Ethan.

Taleena was visibly trembling now, her face a dark crimson. One hand stole to the very thin knife she had in a small sheath strapped to her thigh. As she began to draw it out she suddenly cried out in pain as Murdrock lifted her several feet of the ground by a handful of her long hair. He held her there, dangling for a minute. "Go ahead, wench. Draw your little frog sticker. You may get lucky and be able to stick me with it. But when you try, make sure you succeed with your first thrust. You would not get a second chance. And be sure, I will not kill you quickly. I will first pull out every hair on your head." He shook her harshly, still dangling.

Taleena cried out and let go of the knife's handle, lifting both hands up to Murdrock's arm to lessen the agony of her scalp. Tears were coursing down her face, both from pain and anger. Murdrock laughed again, more of a very dangerous low growl.

"You need to re-learn your place in Dominion life, little girl. You are the least important person on this ship. When we arrive in Kardern you will be the least important person in the whole town. You are far less valuable than your poor overwrought boyfriend over there. I would sacrifice every other person on this ship for him. For you, I would use you as a mop to clean up his sea sickness. You are nothing, will never be more than nothing. You were a slightly useful tool in Freelandia. Back in the Dominion you will be useful for only one thing… " Murdrock looked Taleena over … "and probably not very good at that either." He flexed his arm and effortlessly tossed the small woman across the room to land in a heap amongst the carpets.

Murdrock stamped out of view, but apparently left the door open, since fresh air began to flow through the room. In a minute, a hatch high above also opened and a salty breeze began flowing through the hold. Ethan could just hear a voice bellow "And let's air out the hold – I don't want the stink of that wench in my nostrils. And she had better wash it out of that mop on her head, or by the Overlords I will cut it off, nor will I be all that careful where I cut!"

Taleena slowly lifted herself off the floor, wincing from the bruises. Her tears were nearly stopped, but she was still shaking. "Somehow, sometime, somewhere I will make him pay for this," she muttered. She walked over to where Ethan was still struggling with his bonds, not comprehending what had just happened, but knowing that big brute had hurt his girl. His head was still very fuzzy, but he had heard that they were heading to the Dominion.

"Kaytrina … he's gone now – cut me loose and let's get out of here!"

Taleena ran her hand softly over Ethan's cheek. "Poor young, gullible Ethan. You still don't know what is going on, do you? The funny thing is … I really do like you, at least a little."

"Huh? What is going on, Kaytrina? Help me get loose!"

"No, Ethan, my love. The only place you are going is to an interview with the Overlords. I'm afraid that you may not survive that encounter. And if you do …" A fingernail from the hand that was caressing his cheek dug inward and she drew a trace of blood. Ethan flinched away in horror. "And if you do survive, it will no longer really be you anymore, just a mindless, empty husk that they will strut around, asking for the wealth of Freelandia for your ransom, never expecting a penny but destroying your people's morale. And then when they do invade, they will have you parroting about in front of their army. They may even work enough of their magic on you that you will think your own countrymen are your enemies and … ha … you might even join in, killing your own people.

Poor, poor Ethan, the hero of Freelandia – hog tied in the cargo hold of a Dominion merchant ship, betrayed with a kiss. Ironic, isn't it?

Now how can I get around Murdrock? He found the one stash of jewelry, but I have others. I still have a few tricks, my own magic to work. But I will have to be very, very careful around him. I am still too valuable." She cocked her head to one side, looking down at the tears of barely understood betrayal streaming down the boy's face. "And maybe I would be even more valuable without you. I would have to be very cautious about that, now wouldn't I? Hmm. I wonder what potions I have left to work with?" Taleena walked out of the hold and back to her cabin, muttering something about needing to wash her hair.

Ethan's tears ran hot down his burning cheeks, and stung in the scratch Kaytrina … if that was even really her name … had made. Even though he was beginning to realize he was not thinking very clearly – he could feel that, though not explain it – he had understood enough of what had just been said to know he had been played for the fool. He had been an idiot, and now he would have to pay for his foolishness. And maybe all of Freelandia would have to pay. His tears went from anger to helplessness and bitterness. He was all alone now. No friends – betrayed by someone he thought loved him and in turn he had betrayed all those close to him. He had even turned his back on God, and now, by the looks of it, God had done the same. Not that he could blame God at all. Whatever was coming, he deserved it. How could he have been so stupid?

⚜

Robby waited, but it was not in any way, shape or form of what anyone would call "patiently". He paced rapidly back and forth on the dock. How could he have let her go up in that ... that ... that sack of air? He had watched in anguish as the basket hit the water's surface, too far away to know what had happened to Arianna. He saw the old patrol ship head over toward it, but it seemed to take a very long time. And it was taking an impossibly long time to return to the dockyard. If it was not showing up shortly he would ... he would ...

Robby never had to try to figure out what he might do, for just then the ship came around the promontory that marked the entrance to the main military wharves. It was still thirty minutes from the dock, so he had a bit more worrying to do. His mind was jumbled, alternating between extreme concern for the woman he loved mixed with anger at both himself and Arianna for letting her be put into such a dangerous situation. He figured he still had some time to prepare a carefully worded chewing out he was going to level at that auburn-headed engineer who was causing him such agony.

Soon enough the patrol ship slide up to the dock, barely creeping the last few yards until it gently rocked into the soft wooden beams designed to absorb some of the shock. A gangplank was lowered and Robby raced aboard, heedless of asking the captain for permission. "Where is she?" he blurted out.

A deckhand scowled at him for breaking protocol and pointed toward the rear of the ship where the main cabins were located. Robby raced in that direction, only to be stopped outside the door by someone who appeared to be the captain. "Now hold on there, fella. I think I recognize you. We've got wounded people aboard, both our own and of the enemy. You can't just go charging down there. We need to get some healers aboard to check them out before we can move them, and I want some Watchers to take over responsibility for the enemy sailors. They are all in there right now."

"WHAT? You've got me Arianna in with a bunch o' enemy ruffians? Are ye out of yer mind?" Without waiting for an answer Robby shoved the man aside and barged through the door. Inside was a narrow passageway with a larger door at the end and a ramp leading down below to the hold. Along one side of the passageway was an open area – Robby recognized it as the galley. All the tables were occupied with wounded, with a few able bodied sailors tending to them. There were also several sailors standing guard over to one side, with drawn cutlasses watching over a small group on the floor, most of whom were heavily bandaged.

"Where is she – where is me Arianna?" Robby's eyes were bulging and his jaw and fists were clenched tightly. The captain came bustling in right behind him. "I don't care if you ARE the Chief Engineer – you have no authority to take over my ship! And besides, she is in my cabin, at the end of the hall."

Robby ignored him and barged forward, yanking open the solid door. His semi-belligerent rush ended there as he paused in the doorway, looking in. The room was small and only dimly lit. There, on the narrow bed, lay the still form of Arianna, a dark bruise already showing on the arm lying on top of the light sheet covering her. All the words he had planned emptied out of his head like a stiff breeze blowing away wispy fog. He stumbled over to her bedside, wanting to crush her into a hug yet fearful that the slightest touch might hurt her.

At first he thought she might be dead, so lifeless and pale laying there with closed eyes, but then he noticed the shallow breathing. "Arianna … oh, Arianna! I shouldn't have let ye do it, I should'a been the one up there, not you! I shouldn't have said a word about trying to stop them ships; we should have just done the simple test firstly. I will never forgive meself for you gettin' hurt like this – I'll never let it happen again, I swear!"

"Bobby … is … that …you?" Her breath was very shallow and the words barely seemed to issue from her lips even as her eyes fluttered slightly and only opened to slits.

"Yes me love, yes … it is Bobby … how badly are ye hurt? Oh, if somethin's broken I will never …"

"Bobby …" Her voice was a mere wisp of a whisper and he leaned far over, turning his ear to hear. "Bobby … I …" Her voice faltered off and he turned his head rapidly to look down upon her, panic in his eyes and a face of dreadful woe.

Arianna couldn't hold it in any longer. She giggled and reached up quickly to pull his head down into a kiss on his cheek. At the rank confusion written all over his face as he quickly pulled back, her giggle transformed into hearty laughter. "Oh, Bobby ... you should have seen the look on your face! It was positively dreadful!"

Robby turned bright crimson and began sputtering. "Of all the fool-hardy, manipulative, impertinent ..." his words dissolved into the best scowl he could come up with under the circumstances, though he couldn't hold it for more than a few seconds. "Oh, lass, you had me but good. I canna stay mad as a hornet with you, you know that and used it agin' me! But to think I could have so easily lost you ..."

Arianna, barely controlling her giggles, looked up at the Chief Engineer. "Bobby, I had some time to think out there waiting to be rescued and brought back. To think about us."

Robby leaned forward and interrupted, "Yes lass, and I want you to know ...."

Arianna raised a finger to his lips to silence him. "Let me finish! I had time to consider my feelings toward you. Recall how I asked you to consider me as a sister and fellow engineer?"

"Yes, but I need you to know ...."

Arianna frowned slightly. "Shush! As I was saying, we had an agreement." Robby attempted to begin his protest again, but her frown and negative shake of her head stopped him.

"Now I have noticed you were trying to keep it, but frankly were failing." Robby acquired a solemn look and nodded his head in affirmation.

"I have watched you for some time, Robby. You love God more than anything. You are a man of your word, and while you often lack tact everyone always knows where you stand." At this Robby perked up with a hopeful twinkle in his eyes. Somehow he managed to not open his mouth.

"You have many admirable traits, but also some rough edges." At this Robby's face fell and as he began to protest Arianna's frown once again silenced him.

"You do wear on a person!" Arianna said that with a big smile. "I think someone needs to work on those rough spots. I have considered the problem from multiple angles and have reached a sound engineering conclusion that I am just the right person you need."

"Can I talk now?" Robby gave her a doleful look that made Arianna laugh again.

"I suppose so!"

Robby smiled back. "I had time to do some thinkin' too. I could not bear to see ye in such danger, but I … I loved ye enough to let ye do it, knowing that is what ye wouldst want. There, it's been said." He reached down for her hands. "Arianna, I have come to love ye. I don't say that easily or lightly. With the war coming and all, I fully agree with ye that I am in sore need of help. I would be highly honored if that helper twas ye."

Arianna beamed up at Robby, and something inside told her there was more. "Is that all, Chief Engineer?"

Robby grinned from ear to ear. "Oh yeah, there is one more thingy, a trifling little thing, really. Let's get married … soon."

Chapter 24

Realizations

The fully recovered Master Warden James was pacing back and forth when Chancellor Duncan and Lydia entered his office. They looked at him expectantly, with Lydia speaking first. "What do you know, James … where is our Ethan?"

"We have no solid evidence, but everything points to his being kidnapped. I have merchant witnesses who said they saw several large carpets loaded onto a merchant ship and the seller closed down his shop very quickly. The ship immediately left the wharves when all were on board. A Watch Tower reports seeing it meet up with two other merchant ships and the three made straight away for the channel to the open seas. With our naval fleet still out, there was only one old patrol ship and the coastal catapults to stop them. The captains of those ships knew their stuff – they kept to the center of the channel for most of the route, keeping them out of the shore Cat's range. Our patrol boat captain should be given a medal – his ship was taking on water and substantially out-sized by a merchant ship that suddenly sprouted heavy weaponry – and he still managed to sink it with minimal harm to his ship and only a few lost crew. He was even able to pick up a few of the surviving enemy sailors, who we are questioning now. We didn't know it, but the engineers were testing some new explosive device and coincidentally – more like God's timing! – they were able to test it out on one of the other Dominion ships instead of an old scow. From all reports the test was extremely successful – I can hardly believe what the eye-witnesses have said. I hear they are calling that 'The Thunderclap of God'. It sounds like when the engineering thing went off, it utterly destroyed that ship.

Unfortunately, the third remaining ship got away. The coastal catapults could not reach it – the ship proved to be quite speedy."

"But Ethan … which ship was our son aboard?"

"From the descriptions given to me, he was on the ship that survived – and which escaped cleanly. We are certain it was Dominion, and from what my Watchers are piecing together I would say Ethan's female friend was probably a spy."

Duncan looked grave as he replied, "Yes, Minister Polonos said he smelled something he called 'a love potion' around Ethan – do you think he was poisoned?"

James frowned. "Were his actions odd lately? I checked and he had not been keeping up his work at the Watchers Compound – very unlike the Ethan I knew."

"Yes – he was acting strangely the last few weeks, ever since he starting seeing some girl."

"We are trying to trace that person's activities. One of the merchants said he definitely saw a young woman with Ethan at a carpet seller's stall, and that was the last time anyone saw Ethan. Can you give us a description of the girl?"

"No … no we can't. He would never bring her to meet us, and we did not want to pry and pay him some surprise visit when he was with her …" Lydia hung her head and began to cry. "It is our fault! We should have demanded to meet her; we should have been more forceful …!" She turned and buried her head into Duncan's shoulder. He too looked downcast.

"James, what is next? Where will they take him, and what will they do to him?"

"We don't know their exact intentions, but I would expect they will try to extract as much information out of him as possible, and maybe also try to use him as a bargaining chip against us – such as to try to extract a ransom – maybe even demand that we capitulate our sovereignty. I have asked Turlock for his opinion, as he may be the most knowledgeable on what their plans might be."

Duncan's face went hard. "I would never sacrifice our nation for one person, even if it is my own son." Lydia looked ashen and after a moment of internal struggle slowly nodded in agreement. Duncan waited until that conclusion had been reached in his wife and then continued. "James, what can we do now?"

"Our navy is still out at sea, and we have no idea how long it will be before they return. It is possible they may stop that ship ... but there would be no real reason for them to do so. We have no able bodied war ships to send out after them, even if we knew specifically where they were heading. There is one very important thing we can do, though. We can pray."

Duncan looked pleadingly at James. "There are no fast ships at all that are left at the Keep and which could be sent out after them?"

James pondered that. "There may be a few shipping or merchant ships that are fairly fast, but anything flying a Freelandian flag or even looking like one of our ships would not fare well once they crossed over into Dominion waters. And besides, they have a large head start now, and we do not know their destination – it is next to impossible. No, I think our best option is to get word back to Gaeten and see if he or the Watcher Network can pick up their tracks. I'll ask the Alterians to take ... word ...back ..." his voice trailed off as another thought overrode his speech.

Maria was restless. She was still physically exhausted from the worship warfare of the morning and yet her mind would not give her peace. She semi-dragged herself to the afternoon voice lessons and her effort was tone-perfect, but rather lifeless. The senior apprentice frowned in disapproval, seeing that Maria's mind was really elsewhere. After half an hour the teacher gave up in exasperation and told Maria to practice what she already knew – it was not particularly useful to continue in the half-hearted manner shown so far.

Maria kept at her scales for another twenty minutes, but then she too gave up and sat down on the floor. She kept replaying the morning's events, and felt she had been inadequate and incomplete – that she could have done so much more, been used by God more fully if she only had better tools – and in this case that meant better ability to craft the music. It was not just all fun and games. This was for real. This was serious. War was coming. God wanted her to be ready. She stood and started in again with her practice, determined to do better.

Master Veniti watched Maria in silence. He had come in through a back door very quietly and stood just in the doorway, not alerting her to his presence. He had watched her practice without concentration, and had nearly stepped in to remonstrate her, but then decided to wait. He saw Maria slump to the floor, and from her expression it was obvious something was greatly troubling her mind. Inwardly Veniti wondered if this was 'it' – one of what could be several decision points many musicians and vocalists came to, questioning if they really could continue. In a moment he saw Maria rise and begin her practicing again with forced determination. He smiled. A decision point reached and passed.

He strode into the room with purpose. "Maria, you are progressing with quite good speed, faster than I thought you would." For Veniti, this was about as close to a compliment as he normally would give. "Yet there is something lacking today. You are forcing the sounds out and they sound tense. You must relax and let the sounds flow out more smoothly. Practice is slow and methodical, and it should be. You have time to reach perfection – or as close to it as I can get you."

Maria had stopped singing the notes as soon as she had heard Master Veniti's footsteps. She was tense and she knew it, though she did not realize the grimace she had on her face. "Master Veniti … I had not heard you. I WILL get this right. And I fully admit your lessons are making me a better singer. Yet you are very wrong in one thing. I don't have time."

Veniti's smile froze on his face and he halted in place. He was not used to any apprentice 'correcting' him or disagreeing with him – and certainly not a beginning apprentice such as this young girl. A recollection of a certain very talented and very proud young man who once had stood right here and argued with him flashed through his mind. Was Maria about to embark on a similar pathway? He still regretted the turn of events that caused that aspiring singer, probably the best male vocalist he had ever worked with, to quit the Academy and with inflated ego launch off into his own international career. Veniti had lost him, and frequently wondered to what even greater level of skill might have been reached had the young man not been so stubborn and proud. If he would have just been patient and continued with the methodical precision Veniti had proposed it could have all been so different.

In that former case he had been adamant that his method was the only way to perfection and it must be precisely followed. He wondered if this rigidity had fostered rebellion. With Maria he had not noticed a hint of that same prideful spirit, and she seemed rather frail in constitution and attitude. Yet here was a new side of the girl he had not observed before. How should he react? With a forceful counter? That had been disastrous before, though he knew it was the easiest and normal path he followed. Perhaps restraint was called for, at least at the moment.

"Whatever do you mean, child?" he said in an even tone that was as conversationally pleasant as he could muster.

"The Dominion. They are coming."

"Yes, I have heard that. It is somewhat unnerving. I don't know what they would do with the Music Academy. But what will come, will come. We have no say in it and we are not Watchers nor politicians. We will just have to roll with whatever lot may fall upon us."

Maria turned fully toward him, her chin jutting out defiantly. "No, Master Veniti. We do have a responsibility and a part in defending Free-landia. I have a part."

"What are you talking about Maria? How can a tiny thing like you fight the Dominion?"

"I can do nothing in my own strength, sir. But God can do anything and everything. This morning was our … and my … first battle. I think we won, but we … I … was not good enough, not skilled enough."

"This morning? I did not hear of any 'battle', only that you and a few others had some sort of impromptu recital in the amphitheater."

"Oh Master Veniti, it was far more than that. God spoke to me. I heard Him … in my 'special place' … He spoke directly to me. I think that was the first time that has happened."

"God SPOKE to you? Surely you are jesting … or confused."

"No, Master Veniti. I know what I know. God spoke to me and showed me that He would use our music – our worship really – to stand against the Dominion … that our place was to wage war with worship as our weapon."

Veniti was sorely tempted to add a 'harrumph' to that. It was incredible, preposterous! Music was a skill to be practiced until one achieved near mathematical perfection. As a weapon? Nonsense. Worship … well, Veniti had not had much place for that. He believed in God, but that was in one compartment of his mind. Singing and music was in another. He was a very disciplined and practical person, or at least so he thought of himself. 'One thing at a time' was a personal motto.

Yet ... he had heard Maria sing the Masterpiece, and besides the skill – and a few places he still recalled needed some touching up – he also could not help but notice the effects it had on the audience around him, and he too had felt ... something. There had certainly been more to the performance than just the vocalizations, yet just what that was he did not understand or know. Many had commented on how this girl's singing had brought them into special worship with God, that there was some spiritual element to her singing ... something he had not felt. It had left him wondering what he was missing. Was there something more? Did God really speak to people? Could He have really spoken to this diminutive girl?

And though he did not understand, he had to admit to himself that there was something special about Maria's singing. She put such feeling into it, such enthusiasm. It was so very noticeably absent in her practice – which seemed so dull in comparison. His mind was confused with these ponderings; he genuinely asked, "But how, Maria?"

"I am not totally sure. But this morning somehow in my 'special place' before God's presence I was manipulating the sounds of the instruments and our singing, and directing them at a great evil blackness to the south. I don't know why or what was happening, but it was what God wanted me to do. And while I think it was successful, I could tell ... I just did not have the skill or repertoire that was really needed."

Maria's voice rose in pitch and volume and she began to wring her hands. "I cannot let that happen again, Master Veniti! When God calls me again to fight against the evil of the Dominion, I may not be ready ... I may not have the right music." She took the several steps forward needed to reach Veniti and stretched out her hands to contact him. "You MUST teach me more, Master Veniti! Teach me faster! I will work all day and all night, every night if needed. I must be ready! We must be ready! The Dominion is coming!"

Chapter 25

Needed Changes

Several dozen ships of Freelandia's naval fleet limped back into the main shipyard two days later. The most damaged were sent further along the harbor to secondary docks, since they would require more significant repairs. The commander came right away to James to give a full report of the damage they had both given and taken. "Sir, if the fog had not lifted when it did, we would have either sailed straight past them or gotten so close they would have boarded us. At close range we would not stand much of a chance against those big ships. God's mercy was certainly upon us."

James gave a constrained smile. "Yes, I have heard reports from all over Freelandia of a move of God's Spirit, calling His people to prayer. And I heard that there was some impromptu concert over at the Music Academy, of all places and times! But tell me, how did the new weapons seem to work?"

The commander was looking quizzically at the Master Warden as he mentioned the concert, but figured it would not necessarily be taken well if he mentioned that he thought he had heard faint instrumental music on the wind from the north. He shrugged off the idea for now.

"Well, to be totally honest, I was very skeptical of them at first. But they performed exceedingly well – not perfect by any means … several of my captains reported shots that took out rigging but nothing more, and one never exploded at all. But most did pretty much as the engineers said they would, and against those huge Dominion frigates they seemed as effective as I could have hoped. What seemed even better were those drum explosives – we took out several dozen of their ships with just those, especially when a number of captains figured out to cut the barrels loose from each other up-current from the Dominion ships. The last one from my command ship floated into a Dominion warship and blew out their rudder, leaving it vulnerable to our more conventional attack. We nearly lost a few of our own ships to them though, since once loosed they floated wherever the current and waves pushed them. The engineers told us the fuses would burn out within a day or two, so they will not pose a hazard to shipping after that."

James nodded. "Please give a detailed report on those to the Chief Engineer. I expect they will want to make many more of them. I don't know how much time we have, Commander – so see to your ship repairs and upgrades. God greatly blessed us this time – but I figure He still wants us to be prepared. Was there anything else?"

"Just that the fog was not normal. It was oppressive. It felt … well … evil. " The commander scratched his head. "This is the first large scale battle I have ever been in, but it seemed like I was only seeing part of the conflict – like there was much more going on than met our eyes. There was a spiritual aspect too, a battle in the spiritual realm superimposed over our physical realm. And it seemed … it seemed like something was happening back here in Freelandia, something that was affecting the turn of the battle. Maybe it was the prayer. Maybe that and something else. I don't really know."

James looked at him quizzically. "I have had a few other captains mention that they thought they heard something unusual as the fog was lifting. I find it hard to believe, but several mentioned hearing what they described as music, even hymns." James looked hard at the commander. "What do you make of that?"

The commander narrowed his eyes and shrugged. "I don't know, James. That sounds rather incredible. I don't see how it would be possible. Is that all?" After a nod from James the commander turned and left, wondering just how many contraptions those engineers could make. He also needed to address his tactics – those new plated frigates were very difficult targets, and from what he had heard the Dreadnaughts were in a whole other class larger yet. He was not sure how best to go against them. He had gotten some really good and close looks at the frigates, and so had first hand information to share with his strategists … and with the Chief Engineer.

He also very much wanted to hear more about the Thunderclap of God weapon that had apparently utterly destroyed a large ship in the Bay.

Whatever that was, he wanted it ... it may be the only thing Freelandia could use successfully against a Dreadnaught.

Kory knocked on Vitario's office door. He looked up and beckoned her in, surprised she did not have Maria in tow.

"Yes Kory, what is it?"

"Grand Master Vitario ... I ... I don't want to bother you, but ... it's Maria, sir ... she doesn't seem herself since that outdoor ... event ... two days ago."

"How so, Kory?"

"Well, she seems rather driven now – she keeps saying she has to be ready, that we all have to be ready. She has been playing her instruments with such intensity, trying different chords and combinations. She is at it now – she just told me that something was just not right ... that the music she knew would not do at all. Sir, do you know what she is talking about?"

"Hmm. She said something like that right after we played that morning." At that moment an errand boy came in with a knock and handed Vitario a sheet of paper. He glanced at it, then stopped and read it more carefully. "How interesting – our fleet has just arrived back – much earlier than we all expected. This says they had a great battle ... two mornings ago ... and the commander says they miraculously defeated a much larger Dominion force." He pursed his lips thoughtfully. "Two mornings ago ... right about the time we all felt the call to prayer ... and many of us felt the call to play as well. Maria said God was using us, directing our worship against the enemy. I was not really sure what that meant, but perhaps now we have a clearer picture."

He stood. "I think I need a talk with Maria – I think perhaps my entire staff needs to hear that talk." With Kory in tow, Vitario walked out of his office to his assistant's desk.

"Marcie, my next staff meeting is this evening, correct? Clear the agenda – I want to introduce Maria to them in a more official manner, and talk about what happened in our impromptu concert the other morning. Tell everyone this is important ... I have a feeling it may change the focus of the entire Academy ... it is imperative that all attend."

He turned to Kory. "Take me to her, Kory."

Kory looked at him oddly. What was Grand Master Vitario talking about?

Maria was absorbed in her playing, oblivious to her surroundings. She was rapidly playing strident sounds, with a troubled look on her face. She did not even seem to hear Kory and Vitario enter the small practice room.

Grand Master Vitario stood still for a minute, listening. There was a purpose to the music Maria was playing, but it was heavy, almost forceful and urgent. Even as he listened he could feel his heart rate pick up and his senses become more alert. This went on for a few moments, and then the notes faltered and Maria stopped.

"Ohhhh, what should come next?" Her voice was hard and brittle, and a tear of frustration was slowly winding its way down her cheek. She stood and paced back and forth next to her small chair, then sat again while lifting the practice violin back up to her chin.

"Maria!" Kory spoke out loudly to try to capture Maria's attention, and it only partially worked.

"Oh, Kory – you are back? "

"Maria," began Vitario, "You seem to have changed ... your music has changed."

Maria slumped into her chair. "It just isn't working like it should. I know sort of what kind of music we need, but I don't know how to get there from here. It is different than anything I have heard before. I catch part of it in my mind, but I cannot ... cannot stitch it together coherently. I am SO frustrated!" She bolted up from her chair and made her way over to where she had heard the Grand Master's voice. Along the way she crashed into several chairs, shoving them aside roughly in her haste. She found Vitario and searched for his hands. "Show me, Master Vitario ... show me what I need. You must! I don't know how much time we have ... how much time I have ... to prepare!" She was nearly frenetic in her insistence, pulling on his hands forcibly. Then she whirled around and stumbled her way back to her chair, scrabbling around for the violin and bow which she snapped up once they were found. She started to play again.

Vitario was troubled indeed. Something seemed terribly wrong. "Maria, please stop for a minute. I must speak with you! What is wrong? What preparations do you have to make?"

Maria stopped moving the bow, but seemed to only give the Grand Master part of her attention. "The war, Master Vitario! God has laid a crushing burden on me … and the fate of Freelandia may be in the balance. We must be ready! I must be ready! The Dominion is coming … I can feel the darkness gathering strength!"

"Maria – what must we do? What are you talking about, child?"

Maria's face darkened noticeably. "We are to fight Grand Master. Did you feel what we did two mornings ago? Did you?"

Vitario was not used to being nearly commanded to answer, and certainly not from a diminutive blind girl – this was not the Maria he had known for the last several months. "I did feel something, Maria. I felt you manipulating the music we played – almost as if you were our conductor – and without question God's Spirit was immersed in what we were playing. I felt the music going out toward the south, felt it going out with great spiritual power. And I … I played before God in my own 'special place' in an intimate worship like I don't think I have ever done before! Oh, and I just heard that our fleet is back and …"

Maria cut him off mid-sentence. "Yes, they had a victory against a much larger Dominion force, yet many ships and people were lost … they DIED, Grand Master! Many Freelandian sailors died … we were not good enough, did not play well enough … I was not skilled enough."

"Now hold on there!" Vitario was so flabbergasted at this outburst that he did not even think to ask Maria how she could have known those details of the naval conflict. "It is not your fault, not our fault that those men died! I don't know exactly how God may have used our playing, but the outcome was in His hands, not ours!"

"I SAW it, Master Vitario. It was so similar to the … the bad dream I've had for a long time now. The evil darkness to the south. The little sparkles of light that were our ships, and others that were prayers. How our music beat back against the darkness, stopping it from encompassing the sparkles and then forcing it to retreat and fade – but not enough! I did the best that I could … I really did not know what I was doing …" Tears began to flow in earnest down Maria's face and she gently put down the violin and bow.

"I couldn't stop it fast enough …the music was not quite right … I tried, I really tried! And yet … those sailors died. Some were surely husbands and fathers. Maybe some were only parents … and now … and now there are children who are orphans!" Maria crumpled to the floor in great sobs.

"Maria!" Vitario was not totally sure what to do – he did not have much practice working directly with over-wrought young girls. Kory ran over and kneeled down next to her grief-stricken friend, gently stroking her hair.

Master Vitario was in a quandary. Obviously God had used Maria and their music in a miraculous way – and that was astounding! But somehow Maria was also assuming full personal responsibility for the outcome of the naval battle. "Maria – in a battle it is normal and expected that there will be loss of life. We won a great victory – and that may have saved many thousands of other lives had those Dominion ships arrived into our harbors. The loss of our sailors is indeed horrible, but all gladly risked – and sacrificed – their lives in defense of Freelandia. They are heroes, Maria. And for the part that God used you, you too are a hero."

The sobs were slowing. Maria's head rose off the floor with a fierce look. "Don't say that, Master Vitario. If I had known how, somehow worked harder, some or all of those sailors very well may have been saved. It is like I killed them, or at least they died because of my incompetence. And yes, they were brave and were willing to sacrifice for the greater good. But those who will suffer their loss will not likely thank them for that. They will just want their father to come home! Who will take care of them now? What will happen to those families now without a father? Do you know, Master Vitario … do you?"

Vitario hung his head and his shoulders slumped. "No Maria, I don't know. I assume the Navy or the government takes care of such things." He had never thought of such things before, but realized that right here, right now, it was of vital importance to his ward. A thought came to him. "Maria, remember when I said you had a secret benefactor who left you a rather large sum of money?"

"Ye… yes." The tears stopped and Maria sat up, though still leaning heavily on Kory.

"I will find out what will happen to those families. I will do it tomorrow. If they are not well taken care of – and especially any children who may be left as orphans – how about if we set up a special charity for them with some of the funds? We would need someone to run it, and I bet there are plenty of others in Freelandia who would want to help. Do you think the pastor who ran the orphanage where you were might be able to help out?"

Maria perked up immediately. "Oh Master Vitario! What a wonderful idea! Yes, I think Brother Rob would help out. Can we really do this? Is there enough money for it? Can we really get others to help too?"

"Yes Maria, I think we can. And I am sure your benefactor would heartily approve. I will help you choose someone to run the charity – I think we will need a very good administer. I will ask Chancellor Duncan for ideas also."

Maria rose and gingerly felt her way over to Master Vitario. She hugged him, clinging to his large frame. He felt as good as he could ever remember.

"But Maria – those deaths were NOT your fault. You said you had a burden, which we – and I assume that means the Academy of Music – have much to do to get ready before the Dominion comes against us in earnest again. I don't really know why, but I fully believe you. I want you to explain that tonight at my Academy staff meeting. Your burden is our burden, Maria. You are not in this alone. We are all together working out what God wants us to do. If God has given you a direction, it may well involve all of us."

Maria finally let him go and back up a step or two. "Me? Speak to your staff meeting? I … I don't know if I can. If you want me to I will try to explain. But I still feel responsible. How can God expect so much of me?"

"Maria, is it God expecting it … or you? God always gives the strength and grace needed to do His bidding. We can only work with what He provides. Are you saying that God's preparations were inadequate for the task?"

"No … of course not Master Vitario! God could never be inadequate for anything! But I surely am!"

"Of course you are, Maria. We all are. But if God put you into a position to do a work for Him, would He not also fully prepare you and give you all you needed to do that work? Even if the outcome was not what you expected or wanted?"

"I ... I don't know ... I guess so. I'm so confused and tired. But now that I do know more about the work, isn't it my responsibility to prepare better for the next time?"

"That very well may be so. But only as God leads you. Maria, I think you should ask God to show you specifically what is needed – don't just go off on your own, trusting in your own abilities and knowledge to accomplish His work. Ask for direction. Then do it with the power and strength He supplies."

"But I don't know how!"

"That is part of living by faith, Maria. Faith is moving forward even when you do not know the way, trusting that with each step His Spirit will be right there to guide your footsteps along His pathway."

"Gaeten once said something like that to me too. That he had learned to walk forward by faith and not by sight. So you are saying the losses our navy suffered were truly not my fault?"

"No, Maria, they were not your fault. They were part of God's master plan. I often don't understand, but I have learned to trust that His plan is far better, and that He cares immensely for each and every one of us. There are no orphans in God's sight – He always was, always is, and always will be their Father ... and yours and mine too." Maria sat quietly, pondering. Vitario noted that and continued. "Maria, God seems intent on doing some great and awesome work through music and especially through your music. Yet you are not alone. God has shown me through you that music can be so very much more than I had ever known. And now perhaps He is showing it can be more and mightier still. I don't fully understand that, but I believe it. I did experience some of it two days ago with you.

As you just spoke of your burden, I felt a response in my spirit. I am no discerner, but I believe you. I believe God has appointed you for a great part in our resistance to the Dominion. But I do not think you are alone to bear this burden. The entire Academy is to be involved, I am sure of it.

Now you may want to rest. The staff meeting is right after dinner, in the meeting room near my office. Kory, you of course are invited too. We will all be ready to listen, Maria. Tell us what God has shown and told you."

"I ... I will try, Master Vitario."

"That is all we can ever ask of you, Maria."

At the appointed time Kory led Maria into the main administration building and down a long hallway. At this hour nearly all apprentices were enjoying the sunny evening out in the Commons or enjoying a leisurely meal. The girl's shoes clacked loudly as they walked, and the sound nearly drowned out the beating of their own hearts in their ears. Nearly. Master Vitario had asked them to come about half an hour after the meeting start time, so he would have time to discuss a few other matters with the other Masters of the Academy of Music.

Nervously they approached the room, and as they neared Apprentice Ariel stepped out of a side room to greet them. "Hello, both of you! I expect you are rather apprehensive about stepping into a roomful of Masters and Grand Masters! I sure was the first time. I am their secretary this year – I take notes and help make the meetings run smoothly. Sometimes they even ask me to referee – I have to enforce time limits and even occasionally have to ask one of them to stop talking so someone else can make a comment!" The experienced apprentice grimaced.

"Kory, I am afraid you will need to sit this one out. Grand Master Vitario wanted you to be present to help and support Maria, but some of the others thought the nature of the discussion might become private – so much so that it would actually be better for you not to know all of it. I know that sounds funny, but trust me, sometimes it is better not to know the details. I will take Maria in, and afterwards I will bring her back to your apartment."

Kory looked at the floor for a moment in disappointment, and then suddenly looked up with a big smile. "Hey, that means I don't have to just sit in there with a roomful of old people staring at me … and even if you, Maria, could not see them, I surely could! Maybe I get the better deal!"

Maria laughed. "Yes Kory, I think you do." Then she sobered at the thought of what would come next. Kory excused herself and walked back down the long hallway, but Maria did not really even hear her loud footsteps. A cloud hung over her as she again began to again feel the enormity of the burden she felt God had placed on her, and how she felt she had somewhat failed and caused the death of over a hundred Freelandian sailors. She tried hard to cling to what Master Vitario had said and it did comfort her a little, but it seemed just so easy for the combined weight of the responsibility and guilt to become overwhelming, and she labored to take the last few steps to the door of the meeting room.

"Maria, are you ok ... you look suddenly very pale and weak." Apprentice Ariel put a concerned arm around the smaller girl's shoulder.

Maria tried to smile, but felt like it probably came out more as a grimace. "Well ... no ... I am really not alright. But that does not make much difference, does it? I have a job to do." She tried to square her shoulders and walk in with confidence, but the attempt failed and instead she semi-dragged herself in behind Apprentice Ariel. She was led to a high backed chair that was obviously made for a larger person. Maria sat, feeling dwarfed in the too-big chair, in a too-big meeting room that was filled with too many Master musicians. She had to swallow hard not to lose her dinner and her face went white at the thought of spewing the contents of her stomach all over the fine table top she could feel in front of her.

Grand Master Vitario was to her immediate right at the head of the table, and Maria could hear Apprentice Ariel close the door and take a seat directly behind them. Though of course she could not see who was present (and she was rather grateful for that), she could hear the breathing and slight shifting-about noises of what must have been over twenty people in what must have been a sizeable room.

Vitario began. "Gentlemen and gentlewomen, this is Maria, whom you have been hearing so much about. Truly God's hand is heavily upon this young woman. I can attest personally to the astounding musical abilities God has endowed her with, but I believe there is yet more God has in mind for this small vessel. Our heavenly Father has brought her to us for such a time as we are in. It is no coincidence her talents and abilities are showing up right now, right as the Dominion encroaches on our borders and threatens our very existence.

I have already given you a brief synopsis of her time at our Academy, and some of the details behind the scenes, as it were, when Sir Reginaldo was here and we 'discovered' 'The Singer'. You have heard from Master Tolanard how Maria has described seeing instrumental music in her mind, and how she can manipulate it."

At that Maria heard some grumbling and whispering throughout the room.

"I know, I know – it seems impossible and farfetched. But I want you to hear from Maria herself what happened two mornings ago. I remind you that this was exactly when our naval fleet met the very large Dominion flotilla, in quite an unusual and oppressive fog bank as it was described by the fleet commander. You have also heard of the reports coming in from all over Freelandia and indeed many of you yourselves felt the spiritual call to prayer."

Maria could hear the affirmations. She had not heard of that before. Then she thought of the wisps of smoke she had seen in her special place that joined in with the music – she had suspected that perhaps those were prayers, but had not been sure – and she had not heard that many in Free-landia had been impressed to pray at the same time.

"Now Maria, I want you to first tell us about your 'special place' where you often go with music."

Maria swallowed heavily and held onto the edge of the table to try to keep from trembling so much. "Well, sir, most of the time when I hear or play music or sing, it is like I see myself … in my mind … in a special place where God dwells. I sing, play music and dance before my Maker, wor-shiping Him. The music often has colors and patterns and moves about in ribbons. I can experience the sounds in this way, and sometimes I can touch the ribbons of sound and then make them move into new patterns."

"Wait a minute," said one of the seated Masters, "how can a blind girl see? How would she even know what colors or anything else looked like? I find this hard to believe."

Maria turned toward the somewhat hostile feminine voice. "I was not always blind," she said in a quavering voice. "I remember a bit of what it was like to see, and in my mind I can see the music as plain as … as plain as you can probably see your hand held in front of your face."

Vitario interjected, "Go ahead, Maria – explain what happened on the other morning when you and several others here felt compelled to come and play and sing in the outdoor amphitheater."

Maria summed up what she had experienced, explaining in vivid detail all that had transpired. When she finished, she slumped further into her chair.

Vitario spoke up. "I was there, playing alongside Maria. I felt the power, the anointing presence of God. And I must add – my viola never sounded as sweet and pure as that morning. The others who joined us have told me the same thing – the power of the music was palpable and we could feel the Spirit's power flow through and around us. It was amazing."

One of the Masters in the back motioned with his hand that he wanted to speak. "Vitario, I don't doubt that you and the others enjoyed a spiritual high while playing in the early morning in an impromptu jam session. I think all of us have at one time or another become lost in our music. But you want us to believe that God was somehow bestowing some form of special spiritual favor upon you and a rather select group among us? And that this child – prodigy that she may be – somehow was conducting your music in something that amounts to warfare on behalf of our fleet that at the time was hundreds of miles away? I mean come on … ribbons of light? Wisps of smoke? It sounds to me more like a very over-active imagination that sucked you and other more gullible members of our esteemed group into a fanciful fairytale."

A few others murmured agreement, while others looked very troubled. Those that had been present at the amphitheater were adamantly shaking their heads in disagreement. Master Vitario shook his own head sadly. How could such learned men and women who regularly experienced the beauty of music not see how God could use it in this way? He did have to admit, though, that his own eyes had only been recently opened to a greater sense of God's very personal presence within him. Maria had slumped even further under the sarcasm and disbelief. How would she work on preparations to fight the Dominion if there was such dissention among the leaders of the Academy?

The agitator spoke up again, with added confidence based on the few others who seemed to support his stance. "Now if God somehow wanted to directly intervene on our behalf with the naval fleet, that in and of itself would be highly unusual. From what I heard the new weapons from the Engineers had the largest beneficial impact on the confrontation, and the fog lifting when it did was a fortuitous turn of circumstances that our fleet commander did an admirable job of using to our advantage." He smirked at his own pun, whispering to a nearby cohort "admirable … fleet commander … admiral … get it?"

He cleared his throat. "Now if the Almighty chose to intervene, would He not be able to do it without the assistance of a little blind girl playing some beat-up old violin? And if He somehow stepped into the fight, would we have lost any ships and men? Come now – would God do such a poor job of defending our fleet? Would God really put the fate of all those men into the hands of … her? If so, she certainly did not do that great of a job – I heard we lost over a dozen ships and several hundred good Freelandian sailors!"

Maria crumpled both physically and emotionally. Here was a person condemning her performance, and in her own mind she could only agree.

Vitario stood. "Master Elgin, thank you for bringing up these concerns, which seemed to be shared by a few others in our assembly. Your comments shall surely be taken into very serious consideration."

Maria gasped and the Master in question looked quite smug and pleased with himself.

Vitario continued. "May I please see a show of hands of those who heartily agree with Master Elgin?" A handful of hands rose, and a few others were visibly wavering. A nod to Apprentice Ariel ensured all were dutifully recorded. "Now before anything else, I want Maria to finish." He turned, noticing how mortified and forlorn the little girl looked in the big oak chair. "Maria, please tell everyone who your audience is in your 'special place' and what was told to you after our morning performance." She could not see his eyes twinkle, but she did feel a reassuring squeeze on her diminutive hand.

"My audience? Oh, there is always only one, of course … God Himself." That got a few snickers, presumably from Master Elgin, she thought. "Whenever I sing, I am singing to Him. Whenever I play an instrument, I do so for Him. When I listen to music from others, I enjoy it before Him. When I am overjoyed by the music, I dance before him. Here I have a lot of limitations. In my special place I can rejoice and worship however I want, however I can. Music is so beautiful, so special, such a gift from God! I think it all flows from Him, from some part of Him. Since we are created in His image, some part of God must be musical."

Maria forgot her fears and embarrassment and became animated. "Can you imagine what the music in heaven must be like? Don't you think that God enjoys music? Does He enjoy our music? Is it perhaps some reflection of His beauty? Should not our purpose be to use this glorious gift of music to praise Him, to use it for His honor?" Her face was lifted upward and almost glowed. Master Veniti, sitting about half way toward the back, noted it. He could not recall ever asking himself those questions, and doubted he ever looked that animated, that enthusiastic about music or God. What if Maria were right? What if perfection was not the true goal, though he had striven after all the long years he'd been at the Music Academy? What if the goal was … worshiping God?

"The other morning, after the darkness had mostly dissipated and everyone around me was stopping, I lingered for a few more minutes in my special place, in God's presence. God spoke to me." Again there was a snicker. Her voice dropped to be barely audible and most in the room leaned forward to hear.

"He told me that I was to use music as a weapon against the Dominion. I did not understand, and so He showed me how the music we had just played had fought against the evil from the Dominion in the spiritual realm, and how that also manifested itself in the physical realm. Then He showed me a far, far greater darkness building in the south, one so full of evil and hate I could not stand before it. His presence strengthened me, and He promised it would continue to do so – but that I had to prepare, to get all of us to prepare, for the coming war. Music and worship were to lead Freelandia into battle, and would be used as a mighty weapon against the battalions of the Dominion, and of the spiritual forces behind them. But … but I don't know how. I tried as best I could the other morning – but it was not good enough, I don't think it was the right kind of music."

Master Elgin could not contain himself any longer. "I have patiently sat here listening to this preposterous child's fairytale and her inflated view of her own importance … she is to save Freelandia from the Dominion … maybe with a nursery rhyme! I think we have had our laugh – send her away now, preferably far away! We have had enough egotistical musicians and singers who felt they were too good for us. Maybe she can stick to singing, and hopefully not cause anything else to sink!"

Maria gasped in shock and shriveled into her chair, hurt terribly by the cruel words. She burst into tears. The words sunk in, making her feel foolish and stupid, and worse, guilty beyond what she was already feeling. It was her fault after all. What was she even doing here at the Academy of Music? What could she have been thinking when she tried to use the music against the Dominion? That should have been left for someone much more qualified! She had caused the death of hundreds of Freelandian sailors. That thought reverberated in her head and Maria's thoughts spiraled deeper and deeper into guilty depression.

She did not even hear the loud scrape of a chair being forcefully shoved backward as Master Veniti rose with a fire in his eyes none present had ever witnessed. Maria did not hear the heated discussion that was ensuing in the conference room. Her world had shrunk down to the point where she only knew her own thoughts. This continued for several minutes, and then another, closer chair skidding back across the floor broke into her consciousness. Master Vitario was standing and speaking loudly, but Maria was not listening to what was said. She just registered the angry sounds and knew it had to be about her. It was too much. Now people were angry and arguing over her actions … she was causing problems here too. She just could not stay.

Without warning, Maria bolted to her feet and ran out of the room, retracing the route she and Kory had taken. As she exited the administration building in a stumbling run towards her apartment, Maria's tears mixed with the rain that was starting to fall and the thunder seemed to echo her sobs.

Chapter 26
Self-Realization and Awakening

*E*than was taken up to walk about on the deck for exercise twice a day, being told his captors wanted him in good health. His wrists were connected with a short chain, which in turn was attached to a longer chain that either Murdrock or one of the burly sailors kept a firm grip on. It was not like he had anywhere to escape to. The ship was alone out in the middle of the ocean, and Ethan felt all alone aboard it. No one spoke to him more than gruff commands, and except for these small outings he was kept chained onto the rough plank bed where he had first found himself when he had awakened on this Dominion ship masquerading as a merchant vessel. He was fed once a day, and as a growing teenager he felt starved nearly continually. After just a couple of days a great weakness settled over him. At least they had kept the doors open, and the air down in the hold was clearing, along with the drug-induced stupor that had clung around him ever since Kaytrina … no, he had heard sailors call her "Taleena" had come into his life.

What a fool he had been – that thought never left his conscious mind. And now what harm might come to all he held dear and loved, all because of his idiocy?

Ethan stumbled up the last steps and onto the pitching deck. He had great trouble staying upright – but worked hard at it lest he receive another booted kick as had been liberally administered to him on his first excursion out of the hold. The deck was rolling with much greater severity than before and he could not help but stumble this way and that as the ship made its way through rough waves. A sheet of water crested the bow and slammed into Ethan, who had not seen it coming. He was knocked to the planks only to be roughly jerked to his feet by the chain. The cold water had drenched him, which while startling was also refreshing. It also made him not mind the cold rain that was starting to fall. The sky behind look rather ominous, with frequent lightning flashes. They were at full sail, but the storm was catching up with them rapidly.

At least the weather seemed to matching his mood, Ethan thought. Maybe God was sending out punishment for him already. As he was yanked back below decks, Ethan wondered what it would be like to empty one's stomach in a storm while being chained in place on a board. He could wish the storm would sink them, but he did not feel he could pray for that … and anyway, why would God ever listen to him again?

Maria would not be consoled by Kory, and after a few hours of trying, a very tired Kory gave up and went to sleep, leaving a melancholy and introspective Maria holding herself and slowly rocking back and forth in a small chair. The storm clashed with intensity above them and Maria was drawn to it since it seemed to somewhat match her mood. She found a waterproof coat with a large hood and put on a pair of leather boots. As an afterthought she picked up the flute that Master Tolanard had given her and tucked it into its protective narrow case, slinging it over her back. Quietly so as not to disturb Kory, she slipped out of the apartment and felt her way down the stairs and stepped out onto the covered porch. The darkness was punctuated with lightning, and Maria could just barely sense the bright flashes though she did not truly see them. She certainly did recognize the thunder – it was close enough to rattle her very bones.

The storm began to lessen and the violent thunder subsided and then stopped altogether. The remaining gentle rain made soft pattering sounds that began to soothe Maria's troubled spirit. She could hear the drops hitting leaves, grass, pathways and puddles. The small splashing sounds were especially pleasing to her, and Maria stepped away from the porch, wanting to hear more, wanting to become lost in the simple rhythmic mesmerizing sounds and escape the heaviness that seemed to weigh her to the ground. She recalled Kory taking her to a pond that was no more than an hour's slow walk away, and for her the night was no hindrance to travel whatsoever. She just couldn't stay. The storm around her may have been diminishing, but inside her it was building to a crescendo and she wanted to be alone with her misery.

Maria trudged along in the rain-soaked mud, finding her way slowly, only occasionally using the waterproof flute case to guide her path. She remembered the directions and soon found the rocky pathway that led up a hillside. It was easier to traverse than the muddy low areas and she felt her way confidently around the ridgeline path. The rain was light but steady and she walked with no hurry, almost paced with the beat of the wind and rain. She really did not notice how long she had walked, but shortly the echoed splash of drops hitting standing water beckoned her closer. She now carefully circled around the lake on the groomed path, moving to the west end where Kory had led her to a large rock ledge overhanging the water's edge. A tumble of rocks formed a shallow cave where you could sit, and into this enclave Maria carefully picked her way.

She sat slowly, folding her legs under her. The rain continued unabated. Maria was wet and cold, and it suited her. Why was God doing this to her? What did He want? How could He want her? The thoughts swirled around like the wind driving the rain. Yet without doubt God had been using her. He was always her audience, always seemed pleased with her music and song. She had …had never felt God reprove her, never felt condemnation from Him. So why was she feeling it from others around her – and even from herself?

As her thoughts continued, she began to softly hum, without even realizing it. The tune flitted about, but with the accompanying rain drop background it began to become more coherent.

God had never let her down. Not when she had gone blind, not when her mother had died, not when her father had died, not back in Westhaven … never. He had never made her do something she was incapable of doing. Even playing against the darkness the other morning, she had felt His strength flow and buoy her upward. His power had invigorated and empowered her. Why had she doubted?

Ethan was bucked about as the waves heaved the ship up and down. His wrists and ankles were already raw from the rough movement, though he had not become sick – yet. He was getting his due. Yet a back part of his mind disagreed. He followed that train of thought, clinging to it like a lifeline that it was. God had always helped him before ... but where was He now? Of course, he had to admit, it was he who had left ... he had ditched God in favor of ... of a Dominion spy. He began to sink back into depression.

Even as the black fog of his guilt started to overwhelm and take over, Ethan became aware of a faint red haze in his mind. It had been awhile since he had even noticed that. The redness was all around him, with brighter, congealed spots located nearby. Ethan heard a guttural curse as someone was pitched into a wall and realized the more intense red spot had to be that sailor. A faint blue line, barely discernable, arched off to his right and upward – the pathway up the stairs to the ship's deck. The days when he had used those colored lines seemed like such a long time ago.

Ethan pondered the red and blue he recalled having seen so clearly in his mind when danger was present. He could not remember what it was like to not have them present in time of need – except for the last few weeks. He had ignored them once Kaytrina – Taleena – had come into his life. He could see now how she had enticed him, had lured him away from ... from his parents, his responsibilities and ... and from God too. And he had not resisted all that much. She had made God seem so distant, not really something or someone of his own but instead only something for his parents and others – not for him.

As he considered this, he noticed that the faint blue line showing the impossible escape route did not start out in front of him, but seemed to keep going behind his mental image of himself. He had never seen that before. Where did it go? Ethan had always just known the ribbons of color were there, and typically when they showed up in his mind there was immediate danger to occupy his whole concentration. Well, he thought, he was not really in immediate danger – at least not that he could do a thing about. Time is one thing he had in abundance just now. In his mind he tried to trace the blue line backwards. It seemed to go down deep inside him, and so he mentally tried to follow. In doing so, he did something he had never done before in his mind's image. He turned around.

Ethan found that he seemed to be standing on some solid glass-like surface. He peered back immediately, and saw the faint outline of the ship's hold, almost like it was being viewed through an immense window frame. He was standing, as it were, on the frame. Before him was the world he knew. But where exactly was he? In the quietness of his mind Ethan turned fully around, away from the world he knew. The blue line that had seemed so faint as it traced out in front of him glowed with intensity here and led back to a brightness emanating from … from a cloud? It was hard to look that direction for very long; the brightness was quite intense. It filled him with fear and awe and wonderment. Without any real conscious thought he took a few mental steps toward the light. As he did, he became aware of himself and the guilt and darkness that seemed to enshroud him. The whiteness before him was so pure, so spotless that he could not comprehend soiling it with his own presence. Yet he felt an urge to enter that whiteness.

With each step his own filth became more and more apparent. He saw his lies, his selfishness, his pride and self-centeredness. He could not come any closer. He could not bear the thought of bringing his loathsome dirtiness into that purity. Yet for all he was worth he wanted to enter, to come closer. The attractiveness of that purity was heady.

Ethan looked over his shoulder back at the image of the ship's hold. That was real. That was where he belonged, wasn't it? He faltered and stopped. Without warning an unmistakable thought welled up.

"CHOOSE."

The blue line seemed to be tugging at him, leading into the brightness. Yet his darkness and incriminating ugliness pulled at him to return to the life he knew – as though that was where he truly belonged. The struggle grew in strength, tugging him forward and backward. Yet neither was totally overpowering. He knew somehow that he did indeed have a choice. He nearly stumbled, but with great effort turned his back on the darkness of the ship image and took a step into the outer edges of the intense bright cloud.

Ethan shut his eyes and began to weep, knowing his sin would contaminate the beauty before and now around him. It nearly made him turn and run away. He opened his eyes again, expecting to see the cloud shriveling away, recoiling in horror as it were from his filth. Instead, he saw with amazement that the cloud was … was somehow dissolving the dirt and blackness coating him. Bit by bit the filth began to slough off. Ethan was overjoyed. He tried to gather the bright cloud around him and scrub off the darkness that separated him from the light, but found his actions did nothing. As bits and pieces fell off he felt an intense warmth … and acceptance. He almost laughed as more and more came off. And instead of creating a mess at his feet, the filth appeared to dissolve away as if fell, leaving no lasting stain.

The blue line was now pulsating with life and power. As the last of the dirty coating clinging to him fell away, leaving him wonderfully and wholly clean, Ethan strode more purposefully inward, being enveloped by the whiteness and light. In a moment, he stood before a brightness so strong and consuming he could not go further. He instantly knew what – or who – he stood before and sank first to his knees, and then full prostrate.

"*Ethan, my favored son … finally you come before me.*"

"My … my God!"

"*Am I Ethan? Am I truly YOUR God?*"

Ethan pondered that. His faith had been encouraged by his parents and others around him, so much so that he guessed he had relied as much or more on their faith and belief rather than make it his own. When Taleena had come and shaken what he had always held as truth he had fallen before her lies.

"*Yes, you were relying on the faith of others and had not really learned to trust in ME, to truly give yourself over to me. I sheltered you and gave you a great gift. You used it and lived under my protection, without ever really acknowledging that it was I who gave it to you. You trusted in yourself and in a shallow mental image of what was right. You did not seek the source of TRUTH.*"

"*And look where it got me*", Ethan thought. "*I really am helpless and hopeless, aren't I?*"

"*You indeed are. Without me, you are covered in slime from head to foot and truly pitiful. If you go back to the way you were, you are lost. In your own strength you will fail, for you have no strength. The enemy wants to wring your life, to bring you into a depravity you cannot even imagine – and then use you for its evil purposes against all you have loved and all who have loved you.*

"No Lord!" Ethan was weeping profusely now, crying out between sobs. "No!"

I have given you a choice that everyone has, though few indeed have it set before them quite so plainly. You were created for a purpose, my child. But I will not force it on you. You must choose. My way from this point forward will not be the life of ease you have known. You are an instrument for my Purpose, if you will give yourself to me."

Ethan searched his own heart and mind. He saw where his lust and blindness had taken him. It was ugly. "I … I want Your way. My way is destruction. Your way is life."

The brightness grew impossibly brighter still and Ethan found the cloud had formed a canopy around him that cleared enough so he could again see the ship's hold as though looking through a large window. The presence of the Almighty was directly behind him.

"I am always here, I never leave you. It is you who move away. Stay close, and My Light and Truth and Power will always be with you. Live within those, and no power of evil can overcome you. Come seeking my presence here, for it is where I dwell."

Ethan now saw himself, bound to the wooden frame in the rocking ship's hold. He felt so small and helpless and vulnerable.

"Are you truly willing to be my servant – even when your life seems hopeless? Even when it may seem to go from bad to worse, and then to much, much worse? Are you really willing to fully and truly serve me, Ethan?"

Ethan knew his answer was vitally important, the most important commitment of his young life. Was he really willing to give up his wishes for God's? His time with Taleena had seemed – at the time – to be wonderful, an incredibly tasty morsel that had instead turned incredibly bitter. Perhaps, he thought, that was always the outcome of living for yourself. It was not much of a life, not compared to the infinite beauty and truth that now stood directly behind him. If he could keep that knowledge, keep this area firmly with him, keep himself close to God, he knew he would find true worth, regardless of what circumstances he might go through. "Yes my Lord and my God."

With that statement Ethan felt a power infuse him with hope and direction. He did not want to leave, but knew the direction he was to take. Ethan stepped back to the window and slowly the vision began to fade. He again felt the pain of his bindings, but realized the ship was no longer being heaved up and down and rocked side to side. The storm had passed. But what lay ahead for him? *"Perhaps"*, he thought, *"it did not really matter. My life is not really mine anymore anyway."*

The sky was beginning to lighten and Maria could just barely discern that dawn was coming. She had been thinking, praying and humming all night, but she really had not noticed the time or tiredness – there was something about intimate worship that held your attention and alertness. The rain was lightening, no more than a sprinkle now. The impromptu tune she had been humming almost absently as she was thinking had grown into a more complicated melody. Humming was just not sufficient. Maria unpacked her flute. She had been practicing with it off and on, giving her a break from the violin. Somehow the flute to her was more relaxing, less "serious" perhaps. And it reminded her of the wind and waves, which just seemed very fitting. Now … here … with no other audience than God Himself … she wanted a personal worship with her creator amongst His creation.

The deep pure notes began to sound out, softly at first but growing in volume and intensity. It blended in with the wind and the surroundings, at times almost indistinguishable with the creation with which it now inter-acted, flowing with the wind over the water and through the gently falling drops. As the sun peaked above the eastern forest on the far side of the lake, Maria sensed the light and felt the warmth of it on her cold skin. She played to welcome it and felt her special place opening up within her mind.

There she no longer had the shackles of blindness nor even of gravity. Maria danced within her own music, and the music of the rain and wind and awakening birds. It all blended together into a splendorous unified whole and she was immersed in it, part of it, and it was all directed to her Maker. His power swelled outward and engulfed her. How had she ever felt that her efforts or failures amounted to anything? It was all Him before whom she danced and played, all for Him and all from Him. She realized her true place was here – worshiping Him. The battles before and those coming were not hers – though she knew she was to literally play a part. The battles – and the outcomes – were His and His alone. For some reason He had a purpose for her, but her only obligation was to listen and do what

He directed. The weight was largely lifted and she gave her all to do what He was now directing – to simply worship Him with all her being.

She joyously gave herself to the task. All around Maria it was as if all creation had just been waiting for this and was joining in, all the sounds and movements melding into a concert of incredible beauty. She had not even tried to modify the mighty orchestra; instead it was she who was invited to join in with creation's worship this morning. The sun fully rose above the horizon now and the rain stopped. Maria could not see it, but a rainbow appeared above the lake, completing the concert. Then in her mind the rainbow did appear, composed of the sounds and movements harmonizing in melody before the Almighty.

The thousand-colored rainbow seemed to beckon her, waiting for her to blend and modulate its vibrant life. Cautiously at first, and then with greater abandon, Maria felt God's Spirit within her direct, and she channeled that leading into her own movements. In moments she was gracefully dancing before her audience, twirling amidst the rainbow, her fingers lightly shifting and adapting the colors around her in ever more complicated and complimentary patterns. The light and sound and patterns swelled in greater and greater worship ascending to heaven and, in a way, heaven and earth joined in honor to their Maker in a way so profound that the whole spiritual realm vibrated in resonance.

Vitario was becoming frantic. The staff meeting had been intense, and in the end he had felt the need to relieve from leadership positions all who had opposed the direction that he knew God was leading. Surprisingly, Master Veniti had been one the loudest and strongest supporters of Maria and of the direction Vitario was proposing. To their credit, several in opposition had accepted lesser roles Vitario had offered them, willing to reconsider their positions first and foremost with the Most High. The others had resigned, leaving gaps in his staff that he now needed to fill. There were several apprentices who were in all honesty ready for promotion, and a few Masters might even embrace a change of pace to move into a leadership role within a department.

Vitario had had to preside over the tumult, but certainly had noticed Maria's hasty and emotional exit, though there was little he could do at that moment. Hours later, he had gone to her apartment with Apprentice Ariel – who actually was one of his prime candidates for promotion. They had found Kory sleeping, and evidence that Maria had been there, but she was gone and the rain obliterated any evidence of where she may have headed.

"Where could she have gone?" Vitario spoke as much to himself as to his senior apprentice.

"Sir, she was very, very upset – some of the words spoken were very hurtful and harsh."

"Yes, and Maria is still really just a young girl, especially on the inside. Do you think she would have been so upset as to … to … do something rash?"

"I don't think so … but I don't know that for sure." Ariel looked around the small apartment, and Kory, now fully awake, had fear in her eyes.

"Excuse me," Kory spoke, "but shouldn't we go looking for her – it is already dawn!"

Vitario became resolute. "Yes. Senior apprentice – go find the nearest Watcher and tell them we need an immediate search party. If there is any resistance, tell them I sent you. If there is still resistance, tell them I said this directly affects the sovereign security of Freelandia itself! Go!"

Master Warden James was not sleeping well. He first attributed it to the storm, but that was not entirely it. He rose and dressed, striding out of his apartment within the Watcher Compound. His senior apprentice aide jumped to his feet in the antechamber.

"What is it, sir?"

"I don't … I don't know exactly. Something is nagging at me, like something important is happening and I should know about it."

As he spoke, several of his senior Masters stepped in. "Say James, you cannot sleep either?"

Warden James snapped into full alertness. If it had just been him it would be one thing. A concerned look crossed over his features and he stepped out into the hallway, nearly colliding with three more Masters who were heading toward his chambers. The senior Watchers all looked at each other for just a moment, and an unspoken decision flashed across all their eyes. As one, the other Master Watchers spun and ran out in various directions. His senior aide did not even have to ask. He ran to one wall and strongly yanked on a rope hanging down with a bright red metal plaque. A second later the deep Watch bell peeled out and a signal arrow launched upward in a red flash high above the compound.

Freelandia just went to a Level 1 alert.

All over the capital and indeed all over the country people stirred uneasily. No one knew why, but many went to their knees in prayer.

Duncan and Lydia strode out of their home and over to the nearby stables. They mounted their horses, much to the chagrin of their very senior Master Watcher guardian and his squad. "Something is happening – something spiritual is happening … over that way." Lydia pointed. "This is important – we must be part of it."

They had not gone for more than ten minutes when the great Watcher bell began to toll out an alert. The protective entourage around the Chancellor tightened and a moment later a greater mounted group found them and formed an outer ring while several pushed forward in the direction they were heading.

The Academy of Music was not overly far from the Watcher compound, and the urgent and highly unusual request from Vitario, coming right after the Level 1 alert, was forwarded immediately to James. He had no idea what it was all about, but the timing was much too coincidental. He and a contingent of Master Watchers and senior apprentices hurried off to find the Grand Master of the Music Academy, while several Ready Teams formed for deployment.

Within minutes of Ariel's leaving, Master Warden James burst into the small apartment. Vitario looked steadily at him. "Maria is missing … I will explain later, but I believe she is to have a critical role in the defense of Freelandia from the Dominion."

James looked deep into Vitario's eyes and saw conviction of that statement. He had no reason to question the Grand Master – and from the events of the last few months he was not overly surprised about what was said about that little Singer. He spun around and was about to give orders for the search when they felt something like spiritual shock waves reverberate within those in the little room. They all turned to look at each other in wonder, and then one by one they walked out into the fading drizzle and began to walk and then jog toward its source.

They were not alone. The remaining senior staff of the Music Academy was already moving toward the trail leading to the eastern lake, along with a significant proportion of the Academy apprentices. Many were carrying portable instruments. Ahead, James could see Duncan and Lydia along with their protective team. He turned around and saw a multitude of people coming from the capital, merging into a river of people, oblivious to the light rain.

Far out at sea, Ethan felt the spiritual stirring. A day ago he would not have even noticed, but now he understood and was more aware. Without really knowing why, he began to hum and then to sing a song of rejoicing.

Gaeten too felt the Call. He sat in the small apartment shared with Nimby and lifted his hands in praise and prayer.

Maria was oblivious to all other reality. She was enraptured to another level of awareness in her worship that went on and on without pause. She felt no tiredness; on the contrary she was empowered with might beyond her mortal body. Shortly, new colors and ribbons were blending into the rainbow of worship flowing in her mind. She delightedly drew them in, as they allowed even greater beauty to be formed for her Maker. More and more were adding in, forming a mighty gushing, unstoppable river of pulsating multicolored praise.

Near where Maria sat, a stretch of sand formed a natural beach where the lake's waters shallowed for a hundred feet and which opened up into a large grassy meadow. People had begun to filter in, and the swelling crowd congregated in the open space. Some sat while many stood. Those with instruments joined into the flute's melody, and those without hummed, whistled and contributed however they could. Most had hands raised upward and all rejoiced under the mighty, heavy presence of God and His Spirit.

The crowd grew until the meadow was packed with thousands of worshipers in the greatest spiritual awakening and revival Freelandia had ever experienced. It went on and on throughout the morning. Pastors and laity wandered throughout the crowds, laying hands on and healing people who had injuries and illnesses. What looked like waves of repentance swept over the crowd as the people experienced God's goodness and purity and more acutely recognized their lack and transgressions. Some wailed in the anguish of their realized sins before falling to their faces in confession and then leapt to their feet as they encountered the miracle of God's forgiveness. Dozens of ministers stood in the shallow water, inviting the forgiven to be baptized.

Some people left to go back to their homes and workplaces, telling everyone they met of what was happening. Over the course of the day a large proportion of the capital and of the surrounding towns made their way to the revival.

By noon Maria could play no longer. She got to her wobbly feet and staggered out from the overhanging rock shelter into the now sunny day. Vitario was by her side in an instant, along with Master Veniti, Kory and several others. Someone fetched a canteen of water and others shared the meager food they had with them, and somehow all were filled to satisfaction. Minister Polonos wandered over to the informal area where the musicians had gathered. He was weeping with joy.

"Child," he said as he stooped over the sitting Maria, "God has given you a mission, and the strength and power and giftings to accomplish it. I am blessed to see His hand so mightily upon you. This is a marvelous awakening – a rare gift of God to us. I can feel the shakings and reverberations within my spirit, within the spiritual realm around us. Let those enemies of our souls be shaken too and take notice that we are a People of God."

Maria smiled, not really knowing all that the wizened man was referring to, but still rejoicing in what God was accomplishing. Lydia, Duncan and James, who sat nearby, nodded in agreement. All wondered what the impact might be of this divine outpouring on Freelandia…

Far to the south, the Overlords of the Dominion wondered too, as they all too keenly felt the spiritual tremors from their enemy to the north.

The Overlord Rath Kordoch felt it too, and his scowl was so intensely evil that his assistant closed his eyes in anticipation of a knife thrust or some other death-dealing blow. Assistants were not known to have long job tenures with the Overlord.

When none came he fearfully cracked open his eyes to see Rath Kordoch deep in thought. Violent action could still come at any time, but they were only a day out from Kardern to meet the ship carrying the son of Freelandia's chancellor. The assistant figured that should cheer the Overlord, so he figured he only needed to survive another day in such close reach from him.

Rath knew the Dominion was taking too long; these people were just too timid. They needed a leader to inspire, to be terrified of, and to follow into battle. And he would heartily fill that role. Whatever stirred in the spiritual realm up in Freelandia, it would be too little and too late. They were weak and long peace had made them lazy – his spies had told him they did not even have a standing army, and that their navy was better suited for policing shipping lanes of pirates than for war.

He had also been told of a general spiritual lethargy amongst the majority of Freelandians. That may have changed now, given the reverberations from the north. He wondered what was really happening. Perhaps some mighty prophet had risen up in Freelandia? That could be troublesome

– those pests could sometimes work miracles that the best of demons struggled to overcome.

But even prophets had weaknesses and terror had a way of overcoming all but the strongest faith. Whatever was happening up there, it would not stop his mission, would not stop his terror from spreading out and would not stop him from overtaking Freelandia. His conquest would start in Kardern with one lone boy.

THE END

of book 2 of the
freelandia Trilogy

Get all THREE books of the
Freelandia Trilogy
and SAVE!!!!

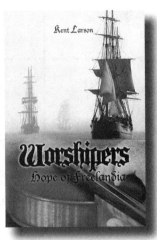

- ○ Great as a Gift for others
- ○ Save on multiple book purchases

Any One book, $10/each

All Three books for $20

Nine or more books for $5/each

MAIL-IN ORDER FORM

Resource	Quantity	Cost each (see reverse)	Total
Watchers: Guardians of Freelandia			
Worshipers: Hope of Freelandia			
Warriors: Darkness over Freelandia			
Tax deductible Donation to ministry			

Subtotal	
MI residents add 6% sales tax	
Shipping add 15% of subtotal	
TOTAL ENCLOSED	

Normal delivery time is 1-2 weeks

For express delivery
increase shipping to 20%

Ship My Order to:

Name: _____

Address: _____

City: _____

State: _____ Zip: _____

Phone: _____

E-mail: _____

Send Form with payment to: Search for the Truth Ministries
3275 Monroe Rd.
Midland, MI 48642